THE ADVE
RAILCAR ROGUES

A murder mystery

Karl Manke

Author of

Unintended Consequences

The Prodigal Father

Secrets, Lies, and Dreams

Age of Shame

The Scourge of Captain Seavey

Gone to Pot

Available at karlmanke.com

To my beautiful wife Carolyn,
for her immitigable patience.

Publisher: Curwood Publishing
Cover Design, book design and formatting: Jeffery Gulick
Editor: Pat Roberts
Copyright ©2017 Karl Manke

ISBN-10: 0-692-89549-3
ISBN-13: 978-0-692-89549-8

The author and publisher have made every effort in the preparation of this book to ensure the accuracy of the information. However, the information in this book is sold without warranty, either express or implied. Neither the author nor Curwood Publishing will be liable for any damages caused or alleged to be caused directly, indirectly, incidentally, or consequentially by the information in this book.

The opinions expressed in this book are solely those of the author and are not necessarily those of Curwood Publishing.

Trademarks: Names of products mentioned in this book known to be or suspected of being trademarks or service marks are capitalized. The usage of a trademark or service mark in this book should not be regarded as affecting the validity of any trademark or service mark.

Curwood Publishing

All of Karl's books are available at KarlManke.com

2nd printing 2019

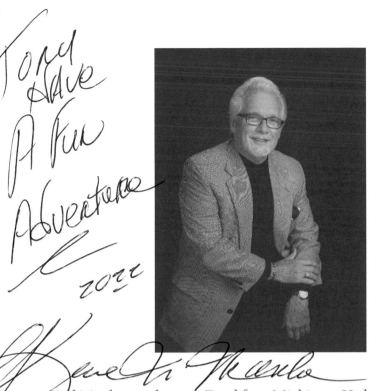

Karl Manke was born in Frankfort, Michigan. He has spent most of his life in the small Mid-Michigan town of Owosso, home to author and conservationist James Oliver Curwood. He and his wife Carolyn have twin daughters and five grandchildren.

A graduate of Michigan State University, the author has been a self-employed entrepreneur his entire working career. After discovering his inclination for telling a good story, he now spends much of his time fine-tuning the writing craft.

CHAPTER 1

1955

Two boys stand anxiously staring at the river's surface. Their eyes are glued on every ripple and bubble. The anxiety builds with each passing moment and the silence only causes more angst. Not able to withstand the fear growing within themselves with every passing second, their demeanor takes on the look of anguish. The blond-haired boy feels the cold chill of powerlessness cascading over his person as an avalanche of unfettered horror causing an outburst, "I think he got so drunk he's drowned!"

The other boy, trying not to react fretfully attempts to be more pragmatic. "Oh hell, he's too mean to drown. He's just showin' off."

Several more minutes pass by. The pent-up level of concern emanating from these two boys has morphed into a dread. One of them breaks into yet another distressful question, "Do ya see him anywhere?"

The other boy demonstrating the same level of disquiet, blurts, "No! I knew we shouldn't a drank that beer! He's drowned. I just know he has!"

A few hours earlier…

Vaughn Kidman is still shy of seventeen years old. He's set himself up as the self-proclaimed leader of his brother, Dace, and a next-door cousin called "Whitey," whose real name is Don, both of whom are fourteen.

Vaughn is on the cutting edge of everything considered by

his peers to be a pathway to manhood, especially stuff a boy doesn't want to get caught engaging in by adults. Vaughn doesn't do well with boys his own age.

He craves attention and finds he can garner more from younger boys who are willing to hand him the reins relegating control of their lives.

He's managed to collect a stash of dirty magazines stolen from a downtown drugstore along with several cigarettes pilfered from his mother's Pall Mall package. All of this is securely stowed away under ole man Franke's barn.

What had begun in the back of this barn as a woodchuck's burrow, situated out of the immediate sight of prying adults, has now been expanded into a den of near iniquity. It's large enough for several boys to crawl into without fear of discovery. Among the supplies stashed within are candles and a butane lighter. Everything from cuss words to examining Vaughn's nearly full grown pubic hairs are fair topics in this grotto. He's the closest thing to a full-grown man in this circle of pubescent boys and is more than willing to display his swagger.

It's a summer day, "hotter than the hubs of ole Billy Blue Hell," a common weather description in this part of northern Michigan. Vaughn is drifting around his backyard, obviously bored, when he spots his cousin Whitey. With a hand motion, he succeeds in bringing Whitey over. He proposes, "Don't tell yer ma, but I'm thinkin' we need to get down to the river to do some skinny-dippin', and maybe a little fishin' if they're bitin'. What say you? Ya up for it?"

The *don't tell your ma* part is how most of Vaughn's adventures begin. Without a doubt, he is a parent's worst nightmare—either as their child or as a companion to their child.

Vaughn is Whitey's mother's younger sister's oldest son. Vaughn's father had been career military and didn't return from the Korean War. Vaughn had been particularly close to his father and continues to have a difficult time adjusting to his absence. Consequently, he acts out frequently in a hostile and anti-social manner.

Whitey is an eager follower of this neighborhood Pied Piper. After all, this is an older cousin. Dace also waits to be coaxed. He's the typical younger brother who depends on his older more aggressive brother to lead. This relationship throws Dace and Whitey together as willing sycophants.

To Vaughn's latest enticement, they reply in unison, "We're up for it, let's go," as they grab a couple fishing poles and a can of worms.

"I got one more thing to do first," says Vaughn. The smirk on his face is telling. With that, he heads for his subterranean hideout. In seconds, he returns with a gunnysack. As he throws the bag over his shoulder, it makes the unmistakable sound of glass containers clinking together.

He quickly looks around and takes the lead hurrying to get out of sight of any prying parental eyes. Dace and Whitey, in their typical way happily fall in like lemmings behind their willing Pied Piper. Hastily the three make their way to the edge of town and down along the brushy path leading to the swimming hole.

The adrenaline rush that comes to young boys convinced they're getting away with pulling the wool over the eyes of those in the adult world is about to become doubly enhanced with this escapade. Within a few minutes, when they're convinced they're out of sight of any prying eyes, they stop. Vaughn exhibits a good-natured impish grin, the kind that comes from the knowledge he's successfully pulled off another caper.

All eyes turn to the gunnysack. The mysterious clinking sound is enhanced with the nearness of the three hovering over the bag. Both Dace and Whitey are nervously giggling at the idea of discovering what secrets are about to be revealed. Vaughn pushes his arm into the bag clear to his shoulder and then slowly withdraws his arm dragging with it a portion of the contents.

"Ta-da!" he exclaims, as his hand suddenly emerges holding high above their heads a bottle of beer.

The excitement only increases when Whitey and Dace discover there are five more bottles in the bottom of the bag. Now all three are giggling and laughing with the prospect they're going to delve into yet another risky venture.

"Where'd you get this Vaughn?" asks Whitey holding a bottle with the fascination of someone holding the Holy Grail.

With the same devious grin, he's held since the beginning of this venture, Vaughn begins his explanation. "I know Rusty Mick's ole man makes home brew. I told him I'd kick his ass if he didn't get me a six pack."

At times Dace and Whitey have both been the target of Vaughn's bullying, but this time they're happy to be on his good side.

None of them have ever had more than just a sip from the bottle of a half-inebriated parent or uncle. Today, those little sips that had been monitored are unfettered, holding the promise of a new freedom as each takes a big gulp of the first opened bottle passing it around among the three of them.

After quickly finishing the first container and not feeling any immediate effect, Vaughn opens another. He's first to tip its contents across his waiting lips allowing its mild effervescence to massage the inside of his throat. Passing it on, each of them chug down another huge gulp. Each patiently takes a turn at getting as much of this elixir down their gullet as they can.

Not the slightest attention is paid to the fact the beer is warm and displaying an excessive amount of foam. Dace suddenly chokes and snorts blowing carbonated fizz out his nose. This brings a moment of concern but with the alcohol's effects gradually taking over their frontal lobes, they roar with laughter at the comedy of the whole spectacle.

In a short time, these unanticipated effects of the alcohol occupy the center of each of their thoughts bringing the laughter to a halt. Each of them become much more introspective as the alcohol clouds their thinking. Suddenly without warning, a numbness begins in their lips and quickly spreads to other portions of their mouths resulting in slurred speech. By now they are laying in the brush without a clue as to what to do next or for that matter what to expect next.

Vaughn once again takes the lead, even with slurred speech, "We outta get to the river and do some swimmin'."

The other two with their own slowed thought processes struggle to their feet only to discover they're having a hard time standing much less walking. With a precarious stance, Vaughn attempts to swing the bag containing the remainder of the beer over his shoulder only to land flat on his keister. Meanwhile, Whitey and Dace are attempting to use their fishing poles as support, but even so, they find they can only stagger.

This phenomenon begins to bring on even more laughter as each discovers his ridiculous exhibition is getting the full attention of the others. The conversation changes to examining how drunk each of them have become and how wonderful it is. They know for sure they have crossed over a new line.

With inhibitions at an all-time low, Dace suddenly breaks into song. The three of them stagger in sync with arms looped over each other's shoulders to the song "Home On The Range." None of them can remember a time they've felt this good drinking Pepsi.

Reeling and stumbling, they soon reach the swimming hole. It's a bend in the river where the current has hollowed out a ten-foot-high bank. Previous generations have left this bastion of young male dominance with a well-used diving board and a Tarzan rope lashed to a branch of an overhanging willow tree. It's designed for a boy to swing nearly to the middle of the stream before letting go to plunge into the depths of the pool.

Not bothering to take his clothing off, Vaughn is the first to dive in. The cool water combined with the effects of the alcohol cause him to remain submerged longer than usual. It's also part of a daredevil stunt to cause others concern.

With his eyes glued to the surface and not seeing any sign of Vaughn, Whitey is particularly concerned with this display of careless bravado. His anxiety is increased by the alcohol.

"I think he got so drunk he's drowned!" exclaims Whitey.

Dace knows his brother better and reassures Whitey, "Oh hell, he's too mean to drown. He's just showin' off."

After several minutes, when Vaughn still hasn't emerged, even Dace is becoming concerned. At this point his eyes are also fixed on the water's surface. The guilt of being helplessly drunk is causing him a near panic attack. He blurts out, "God please don't let him drown and I'll never drink again." Their eyes are glued on every ripple and bubble in the river hoping Vaughn will be right behind it.

"Do ya see him anywhere?" Dace questions Whitey. The

dread in his voice is clear.

"No! I knew we shouldn't a drank that beer! He's drowned, Dace. I just know he has!"

They're both struggling to sober up and begin to shake. They're beside themselves with worry; worry that Vaughn has drowned; worry over what's going to happen to them for letting him drown; worry over how they're going to find his body.

"What we gonna do, Dace?" questions Whitey.

It's clear after this long with no sign of Vaughn, something big has changed in their lives. They're both near collapsing and have tears running down their tanned faces.

"I don't know. What am I gonna tell my ma?" bewails Dace.

It's obvious this is bigger than anything they have had to deal with in their young lives. A good fifteen minutes have passed with neither of them able to muster up the strength to make a move. They're frozen, not able to think straight. They finally collapse on the ground silently trapped in their own fears.

"Maybe you can tell your ma that Vaughn took off and ran away from home," says Whitey.

Dace, buried in his own depressing notions perks up for the moment at the thought of pulling off this lie. "You gonna stick with me on that, if I do?" questions Dace. It's clear from his whole demeanor he's worrying about how to rid himself of any responsibility for his missing brother.

"Hell yeah, Dace. We're family ain't we? We'll just tell our ma's we told him not to take off, but he said he was gonna go anyway."

In their minds this easy fix will give them a reprieve from

yet more guilt added to what they already feel. Agreeing they need to get themselves off the hook in the adult world, they agree to support each other in the deception. Both are hoping this agreement will make all of this go away.

Buried in their own stresses, they silently begin the trek back toward town when suddenly a hand grabs both their necks from behind with the accompanying shout, "BOO!" Both unsuspecting boys jerk and gasp, startled at the thought of being caught by some undetected intruder. Swinging around they're even more startled at what they see.

Standing before them, soaking wet but very much alive, is their incorrigible brother and cousin. The grin on his face tells the whole story. He's successfully pulled off another successful illusion.

"So, you punks were gonna tell Ma I ran away, eh?"

It's unmistakable. Vaughn is aware of their deliberations over the past half hour. He reveals that he had emerged undetected in some overgrowth along the shore line, then hid in the brush where he could take great delight in watching the agonizing response of his brother and cousin over his seeming demise.

With the remnants of alcohol still lingering in their brains, Dace and Whitey have a conflicting mixture of relief and anger. Dace is the first to respond. He stands for just a moment with a blank stare. With the full awareness his older brother is taller and tougher, and quick with a reprisal, he nonetheless unexpectedly lashes out with a punch that catches Vaughn right on the jaw knocking his head almost completely around.

Vaughn's whole demeanor changes from cockiness to anger. In a split second, he has his younger brother on the ground viciously whaling on him. Although this kind of behavior is frequent between the brothers, Whitey stands by in his usual state of helplessness.

He's experienced it all before and knows the fight will sooner or later come to an end.

Within a few minutes, both brothers are standing up cursing the other while brushing the dirt, leaves, and twigs from their hair and clothing.

With the skirmish behind them, they make their way back to the swimming hole. Having dodged what had been perceived just minutes before as an apocalyptic happening but is now quickly dismissed as an overreaction, they're soon back to their original agenda—drinking the rest of the beer, swimming, and fishing.

CHAPTER 2

It's a delightful thing to have days like these. They're only for the young. With their lines in the water, it isn't long before there are fish on the bank.

"We gotta do somethin' with these fish. I'm gettin' hungry. What say we get a fire goin' and cook these buggers up," suggests Vaughn.

With all in agreement, they get in a little more skinny-dipping while the fish cook in the now empty worm can. After eating, they smoke a few cigarettes and drink the rest of the beer. The effects of the alcohol create a drowsiness they can't resist and one by one they fall asleep.

Soon a breeze has picked up. Whitey is the first to sense something is amiss. The fire they built to cook their fish is beginning to catch the dry grasses. The sting of fire on his bare foot brings him out of his stupor. "AARRGGHH!" is the only sound his stupefied brain can conjure. Jumping up and away from the cause of the pain is strictly primordial. It comes with no thought.

His alcohol-drenched brain battles to catch up with the immediacy of the crisis. Seeing the other two sleeping naked bodies also lying in the path of the fire forces a decision. His first thought is to run and save himself. His second thought is that he's naked and needs to grab his clothes. Finally, his third thought clicks in that he needs to alert his cousins. Scurrying round with an armload of clothing, forcing his hands, legs, and mouth to work in unison, he shakes first one then the other, and sounds the alarm, "Get up! We gotta get out of here!"

Dace is the first to respond. Struggling with the same dilemma as Whitey, his first reaction is to get himself out of the line of danger, his second is to wake his brother. He begins attempting to drag the larger boy out of the path of the quickly advancing flames while shouting, "Vaughn, wake your drunk ass up! We gotta get the hell out of here!"

Not accustomed to Dace's brave intrusion on his sleep, Vaughn's first reaction is to pummel his younger brother again. It doesn't take him long to discover the cause behind this rash behavior. Quickly gathering up his clothing, he begins to look for an escape route.

The breeze has changed to a wind and is now whipping the flames into a brush line along the river. By now, it's all these young scallywags can do to save themselves. It would be a rare sight indeed for anyone to see three boys each with an armload of clothing fleeing naked down the path. Fortunately for them, there is no one.

As usual, Vaughn assumes the lead. Because of his less than upstanding lifestyle, it has become second nature for him to always be on the lookout for "escape routes." He quickly directs them to another brushy secluded area well out of danger and out of sight. From this vantage point they can safely watch the aftereffects of this quickly spreading disaster.

It doesn't require an expert to realize this fire is totally out of control. The billowing smoke churning its way toward town with the energy of an escaped genie, strongly suggests it's more than merely a citizen burning trash. What's more, it is coming from an unpopulated area.

Within a few minutes the blare of the town's fire siren is heard calling out to all available volunteers. Adding to this commotion are the wailing sirens of first responders from all over the area.

Alwin "Smokey" Beardsley is Elbertport's fire chief. It's not clear if he gained that nickname from his fire experience or from the never-extinguished pipe resolutely clamped between his teeth. Smokey is a portly man somewhere around sixty years of age. He's famous for his unequaled firefighting abilities in saving many of the community's *basements*.

"Looks like we got us a real grasser," says Smokey in a knowledgeable voice. "We gotta get that sombitch out afore it gets away from us."

Like bees heading into the opening of a hive, the members of the volunteer fire department make their way toward the town fire hall ready to take to the field. Experience levels range from decades to first-timers—all have been personally trained by Smokey. The men vary in ages all the way down to some third-generation guys barely out of their teens.

Dwight Skittle has been in the department nearly as long as Smokey, but has never challenged him for the chief's position. He's content to let Smokey take all the heat for never saving a building in the thirty years he's been a firefighter.

Homer Rogers is also a long time veteran. He quietly fills the gaps in firefighting Smokey leaves open. This faux-pas occurs either out of Smokey's ignorance or because he's too fat to expend much energy for a sustained period. Homer's been overheard to say, "If Smokey gets much fatter they're going to have to grease his fat ass ta get him in and outta his truck."

Smokey continues to struggle into his firefighting equipment, while the others patiently keep one eye on his progress, all the while pretending to fuss with things that don't need attention.

The equipment is a montage of fire trucks left over from WWII and donated by the federal government to the community. Finally, with one final grunt, Smokey mounts his position behind the wheel of the largest truck, a fifteen-hundred-gallon tanker, and slams it into gear. The others in various vehicles fall in behind as they begin the short trek down the two-track trail leading to the now raging inferno.

Meanwhile, the three instigators are far enough away to be both out of harm's way and not risk discovery, while still able to observe. Their interest has changed from fear to excitement. All these fire trucks making their way down the lane are giving them a sense of power they have never felt before. They break out into shameless grins at the sight, giving each other back slaps as though they had just won an Olympic event.

Their vantage point is a tree house left behind by a previous generation. It's some fifteen or so feet off the ground, accessed by a ladder made of wood strips nailed to the trunk. From this platform, the trio has clear view of all the action.

"Looket ole Smokey. He's havin' the time of his life!" says Vaughn. "I think we made his day!"

Dace and Whitey are not quite as pumped. They're just happy they haven't gotten caught.

"I don't care if we make his day or not. Ma and Dad find out about this, my ass is grass and my ole man's the lawn mower," says Whitey being as introspective as he can be at fourteen.

Dace has removed himself, going a bit further into the brush to take a dump. This always happens to him when he gets under stress.

"Damit, Dace. Yer stinkin' the whole damn woods up! Make sure you bury it," says Vaughn from his perch.

Within a couple hours the fire has been extinguished. The action now behind them, the frontal lobes of this discordant trio of young teens are soon drifting into boredom. With the day nearly over, they find themselves sitting at their family supper tables, typically sullen and bored. Each of their parents pose the same question. "So, what have you been doing all day?"

"Nothin'," is the duplicated answer from each of them portraying the same disinterested demeanor.

CHAPTER 3

Elbertport is a small community tucked behind a barrier of dunes protecting it from the ravages of Lake Michigan. It's not really on the way to any place. For the most part the highway comes to a dead end. It's developed its own way of doing things without much concern if it's inside or outside the parameters of the law.

"Hell, we do stuff by common sense around here," says Alec Raymond.

"Yeah, well yer common sense ways is most time very uncommon, Alec," says Ike Mosler.

The most frequent type of infraction generally has to do with someone cheating on a spouse. The last person known to go to prison was Jerry Brockway for stealing the radio out of the fire truck. Elbertport is a small bit of 1950s Americana.

Most of the income in this spirited town of seven hundred-fifty comes from one of two sources—a railroad and a Great Lakes car ferry service both owned by the same company. The company's claim to fame is they can bypass Chicago rail yards and have southern grown produce in the northwestern part of the United States in twenty-four hours. The rail line stretches all the way from Toledo, Ohio to Elbertport. From here the ferries carry cargo laden rail cars across the lake to Wisconsin.

Whitey's father is a railroad engineer, the son of German immigrants who found their way to this port town in search of the American dream. His name is Heinrich Schultz and he goes by the nickname of "Heinie." His mother, whose maiden name was Ethel Wexler, is a native of Elbertport. Her background is truly what America brags about as a melting pot of ethnicity. Although the family was part of a Jewish community immigrating from Poland a century ago, through marriage this branch of the family has become Lutherans.

The lifestyle of these families is categorically a reflection of the protestant work ethic of hard work results in a God pleasing life. Whitey, as a teenager is expected to get his feet wet in the workaday world. Presently school is on summer break and Whitey is being driven around the community by his father with the expectation of getting some sort of summer work.

"If you tink you gonna lay round all summer doin' notin',

you got nother tink comin' boy," Heinie says repeatedly in his broken English. Several stops offering his services from yard work to running errands have produced nothing. It's not until Floyd Tomkins at the grocery store suggests, "Ya might wanna check over at the bowlin' alley. Word has it they're lookin' for pinsetters. Ya might find somethin' there."

Whitey isn't thrilled at the prospect of having his summer disrupted by his father's crazy obsession with work, but he knows better than to kick about it too much or he'll end up working in his father's giant vegetable garden for the season.

Especially since his father's dislike of power tools leaves the only alternatives—hoes, shovels, and rakes.

Heinie makes the Riverside Bowling Lanes their next destination. Whitey is met by Herb Wilkins, a young man still in high school but who has worked his way up to manager. Herb is more than anxious to impress Whitey with the importance of his position.

"Ya think you can handle this kind of work?" asks Herb in a very condescending tone. "Ya know ya gotta work Friday and Saturday nights."

Not willing to be regarded as a kid, using his deepest voice, Whitey says, "Hell yeah, I can handle it."

"Oh yeah, where else you worked?" continues Herb with even more condescension.

"I worked for ole man Ash, cleanin' his damn calf barn. I also worked at the clock factory, shovelin' shit outta cuckoo clocks." The last part of this resume is intended to let Herb know he's not the only wise guy on the block.

Not willing to acknowledge this kid could probably "out

wise guy" him, Herb, moves on to the next part of his interview. "When can you start?"

"Hell man, I was born ready. I can start today," says Whitey, mustering up all the bravado he can bring into play.

"All right. You think you can handle hard work, I'll give you a try startin' tonight at six," says Herb using his most authoritative voice. "But you let me down and your ass is out the door!"

Even with all Herb's tough guy posturing, it's quite evident Whitey is pleased with the results of the last few minutes. "I got the job!" he readily reports to his waiting father with an air of manly confidence.

Even though he is a late comer to America, Heinie nonetheless has a solid connection to the American dream of hard work equaling good results. "You do goot job son, someday you own 'Schultz Bowling Lanes'," he says. The pride in his voice is unmistakable.

At five o'clock that evening, Whitey eats an early supper. The family traditionally eats at six, but his new work schedule demands a different timing. Whitey walks through the door of the bowling alley five minutes early. The pronounced low roar of bowling balls rolling down a wooden lane with the resultant crashing sound of pins tossed in every direction, echoes throughout the environment.

He's met by Herb and immediately escorted down a walkway leading behind the bank of pin setting racks. Whitey's eyes are fixed on the action taking place immediately following the crash of pins. All that can be seen from this vantage point are arms and legs descending like so many darts into the pit to gather up the spent pins.

The intimidation he's feeling increases as they make the turn behind the machines. Here he's faced with a long bench above and behind the turmoil of disarrayed bowling pins. Each lane is attended by a shirtless boy in various stages of attention to the action going on below and in front of him. Dexterous fingers are picking up several pins with each hand and methodically directing each with a hard slam into the proper empty slots of the waiting pin rack. With a single pin left in hand, the boy hits the lowering cord. As the rack drops toward the floor, his last move is to skillfully direct this last pin into the head pin slot before the rack can release its cargo. This seeming chaos is all an esoteric skill that relies strictly on precise timing.

Herb directs Whitey's attention to one lad in particular. He appears to be about eighteen. His dark brown hair is well greased and combed back into a ducktail. He has a cigarette sophomorically placed over his right ear. His shirtless physique is striking and his well-cut muscles ripple with each move. His set jaw and cold eye say he doesn't take any guff. "Whitey, I want you to meet Frank. He runs the pin boys, he's gonna show you the ropes."

Whitey stands slack jawed staring at this manly appearing young man. Frank stares back sizing up his new pigeon. He pulls his Camel cigarette from behind his ear, places it between his lips, and extends his hand toward Whitey.

Whitey is struck by how cool this guy appears. He's everything a young boy imagines a man to be. He notices how large Frank's swollen knuckles have become and how yellow his nicotine-stained fingers appear—all this is due to picking up pins and smoking cigarettes. Whitey can't help but feel mediocre in contrast to Frank's worldly brashness.

With a somewhat intimidating tone, Frank says, "So your

skinny punk ass thinks you can do this work." Staring even harder, Frank adds, "Well, we'll give ya ah try." The skepticism in his voice is telling. After all, this work is demanding and he goes through a lot of boys who can't make the grade. To monitor Whitey's progress, Frank places him in the lane next to him. He's still apprehensive of his ability to make the cut.

Sure that he can adapt to this new environment of swashbucklers, Whitey keeps a wary eye on the actions and reactions of the rest of the boys. They all smoke and cuss for the most part. Frank, in particular, holds Whitey's attention. When Frank cusses, it rolls off his tongue like poetry. Within a week, Whitey is not satisfied to merely become *like* Frank, he wants to *be* Frank.

The pin boys have a strong camaraderie. They stick together against drunk and abusive bowlers who sometimes throw a ball at a boy who isn't quick enough in returning their ball or in the case of a boy working doubles while a co-worker is on break and doesn't clear the downed pins quick enough. It's not above the pin boys to return the culprit's ball on another lane.

* * *

On this insignificant Sunday afternoon Jake Davis, a former pin boy who had quit the summer before to travel with the carnival, has returned. He is entertaining all the boys with tales of his time on the road. He's garnering quite a crowd with word getting around that not only has he returned but he is about to show off his newfound ability to eat light bulbs and double-edged razorblades.

Zeke Allen is beyond fascinated by the prospect of personally watching someone do this. He has nearly single handedly got the word around that Jake is going to demonstrate how he can do this with no damage to himself. With nearly equal anticipation, the boys begin to gather in front of the bowling alley.

Jake has already swaggered in and is leaning against the building supporting himself with one foot on the ground while the other is angled so his foot is flat against the brick wall behind him. Totally basking in the attention, he takes a long drag on his Pall Mall, blows a smoke ring and exhales the rest in two streams through his nostrils. At the same time, he reaches in his shirt pocket and pulls out a packet of Gillette double blades. "Somebody get me a Coke, I need a Coke for this," barks Jake.

Zeke is in a near panic that this long-awaited feat may not be coming off if he can't come up with a Coke. "Come on you guys, chip in and get the man a Coke."

Begrudgingly, with a few pennies from here and there and a nickel from Zeke, a dime is at last raised to cover the price of a Coke. Now with payment satisfied, Jake slowly and methodically removes a razor from the small cardboard box and begins to unwrap it. The small crowd of teen-age boys are completely enraptured with Jake's every move. To demonstrate the authenticity of the razor, Jake holds it up in everyone's view. Satisfied he has the attention of the crowd, he makes a slice through the wrapping with the flamboyance of a polished carnival hawker. With his next move, he places the blade into his mouth. His tongue is seen moving it into position. SNAP! SNAP! goes the steel as Jake's teeth break it into smaller pieces. At last satisfied it's small enough to swallow, in true sideshow tradition, he places his hand on his throat as if to massage it, takes a drink of Coke and swallows. He then opens his mouth to demonstrate it's indeed empty and furthermore there are no cuts.

In the way of young boys regarding things that strike them as unusual, they want to see it performed again. Not ready to dismiss his crowd, Jake orders another Coke. This time there is enough enthusiasm that the money is raised immediately. This time instead of a razor blade, Jake produces a light bulb. With a recently acquired flair of the wrist, he cracks the bulb against the brick wall. It produces several bite size shards. With another showy wrist move, Jake picks one shard and places it on his tongue. The next sound is of glass being crunched. In this case, it's Jake's teeth that are doing the crunching. CRUNCH, CRUNCH goes the glass until it is pulverized into a consistency Jake deems a swallowable uniformity. Repeating the same showmanship of massaging his throat, he takes a gulp of Coke and sends the glass to mingle with the razor blade somewhere in the recesses of his gullet.

Satisfied he's gotten all the attention these young swags are willing to give him, Jake lights a Pall Mall and saunters off with his Coke in one hand and the cigarette in the other.

To say that Whitey doesn't find this feat dangerously alluring would be an understatement. "I can't believe he just ate all that stuff and it din't kill 'im," says Whitey.

"I'm thinkin' them Cokes he was drinkin' proly dissolved all them razorblades," says Zeke in a condescending tone, as if this attitude will normalize what only seemed dangerous.

"Well that ain't gonna make me wanna try it," says Whitey still not satisfied Zeke's explanation is convincing. With a moment more of contemplation, Whitey adds, "I'm thinkin' Jake's gotta be a loon ta do all that crazy shit."

"Maybe, but at least he's our loon," says Zeke.

CHAPTER 4

As since the beginning of time, summers are eternal for youths and too hastily come to an end for adults. This is also the case for the residents of Elbertport. The adults gather in groups around places like Burt's Bar, a local watering hole where everything from soup to nuts is discussed. The youth, on the other hand, gather at such places as Joan's Restaurant. The draw for the boys is the girls and of course it follows true for the girls to be checking out the boys.

Saturday afternoons the youth are especially devoted to implementing creative methods to dodge the watchful eyes of adults (not that this endeavor isn't at the forefront of most of the Elbertport teens every day). On Saturdays, Whitey has a distinct advantage. He's required to attend Reverend Johnson's Catechism class from 10:00 A.M. till 11:30 A.M. every Saturday until Confirmation the following spring on Palm Sunday. After class, he's allowed to hang around for the church youth group which meets in the parish house next door to the church. They plan different youth entertainment events for themselves and are also allowed to use the kitchen facilities for making lunch, providing they leave it as they found it.

Much to the satisfaction of his parents, Whitey has not missed one session nor has he grumbled about having to attend. As a matter of fact, he is up and ready to go before early every week. Heinie is very pleased over this turn of events in his young son's life.

"You know Ethel, ve maybe gonna have a pastor in da family," says Heinie with an air of satisfaction. After all, back in Germany, Heinie's great grandfather had been a bishop. "Ve gotta lotta peoples go all vay back to da Sainted Marteen Luter," he adds with a flair of pride.

The truth behind all this attentiveness is Whitey's attraction to Melody Swanson. She's a blond-haired beauty of Swedish descent also attending the Catechism class. All of Rev. Johnson's emphasis on how much Jesus loves each of them and whose love therefore should be reciprocated can't hold a candle to the stupefying attraction he feels for this fair-haired peach.

Melody is a year younger than Whitey and is as smitten with him as he is with her. She hails from a neighboring community a few miles from Elbertport. Since neither of them have a driver's license, the only time they have together is on Saturdays. In the past, Whitey had sneaked a few phone calls to Melody, but because they were long distance calls and after seeing the cost on his phone bill, Heinie's German frugality soon put a stop to that expense.

The dozen or so other kids in the young people's group are well aware of the budding relationship between these two love birds and are willing to cover for them, knowing it could soon be their turn at romance.

Taking Melody by the hand, Whitey leads a compliant partner from the parish house back across the empty yard to the church and into the sanctuary. Passing the altar with the crucified Christ hanging there all alone, they make a quick genuflect and quickly continue unseen up another flight of stairs to the organ loft. They are following what has become a well-rehearsed weekly ritual of excitement.

After arriving at the top of the steps with both being nearly out of breath, they head to a secluded corner near the back side of the huge organ pipes. Here they slide into a familiar pew.

In whispered tones and shaking a bit, Whitey says, "We made it!"

Melody responds by placing her cupped hands over her mouth, attempting to smother an unceremonious nervous giggle.

She's also shaking a bit. Neither are trembling from fear, rather from the long anticipation of being alone once again. They both sit staring straight ahead with their own thoughts for a few moments as they try to compose themselves. Even the "all seeing eye" painted above the chancel is overlooked.

Heaven must be a lot like this cause if I were any happier, I'd pass out! thinks Whitey.

Melody is also lost in her own thoughts. Feeling the nervous sweat running down her sides, she muses, *I wonder if I stink?!*

The thought of being personally responsible for anything that can sabotage this rendezvous is making her very uptight. Just as this speculation works its way through her thoughts, she suddenly catches a whiff of nervous perspiration. Not realizing Whitey had just raised his own arm to place it over the back of the pew and around her, a feeling of panic overtakes her as she shudders. Realizing it is Whitey's sweat and not hers, gives her a moment of relief. In another second, Whitey is placing that long dreamed of kiss on her lips sending her blood rushing into all parts of her person. It's overstimulating every organ in her young body, causing her to swoon limply in his arms. The previous concerns over sweat are lost in the moment, never to be given another thought.

Both are breathing so rapidly and their heads are twisting on each other's lips hard enough that any would be onlooker might question if their mouths may have locked together and they are having difficulty pulling apart.

Regardless what others may make of this spectacle, for these two, nirvana could not be closer. This meeting is the culmination of a weeks' worth of pent up dreaming for this very moment and to them it couldn't be more perfect.

They come up for air for a moment and to assess where they

are going next. Words are coming in gasps.

"I really missed you Melody," says Whitey, tightening his hold on her.

"I've dreamed about you all week. I've missed you, too," says Melody sinking deeper into his arms.

With hearts filled with adolescent passion, they fall back into a long and passionate kiss. Accompanying these beguiling sensations, Whitey and Melody are enjoying a sense of timelessness. This making out is complete enough to affect them physically, mentally, and spiritually. They feel a oneness with themselves, with God, and with one another.

"Melody, I want to ask you something." Whitey clears his throat. It's obvious he is nervous. "Will you go steady with me?" asks Whitey, while removing his ring.

There is a moment of hesitation on Melody's part as she processes this proposition. "I will—but I can't wear your ring. My parents told me I can't go steady until I'm sixteen," says Melody with a bit of remorse.

Hoping for the best, but ready for the worst, Whitey is partially gratified with this compromise. What he would have preferred is that she wear his ring as a symbol that her heart is given exclusively to him. Nevertheless, and regardless of parental concerns, they each share the similar opinion that they have deep feelings for each other that are as full-grown as any adult relationship. As young teens with this mindset, it is nearly impossible for anyone to tell them differently.

Having finished professing their love for one another in this more profound manner, they wrap their arms around each other in a final embrace.

Without as much as a stair creaking to warn of an intruder, they are suddenly interrupted by the unmistakable form of Mrs. Norwald, the church organist. With an armload of sheet music, she's standing at the top of the stairs gazing at the two of them completely dumbfounded. Finally assessing what is obviously, but unbelievably going on in her loft, she blurts out, "Well for the love of God! What are you two kids up to?!" Her words penetrate the air like bullets.

Caught totally off guard, Whitey quickly readjusts himself tipping Melody's head back, he proclaims, "I'm trying to get something out of her eye Mrs. Norwald. Honest that's all that's going on."

In the next moment, the two of them are giggling as, hand in hand, they fly down the stairs hoping to avoid any other adult scrutiny.

CHAPTER 5

1959 (four years later)

Since most of the people living in Elbertport are made up of some western European descent, lines of division are not drawn because of ethnicity. But that doesn't mean divisions aren't drawn. In this region of Norwegians, Finnlanders, Swedes, Germans, and Danes, most belong to Trinity Lutheran Parish, a member of the Augustana Synod. Those that don't are usually members of St. Ann's Catholic Parish. Suspicions between these two denominations can run deep enough to provide parishioners exclusive denominational cemeteries so even the dead don't mingle.

The young people of Elbertport couldn't care less about

these denominational schisms. After all, these divisions were set by their parents' generation or even earlier. This doesn't mean they don't have their own rifts. The major concern of the youth of this community is whether you're a town kid or a country kid. The discord over this issue runs just as deep as that of their parents' religious issues. The town kids have set the bar of town sophistication so high that a country kid is unable to measure up. Consequently, the country kids have formed their own clique. This begins in grade school in the only common place they meet as a group—riding the school bus.

School has been in session since the day after Labor Day. These groups are mostly separated through the summer months, but now are daily thrown into close proximity. Tensions are rising between these opposing clans.

Buck Ackerson is nearly twenty and has been out of school since he quit in the eleventh grade. He's been known to hit guys so hard he breaks their jaw with one punch. He has a plan to get a fight going between the groups and has drafted Dace, a senior this year, to set it in motion this coming Friday night at the dance.

Orin Anderson is a tough farm kid who has let it be known he isn't going to be pushed around by any "Townies," as the town kids are known in country circles. Buck has selected Orin to be his target.

Friday night finally rolls around. Buck pulls Dace aside in the parking lot. "Dace you get something going with that prick Orin. I need you to rile him up until he is good and pissed, then get him to come outside and I'll take over from there," says Buck, "Oh and by the way, you do a good job and there's a couple beers in it for you," further promises Buck.

The dance is being held at the local community center which

also doubles as the school district's gymnasium. The funding for such a building came from a grass roots grant given to the community after WWII.

Jim Dingman is the twenty-something young man hired to check the sobricty level of the attendees. The dance organizers have placed him on a stool at the entrance. His job is to smell everybody's breath for alcohol. He's also in charge of keeping order among the students—sort of a bouncer.

Making his way past Jim's unfettered alcohol sniffing nose, Dace spots Orin with a gang of four other country boys hanging out in the back of the gym. They're trying to make some time with a couple of town girls. One of the girls is his cousin, Sheila, Whitey's sister. Orin is particularly trying to make time with her knowing full well she is dating Buck.

This might be just the thing I need, thinks Dace as he makes his way toward the cluster. "Hi Sheila, how you and Buck doin'?"

"We're doin' okay," says Sheila. She is wise to the animosity building up between Buck and Orin. She also has a feeling Dace may be up to something more than merely stopping by to say hello

"Sheila, do you smell somethin'?" asks Dace holding his nose. "I know I do! It smells like country boy pig shit!" Dace feigns not seeing Orin, then says, "Oh I guess it's just you Orin. I guess I didn't see you right away."

Sheila has a feeling she knows where this may be going. Not wanting to be a part of it she rolls her eyes at her cousin and walks off.

It's clear Orin heard every word Dace has dared to say. "You losin' yer mind little man? You think you can piss an alligator off afore you get through the swamp and not have a piece ah yer ass bit off?" questions Orin with more than a menacing look.

"Why, you thinkin' yer the big bad alligator gonna get a piece ah me? You ain't nothin but a shit kickin' country punk," states Dace with a smirk. Dace is enthralled with the idea of starting a fight with a tough guy like Orin without having to finish it.

It's clear Orin's rage is beginning to rise as his face turns red and takes on a nearly demented twist.

"I'm gonna kick yer skinny ass so hard yer bastard grandkids 'll feel it," says Orin in a near whisper not wanting to draw any undue attention.

"I bet a buck if you meet me in the parkin' lot, I'll have yer ass chewin' gravel before you know what hit you."

"Put yer money where yer mouth is little man," says Orin.

Sheila hasn't gone beyond hearing distance. Dace motions her back. "Here Sheila, hang on to this buck for a while." Looking boldly at Orin, Dace says, "Give'r yer buck big man and meet me out back."

With that all settled, Dace makes his way to the door like a man on a mission only to be told by Jim if he leaves he can't get back in. Ignoring the warning, Dace steps out of the door with Orin and his four companions close on his heels.

Realizing he's outside the safety of the crowded gymnasium where any ruckus could hardly get started before Jim would have put a stop to it, Dace can't get to the protection of Buck waiting in the parking lot fast enough. Rounding the corner and expecting to see his waiting allies, he's startled to see only a couple latecomers making their way to the dance. *Where in the hell are you Buck!?* is his terrified thought.

Without even looking, Dace knows Orin is much closer than he wants to have to deal with alone. Just as this thought is soaring through his mind, he's aware of a blow that feels more like a ham coming down on his back knocking him to the ground. He's panicked by the thought that Buck has set him up and then decided to abandon him to the revenge of those he provoked.

Lying on the gravel parking lot with the wind knocked out of him, paralyzed by fear, without a plan "B," and fully expecting to be beaten within an inch of his life, he hears a familiar voice. It's as welcome as the voice of Jesus coming to save him from the pits of hell.

"Hey there, Orin. Why don't ya pick on somebody yer own size?"

Buck has been lurking in the shadows waiting for just the right provocation to confront Orin.

Orin swings around startled to be confronted by a surprise attack in the person of Buck. He's hardly prepared for what comes next as Buck sucker punches him. Orin falls to the ground with blood spurting out of what appears to be a broken nose. Buck seeing, he has an advantage, kicks him with the full brunt of the heavy engineer boots he purposely wore for this occasion, often referring to them as his "stompin' boots."

Orin reacts with a gasp of desperation as he tries to scramble on all fours to some undetermined haven of safety. The four with Orin decide it's time they weigh in on this brawl. Seeing their compatriot compromised so quickly hardly allows them the luxury of a plan. Instead, they gang rush Buck pounding him indiscriminately with fists wherever they land. Meantime, both Dace and Orin are getting back on their feet. Each quickly surmises what's going on through different lenses.

Buck has lost the element of surprise and is now busy attempting to fend off the other four boys.

Orin instantly takes advantage of the superior numbers and piles in with the vengeance of a wounded bull on the merciless pounding started by his companions.

Dace is at loss as to what to do. His mind is racing at lightning speed. He finally finds himself jerking open the door of a parked car looking for any kind of object that can be used as a weapon. Searching frantically under the front seat, his hand grabs something solid. Pulling it out, he discovers he is firmly gripping a tire iron.

Without a moment's hesitation in thought or action, he begins to bash the skulls of all those piling on Buck. The sound of iron meeting bone has its own distinct sound. It's a sound those on the receiving end may never hear as they crumple unconscious to the ground. In seconds, there are five seriously wounded boys in the parking lot.

A winded Buck has managed to get to his feet, unaware of why he can. Along with the crowd that has gathered, he stands looking at the carnage. Dace also near breathlessness, is standing quiet and stunned, still gripping the tire iron, looking at his five bleeding, unconscious, hapless victims lying in a pile around his feet.

Jim Dingman is in the forefront of the crowd. He is frantic. He knows somehow he's going to be held responsible. Looking for a scapegoat of his own, he begins to bellow, "What the hell is going on here? Who the hell did all this?"

No one is paying much attention to him. Rather, a few in the crowd begin administering aid to those lying in what appears to be a mortal situation. "I think he's dead," states a girl attempting to revive Orin.

Hearing this, Dace drops the tire iron and bolts off into the darkness.

CHAPTER 6

Reduced to a state of shock, Dace wanders around mindlessly in the darkness trying to sort out all that has taken place. The words spoken by the girl regarding Orin, *I think he's dead*, continue to plague him.

He feels alone and in need of consolation. His cousin, Whitey, wasn't at the dance because he is working tonight. Eventually, Dace finds himself behind the bowling alley. Checking his watch, he decides: *It's 11:30. I'll wait til midnight when Whitey gets off work, he'll know what to do.*

With his eyes firmly fixed on the bowling alley door, he remains in the shadows. Chain smoking cigarettes seems to be at least a temporary elixir as he waits for the familiar form of his cousin to emerge. "It's midnight Whitey. Where the hell are ya?" questions Dace in a desperate whisper heard only by himself.

No sooner has Dace demanded an accounting when a wave of security flows over him as Whitey appears on the street. Cupping his hands over his mouth he blows through them giving a low, mournful whistle. It's a signal they have used with one another since early childhood. Recognizing this alert, Whitey instantly turns around searching through the darkness for its source. Not able to see, he in turn responds back employing the same signal. In a moment, Dace comes up to him.

"Wadda ya doin' out here spookin' around this time ah night?" asks Whitey.

Taking his nearly empty package of Pall Mall from his shirt pocket, Dace offers Whitey a cigarette. Never refusing an opportunity to add even more yellow nicotine stains to his already embossed fingers, Whitey accepts. Now sure he has Whitey's full attention; Dace's sense of desperation quickly resurfaces as he stumbles through the telling of the events of the evening. The bond between these two cousins is closer than the sisterly bond of their often-bickering mothers. Whitey listens with the ear of a spiritual adviser.

"Do ya think ya really kilt any of 'em Dace?"

"I dunno, Whitey. I just kept hittin' on 'em til they wasn't movin'. Whadda you think is gonna come outta all this?"

"I ain't got a clue, but we gonna have ta do somethin'," says Whitey, fully engaged. He pauses for a minute in deep thought. "You remember that shack Dud Olsen built up in the hills when he ran away from home?" Not waiting for Dace to answer, Whitey continues, "You gotta get up there until we can figure things out."

"Yeah, but Dud ended up hangin' himself in that shack rather than go home. His ole man beat him every time he got drunk, but findin' him hangin' there like he did, he wailed louder than a dyin' calf in a snow storm. You know damn well his ghost is still seen by a lot of people goin' up there," says Dace apprehensively.

"I never heard of him hurtin' nobody though," says Whitey. There's a hopeful note to this statement and no trace of anxiety because he's not the one who must discover the truth supporting this belief.

Considering the alternative, Dace says, "I think I can deal with it. You go on home and keep yer ear to the ground as ta what's comin' down. Don't tell my ma what's happenin'. Just tell her I'll be back later. Oh, and bring me a can of beans and a pack of cigarettes tomorrow." It's clear having Whitey tell him what to do has calmed him some.

Quietly, they both slip into the silence of the night. With his first step up the hill that leads to Dud's shack, Dace is fully aware he's stepping into an unknown world. These hills have been the playground for generations of Elbertport's youth. But during the night, these same spaces become the domain of those creating sounds not heard at any other time. It's the sound of woeful spirits breathing their breath of despair through the trees. The trees in turn, reverberate with a labored creaking sound. Some swear these sounds resemble the moans of those troubled spirits left to languish in their fate. It's enough to send a chill down his spine.

As frightening as facing this nocturnal junket is turning out to be, Dace finds he's at a juncture. Not granted another option, he must continue forward or suffer the consequences of turning back. Dace remembers from his Sunday School days the part of the twenty-third Psalm that says, "Yea, though I walk through the valley of the shadow of death, I will fear no evil for Thou art with me." He attempts to get through it from beginning to end but when this isn't helping as much as he'd hoped, he begins to recite the Lord's Prayer. Afraid he's getting the words mixed up and the prayer will end up rejected, he goes back to the Psalm. Concerned that his improper efforts are the reason he still has a lot of fear, he tries harder to remember the words he had little use for at the time.

Nonetheless, through this exercise, the time races by and he soon finds himself at the tangled path leading to Dud's shack. Grateful he's made it safely inside, he thanks God and uses his lighter to locate a candle. He's in luck, there is barely a stub of one next to the window. With the room illuminated, it presents a pile of semi-fresh garden produce. It's obvious this shack has been recently inhabited. After a rather nervous speculation as to whether they may still be around, he decides the stuff was probably picked earlier and left behind and makes his way into the waiting bunk.

* * *

Back in town, Whitey is at a loss as to how he's going to break all this to his aunt, Brina. She's the younger sister to his mother and widowed. Since the government pays very little support to surviving family members of those lost or killed in war, she has to depend on her family for financial and moral support in raising her two boys. Most of the time she's beside herself with each of them tormenting her in ways only teenage boys can—it comes with no effort.

It's late when Whitey arrives home. He chooses to sleep on Dace's request to alert his aunt, deciding to wait until morning to talk to her.

Morning arrives sooner than he had expected. Usually he sleeps in on Saturday, but he's awakened by his mother at 7:30 A.M. "Whitey, your aunt Brina is on the phone. She is saying Dace didn't come home last night. What do you know about this?"

Ethel and Brina are the only two living sisters out of four girls. The other two sisters died in infancy of pneumonia. They love each other and would do nearly anything for the other, until it comes to blaming each other's boys for the way their own children are behaving. This morning is no different. Brina is sure that Whitey is more than culpable for knowing Dace's whereabouts. Ethel, on the other hand assures her sister she has no business blaming Whitey because he spent the evening working at the bowling alley.

"What do you know about Dace not coming home last night? And don't you lie to me!" demands Ethel in the unmistakable voice of one who will mete out repercussions if she suspects this last imperative is violated in any way, shape, or form. Because Heinie's railroad work leaves him absent much of the time, it's been left mostly to Ethel to keep the family in line. Consequently, she has developed her own methods.

Whitey is only half awake as this bombardment of questions from his mother begins to relentlessly assail him. Desperate in his attempt to sound convincing without giving too much information, Whitey struggles with a half-geared brain. "He said he got in a fight at the dance and thinks he may have kilt a kid so he's taken off."

Sheila is also awakened by the sound of her mother's agitated exchange with Whitey. She listens as Whitey tries to answer questions he doesn't know the answer to. After a few futile attempts by his mother to get to the bottom of what he means by "he may have kilt a kid," and "he's taken off," Sheila decides it's time to weigh in with what she saw with her own eyes and ears.

"Mom, I know what happened."

Hearing these words from a daughter who is a straight-A student and has never given her parents any reason to suspect she is anything other than the princess they have always believed her to be, Ethel swings her full attention toward her daughter.

"I was there at the dance when all this took place—I saw it all," confesses Sheila. She's not capable of telling a lie even if it meant she could save her own life. Whereas, Whitey will tell the truth, if he has to lie to do it. Ethel knows her children well enough to put much more credibility into her daughter's words than to spend hours trying to untangle Whitey's attempts to dodge a straight answer.

Now wholly absorbed in what her daughter is about to tell her, Ethel's demeanor changes from hostility to affability knowing full well with this daughter, she doesn't have to engage the mind of a prosecutor to get to the truth. Over the next fifteen minutes, Sheila goes into great detail, trying hard to leave nothing out. Whitey is also paying close attention. Sheila's account pretty much interlaces with Dace's description except for the part of Orin being dead.

"Did you say Orin isn't dead, Sheila?" questions Whitey showing a bit more than a passing interest.

"No, I'm saying he was alive when the ambulance came and took him away, but Sheriff Miles Peleton said it'll be a miracle if he pulls through," continues Sheila.

Ethel listens with the keen ear of one who won't be fooled unthinkingly. She gives Whitey a stern, hard no nonsense look and grabs a fist full of his hair. Not quite finished with him, she twists his head to meet her gaze, then follows up saying, "Don't even try to lie to me! What exactly do you know about where Dace went?"

This is the part of his mother Whitey has never been able to lead on with some complex off the wall deception he may attempt to weave. Whitey has always been able to read how deep he can sink a lie or stretch the truth. Mrs. Bigsly, one of Whitey's teachers, maintains, "If that boy can't dazzle me with brilliance, he'll definitely attempt to baffle me with his BS."

Still not ready to roll over on his cousin, Whitey measures his words, careful not to give any indication that Dace is holed up in Dud Olsen's shack. "I don't know where he went. All's he tol' me is he's gonna take off."

"I don't believe a word you're telling me, Whitey. I don't care how much you think you can come and go as you please, you're going stay right in this house until you tell me the truth."

Remembering he did tell Dace he'd bring some supplies, the thought of being a prisoner at home is more than he can bear. "Ma, I'm tellin' the truth. Dace said that he had to get away to think things out and that he'd be back. Please don't torture me with all these questions!" pleads Whitey.

"You can decide for yourself to be "un-tortured" when your desire to tell the truth becomes greater than your desire to tell a lie, young man," says Ethel with the resolve of a Fuller Brush salesman.

Knowing his mother's unwavering resoluteness, Whitey realizes there is no sense in groveling, begging, or sniveling in the hopes of receiving an early out. He's just going to have to take the bull by the horns and move on to plan-B.

Rather than phone Brina, Ethel has opted to go across the backyard to her sister's home and personally give her what she has learned. Whitey is weighing his options.

Not wanting to leave his family totally in the lurch, Whitey composes a note. His thoughts are precise. *"I can't sit here and let Dace struggle alone with this dilemma. I've got to give him my support. We've always been there for each other. I just can't desert him now when he really needs an ally. Don't worry about either of us, we'll be fine. Whitey"*

Finishing his note, he cautiously leaves the confines of his room. Making his way to the kitchen, he spots Sheila taking advantage of their mother's absence to make some phone calls to her friends. She is so engrossed in her phone gossip, she doesn't even notice Whitey as he fills a bag with some canned goods and a package of his mother's Winston cigarettes. He then makes his way back to his bedroom in time to hear his mother return. She's busy admonishing Sheila for tying up the phone.

Realizing it's now or never, he places the note on his bed, grabs his buck knife and a rolled up sleeping bag, opens the window, and shimmies out to the ground. With provisions in hand, he stealthily makes his way through the neighborhood as quickly as he can, hoping to make a clean getaway without drawing any unnecessary suspicion. Soon, he's at the foot of Church Hill. Looking around for anyone who might spot him, he only sees ole' lady Jensen working in her garden. She pauses, taking a moment to look him over, then runs to her house. Despite her odd behavior, he nonetheless begins his trek up toward Dud's shack.

The sun is making its way higher in the sky, promising a beautiful day. These hills are challenging enough without carrying an extra load of the pilfered canned goods over his shoulder. Putting one foot in front of the other he counts his steps—1-2-3-4----. This has always made these steep treks bearable and makes the time it takes conquering them seem less burdensome. All the same, he finds himself panting and breaking into a sweat as he crests the first summit, periodically looking over his shoulder for any followers.

Only a few boys from town have taken the time to explore the many ridges and deep ravines the last ice age cut through this region. They're densely covered with at least fifty years of growth, since the last logging expedition took place. Parents have systematically discouraged their children from entering this dense wilderness with stories of bears, wild cougars, kid eating coyotes, as well as an assorted number of restless spirits still roaming the area ready to rip the heart out of those foolish enough to enter their domain.

Dace and Whitey are among the few boys who are sure these warnings are for sissies. Whitey especially is inclined to believe he can pee right into the wind and not get wet. Dace on the other hand is a natural follower rather than a leader. In spite of their differences, in many ways they have become the living embodiment of dereliction in the eyes of many Elbertport's parents.

Stopping to rest, Whitey takes advantage of the moment to

cup his hands around his mouth and sounds three low toned whistles signaling his presence. This low mournful pronouncement penetrates the trees. Within seconds the returned signal gives Whitey the assurance he has not made this expedition in vain. In matter of seconds, Whitey enters a familiar ravine he quickly recognizes as the portal to Dud's shack.

An hour has passed since Whitey made his flight from the comforts of a modern home to a wilderness setting presenting itself as his only bastion of safety and comfort. It's well hidden beneath a group of cedars surrounded by thick vegetation consisting of bramble bushes, fallen trees, and wild grape vines entangling everything in their path.

Any upgrades on this hundred-square foot shack have been an attempt to solve an immediate problem. This has resulted in roofs, doors, and walls in various stages of disintegration—but nothing a prop pole can't fix. As a matter of fact, if all the prop poles were removed, the structure would collapse like a house of cards. Much of the building materials are cut from the surrounding trees and turned into a series of pillars and rafters. The only exception is the severely rusted metal roof that had been found abandoned years ago, with some mysterious provenance having to do with the logging industry. The environment around the structure is littered with signs of the modern world with a full complement of empty cans and bottles, all indicating it's had some ongoing use.

The interior is hardly a place someone with allergies would care to spend any time. It has the damp smell of rotting wood. A bunk built a foot or so off the dirt floor serves for both sleeping and sitting. It is cushioned with cedar boughs and blanketed with a tattered sleeping bag that looks as though it's been here as long as the shack has. The only window is fashioned with a leather hinge on one side of the top and the other hinge is fashioned from what appears to be a shoelace. It is designed to be propped open from the bottom with a stick.

The shack bears all the accouterments of a primitive dungeon, but for a young boy escaping the confines of the adult world, it's a chunk of heaven. All in all, every part of this glorious outpost suggests wear and tear.

The attraction of this outstation is the freedom it provides. A boy is totally unsupervised. He eats when he wants, sleeps when he wants, and any other activity—all with no adult hanging over any of his decisions. There's a clay cut with the purest water on the face of God's earth not fifty feet from the shack for drinking only. To do anything as unimaginable as using this pristine source to bathe would be all but a sacrilege.

Canned goods of anything but vegetables are welcomed, with the exception of baked beans which are the only plants deemed suitable to eat. Many have talked about how they could set out snare traps to catch rabbits, but to date no one has ever made that work. Canned spam, ham, hash, all snagged from some unsuspecting mother's pantry are acceptable staples of camp life.

Dace couldn't be happier to see Whitey, especially with the stowage he's bagged up.

"Whatchu got in the bag?"

"I dunno, I jus grabbed stuff hopin' I had enough ta last a couple days," reports Whitey.

"Lemme look, I'm damn near starvin," says Dace as he paws through the bag. "Ah here we go," he says pulling out a can of pork and beans. Within a minute, he has the can cut open, tipped up, and dumping a load into his waiting jaws. After two more mouthfuls, he sets the can down. His mood is pensive.

"Is he dead?" is all Dace can manage to say. His voice is hesitant, his gaze reticent. Both know exactly to what he is referring.

"No, but if he ain't, they're sayin' he outta be, he ain't outta the woods yet," qualifies Whitey, with an equal amount of concern. "The Sheriff's lookin' for ya. He's claimin' that tire iron is a deadly weapon."

"I spose it is. But so is five guys beatin' on Buck. What was I sposed ta do, let 'em kill 'im?"

"I ain't blamin' ya. I'da done the same if it was me. You got a plan for what we're gonna do now?"

"I'm figurin' I gotta get the hell outta Dodge afore somebody puts two and two together and comes lookin' for me up here."

"Well count me in. I'm goin' with ya."

"You take off with me, yer ma's gonna be really pissed," says Dace with a knowing grin.

"Not nearly as pissed as yer ma's gonna be." Whitey has the same grin. "'Sides, I left my ma a note."

"I always knew I could count on you. Yer the best cousin a guy could have."

"We gotta come up with a plan though," says Whitey, looking around as though they can't be too careful. "Who do ya suppose knows we could be up here?"

"I'm sure Vaughn will figure it out soon enough. He's just enough of a weasel to want to be a big shot and turn me in. He'd turn our grandma in, if it made him look important. He lives fer glory," says Dace with a tone of disgust for his brother's shortcomings. Pausing for a moment's thought he adds, "Maybe we should set up a watch so we ain't caught with our pants down."

Whitey's mind is already churning in a different direction. "I agree about gettin' caught with our pants down. But I think we gotta move outta here real soon. Maybe we can wait til tonight and hop a boxcar they're loadin' on a car ferry headin' fer Wisconsin," says Whitey with a confident air suggesting he's done this many times.

Dace contemplates this for a moment. After all, this is a bigger move than either of them have ever made. The only thing that comes close is when they told their parents they were going down to the outdoor free show one Tuesday summer night, instead they jumped into Terry Steelson's chopped and channeled 1949 Ford and headed for a grasser in the middle of Abby Allison's orchard some ten miles from town. The cops came and everybody ran in all directions leaving nearly a full keg. Those that had cars took off through the orchard leaving everyone else to fend for themselves. Dace and Whitey, too scared to move, stayed hidden in the woods until daylight.

Both were supposed to be grounded for the rest of their natural lives or at least until Jesus came back.

Living in the glory of having done something this daring gained them a new place in the minds of their peers who consider their own lives mundane and ordinary. This new plan will top that orchard fiasco forever.

"I'm with ya, Whitey," says Dace picturing the looks on the faces of all the kids in the senior class when they discover how this daring feat took place.

They begin to plot their great exodus. "Let's make our way down toward the boat landing and check it out. I know they got boats leaving all day and all night," says Whitey. "It'll just be a matter ah which one we can get out on without gettin' caught."

By the time, they get themselves organized, the sun is much

lower, promising the end of another day. The decision is made, they pack up and move out. Whitey has prepared himself before arriving here. Dace on the other hand is left a little shorthanded. He has decided to abscond with the only sleeping bag available—the tattered one left in the shack. Making the trek across forest covered dunes and deep valleys is not an easy task even for those who know the terrain, much less doing it in the dark. It's easily a two-mile trek as the crow flies, but now with these added obstacles it's going to be a two-hour hike at best.

The light is continuing to gradually fade, leaving them yet at least a half mile from the harbor. With twilight turning to darkness, the strange sounds of the night forest are returning, reminding them this is not their jurisdiction. Both find comfort in the presence of the other so they don't have to deal with their hair-raising goose bumps alone.

"You spose Dud's ghost is still roamin' around up here?" asks Dace with a nervous little titter.

"Hell, I don't know and don't care ta find out fer sure," replies Whitey with the same nervous concern in his voice.

"You spose ghosts wear the same clothes they was wearin' when they died or are they naked?" further inquires Dace

"Jeez oh Pete Dace, will you stop 'for one ah these guys decides ta show ya. Don't be foolin' around kissin' the devil good morning 'for ya meet 'im!" says Whitey with a more than impatient sigh.

CHAPTER 7

Small towns stay true to themselves. Wherever people in these communities gather, they sift through the doings of the day. There is never a shortage of opinions on any subject. Many a person who has managed to escape the judicial system is categorically sentenced to suffer some form of public retribution regardless of the official evidence or lack of.

By afternoon the victims of Dace's tire iron have been declared dead and resurrected many times by the summations of the crowds gathered in the barber shop, the coffee shop, the tavern, and even the Methodist men's club. The truth is, the injuries in this fight are all likely to heal, even Orin's, but nevertheless, the Sheriff is threatening to obtain a warrant for Dace Kidman's arrest for assault with a deadly weapon.

In this small town, there is never a lack of judgments. Opinions are much like rectums—everybody has one.

"Sumpins definitely wrong with this generation. Why hell, when I was a kid we'd put the gloves on and settle things like men. We didn't go around beatin' each other with a goddam tire iron," says Barley Evans.

Not to be out sanctified, Cecil Lemke recalls how a wrestling match would be set aside on a given day. When it was over, the winner and loser shook hands and parted friends. "Hell, that's the way we done er. We didn't need ta use any of the brass knuckles, switchblade knives, or fer god's sake a goddam tire iron these kids use nowadays."

"Somebody should get aholt ah that Kidman kid and give 'im a damn good thrashin'," says Butch Sorenson.

"Word has it, he lit outta town. Nobody's seen 'im since last night. If he hooked a ride with a truck driver, he could be clear down state by now," says Tom Lunderman.

Meanwhile, Ethel has discovered Whitey's note. She is beside herself and is displaying her usual sense of frustration with her son's predictable unpredictability. Sheila has never given her parents even a hint of trouble and they rather expected this second child would follow suit. When their blond-haired boy began to run away at two years old, it became apparent they were dealing with a different creature.

Heinie is more optimistic and willing to hang to the hope, "Give da boy a coupla missed meals and he come crawlin' home."

Sheila isn't so sure. She bears the emotional scars of dealing with her younger brother over the years when he had been left in her charge. Remaining as captives in her thoughts are events that only an older sister with a younger brother would have to endure.

One specific memory stands out. Since their parents would not allow locks on their children's bedrooms, Whitey delighted in accessing her private things. She particularly recalls the torment he caused her emotionally the day he sneaked into her room, forced the toe of his shoe against the inside bottom of the door preventing her from entering and then read a love note from Buck back through the closed door.

By the time she managed to get the door opened, Whitey had made his escape through an open window.

Sheila prides herself on her long suffering with this recalcitrant brother and hopes God will be pleased with her behavior and will grant her a better place in heaven. She also is very aware of the bond between her brother and his cousins and what hellish antics they can conspire to bring to life.

Since Sheila was a witness to what took place in that dreadful parking lot the night before, the sheriff comes to take a statement as to what she saw. He is interrupted in the middle of his interview by a call on his radio involving a suspicious death at the Dennis Walden residence. To say Sheila is less than happy to be rid of this intrusion is an understatement.

She is a truthful girl, prone to tell more of the truth than she's been asked. This inclination has particularly been to the detriment of all those sharing with her in mutual wrongdoings and who are perfectly willing to lie their way out of trouble. More than once when confronted, Sheila has pulled those sharing in her breaches of conduct down with her, only to make a bad situation even worse—especially when her compatriot's testimonies are exposed as lies.

"I can't help it. When I'm asked, I have to tell the truth," says Sheila. "I just don't want to get in any trouble."

"Yeah, but you don't have to tell so much of it," laments Buck when he's finally gotten the opportunity to confront Sheila as to what she has told the sheriff. "You made it sound like poor ole Orin was getting set up."

"Well??!!" she responds with a look of one who was smart enough to figure out what Dace was up to in luring Orin outside the dance. At this point, she has no intention of compromising her position.

"'Well??!!' is not going to make this situation blow over, if you keep feedin' the sheriff with more information than he's askin'. Let him fill in his own blanks," says Buck with a little more male bravado. "As bad as it may ah looked ta you, Orin and the rest of 'em are all gonna live. Besides I was gettin' the worst of the deal."

Sheila is always torn as to where truth and her allegiance to Buck begin and end. Buck is her boyfriend and though she considers herself a good girl, she is drawn to Buck's "bad boy" image. It's as though she feels because of her goodness and forthrightness she can compensate for Buck in his wayward ways, and maybe even bring about a change in him.

CHAPTER 8

By now the light along the path has diminished to the point Dace and Whitey can only see a few feet—anything further is lost in the darkness. The sounds of the creaking trees are suddenly disrupted by a sound not associated with anything the forest usually produces. It's a low moaning sound accompanied by a form that has somehow found its way in front of them. It gives the appearance of being a human male with a rope around his neck. His face cannot be seen since his back is turned toward them.

Dace and Whitey stop in their tracks frozen with terror. The thought races through both their minds like a bolt of lightning that this is the unmistakable apparition of Dud Olsen. He's come back to claim a bizarre kind of reparation for staying in his cabin. Both gasp as the form stops not five feet in front of them, lifting its arms as it slowly turns its rope collared neck around all the while moaning until suddenly it shouts "Wooooh!" This outburst turns their legs to jelly as they both collapse to the forest floor. The form is now hovering within inches over its hapless victims and lets out a very familiar laugh.

"Damn you Vaughn, I shoulda known it was you," says a much-relieved Dace. "You're one sick son of a bitch. You know that?"

Whitey is barely recovered as he too rips out an epithet

against his cousin. "Your nothin' but a dickhead, Vaughn. Why you keep doin' this creepy crap?"

Vaughn couldn't be more delighted. "You guys can thank me you're still on the run. The sheriff's been nosin' around asking everybody if they know where you went. I knew damn well where you'd go, but I never squealed on ya. I just had ta let ya know ya may have fooled a lot of other people but ya never come close ta foolin' me. Besides the sheriff got busy with a real murder. Rumors say it was out at Dennis Walden's place. Sumpin' ta do with Sid Powell's ole man."

"So wadda ya gonna do now? Play the hero role like you're some kinda Sherlock Holmes and turn us in?" asks Whitey.

Whitey is well-experienced in his cousin's ways and knows how much Vaughn seeks attention. He knows Vaughn could turn on his own mother, if there was something in it for him.

"You guys give me a pack of cigarettes and I may change my mind and let ya go," says Vaughn.

"I ain't got a pack, but I'll give ya one," says Dace as he processes his brother's intentions.

Taking the cigarette, Vaughn flips out his Zippo, lights the end, takes a long drag, exhales, and pulls out an open beer from his pocket. Taking a swig he asks, "Whatta you guys gonna do now?"

Knowing his brother as he does and before Whitey can answer, Dace quickly replies, "We plan on hangin' around up here till things blow over." This lie is said in the hopes his brother will find this choice way too boring and decide to leave.

From the look on Vaughn's face, Dace's assessment is correct, this decision is proving to be way too dull for him. He takes one last drag on his cigarette, butts it, reaches into Dace's pocket, pulls out what's left of the pack of Pall Malls, and takes one more of the remaining cigarettes. Handing the rest of the pack back to Dace, he says, "Well, you little boys have a good time. I'm outta here." With that, he turns and disappears into the darkness.

Dace and Whitey stand quietly for a moment, hoping Vaughn means what he said. Without any evidence of his return, they soon grow confident they're rid of him and feel safe enough to resume their secret trek to the harbor.

Within the hour, they arrive at the top of the dune overlooking the railyard serving the boat landing. The place is ablaze with lights and filled with movement. The humming sound of a diesel-powered yard engine loading the waiting Great Lakes car ferry is unmistakable. Men with swinging lanterns signal engineers to move the train to various places. Others, on board the huge three-hundred-foot boat, scurry around inside its belly securing loaded rail cars in hopes of preventing them from breaking loose in rough seas.

Whitey immediately recognizes his father as the yard engine's engineer. His intuitive reaction is to duck as though his awareness is also his father's awareness.

Satisfied he remains unseen, his thoughts turn back to their escape route. Their task is to get into the yards, find an open box car, and climb aboard. The trick is that it must all be done with precision and totally undercover. Remaining in the shadows, they sneak down from their inconspicuous perch above the frazzle. Stealthily, they slip across the tracks to a line of rail cars standing by to be placed in the ship. With one eye open for any railroad personal and the other for an unsealed box car, the two boys hurry from car to car.

"Bingo!" says Dace in a muffled tone grasping an unsealed door. Whitey is directly behind him. In concert, they muscle open the sliding door along its track. Hoping to remain concealed, the two of them manage to get aboard and slide the door back to its closed position. It's black as pitch. Nonetheless, they remain as quiet as a grave, listening for any indications they may have been caught out. Without warning the car suddenly jerks forward tipping them from their seated position to lying on their side.

"Holy crap! We're on our way," says Dace.

It's an odd feeling to be moving without being able to see. It is impossible to determine what direction they may be going— forward or backward. Not willing to slide the door open, Whitey places his eye to a crack in the wooden planking making the walls.

"Good grief, we're going in the wrong direction!" says Whitey daring to speak out loud.

No sooner has he made this revelation than the container is brought to an abrupt stop, throwing them once again to the floor. Still not exactly sure what may be happening, another jolt is felt, followed by the sensation of moving once again. From the noise level it becomes obvious Whitey's father has taken the car off a side track and is now repositioning it to be loaded onto the waiting boat. The click of the car's steel wheels at the joints of the steel rails is pronounced. CLICK, CLICK, CLICK... only to change to a more subdued *click, click* as the wheels meet the rails on the boat.

When they come to a stop, the two lie on the floor in case a stray wave might bounce them around. They are totally at the mercy of whatever is going on around them. They dare not risk any unnecessary movements or sounds that could in turn bring about an unannounced intrusion by boat or railroad personnel. They find themselves as helpless as babies and can only hope all will end well.

At least another hour goes by without any sensations of movement. The only sound heard is the throaty blast from the boat's horn. Many times, over the span of their lives they have sat on the crest of the giant dunes overlooking the yards. Whitey and Dace have both become somewhat familiar with the process of a Great Lakes steamer as it embarks.

"I think we're leavin' the harbor," announces Dace.

"I hope you're right," says Whitey, somewhat uncertain.

"They only make that last horn blast when they pass through the breakwater into the lake," further reports Dace. His voice is more relaxed than it's been for a couple of hours.

The cracks in the walls allow only enough light to inform them the lights of the cargo hold are on. It avails them nothing. Scrounging around in their bag of supplies, Whitey produces a candle and candle stand. He puts the stand on the floor while digging around his pocket for his lighter. With the flick of a lighter the sitting candle is lit—however, it's by the hand of neither Whitey nor Dace, but rather by a strange hand poking its way through the darkness. Once again, they both gasp at the uncertainty of something alien. Their heads jerk in the direction of the now shadowed, bearded face of a young man they both have a passing recollection of from years ago. The near haunting specter of what neither of them ever want to be stares back at them as they endure a moment of fear. It's the character of Sid Powell, the AWOL guy; the military deserter.

"How ya doin' boys?" says Sid in an almost inaudible voice. His breath holds a distinct smell of alcohol. He has an unmistakable sinister smirk that's been an integral part of him since he was a kid.

"Holy shit is that you, Sid? What the hell ya doin' here?" asks Dace. Vaughn had often hung around with Sid and had him at their house occasionally when they were much younger. Dace feels he is more acquainted with him than Whitey. Although, he hasn't seen him in years, he feels free to pry.

Without answering and taking another pull off a bottle he's cradling inside his coat, he considers the question. "I might ask you boys the same damn question. Most people sittin' in a boxcar in the middle ah Lake Michigan generally ain't out here on no picnic are they now?"

Avoiding answering the same question and with a little less bravado and a little more caution, Dace reacts with, "We heard you was back in town, Sid."

"Ya, I stopped back ta pick up my '50 Plymouth coup, but my drunken ole man sold it," says Sid.

Sid's mother had been a young runaway from an Irish Traveler's community in North Carolina whose parents had an arranged marriage in mind for her. She made her way to Elbertport, where she met and married George Powell. She left George and took up with a traveling salesman from Florida when Sid was twelve. The man had been visiting Elbertport on business selling boats. She saw it as an opportunity to get out and abandoned George, her son, Sid, and Sid's younger sister, Stacy, who is now nineteen years old and lives with her boyfriend, Dennis Walden. No one has seen nor heard from this wayward wife and mother since. Soon after that, Sid's father George Powell abandoned both children for the bottle. Gossip in town has it George has now moved in with Stacy and Dennis.

Many believed Sid became malicious after his mother left, but the truth is, Sid and his father regularly abused her, and if that weren't enough, both father and son hated each other. Sid left when he was old enough to join the army. To say the family was anything less than destructive would barely describe them.

Sid is at least in his early twenties. That's several years older than Whitey and Dace. Being their senior, he automatically fills the vacuum left by Vaughn. At this point neither Dace nor Whitey are aware of how toadyish they are around these older boys. It just seems natural to let an older boy take the reins of their lives.

"You guys bring any food? I ain't ate since this afternoon," questions Sid in a menacing nearly inaudible voice. Before he has allowed either of the boys to answer, he snatches their bag and begins to sort out what he wants. Although this is not the way they wish to respond, neither has the guts to oppose Sid. After all, it's been rumored he may have killed a guy on the army base. Supposedly that's why he went AWOL.

"So, where you guys goin?" asks Sid wiping his mouth with his sleeve. Barely looking up, his eyes have taken on an even more ominous look in the dimness of the candle light.

Whitey takes the lead. "We're headin' out west. Maybe Wyoming or someplace like that."

"Yeah, I heard a guy can get a job on a ranch out there pretty easy. Where you headin' Sid?" asks Dace.

Sid licks some food off his fingers using the time to measure an answer. "I dunno yet. I'm just playin' it by ear."

With his usual sinister smirk and a laugh that has always made Dace uncomfortable, he says, "Who knows, maybe I'll do some ranchin' myself." At this point it's obvious none of them want to talk about what has brought them to this juncture in each of their lives.

Whitey has a very uneasy feeling about Sid. He's never heard his name mentioned unless it pertained to something illegal, immoral, or just plain mean. He feels a little more secure having his buck knife strapped across his chest and hanging under his left arm. Reaching into his shirt, he unsnaps the security strap allowing him quick access should he need it. Without a word, Sid slips off into the dark recesses of the car leaving Dace and Whitey to themselves. Soon, the two boys prop themselves into a corner at the opposite end, and leaning on one another, they fall asleep.

CHAPTER 9

Not exactly sure what's going on, they are awakened out of a dead sleep by a jolt against their wheeled quarters. It takes Whitey and Dace a moment to remember where they are. The car is still dark except for the light from outside attempting to penetrate through the cracked wooden walls. They're not sure what time it is or whether they have reached the Wisconsin side of the lake. Both know they may have some ways to go before it's safe to open the big sliding door and investigate.

Not able to see clearly the whole length of the boxcar, neither of the boys know the whereabouts of Sid until they hear the sound of water hitting something. On closer inspection, they can make out a pair of legs faintly outlined by the crack of light coming through the gap under the big sliding door. It's Sid attempting to urinate through the opening. Taking this as a cue, Whitey and Dace do the same.

So far this morning, relieving themselves has been their highlight. The mundaneness of a darkened boxcar is akin to being sentenced to "the hole" in prison. They each sit silently with folded arms. There's nothing to stimulate any kind of conversation. For the next hour, the still darkened boxcar is jostled and jolted first in one direction then another. It's obvious the yard crew is either assembling or disassembling a train.

Finally, all the movement has seemingly stopped. Whitey

takes the lead. Rising to his feet, he cautiously slides the door open a crack. Peeking from behind the protective barrier they've utilized for their free ride across Lake Michigan, they're greeted by a beautiful day. The brightness of the sun forces him to place a hand across his brow to shade his already squinting eyes.

Even though the sun is bright in the sky with the promise of a balmy day, the breeze off the lake is cool. Jumping from the car's platform with stiff legs, the boys look around cautiously.

When their eyes finally return to normal, they discover they're on a siding along with a dozen or so other boxcars. With daylight forcing its way into the recesses of the rail car, they find Sid to be as elusive as ever. Hunched up in the rear of the car, he remains out of the light preferring to hang back in the shadows a bit more.

Still unable to get a good look at Sid, they can only determine his hair is an untidy grown out military cut covered with a military issue cap with the brim pulled down low shadowing his face. His cheeks and chin have at least a week's worth of stubble. His clothing is green army issue as well as the bed roll he has roped over his shoulder. He's proven by his body language not to want a lot of questions coming his way. He has a manner of avoiding any direct eye contact with anyone. When confronted, he holds his head down with only his eyes rolled upwards barely enough to acknowledge the person. With deceptive eyes shifting in a distrusting fashion, his gaze possesses a disturbing contempt. Whether he does this purposely to avoid interacting or if this is unintentional is questionable. Either way, he gives Whitey and Dace the creeps.

Once on the ground, the first thing that catches Dace's attention is a diner. It's straight ahead across the tracks. Red roof shingles spelling out the word EAT are boldly embossed across the black roof. With empty bellies and a singleness of purpose, they sling their bags over their shoulder and head for what they hope to be an inexpensive hash house.

This eatery is a hideaway named Maynard's. It's on the edge of the main part of the town of Kewaunee, Wisconsin. The lettering on the sign is as weather-beaten as its patrons.

The major frequenters are either railroad workers or those hanging around waiting for a freight going their way, or as in this case, the motley crew of Whitey and Dace disembarking after their short ride.

There is already a line of hobos waiting in front of a take-out window. The menu is listed on a fading weather-worn sign offering free coffee with an order of two scrambled eggs, and a slice of toast. All for 15 cents.

Whitey finds it difficult to make eye contact with any of these men. They seem to be the most comfortable remaining in a withdrawn state of mistrust. Many of them have chosen this often-solitary lifestyle as a way of insulating themselves from a constantly changing culture. Others are more than likely hoping to leave some unpleasant occurrences in their past behind. Still others, like Sid are avoiding the law by remaining in this near underground existence. Then there are those like Whitey and Dace who are using their unseemly circumstances as the catalyst to seek adventure.

The only commonality in this assemblage of wild, tattered, eccentric men is that none of them are by any characterization "common." They are all huddled like so many lonely exiled birds flocking together.

In the midst of this crazy conglomerate, Dace spots a younger man. He's just arriving. There is an odd sort of familiarity about him that he can't readily put his finger on. The fellow is sporting a well-worn cowboy hat, a pair of aviator sunglasses that nearly covers the whole top part of his stubble-laden face, a young mustache barely curled upwards at the ends, a western shirt, cowboy boots, and a large belt buckle sporting a bucking bronco. His face tells a story of a carefree life. He's a few years older, but the youngest of this whole bunch. Feeling a bit more akin to this younger man than to the grit of the rest, Dace says, "Howdy."

The young man returns his greeting with a broad smile and an affable enough "Howdy" of his own.

Dace decides to let this fellow make the next move. With the ice broken, the cowboy asks with a distinct western drawl and pointing back toward the rail yards, "Din't you boys jus' get off that freight?"

"Yeah, we came across on the car ferry," admits Dace.

"Yer lucky them railroad dicks din't throw yer asses overboard."

By this time, Whitey and Dace have gotten their order of eggs and are listening to the others, hoping to get some information on what freights are leaving and for where.

Whitey feels comfortable enough with this seemingly affable younger man to ask him a question. "Where ya headin'?"

The young man considers the question for a moment, tips his hat back revealing the contrast of a white forehead to a sunburned face. "Depends on which way the trains goin'," he discloses. Watching the ensuing confusion within these burgeoning greenhorn hobos, he senses this answer may be too vague. In an attempt to clear it up he says. "If the first freight outta here is headin' south, I'll be headin' fer the oil fields. But if the first freight outta here is headin' west, I'll be lookin' ta do some kind of ranch work. Don't really make no never mind ta me one way or ta other."

Feeling more confident with this easy exchange, Dace questions a little deeper. "You mind if we tag along?"

The returned look from this natty cowboy is a puzzle Dace finds difficult to process. "I hope you don't mind me askin'—I mean we don't know what in hell we're doin' much less where in the hell we're goin," he adds noticeably embarrassed with this further encroachment into the private life of this stranger and even more so with the disclosure of their own helplessness.

Fussing with his hat brim, the stranger blinks a couple times. "Ain't nobody ever asked me a question like that there before," he confesses.

Trying as best he can to not sound as though he wants to put this friendly stranger on the spot, Dace attempts to rescue himself, "I don't mean fer you ta carry us, just show us a few of the ropes we need ta get along."

The young man is noticeably nervous that this conversation isn't overheard by any of the other hobos. He motions them a little further from the rest of the crowd. Dace and Whitey follow dutifully. Getting them aside, he looks them directly in the eye. "You boys consider yerselves hobos, tramps, er bums?" he asks this question with the earnestness of a trial lawyer.

Dace looks at Whitey, Whitey looks back at Dace. It's obvious neither knows the difference.

"We're whatever you are," says Whitey hoping this answer will suffice.

"I'm a hobo," says the stranger with an air of pride. "I'm willin' ta work at jes about anything somebody's got ta do. Them damnable tramps is lazy. They's jes lookin' fer a handout. The bums is the worst though, all's they wanna do is drink."

"I'm sure we're hobos," says Whitey. "We're both willin' ta work." Both boys are still hoping on the face of it this seeming expert rover will take them under his wing.

"That there is a good start. What kinda work ya done?" he asks continuing to call into question Dace's and Whitey's statements.

Whitey is the first to respond. "I been settin' pins at a bowlin' alley fer four years."

"That's damn good, kid, I done that myself," replies the young stranger. He continues his interrogation looking directly at Dace. "What about you kid? Whatta you done?"

Not to be left out, Dace quickly comes back with, "I'm a domestic engineer." He says this in the sincerest manner he can muster up.

"Who the hell ya tryin' ta discombobulate with that bullshit?" says the young stranger all the while working up a knowing chuckle.

Realizing he's caught trying to BS, Dace tries to rectify the situation. "Well, I guess I mean I can mop, sweep, haul trash, mow lawns, garden, and about anything else somebody wants done."

"That's better. At least now I know what the hell yer sayin'," says the drifter. "So, what's yer moniker?" he continues.

Again, the two boys look at one another with a perplexed gaze. It's obvious they don't know what a moniker is. Realizing these two greenhorns, who are literally right off the boat, don't have a clue as to what he's asking, he puts the question another way, "What do they call you boys?"

Both are stumbling for an opportunity to rectify themselves. In doing so, they begin to talk over each other attempting to get past the moment. Finally slowing down enough to sort out their words and the order in which they're presenting them, they look at one another once more to establish who will go first. Whitey takes the lead. "My name is Don, but I go by Whitey," he blurts out in an attempt to come across more capable than he feels inside. Quickly following up with, "And this is my cousin Dace," hoping this will be enough to satisfy the question.

Much more relaxed after Whitey's forthrightness, the stranger shifts from one foot to the other without the slightest hint of curbing the conversation. Hobos generally don't share real names until they get to know somebody long enough to make it awkward not knowing; even then they prefer either first names or a nick name.

"Nice to meet you boys. They call me Cowboy—you can do the same." It's as if his acceptance of this easy introduction gives permission to get on with other things.

Whitey takes the lead once again leaving no gap in the conversation. "So, you think we could hang with you till we get a handle on this hobo thing?" There is a sense of adventure rather than desperation in this question. On the other hand, it's only Dace who has a possible arrest warrant hanging over him, and for him there is still more desperation than adventure in this journey.

It's apparent Cowboy is considering this alignment, but for different reasons. He's new to these parts himself and doesn't have anyone to watch his back in the event circumstances might demand an ally. After a moment of pondering, he broadens his grin. His words are deliberate and measured. He's making certain he's appealing to their sense of obligation.

"Yeah, I think we can work somethin' out. I ain't no chump who's gonna do somethin' fer you boys without gettin' somethin' outta the deal. You boys wanna team up with me, it means we watch each other's back. A lotta these guys ain't 'bos. They been in prison and are more 'n likely drunken bums or lazy good fer nothin's. Either way, they can't be trusted. You boys agree ta do this, I believe we got a deal."

Dace's stronger sense of desperation surfaces as he hardly gives a second thought to Cowboy's proposal. His voice betrays an unspoken fear. Without as much as a glance in Whitey's direction, he says, "Hell yes." In giving his personal allegiance to this newborn alliance, his hope is to begin to feel more at ease with his own predicament.

Whitey also agrees. "Why not?" is his affirmation. This adventure has a life time of bragging rights. It sure beats living in Elbertport and going to school. He considers himself the lucky one. This is an opportunity to be free from the watchful eye of adults— at least the kind that make his life accountable to their "churchy" values. The only other person he would like to have with him is Melody. In many ways, he wishes he could share this adventure with her.

CHAPTER 10

With breakfast being an ongoing affair, the string of patrons continues to increase including railroad personnel, hobos, bums and tramps. Each group seems to have the ability to discern their own and gravitate toward one another forming loose groups. The railroad workers choose to utilize the indoor seating while the others gather around outdoor picnic tables. Some of the outdoor gatherings are playing cards while others are rolling dice. Some are reading well-worn pocket novels written by Zane Grey or Louie Lamour.

The railroad staff opting to mingle among the outside assemblers are the "Dicks" or "Bulls." These men are hired because of their intimidating size and no nonsense mind-set. They are not much liked by other railroad personnel because they are also expected to keep them in line as well as hobos and the like.

A burly man in his forties wearing a standard dark suit and a badge pinned to his vest makes his way to the table where Whitey, Dace, Cowboy and several other hobos have seated themselves. He's made his way from group to group with only a single warning. He's making it clear that if caught playing cat and mouse with him, the repercussion won't be pretty. "Any ah you boys considerin' hoppin' one ah my freights is breedin' a scab on the end of his nose, and I'm damn sure it'll be me pullin' it off. Ya hear me now?" All the while he passes on this dissuasive suggestion, he keeps his coat pulled back to display a lead filled blackjack attached to his belt.

As the day drags on, the rumbling sound of switch engines permeates the air. The mood around the groups is hopeful that a long hauler will be assembled before too long. One thing is certain—no one can ever hurry a train. From time to time various groups scurry to different sidings they believe may be assembling the anticipated for long hauler. Before committing to this activity, a careful eye is lent to scan the area for the ever-elusive bulls.

"I think the first chance we get, we gotta get outta here," says Cowboy.

Later in the morning it's apparent something different is beginning to take place. A new work shift has turned up. The new crew are beginning to assemble what only can be described as a train.

All three are looking at this, as a window of opportunity beginning to open in their favor. Things are set in motion to develop quickly with almost no time for debate. With little encouragement needed, the decision is quickly made.

They stealthily make their way across several sets of tracks with an ever-watchful eye for any vigilant bull ready to thwart their effort. With determined haste, they quickly duck between two sets of tracks lined with boxcars. Here it will be more difficult to be spotted.

To reduce the slack between boxcars, the head engine powers up sending out two short toots followed by a thundering reverberation through the entire mile long train resulting in each rail car individually jerking like a falling domino. With this maneuver completed the screeching sound of steel wheels on steel rail leaves no doubt, the train is already moving.

Whitey and Dace are still side by side. Cowboy is a car length ahead of them and already hopping aboard. Well aware they are out of their element, Whitey and Dace spot the next open car. With the most intense effort either has ever expended, they clumsily grab onto anything that assures them leverage to pull themselves up the four-foot gap between the car's flooring and sure death under a steel wheel. Dace is hanging on, but unable to get into a position to hoist himself onto the decking. Next to him, Whitey manages to get himself inside. Safely on board, Whitey answers the call to help his cousin. Reaching down and grabbing Dace by his belt, he gives him enough of a pull to jerk him face first across the grungy floor.

In another few seconds, they would have lost any possibility of boarding as the train is quickly picking up speed. Lying flat on the floor, Dace takes a moment to catch his breath and try to put out of his mind how panicked he was when he was unable to pull himself out of danger.

Satisfied his cousin is safely on board, Whitey extends his hand to Dace once again—this time to pull him to his feet. Both are still gasping, attempting to catch their breath. "Thanks, cuz. I'da been ground bologna if it hadn't been for you," says Dace.

Hanging their heads out the open door with the wind in their hair, they manage to pass along a hand wave alerting Cowboy in a car ahead of them of their success. It's not long before this event is behind them and the freedom of a spontaneous adventure once again overwhelms them.

Under different circumstances this adventure would be considered boring. After all, the adrenalin rush that readily accompanies motorcycle riding is certainly on a different level than freight-hopping. This quest has more to do with getting away with something marginally illegal and undeniably dangerous but different than that of racing fast cars. It requires a combination of endurance and fast thinking. There is more than one man whose last sights and sounds on this earth were from the screeching pronouncements of steel wheels before they indiscriminately severed his earthly life between wheel and track.

Sharing a can of Spam, Whitey laughingly says, "Huck Finn ain't got nothin' on us." It's amazing how much adventure a grimy, empty boxcar can provide when it's been conquered against overwhelming odds. It's not much more than a small warehouse on wheels, even so, there remains a sense of hominess when one has it all to themselves.

The day passes quickly as the freight train races at a high speed non-stop, straight through Milwaukee, with a probable destination of Chicago. With a certain degree of peace and contentment, the two boys are able to watch through their open door the bountiful farm crops beginning to ripen, an occasional abandoned home with trees and brush overtaking it, or a post war subdivision with cookie-cutter homes reflecting the nation's new burgeoning economy. In any case, as Spartan as this rail car is proving to be, there, nonetheless, persists a perception of freedom neither of them could ever have experienced in Elbertport.

The steady monotonous clicking of the wheels along with every nut and bolt creaking in rhythm with the sway of the car soon brings on heavy eyes. Looking for a place to fall asleep, both soon give in and wrap themselves in their sleeping bags to drift along with the susurrus rhythm of the train. The afternoon soon becomes evening which then becomes night.

What awakens Whitey is an ominous sense of stillness. The train has stopped. It's dark except for a grayness created by a full moon filtered through a layer of fog. Dace also begins to stir. *Where the hell are we?* is the silent thought forming in both their minds. Whitey takes the lead, making his way to the open door in hopes of some telling hint as to where they've arrived. The darkness and the fog make it difficult to discern anything beyond the length of a rail car.

What meets his eye is an obscured form leaping out of the car next to theirs and quickly being hidden by the white mist. Because of the murkiness of the night, Whitey only has a vague impression but, there is something familiar about the way this shadowy figure appeared hunched over almost lurking like a prowler. Dace joins Whitey just as this figure is disappearing. Fearing his eyes may be playing tricks, Whitey calls out in a whisper, "Did you see that guy?"

Dace considers the darkened stillness with the same trepidation he would if he were told to look for an apparition. His tone possesses the same apprehension, "I dunno man, what you seein?"

"I swear, I just saw what looked like Sid."

Dace looks a bit deeper into the void. "I don't see nothin' but murk. Besides we left Sid back in Kewaunee," declares Dace.

A person's voice tells a lot when they are fearful and neither of these boys are the exception. When it comes to the subject of Sid, there is no doubt they're both uncomfortable with the likelihood of him still lurking about.

They don't know what time it is. There's nothing to see and nothing to do but wait. Having no other choice, they resign themselves to returning to their sleeping bags. Once more sleep overtakes them. Next, they are abruptly awakened by the forthright voice of Cowboy. "You boys rise an' shine 'for one them Bulls catches ya sleepin'. The crack ya hear won't be the crack ah dawn, it'll be a crack 'long side yer noggin!"

This familiar voice is very welcome in the bleakness of this desolate place. The fog is beginning to lift enough to see they're on a rail siding. More than ready to have this inhospitable place behind them, within minutes both boys are up and ready to follow their new mentor.

"There's a hobo jungle down the tracks a ways. We can proly get us a cup ah coffee," says Cowboy while leading out.

The new alliance is, on the face of it, still in place—but then it's yet to be tested. A quarter-mile down the track, the trio find themselves entering a nearby brushy area. It turns out to be a hobo jungle deep in the Chicago yards.

These aren't typical railyards. They are made up of miles and miles of complex rail sidings and thoroughfares. For a freight train to make its way through this maze is easily a twenty-four-hour ordeal. Horns are blasting every few minutes along with clanging sound that only trains can make. The voice of distant train whistles is a rather mournful, innocuous sound. This is a much different experience than the terrifying sensation these iron monsters present up close.

The trio are met with a hubbub of incomparable magnitude. Two men are seated in front of the campfire with bloodied rags wrapped around their heads. They both have the same tale. They were awakened when they sensed someone rifling through their belongings. The intruder immediately put a knife to their throat and demanded money, or as he said, "I'll slit your worthless throat and take it anyway." After successfully robbing them, he knocked them out with a rock to their head.

"The sombitch rolled me fer four bucks," says a hobo going by the name of Blackie Miller.

"He got me fer six," laments the other hobo named Lonesome Lou from Kalamazoo as he rubs his hand across his bloodied head.

In this community, the idea of involving the police is unthinkable. No one uses their birth names as a good share of them are wanted by the law for various infractions. Besides, none of them will be here long enough to complete any kind of investigation. The rule remains, "Watch yer own ass, nobody's gonna do it fer ya!!"

By mid-morning, Cowboy has decided to do a bit of nosing around on his own, leaving Whitey and Dace to fend for themselves. The two newcomers have aligned themselves with a couple other hobos waiting for the opportunity to be on the move by evening. One of these men is an older toothless, grizzled man with a rounded back caused by years of poor diet and hard work. He is referred to as Pappy by the other hobos. It's obvious Pappy has been on the road for much of his life. He passes the time either singing old gospel songs or playing his harmonica.

The other man appears to be much younger but not without

his share of the grimy lines of time encrusting his face. He is referred to as "Tiger." It seems he has a penchant for the Detroit Tiger baseball team and is a walking baseball encyclopedia. He knows batting averages of obscure players from as early as the late nineteenth century and is inclined to engage anyone in conversation providing it's concerning baseball. He has a unique ability to hear a ball game on his little transistor radio and announce it from memory word for word. "I don't fit nowhere in town. Some people say I'm retarded, but I know more about stuff than they do," laments Tiger. He had spent a good portion of his life in the Traverse City State Hospital for the mentally retarded located in northern lower Michigan. Somehow, he managed to skip out on a furlough and never returned. It's obvious Tiger isn't quite right, but it's hard say exactly what his problem is. One thing is for sure, with his ability to memorize, he's a long way from being retarded.

Whitey and Dace are quickly discovering this band of misfits are head and shoulders beyond them in the ways of the world. Up until this point, their world has consisted of working on personality traits that make them cool in school. This school boy mindset has no place in this environment. They're finding very quickly there is life beyond high school and it's best to try and fit in without annoying anyone. It's better to sit quietly and listen, rather than try and impress these road veterans with their teenage prattling.

What they are discovering is a wealth of information about what has occurred down the tracks over the past few days. A hobo calling himself "Gabby" is holding everyone's attention. "That goddam Milwaukee yard got more damn bulls than dogs got fleas. They catch a 'bo, they beat 'im near ta death, then steal his money. They calls it a fine fer tresspassin'. I know damn well it stays right tight in they own pocket."

Another hobo named "Watervliet Pete" after a town in

southern Michigan is passing on another piece of news. "Ole Stub got hiself kilt up in Duluth. Poor ole bastard had one to many drinks 'for he caught out. While tryin' ta hook a ladder, he missed an' 'stead shot hiself under a wheel. I saw the whole damn thing— cut 'im clean in half—he never bled much cause the wheels pinched his damn veins tight. I still ain't over it."

Another thing noticed by both boys is the number of newspapers that are read before they become cigarette rolling papers or toilet paper. Political issues are discussed with the clear intention of finding fault with all politicians, government programs, people's rights being taken away, or even the incoming weather. To sum up a discussion someone will frequently say, "With all this horse-shit you'd think there hadda be a pony somewheres. Right here's the reason we live the way we do!" It is as if all other choices have evaporated because of decisions made in Washington D.C.

From time to time one of these old timers will hear the whistle from one of the engines and determine it to be merely a yard engine moving cars, or a pair of grand old mainline diesels being positioned to move a hundred-fifty freight cars out of a siding to a main track. When it becomes clear a train is moving, the trick becomes keeping one's eyes and ears open to know where to "catch out."

Pappy is one of these clairvoyants. He suddenly has stopped singing and playing his mouth organ. Instead he is staring down the track as a huge line of diesels hooked together is making its way from a turn table. It's become obvious to him something different is beginning to play out. Without a word, he gathers up his meager bedroll and makes his way across a group of tracks toward a line of freight cars that have on the face of it formed a train. As if on cue, a horde of men fall in behind the lead of this old vagabond.

Also, as if on cue, two concealed bulls step from between a pair of connected boxcars. It's as though they knew beforehand this would be the time these drifters would make their move. The bulls unfasten their blackjacks as they begin to make their way toward the swarm of men deftly hopping over rails and between rail ties. It takes a degree of skill to run betwixt these obstacles. It seems the ties are always spaced just enough to challenge the stride of any human gait regardless of leg length.

The bulls are now in hot pursuit, indiscriminately swinging their lead filled persuaders, laying heads open wherever they make contact. Dace and Whitey find themselves near panic. With no time to wait for Cowboy, they try and keep an eye on the railroad cops and the other men, all the while watching for an open car. As luck would have it, they spot Pappy and Tiger just ahead. Pappy's age has left him with knees that cause his gait to be bowlegged. What he has lost in speed he makes up in expertise. In a single motion, they toss their bed rolls onto the deck of an open boxcar and Tiger is up and in. In a well-rehearsed move, Pappy reaches for a little help. Just as swiftly, Tiger meets his extended hand. With the skill of a man who has done this more times than he can recollect, he has him snatched on board.

Whitey and Dace have the same idea as they follow suit. Throwing their gear on deck they run along the car terrified by the thought they may stumble and find themselves under a wheel. Both continue to run until they convince themselves it's now or never. Both Pappy and Tiger have extended a hand and help Whitey and Dace clumsily struggle on board. At last they're inside, but not without bruised knees and skinned elbows.

Barely aware of their injuries they look out through the open door scarcely believing they made it. They can't believe what they see. One of the bulls is chasing a man that is unmistakably Sid.

Where the hell did Sid come from? is the thought ricocheting through both their minds. Still not convinced Whitey had really seen Sid in the fog that morning, they had assumed he'd gone off on his own.

They never in their lives had expected to see what happens next. The bull is in full pursuit with his arm raised and his blackjack ready to meet the top of Sid's head. Suddenly the golden glow of the setting sun is reflected from something Sid is carrying in his right hand. With no warning, Sid stops cold in his tracks, swings around and lunges at the still pursuing bull. The bull stops suddenly while falling to his knees, grasping at his abdomen. In the next moment, with the precision of a trained assassin, Sid is pulling a bloody knife out of the belly of the fallen man leaving him writhing helplessly between the tracks. Whitey and Dace are stunned. Only a psychopath could carry out the maneuver they just witnessed with such exactness.

The train is beginning to pick up speed. Peering out of their rail car dumbfounded, Whitey and Dace momentarily meet Sid's riveting eyes. With a stare only Sid can impart, he glares back briefly before leaping aboard the next open car, leaving several separating them.

In all the commotion, what has transpired between Sid and the bull happened so quickly it went undetected except by Whitey and Dace. They are horrified. Too stunned to bring it up with their new boxcar companions, they opt not to discuss it.

CHAPTER 11

Having missed this skirmish, Pappy has been busy checking out potentially useful materials that are strewn around the boxcar.

He patrols this moving, rocking turf with the expert balance of a tight rope walker. The rolling uneven rails would throw an initiate like Whitey or Dace to the floor. It seems everything these seasoned hobos do has a hidden purpose. Often, it happens when a cargo is unloaded packing materials are left behind for someone else to clean out. In this particular instance, there are reams of packing paper and binder twine.

"They ain't no sech thing as refuse when a man is on the road," says Pappy as he wraps a length of rope from thumb to elbow before placing it with his belongings. Next, he folds a strip of the discarded paper as one would a strip of toilet paper, he demonstrates its use across his rear end. "And this here paper gonna make my ass feel sweeter 'an a mother-in-law's kiss," he further adds sending an elated cackle across his toothless gums.

Tiger, on the other hand is busy with a more immediate need. He's also gathering up paper, fashioning it into a comfortable cushion. These boxcars are not designed with human comfort in mind, hence any materials capable of absorbing road shock are greatly appreciated.

The clicking sound of the steel wheels meeting the uneven adjoining steel rails is merging to a constant hum as the train picks up speed. Dace and Whitey mimic the activities of their much more adept companions. Folding, wading, or stuffing the paper to mold into useable shock absorbers, they have managed to make themselves relatively comfortable. With the afternoon waning, Whitey and Dace grow quieter as they reflect on the events of the past few days.

Pappy recognizes just how green these greenhorns are when Dace begins to slide the door closed. "Better ta stay a little cool 'an dead boy," he says, quickly blocking the door before it closes.

Dace gives him an embarrassed glance as he realizes he's done something to bring this old headmaster to his feet in a hurry. Staring back hard, Pappy points to the latch on the door. "See this here kind ah latch? Oncet that door closes, 'at there latch stays shut till somebody on the outside decides they need ta open it an' discovers they jes let the light a day shine in on a bunch ah dead bodies. Rightly so, they ain't all like this un here, but ya gotta learn the difference lessen ya don't mind starvin' ta death in a boxcar."

With that rebuke needing one more modification, Pappy pulls out a rail spike, holding it between his fingers where Dace can see it, he then jams it in the sliding door's track preventing it from completely closing.

It's become obvious to Whitey and Dace they don't know much about the hobo life. Staying alive often means having the sense to avoid unnecessary and obviously deadly pitfalls like this one, which they could not even recognize until it was pointed out.

To show his appreciation and hopefully make amends for his near act of carelessness, Dace reaches into his bag and pulls out his highly treasured last can of pork and beans and hands it to Pappy.

What a moment ago, had been a stoic reaction has just as quickly turned into bright smile. Elevating the can as if he had just received a sacred object, Pappy exclaims, "Boy, how'd ya know this here's my choicest. Yes sir! This here's nectar of the gods."

In a matter of a few strokes from a well-rehearsed arm, Pappy produces a can opener and a spoon. The look of satisfaction cannot be mistaken as he samples a spoonful of his favorite ambrosia. After a couple mouthfuls, he passes the can to Tiger, who gladly accepts the shared gift. There is a special relationship between Pappy and Tiger. Whatever Tiger's disabilities may involve, Pappy makes allowances, always continuing to befriend him. Tiger in turn takes a couple spoonsful and passes the can to Whitey. Not quite sure how all this works, Whitey fumbles around in his bedroll until he comes up with a spoon. Quickly catching on to the tradition of sharing with cabin mates, he takes a couple bites and passes the last few spoonsful back to Dace who started this whole procession. With this action in play and without hesitation Pappy has produced a can of Harvard beets taking a few spoons and starting the whole process all over again. Rather than eat beets Whitey would prefer to starve, but realizing the seeming importance of this ritual, he manages a single spoonful and passes the jar to Dace.

After all this sharing of canned goods, Pappy digs around in his pockets for his tobacco. Since Pappy generally wears several layers of clothing this can be a long drawn out affair. Eventually a can of Prince Albert smoking tobacco appears. With the dexterity of a surgeon, he soon has rolled a pile of cigarettes.

In the meantime, Tiger has lit a can of Sterno and is boiling a pot of water. He next takes a handful of used coffee grounds he has carefully pulled out of the garbage can behind some restaurant. Still wrapped in the filters in which they were dumped, he tosses them into the boiling water. In seconds the water takes on the dark brown look of coffee. After filling his own cup, he unwraps a rag with a dozen or so absconded sugar cubes from God only knows where, and drops a couple into the steaming liquid. Satisfied the action is completed, he passes the coffee container to Pappy and then on around until each has a filled cup. Immediately following this gesture are Pappy's hand-rolled cigarettes.

Hobos are much more willing to share these material kinds of goods than they are personal information. There is an unwritten and unspoken code of privacy among these vagabonds. Any personal topics are kept close to the vest. Exposing a personal secret could fall into the wrong hands and come back to bite. Unwanted trouble is avoided like plague. But because Whitey and Dace are young and new to this life, they pose a lessened threat and are given more leeway than an older man. So with this understanding, when Whitey takes license to pry into Pappy's life, he's given a pass.

"How'd you get into this kind of life Pappy?" asks Whitey with the innocent curiosity of a kid.

Pappy ponders the question for a moment. Most hobo's have more than one answer to whatever personal question may be asked. A twinkle is visible in his eye. He's like everyone else in wanting to talk about himself. Considering Whitey's and Dace's naivete, he allows them to breach the wall of his privacy. Feeling safe he begins.

"It were back in '37. There weren't no jobs anywhere. Me an' my older brother Guy decided we was gonna head fer Odessa, Texas an' work the oil fields. We hopped freights till we made it down there. They was hirin' an' we got us jobs swampin' up oil comin' up 'roun' the rig. Later on, Guy got him a good job roughneckin' til he got cocky an' fell off the rig an' kilt hiself. He found out too late his neck weren't 'at rough. I never went home after that. Been ridin' freights an workin' 'ever I can since them days."

"Do ya think you'll ever stop bein' a hobo?" asks Dace.

Pappy gives a little chuckle, "Yeah. The day Jesus comes, either for me or fer everybody. I tried town livin' fer a while. Trouble was ever time I'd hear the whistle of a train, I'd get antsy. It weren't long afor I was back on the rails. That were back in '49. 'Ats when I met Tiger. He busted outta that jitter-joint they had him locked up in an' got hiself outta town on a fast freight. Sometimes his noodle ain't workin' real good an' he needs my help. We been hangin' out ever since."

Most relationships among hobos usually are short-lived

because of the transient nature of their lives, but this unlikely relationship between these two has been ongoing for ten years.

"'Sides I'm sixty-five an' proly retired, so now I jes work when I needs ta," he says with a chuckle.

This is a whole new chapter in the lives of Whitey and Dace. Being exposed to the underbelly of this flourishing culture they never realized existed, is quickly becoming an exercise in adaptation.

Shortly, they find they are not only satiated physically but also mentally. Along with the clicking of the rails, and with a sense of fulfillment, they are content to sit quietly smoking and listening to their own thoughts. It's a form of solitude that can often be found without becoming lonely.

Deciding after nearly two days of being cooped up in a boxcar getting out of the Chicago yards is plenty long enough. They agree with Pappy to be ready to hop off at the first opportunity. It's not until they are coming into what Pappy declares to be Terre Haute, Indiana south of Chicago that the train shows signs of slowing enough to make a reasonably safe leap. The four of them hit the ground uninjured.

Taking one step of this risky venture at a time, Whitey and Dace try to stay in stride with Pappy's next move without revealing they don't have a clue what to do next. Without missing a step, Pappy and Tiger make their way down the tracks to a brushy, wooded area. There suddenly appears a well-worn path off to the side of the rail bed. It's the kind of path that didn't just recently get this worn down. It's obvious this trail is used regularly. It's littered with a plethora of empty cans, bottles, and every article of discarded clothing from sweatshirts to underwear. In a couple of minutes Pappy lets out a hoot, "HOBO!" A hoot is returned, 'HOBO!"

Whitey is nervous enough to reach inside his shirt and

unsnap the small leather strap holding his buck knife in the sheath. Dace is also showing signs of apprehension about what they are walking into. Both boys hold back, more than willing to give Pappy and Tiger a good lead.

What comes into sight is a conglomeration of men milling around among old army surplus tents. Others are in shacks put together from pieces of every conceivable cast off piece of tin or scrap lumber that has found its way into this hobo jungle. In surprisingly creative ways, it's all been re-purposed and retrofitted to become a roof or a wall or maybe even a door.

It's all jammed in like a tiny village into a thicket of fifteen to twenty-foot-high box elder trees. The ground is worn thin of any vegetation except for the dead leaves beginning to drop from the box elders. Adding to its surrealism, the lingering smoke from several burning fires fueled by what appears to be the remnants of old cast off railroad ties is trapped beneath the trees, giving the camp a smoky eeriness.

Behind this colony is a creek providing fresh water. At present, a few men have decided to bathe. Some strip down and wash their clothing as well as themselves, others lay down in the water still wearing anything that's washable with the intention of bathing and doing their laundry all in the same movement.

Pappy is greeting a near-naked man. He's plainly an old acquaintance. His name is Buckweed—at least that's the only name anyone has known him by since he hit the road back in the thirties. The men embrace one another like long lost friends. "Pappy you ole sumbitch, you still livin'?" addresses the man wearing only what appears to be some kind of makeshift loincloth. It's the only covering on a nearly emaciated, pasty white body adorned with a few jailhouse tattoos set off with a tattered straw hat over a pile of shoulder-length snow white hair, and a chest-length white beard.

"Hell yes, I'm still a livin'," maintains Pappy. "The devil ain't never in a hurry fer them he's sure of, now is he? An' what in hell you doin' runnin' 'roun here like you some kinda Jap rassler?" further needles Pappy.

"I'm boilin'," (boiling the lice out of his clothing) pronounces Buckweed pointing to a large wash tub sitting on top of a fire, all the time looking Pappy over like he should be doing the same.

"'Bout time ya rid yersef ah all them blessed chiggers ya been breedin' on ya all these years," says Pappy with a grin.

"Yeah, I know. I kill this bunch and another bunch jes as big shows up fer the goddam funeral," evaluates Buckweed with a similar grin.

This camp is a transition point. The big diesel locomotives have to stop and refuel at a nearby siding causing the train to slow and eventually stop. This allows fairly easy access for anyone wishing to hop on or off.

Most of the men sitting around act as though they aren't particularly interested in the new arrivals. Some are poking sticks as if tending a fire, while others are propped against anything that will support their back, smoking tobacco in any receptacle that will hold fire from rolled papers to pipes.

What isn't readily noticed is as these new arrivals are gradually assessed to be non-threatening the earlier inhabitants of camp begin to put away the open knives they've inconspicuously had sitting beside themselves.

Many of these men are ex-convicts. It's not unusual for each to carry a reasonable suspicion of anything that seems threatening.

Moreover, more than a few are capable of any type of crime a human can imagine and a few they can't. Others are men who find they can survive the anomalies of the hobo life if they guard against any kind of changes that come their way. Still others like Tiger have mental problems.

As suspicious as they are of one another, they seem to have a need to herd up in these camps, sharing stories and what little possessions they may have. Whether they are hobos, tramps or local bums, they're all on the fringe of society. What they have in common is they seem to accept—or better yet—ignore the idiosyncrasies of others as long as their own strange ways are accepted or ignored. There is a silent agreement to mind one's own business and to stay out of each other's way.

On any given day during this time of year this camp may have as many as a dozen or more men. Presently, there are about fifteen or so. Like with all groups, there is a tendency to join with like-minded folks. The hobos are gathered in their own area around their own campfire, as are the tramps and bums. The hobos aren't much disposed to excessive drinking.

The bums, on the other hand, have given themselves over to just about anything that contains alcohol. Some are mixing Benzedrine soaked cotton swabs found in Vicks inhalers with their wine for a kind of hyperactive drunk keeping them up all night.

From time to time violence can break out—usually between a couple drunks arguing over everything from who one may believe is the greatest country singer to ever live or something really important such as whether a man could become an alcoholic by just drinking beer. This breed of men rarely hop freights and have never been known to work. Before the night is over, they will usually end up arguing and fighting among themselves, leaving the others to find ways to put up with their drunken nonsense.

Whitey and Dace are sticking pretty close to Pappy and Tiger. Buckweed has been here for several weeks waiting for a train heading for Florida. His story is much like many in this camp. Years ago, he had been unable to find work in his home town and was on the edge of losing everything he had worked for. Choosing to be proactive, he left his wife and daughter at home while he struck out for work in the copper mines in Michigan's upper peninsula. This worked for a time until the mines ran out of copper. Returning home, he was met with divorce papers. "After my ole lady met Mr. Wonderful, she lost her sense of humor and divorced me. She went one way an' I went another," is the way Buckweed lays it out. "That's been nearly twenty years ago, I been ridin' the rails ever since."

In the short time Buckweed has been here, he has fashioned a lean-to shack for himself. It's made from a combination of wooden crates, corrugated tin, and odd pieces of canvas left over from an abandoned tent.

Considering that necessity continues to be the mother of invention, Buckweed has ingeniously put together a cooking stove from all kinds of stray pieces of scrap iron. Presently simmering on this makeshift stove is a pot of Mulligan stew. "I been hittin' the churches pretty damn hard 'long with everybody else. A grocery store gimme some stuff they was plannin' ta trow out and a guy at the butcher shop gimme a ham bone." To complement Buckweed's hospitality, many in turn are coming up with things they can throw into this conglomeration. Not to be miserly, Dace has found a can of hash in his bag to add to the brewing pot. Pappy and Tiger each contribute a can of corn.

While enjoying Buckweed's hobo cuisine and with the sun

flowing directly through the door a shadow of a man appears blocking the light. It's a familiar silhouette. "You girls gonna invite a starvin' hobo in?" The voice is also familiar, so is the infectious smile.

"Well I'll be, it's Cowboy," says Dace. "Where the hell you been?" is his next question.

"Been ridin' the rails like the rest ah ya, yup jes ridin' the rails," answers Cowboy as if the question is unneeded. "When them railroad dicks come after us, I jumped into a car and hid in the back 'for he come after me," he further reveals. Pausing for a moment, he asks, "Any you boys get hurt?"

"Nah, we're okay but we saw a guy we know stab one of the dicks," reports Whitey.

Pappy, Buckweed, and Tiger stop dead in their tracks. They're not believing what they're hearing coming out of the mouths of these greenhorns. The hobo code of seeing, hearing, and knowing nothing is falling into disarray before their very eyes and ears. These greenhorns are talking about things they saw that will absolutely, in a heartbeat, bring the law around.

Doing anything to attract the law is the best way to get thrown out of a hobo camp. The discomfort of these veterans of the road is obvious by their sudden movements to distance themselves from the rest of this conversation. Each of them are taking their bowl of stew and choosing to sit outside around the fire leaving Whitey and Dace to disclose the details of Sid's actions to this other stranger by themselves.

"What's this guy, Sid, look like?" asks Cowboy.

Dace goes into a long description of what he could see of Sid, finally bringing the whole verbal description to a head. "Other than his clothing and the way he walks and talks, he's impossible to describe. He wears that damn hat so far over his forehead not letting anybody see his whole face. When he does look anyone in the face, he either cocks his head to one side with one eye closed and squints through the other or looks up through his eyebrows. Either way, I haven't seen him full faced since I was a little kid when he hung around my brother Vaughn. The only reason Vaughn liked him was he was older and taught him how to siphon gas."

Dropping his signature, dark aviator glasses down on his nose, and looking over them, Cowboy says, "Sounds like the guy 'at jumped on my car an' rode with me."

"No shit, Cowboy, you think we're talkin' about the same guy?" asks Whitey. The fear of this possibility is plain in his question.

"Did he say anything about stabbin' that dick?" follows up Dace before Cowboy can answer Whitey's question.

"No, hell no, he didn't say much ah nothin'. He stayed to hiself. He didn't seem ta wanna talk much. I decided to get off here, as far as I know he stayed on the road," says Cowboy. There is a matter-of-fact air to his report that seems a bit casual, now that he knows he was riding alone with a killer.

CHAPTER 12

The night passes without further incident. Morning brings about an awareness of change. People in this world are private to a fault, tolerating very little when it comes to questions concerning their comings and goings. Much of hobo life is solitary. Being alone is sought after. Those that have persevered in this life are those who can be alone without becoming lonely. In keeping with this impassive style this morning, there are those who without speaking or being questioned make it obvious by their actions they are either getting ready to pull out or are hanging around for a while. The three old-timers, Pappy, Tiger, and Buckweed have made it clear they don't want to hear anything more about some cop getting stabbed. It's clear this revelation has strained their relationship making it easier for Cowboy, Whitey, and Dace to agree to get back on the road alone.

Cowboy has a certain appeal about him. Whatever that quality may be, Whitey and Dace find it compelling.

He takes advantage of every circumstance to pull rank on these two greenhorns.

"You guys know what town we're on the outskirts of?" asks Cowboy.

"I think I heard somebody say they thought it was Terre Haute, Indiana."

"They were tellin' the truth," says Cowboy with an air superiority. "I'm plannin' on goin' inta town. I think if we play our cards right, we can pick up a few bucks here."

Whitey perks up when he hears him use the word *we*. "Does that mean Dace and I are goin' with you?" he asks.

"Well hell ya, we're a team ain't we. I pledged I'd stick with you guys and show ya the ropes. I'm a man ah my word so let's get inta town and see what's shakin'," says Cowboy with the same assurance he has maintained since he first met these boys.

One thing is for certain, the demand for hobo labor in this area is scarce to none. Back in the thirties and even into the forties many farms depended on transient laborers to fill the demand for a human work force. But this is the fifties, mechanization has replaced a good share of this market. Nonetheless, this trio begins a trek into the city with the confidence they can get enough of a grubstake to carry them a couple days.

"You guys hit every business. Tell them you're on the road and you've run out of money and you're willing to work. Offer to mop floors, clean bathrooms or anything that will give you a buck. Some will have you work others will give you fifty-cents or more just to leave," alleges Cowboy with a cocky smile. "I've got a few ideas of my own and I'll meet you back here at four o'clock," he adds.

Whitey and Dace have worked hard all day and managed to make a couple bucks apiece. "Well, here we are, it's four-o'clock but where the hell is Cowboy?" says Dace. The hint of worry is unquestionably in his voice.

"I don't know. I haven't seen hide nor hair of him since we split up this morning," says Whitey trying to act a little more cavalier than his cousin.

Both are anxiously looking up and down the street when they hear a car horn. It's coming from a car parked across the thoroughfare. Behind the wheel is a barely recognizable form. There's just enough of a hat and sunglasses to hint that it's Cowboy peeking over the wheel. It's a brand new 1959 two toned red and white Buick Roadmaster four door sedan.

Both boys rush across the street and pile in. "Where the hell did you get this boat?" asks Dace with a laugh that reflects Cowboy's good taste in cars.

"I know a guy here in town. He wants this car delivered to Wichita Falls, Texas. I volunteered. The only thing is we gotta get on the road right away, we only got a couple days," says Cowboy.

"Hell yeah man, let's get on the road," says Whitey, hardly able to contain his excitement. This is a real luxury car. Neither Whitey nor Dace have ever ridden in such a glorious car. Dace's mother has never learned how to drive and Whitey's parents are still driving a 1949 Ford. This thing has power windows, power steering, and air conditioning.

Sitting comfortably in the backseat, Whitey can't help but feel he's being chauffeured. "Holy crap!" he exclaims pointing to the ashtray, "This thing's even got a cigarette lighter in the backseat." Hardly able to believe the luxuriousness, he's getting a notion of what it must feel like to be rich. Reaching into his pocket, he pulls out a cigarette. Just to enhance his sense of wealth, he lights it with this impressive backseat piece of equipment. Sucking the fumes deep into his lungs gives him a wonderful pulmonary orgasm as he exhales. He can feel the world and all its cares leaving along with the trail of smoke.

Nostalgically, he wishes the guys back home could see him now. For the next few moments he relishes the thought of how envious they would be. He even begins to envision picking Melody up in such a fine car and how impressed she'd be at the thought of being seen with him in such luxury.

Dace also harkens back to Elbertport. It's only been a few days since he and Whitey made their middle of the night getaway but it seems longer. It saddens him a bit to imagine what all this mayhem may be doing to his mother. However, as it often goes with the young, this kind of guilt dissipates with the allure of new undertakings. After all, isn't there always some mysterious adventure beckoning on the next horizon?

For Dace and Whitey, Cowboy carries a peculiar kind of

familiarity in some strange way. The boys still can't quite put their finger on it, but for the time being he's hitting a home run. A new car, a tank full of gas, cigarettes, a sunny day, a couple bucks in their pockets, and the promise of an adventurous road trip makes life as perfect as it can get.

"This sure as hell beats a goddam boxcar," says Whitey, as he pushes the button lowering the window enough to let the warm Midwestern air blow through his hair.

The afternoon wanes into evening, which flows into nightfall, and soon enough waxes into morning to begin all over again. They have driven through the night with Whitey and Dace taking a turn at the wheel. They've reached El Reno, Oklahoma. It's six o'clock in the afternoon, they're dead tired and this luxury automobile has turned into all but just another boxcar.

"I need to get a room and a bath," acknowledges Cowboy, "I can't go another mile."

They have pulled into the parking lot behind a hotel near the downtown area. Hotel Southern has its inviting inscription painted in huge letters across the top of what appears to be a four-story building. It holds a promise of comfort and a reprieve from the rigors of travel. Each of them have their own idea of what amenities could be awaiting them. The single thought of a shower and a real bed are as gratifying as winning the major prize on the TV show *Queen For A Day*.

After agreeing to pool whatever monies they have between them, they begin digging in their pockets only to discover they have what amounts to enough for another tank of gas. Certainly, not enough to rent a room and a tank of gas. Surveying the situation, Cowboy speaks out, "We're gonna have to do some fancy sidesteppin' if we're gonna make this all come together. You boys let me do the talkin' and follow my lead."

Both boys agree. Not sure how this is all going to "come together," they silently gather their few belongings and follow their persuasive leader. He leads them to a telephone booth down the street from the hotel. Dropping a nickel into the slot he dials the number clearly seen on the side of the hotel. In a moment, he's speaking to someone on the other end of the line. "Hello. May I speak with a manager? Oh, good you're the manager. My name is Cloyce Pardee. I'm the financial manager for Texas Amalgamated Gas and Oil. We have three of our employees in your area that need lodging. We would like to set up an account with your hotel to accommodate not only these three, but several more over the next few weeks. Is that something you can put together for me?"

Dace and Whitey are doe-eyed listening to the audacity of this young man dealing with their dilemma. With a few more convincing words exchanged over the phone, Cowboy hangs up and with a wide grin makes the announcement, "Everything is cool man. It's all cool we got ourselves a room. I think we can get at least a night's sleep and a shower before they figure all this stuff out."

Dace and Whitey are overjoyed with the success of this ploy. Both agree their alliance with Cowboy has paid off in ways they never would have been able to produce. Cowboy has opted to bunk alone in a single room, whereas Whitey and Dace feel more comfortable rooming together. Not only do they find a shower refreshing, they wash their underclothing and lay the wet garments over the radiator to dry. The only thing left to do is to climb into bed and let the night overtake them.

About six o'clock the next morning, Whitey awakens with an urgent need to relieve his bladder. On his way to the toilet, he glances out the window and sees a familiar figure. "Oh, my God! Is that him again!? What the hell is he doing here!?" he exclaims. At the top of the list of all the people he and Dace would prefer to never encounter again is Sid. And here he is big as life skulking out on the street in front of the hotel in his usual hunched, slouchy gait. Being only on the second floor, Whitey watches until he disappears down the street.

These continuous 'Sid sightings' are a disconcerting distraction. Not sure how to react to this new development, he returns to bed hoping Cowboy will have a solution when they meet up later in the morning.

At nine o'clock Dace is awakened by a barely audible knock on their door. Afraid it may be someone from the front desk with security to throw them out, he awakens Whitey. Dace's sentiments are quickly shared with Whitey. As they race around getting their clothing on and their bedrolls pulled together, the knock sounds again. They're on the second floor, Dace opens a window nonetheless, with the plan of dropping to the ground in the event this is the hotel management.

Meantime, Whitey hesitantly approaches the still closed door with the obvious question, "Who is it?"

"It's me, Cowboy. Hurry up and let me in."

Relieved beyond description it's not hotel personnel, Whitey unlocks the door allowing Cowboy to enter. "Why in the hell didn't ya say so. For all we knew you were security come to throw our asses outta here."

Dace is still poised on the windowsill expecting to have to drop into the bushes below. Seeing it's indeed Cowboy, a look of relief quickly replaces the panic he was experiencing only a moment before.

"Well, they may indeed be planning to do just that. I got another plan, but we gotta be quick and quiet. Just follow me and do as I do," says Cowboy in a hushed tone. With that, he carefully opens the door, peeking around the corner and down the hall. With a hand signal, he motions the boys to follow. Not at all sure what may be going on, they willingly and promptly fall in line behind their leader.

Looking once more behind him and down the hallway, Cowboy quickly and with a purposeful stride leads them down the hall to an open window. Satisfied they're undetected, he slips through the opening onto a fire escape. It's a rickety thing that probably hasn't had this much weight on it in years. Whitey and Dace are right behind him, adding an even more of a load to the already creaking contraption.

With as much haste as this rusty, aging device will allow, they make their way down to a just as dubious fold-down ladder. With a little luck, this will take them to safety. Still leading the way, Cowboy is the first to drop safely to the ground followed just as sprightly by Dace and Whitey.

No sooner are their feet on solid ground than Cowboy pushes forward in a near sprint toward the back of the building. The boys assume they will be heading for the Buick still parked where they left it the night before. Cowboy, on the other hand has another plan. He passes right by the Buick without a word. Instead he motions them toward a delivery van parked few spaces beyond. With one more wave of his hand, he motions them to get in. Having no idea what is going on, both boys pile in as best they can without slamming a foot in the door.

The smell of fresh bread is overwhelming. Obviously, this is a bread delivery wagon. Wasting not a second, Cowboy gets the contrivance in reverse and backs out of the space. The number of unanswered questions begin to mount.

CHAPTER 13

The anxiety level on these three is rising. It's especially high on Dace. Agreeing to skip out on a hotel bill is hardly the same as making a getaway in a very questionable delivery van. Assuming they're far enough away from the hotel to not encounter any trouble from that source, he soon voices a new question, "What the hell are we doing in this piece of crap and why ain't we back in the Buick like you said we was gonna be?" asks Dace.

Remaining focused on the task at hand, Cowboy is grinding the van's gears. It's obvious he's not well prepared to be driving a vehicle with a standard transmission, nor is he ready to give them a reassuring answer.

Whitey is surveying this situation as carefully as he can. He ultimately jumps in with his own question, "Hey man this has gotta be joke—right?"

Noticeably, Cowboy is avoiding all questions as he continues to focus on what appears to be a prescribed path. The trust Whitey and Dace have put in Cowboy is quickly slipping away. As young and inexperienced striplings, they are feeling more and more like complete strangers in this clandestine underbelly of the culture. Now with this latest turn of events, where they had once seen rainbows on their horizons, they are beginning to see storm clouds.

It's immediately apparent to them both that Cowboy hasn't gotten a new career delivering Wonder bread. Without a doubt the truth is they are riding in a stolen vehicle. On the other hand, this new development is happening so fast they feel they are being sucked into strange new circumstances without a choice. For the present time, the questioning glance they give each other says, at least for now they are along for the ride—and hoping for the best until they can figure out what to do differently.

The next fifteen minutes are endured without a word spoken. It's apparent Cowboy is struggling with an explanation. Finally, on a back road hopefully leading south toward the small village of Union City, Cowboy breaks the silence. "Sometimes a man's gotta do what a man's gotta do! If you boys can learn to go with the flow, you'll make it in this kind of life. If not you'd be doin' yerself a favor ta head back ta where ya come from."

Not really listening to Cowboy's latest pronouncement, Dace's question takes more the form of an interrogation rather than a simple inquiry. "You stole this van din't ya, Cowboy? An I bet ya stole that Buick too, din't ya?"

Cowboy's hands begin to nervously twitch as he grips and re-grips the steering wheel. Beneath his sunglasses his eyes are blinking erratically. Then he twists his neck from side to side letting it crack as if attempting to work out a kink, or maybe it's an attitude he's adjusting. It's plain to see he's having tangled thoughts.

Whitey is watching Cowboy's nervous reaction. He's beginning to share Dace's sentiment. He too is waiting with more than a little expectancy for a reassuring explanation.

Cowboy formulates his response. "Yer right. Both these been stole, but I din't steal 'em." With this confusing affirmation, he briefly takes his eyes off the road to look at his interrogators. It's long enough to garner a response.

"Well, if it weren't you that stole 'em, Dace an' me know fer damn sure it weren't neither of us, so who the hell are you gonna tell us done it?" says Whitey. The questionable answer they expect earns a sarcastic grin from both boys.

With both hands on the wheel, his eyes locked on the road and with the confidence he is at last going to clear up this enigma, Cowboy very deliberately says the name they least expect to hear, "Sid. Sid done it," he repeats it once again, sure this reinforcement will be convincing enough to pull the heat away from himself.

Instead of this explanation clearing the air, it serves only to muddy it more. Dace retakes the lead with this admonition, "What the hell you sayin', Cowboy. You've been comin' on like you din't have a clue who *this guy, Sid,* is. Now we find out all along the two ah you been in some kind ah secret cahoots behind our backs."

Whitey isn't about to stand on the sidelines either. He's quick to pick up where Dace leaves off. "How the hell you get so damn cozy with a guy like Sid an' what the hell kind ah alliance the two ah you weaselin' bastards got goin' anyhow?"

Cowboy is prepared to put the mystery to sleep. With a moment of silence, he looks off into some distant place. "He's my cousin."

There's dead silence between all of them for another moment. Suddenly they realize why Cowboy looks familiar, it's because of the family resemblance to Sid.

Cowboy continues, "We was in the same barracks at Fort Leonard Wood and both went AWOL together. I been meetin' up with him from time to time. He don't mind doin' a little dirty work when I need it done. He can steal a car faster 'an anybody I've ever seen."

"He's also capable ah killin' ya know, or did you forget what he done ta that railroad dick?" presses Whitey.

"No, an' he ain't forgot it neither—much as he'd like to. He knows both you guys seen him do it. That there is one ah the reasons he keeps poppin' up. He don't come right out an' say it, but he ain't sure what you guys plan on doin' with that kind ah info. In other words, he ain't sure he can trust ya ta keep yer mouth shut," says Cowboy.

This revelation is enough to send a cold chill down the backs of these two boys. Dace is always a bit more responsive than his cousin and doesn't usually let things brew inside too long before he reacts. "What the hell is that spose ta mean 'he ain't sure he can trust us'?" This is followed by an obvious look of great concern.

"He ain't gonna mess with you boys as long as I'm with ya," assures Cowboy.

Whitey is a bit more reflective. "So, what's he plannin' if you ain't here?"

"The only thing I can say is he spose ta have kilt a guy on base. Nobody saw it happen but everybody knowed he done it alright," says Cowboy.

"So why you keep hangin' with a guy like Sid?" questions Dace with the same puzzled look he's had since this whole discussion began.

"Cause, like I said, he's my cousin and besides a guy like Sid is handy ta do a lot of dirty work I don't wanna get caught doin'," reiterates Cowboy.

Whitey is paying close attention to what's being revealed. "So yer sayin' Sid's lookin' fer a chance ta off me an' Dace?"

"Without scarin' the crap outta you guys, I'd say that's how Sid operates," says Cowboy. Both boys are somewhat taken aback by Cowboy's cavalier attitude. "Don't worry. Like I said, as long as I'm around he ain't gonna do nothin'," adds Cowboy.

Whitey lets this piece of the puzzle bedevil him for a moment before throwing out the next question. "I saw him earlier this morning leavin' the same hotel we was in. How the hell's he keep knowin' where we're at?"

Remaining nonchalant, Cowboy forms another thought, "He crawls around like a huge goddam spider. He's like a bad penny, he just keeps turnin' up."

"So, what the hell are we sposed ta do, hang out till he gets around ta killin' us?" questions Dace.

"He ain't gonna do a damn thing if we all stick together," drawls out Cowboy.

"What the hell makes you so cocksure?" demands a more pragmatic Whitey.

"Cause, like I said, I know how he operates," says Cowboy.

Neither Whitey nor Dace are gaining any comfort from this latest revelation. But as with all things, new developments soon overshadow unresolved events only to shove them off to the side. New concerns are quickly overtaking the trio as it's becoming apparent the bread truck may be a common sight, but with the big bold lettering on the side is also very noticeable.

"We need ta ditch this truck an' get back on the rails," says Cowboy with the definitive air of one who knows when he's pushing his limits.

Whitey and Dace shudder at the thought of getting caught with a stolen vehicle. As much as the two would like to be free of Cowboy and all his shrouded and clandestine movements, they find they are still up to their armpits in uncharted waters. This leaves them with no other choice than to keep the status quo. Consequently, they remain a hundred percent dependent on him to keep them from all their unanticipated pitfalls.

Moving fast is going to be the biggest defense they have against an unscheduled brush with the law. An even bigger problem is once the truck is ditched how are they going to arrange getting to the rail yards. As usual Cowboy has a solution.

"Pay attention boys, we're goin' in the bread business."

With that said, he swings the step van into the next small mom and pop grocery store. Putting on a company hat and jacket found in the truck and placing a couple dozen loaves of bread in a delivery cart also found in the truck, he makes his way to the delivery entrance at the rear of the store. Within a few minutes, he returns with an empty cart and waving a dollar bill in his hand.

With the same curiosity known to kill cats, Whitey asks the obvious question. "How the hell did you manage that?"

"I gave them an offer they couldn't refuse. I told them the company was offering a promotion. For every loaf, they purchased, they received one free. They bought all I brought in," says Cowboy with his signature grin.

Within an hour, they make enough stops around the area to empty the truck and collect close to ten dollars in cash. Leaving the truck in the parking lot of their last stop, they make their way to the bus station. Once there, they purchase tickets back to El Reno. Before half the day is spent, they have made their way to a hobo jungle near the Rock Island railyards.

CHAPTER 14

With a comfortable night's sleep behind them (compliments of the Hotel Southern), a fairly substantial horde of cash (compliments of the Wonder Bread Company), and a successful getaway, the trio take the opportunity to relax in the comparatively stress-free atmosphere of this hobo jungle. It's hidden away near the railyards beneath a canopy of cottonwoods. It's the customary mix of hobos, tramps and local bums. As usual the hobos have separated themselves from the others as they patiently wait for a chosen train to leave.

This trio of Cowboy, Whitey, and Dace have picked out a spot off to the side in the shade. Aware of several hobos passing a bottle between them, Cowboy chooses this time to produce a bottle of wine he had bartered for earlier during one of his bread selling stops. The three of them pass the bottle among themselves and even offer a couple other hobos a drink. Taking notice of this fresh influx of alcohol, one of the local bums makes an ill-judged decision to cross the unspoken barrier between groups and invites himself to the drinking. It's obvious he's had way too much to drink to be sensible.

"I see you boys got a fresh bottle there. Mind if a man dyin' ah thirst takes a pull?" The silent code of hobos keeping their distance from the local bums has been violated by this overly inebriated interloper.

Cowboy, Dace and Whitey sit silently staring at the man as he stumbles around their camp. The other two hobos also stare at this intruder until one of them called "Studs"—a rather robust man—says to the invader, "Mister, I'm only thirty seconds away from flyin' into a fit an' yer right in the middle ah my road. I strongly suggest you get yer bum ass outta here an' get back where ya belong!"

The intruder takes only a moment before he throws his mouth into gear hoping to rebut the dismissal. "You goddam hobos think yer better 'an the rest ah us, but you ain't shit ta me."

With that defense, the man pulls out a handful of cash, and waves it in the faces of his tormentors, shouting, "You dickheads ain't never seen cash like this here, an' proly never will." Sure that he's made his point, the man crosses back to his assigned side of the camp.

As the day passes, the local bums have made several booze runs to a handy party store not more than a quarter mile from the jungle. By nightfall, those that haven't left are beginning to show the effects of their bender. One by one they begin to pass out. The hobo section of the camp is also beginning to slow down with each man claiming a suitable spot to lay out his bedroll.

Dace has opted for a place near the fire. He's sure he'll get less mosquito bites by allowing the smoke to drift around him.

Whitey, on the other hand, has found a piece of mosquito netting left tangled in the brush. Wrapping it around his head allows him to find a more private spot and be free of the smoke. This also assures him he won't be bothered by a drunk stumbling around in the night. But nonetheless, as a precaution, he continues to keep his hand on his buck knife under his shirt. This gives him some assurance that no unforeseen harm will come his way.

Cowboy has also drifted off to a nearby thicket allowing himself the privacy he seems to crave this time of day. His persona is in high gear throughout mornings and afternoons, some might even describe him as manic, but as evening approaches, he runs out of gas and begins to display a moodiness that prefers isolation.

Quickly learning the hobo code of not questioning others' idiosyncrasies, Whitey and Dace are more inclined to accept this oddity than pry into the reason behind it. The three of them have shared many hours together for several days. For most hobo relationships, including those that have lasted through many years, the individuals may have only spent brief periods of single days with that person. The relationship these three are developing is highly unusual in this sort of community.

The night is clear and cool. About 3:00A.M., Whitey is abruptly awakened by a strong urge to urinate. Forcing himself out of his warm sleeping bag and not wanting to make a toilet out of his sleeping area, he stumbles some twenty feet away. In the early morning stillness, he hears the sound of two voices over toward the thicket where Cowboy had chosen to bed down. Quickly finishing his toilet duty, Whitey quietly takes a few more steps in the direction of the conversation.

One voice sounds like it could be Cowboy's. "Why do you always have to take things to the extreme? He weren't nothin' more than a mouthy bum!"

It's clear this is Cowboy's voice, but because of the thickness of the foliage, it's impossible to see the two speakers.

The other voice is also familiar. "The som-bitch had it comin', you know that as well as I do!" says the mystery voice. In a moment of clarity, Whitey suddenly realizes the origin of the other voice. *It's none other than Sid Powell!!* This awareness piques his attention to the point he is willing to risk detection and draws closer. But this ploy still prohibits him visibly making out the speakers.

"Well, he may have, but ya didn't need ta kill him while I'm still here!" continues a clearly upset Cowboy.

"The som-bitch had over forty dollars on him and you sure as hell need that a lot more than his dead ass," says Sid in his usual sarcastic tone. "Besides, bums like him ain't got no way ah havin' money like that lessen he stole it."

"I want you gone by morning, Sid. There ain't no sense in you bein' 'round ta muddy up what's gonna bring every goddam lawman in sixteen counties ta this area."

"That ain't never been a problem, Cowboy. You know when I need ta, I can disappear at the drop of a hat," says Sid.

As quickly as the conversation began, it is now silent. Whitey waits for a few minutes to see if it will begin again. Still unable to see, he's satisfied he's eavesdropped on Sid confessing to another murder. Cautiously he makes his way back to his sleeping bag.

Finding it nearly impossible to fall back to sleep, he's just beginning to doze off when he's jolted awake by Cowboy. "Get yer ass in gear! We gotta get on this south-bound 'fore they get outta the yards an' pick up speed," shouts Cowboy.

Dace and Whitey get busy rolling up their bedrolls. Within minutes, they quickly join the others as they break out from a trot to a run to catch the moving train. Whitey realizes everyone is so wrapped up in catching out no one has become aware of anything unusual going on during the night. He's relieved they're leaving before another dead body is discovered.

Paying close attention to the type of railcars being moved, they realize luck is on their side. They've hit the jackpot for railcar hopping. This whole train is made up of grain cars. Each car is indented on both ends creating a cave like porched in area with enough room for one man to ride fairly comfortably.

The ladders from a pair of these grain cars present themselves. Dace and Whitey, with the adeptness of youth, place one foot on the lowest rung along with both hands positioned on a higher rung, and manage to launch themselves to safety. Even novices like these boys have very little struggle boarding. They don't have the luxury of being inside a boxcar with a floor. Nonetheless, on nice days, the ride is exhilarating.

Looking back along the track, Cowboy is nowhere to be seen. They assume he also hopped on at some point, but as is his pattern, he prefers to ride alone. Whitey waits for himself and Dace to settle in before he reveals the conversation he had overheard involving Sid and Cowboy during the night.

There is no question Whitey has Dace's full attention. "That damn Sid is nothin' but trouble, always has been, always will be! He's gonna be the downfall of all of us!" deplores Dace, fidgeting around as though making his body more comfortable will also quiet his fearful thoughts. The pressure hanging over him from his bruhaha back in Elbertport along with Sid's behavior keeps him in a state of high anxiety.

With Sid dogging their every move, what had started with all the hopes of an adventure has quickly turned into ongoing crises in which Dace and Whitey have little or no control.

The train could care less. It rumbles on as if nothing has happened. The clicking of the wheels is barely noticed as each of the boys are buried in his own thoughts.

The miles and miles of wasteland making up this near desert environment is far removed from the lush vegetation both have taken for granted in Elbertport. Despite having the company of one another, a kind of loneliness matching this sere environment is creeping over each of them.

For the moment, hunger becomes a welcome distraction. Whitey digs around in his supplies long enough to come up with a can of sardines. Responding to this, Dace has some crackers left over from the abandoned bread truck. Nestled in the protection of a train speeding away from the mayhem that has barged into their lives, they enjoy a simple breakfast in the hopes of a better day.

Only a few days have passed since leaving the community in which they were born and raised. Now finding themselves neck deep in a world they never knew existed, Whitey and Dace are discovering a different kind of change coming over themselves. The awareness that they are not in control of this recent reality is apparent.

They feel a weighty need to begin to adapt to whatever these new, nameless developments may be called. To call it *adulthood* is probably stretching the definition of maturity beyond its limits. To overcome their youthful naivete is going to require a shift from dealing with familiar youthful goings-on to successfully understanding these unfamiliar pseudo-adult behaviors. It's paramount they succeed; to fail could mean their lives.

CHAPTER 15

Meanwhile, back in Elbertport, life goes on as usual. Faces may change with time, but similar personalities tend to transfer from one generation to the next. There is always the gossip—those who develop it, and those who listen to it. Humans have always found the lives of others more interesting than their own and will willingly spend hours attempting to control the behaviors of everyone else.

Until these recent events, the only legal concern was to be on the lookout for Sid Powell—AWOL from the army. He's been reported to be heading back this way. He has a reputation for having a mean streak and law enforcement are asked to be cautious in dealing with him.

It's been several days since one man was found dead in Elbertport and a young man was nearly beaten to death. Sheriff Peleton has never been this busy in his two terms as the county's lead law enforcement officer. His attempt to keep the investigation isolated and away from inquiring minds is a practice in futility. What one has heard from "a damn good source" is passed on as gospel. The clamor for justice is in the end spiced with the mindless injustice of a lynch mob.

Joan's Restaurant is alight with the latest developments as is Bob's barbershop. Each contributor is clamoring to add their personal twist to what they've heard and what they're concluding. Pieces of the stories considered as facts are measured by the verbal intensity of the narrator rather than by anything resembling a scientific investigation. As most stories go, they often become convoluted. To mix parts of one event with parts of another is common practice with the ill-informed.

Generally, whatever conclusions are drawn in the restaurant, more often than not do not match those in the barbershop and these recent events are no exception.

An idler named Ed Higman is on these two cases full time. He spends a few hours in the morning kibitzing at the restaurant, then reassigns himself to the barbershop in the afternoon, and finally caps his evening off at Burt's Bar. He has become quite an authority on both the horrific murder out at Dennis Walden's place and the attempted murder perpetrated by young Dace Kidman all taking place within the past few days.

"Yeseree Bob! If ya ask me that Kidman kid's gotta hand in all this. He ain't got an ole man ta put a foot in his ass when he needs it, an' his ma ain't never been able ta control either ah them boys fer a minute."

The sheriff is trying his best to keep a low profile concerning what he has uncovered in both cases. Unlike the general populace, he is very much aware of how the cases differ. The sheriff's temptation to put rumors such as these to rest must be put on the back burner until his investigations are completed.

It seems the murder victim at the Walden's was Sid Powell's father, George Powell. The details are still unclear at this time. What Sheriff Peleton is keeping close to the vest is his search for Sid. He has received information of Sid's probable involvement in the murder on the army base and a strong possibility that he is involved in this latest murder of his own father.

To release too much unsupported information to the public in this small town is certain to trigger some of its citizens to put together a vigilante group—all under the guise of performing their civic duty. After a few beers, it's amazing how people with different sober opinions find a commonality in thinking; Sober thoughts quickly erode and soon give way to damaging impulses. Within a very short time a public conviction and a swift penalty all begin to make sense.

At the same time, Sheriff Peleton would like to draw on as much support from the public as he can garner, but not at the expense of compromising either case. He realizes this struggle is a fine balancing act that needs a careful steadiness.

Meanwhile, Peleton is on his way to respond to a citizen's concern with an intruder she had earlier encountered. Mrs. Jensen lives behind the Methodist Church at the bottom of Church Hill. She had been startled by a young man raiding her vegetable garden a few days earlier. She reported it to the sheriff department, giving them a description and was told they would check it out and for her to monitor any further trespassing.

Without a lot of fanfare, but never without someone taking notice, Sheriff Peleton calls on Mrs. Jensen. Carefully beginning his inquiry with reassuring words of apology, he begins, "I'm sorry it's taken so long to get back with you Mrs. Jensen, but as you have probably heard we've had quite a bit of turmoil in our county the past few days."

She is so stressed over the startling discovery of a bedraggled young man in the early morning hours invading the sanctity of her property that she hears nothing of his wordy apology. She is so overwhelmed with concern for her personal safety, she can only be consoled by the calming individual attention the sheriff is giving her.

"That man scared me so bad, I've barely left the house since!" she says.

Realizing he first needs to patiently listen to her fears, if he hopes to get any worthwhile information. He lets her recount all the feelings she is experiencing without interruption. Ten minutes pass before he perceives she has vented her frustrations enough he can begin to ask some relevant questions about the man invading her garden.

"Mrs. Jensen I'd like you to tell me what you remember about his looks—for example what did you imagine his age to be when you first saw him?"

Not hesitating for a moment, she begins, "The same age as my grandson, Jimmy. He lives down in Thompsonville—at least he used to, but now he's going to school downstate."

Not wanting to be overly aggressive in his interrogation, he gently leads her back to his original question. "And how old would you say he seemed to you?"

"Oh, I guess maybe twenty-two—three maybe, not more than twenty- five. All these young people look the same age to me nowadays," she confesses.

Sheriff Peleton is scribbling notes in a small pocket tablet he can flip from page to page.

"I want you to think for a moment on this next question," says the sheriff. "What did he seem to be wearing?"

Again, not hesitating, Mrs. Jensen says, "It looked ta be some kinda army stuff—you know like green colored."

Looking back through his notes, Peleton takes a moment before he offers his next query. Looking up as though he needs something clarified, he continues, "Did you notice which way he came and which way he left?"

"I know for sure he went back up the hill?"

"You say you *know for sure he went back up the hill.* Did you see him come down?" belabors Peleton.

"No, but I already noticed the sand on the hill was turned over showing the damper stuff before he made his get-away," says Mrs. Jensen, with the firmness of a soil expert. After all, she has been a gardener all her life. Since her husband died several years ago, she takes great solace in working long hours in her raspberries, strawberries, tomatoes, sweet corn and an assortment of all God's vegetables. Now to have this sacred place threatened by the likes of a suspect believed to be Sid Powell, who has been a troubled person all his life, is devastating.

Writing as fast as he can, Peleton finishes his notes and assures Mrs. Jensen she has been a great help. He doesn't want to concern her unnecessarily about Sid also being a suspect in his father's murder, so he plays into her own concerns about him raiding her garden. "I want you to call my office immediately if he shows up here again," says Peleton, using his most official and most reassuring tone.

"Don't you worry for one minute about that! I'll be on the phone so fast he won't have a chance to turn around," decries Mrs. Jensen.

"Well we can only hope it will be that easy, Mrs. Jensen," returns Sheriff Peleton.

Pausing for a minute, she adds, "I also saw Heinie Schultz's boy going up the same hill carrying a whole bunch of stuff yesterday."

Sheriff Peleton adds this notation into his note book.

Thanking her for taking the time to allow him an interview, she in turn thanks him for taking the time to answer her complaint. Both close on a good note.

Back in his office alone, Peleton sorts through all the information he's accumulated over the past few days surrounding the disappearance of the three Elbertport young people. All of them suspects in some sort of felony or another.

Rumors aren't always forgotten or ignored by Sheriff Peleton. There is one in particular, he recalls where Vaughn Kidman was bragging how he could track his brother down in a heartbeat if need be. Playing on a hunch, Peleton decides to pay Vaughn a visit. He finds him in his mother's backyard tinkering on his '49 Mercury—a car Vaughn has built with stolen parts. Not that he needs to identify himself, Peleton, nonetheless introduces himself.

Vaughn is more than a little intimidated by the appearance of this heavily uniformed lawman. He begins to blink and swallow to a point where he finds it impossible to speak. His hands are shaking so bad he lets his wrench drop to the ground. All he can do is nod.

He is sure this visit has something to do with all the gas he has siphoned from unsuspecting citizens around the county or all the questionable car parts lying about. His guilty conscience makes him extremely aware of his siphoning hose and gas can sitting in plain sight in his open car trunk. Trying to remain nonchalant, he makes his way to the back of his car and slams the trunk shut. After clearing his throat several times in an attempt to speak, he manages to squeak out, "What can I do for you, sir?"

As a career lawman relying heavily on his ability to read guilt in people, Peleton plays into this advantage with Vaughn.

"I've gotten information from very reliable sources that tell me you aided and abetted your brother Dace in avoiding a possible felony warrant I have for his arrest."

It's readily apparent this selective information the sheriff has been privy to is shattering Vaughn's usual cavalier reaction. He's more accustomed to dealing with much less authoritative figures where he can maintain an advantage. With the sheriff personally making this accusation, he realizes he is out of his league.

The color drains from Vaughn's face and his shaking worsens. Because of his involvement, he's aware he may be in more trouble than he had planned or imagined. All the same, it was his own need to brag about his detective ability in locating his brother that has brought this trouble to his door.

Still not able to put enough thoughts together to sidetrack the sheriff, Vaughn tries not making eye contact with this seeming nemesis. In doing so, his eyes dart everywhere except toward the sheriff making himself look guiltier than if he held his ground. He's quickly becoming putty in Peleton's hand.

Peleton is no stranger to these showdowns. Seeing he has Vaughn against the ropes, he offers a way for Vaughn to exonerate himself. "If you choose to co-operate we can make these charges go away. On the other hand, if you choose to lie and try to make me believe I'm an idiot, then I'll throw the book at you and you can swing in the wind alone."

It would be totally in character for Vaughn to sell out his grandmother to protect himself. Aware the sheriff's holding all the trump cards, Vaughn has a moment of clarity. He realizes the sheriff is giving him an opportunity to weasel his way out of this predicament. "What do you need from me?" he humbly asks.

Assured he has this interview going his way, Sheriff Peleton follows with his first mandate, "I need the truth about where this shack is up in the hills and for you to lead me to it."

"I'll do it, sir, but I already know they ain't there anymore. I was with 'em when they took off outta there," confesses Vaughn.

"Who's the *they* you're talking about?" questions Peleton.

"Dace and Whitey, sir."

"Was there anyone else with them when you last saw them together or separately?" further questions the sheriff.

"No sir. They was all alone together. I never saw nobody else," professes Vaughn.

Wanting to keep Vaughn on the defensive, Sheriff Peleton gives him the evil eye as he throws out the next question, "You're sure they weren't associating themselves with anyone else?"

"No sir! I'm double damn sure they was alone the last time I saw 'em."

"Well suppose you and I take a little jaunt up the hill to this famous little shack and see for ourselves what's going on," says Peleton.

"Right now?" says a surprised Vaughn.

"I can't think of a better time to get started, can you?" says Peleton with a steady gaze on any reactions Vaughn may be displaying.

"No sir—I guess now's as good a time as any."

It's not beyond Vaughn to shift his gears of allegiance when the winds of fate blow against him. Finding himself riding in the front seat of Sheriff Peleton's patrol car and not the back seat gives him a sense of importance. To further enhance the appearance of a friendly acquaintance with the sheriff, Vaughn casually rests his elbow on the open window. He's always had a sense of prideful arrogance. In this cruise through town, he hopes to present himself as being on the inside of important town events. And even more so as he discovers he's being witnessed by many of his peers.

Soon, he and the sheriff make their way to the trailhead leading them up the dune to Dud Olsen's shack. Viewing this uphill trek as any smoker in his late forties and slightly overweight would, Peleton is not looking forward to the fatigue that inevitably awaits him. Not wishing to display any sign of weakness in front of this young man, he makes a forward hand gesture suggesting Vaughn lead the way.

Within a hundred feet, Peleton has no choice, he needs Vaughn to slow the pace. Trying not to gasp in an attempt to make light of his lack of conditioning, he says, "Hey kid this ain't no foot race ya know. Slow it down a bit, we wanna get there in one piece."

Vaughn looks puzzled at this unseemly request. Being young and self-absorbed, Vaughn has no idea how this type of physical exertion is affecting Peleton. For Peleton, placing himself on this kind of assignment makes him more aware than ever that at best his youth had been very temporary.

With nothing left but sheer determination, the huffing sheriff crests the top. He not only feels the fatigue, but has also become lightheaded. Very clearly without adequate oxygen getting to his brain, he's seeing stars and feels he'll pass out. Taking in some deep breaths while cupping his hands over his face, and not able to say a word, he manages to recover enough to throw a hand up in the international signal to halt.

Still puzzled at this interruption, Vaughn has no clue what struggles Peleton is undergoing. He takes the break to mean it's time for a cigarette. Popping a Pall Mall between his lips, Vaughn flips out his Zippo, and in a single ostentatious presentation, he lights an ordinary cigarette as though it was one of a kind. He then takes in a long drag only to exhale it moments later in a perfect plume of white smoke. As routine as smoking is for Vaughn, this procedure is not merely a habit, but a well rehearsed ritual.

With this brief interlude Peleton's lungs begin to return to normal. In the hopes of not giving Vaughn an indication of his lack of conditioning, he takes advantage of this break to light a cigarette of his own. Ten minutes elapse. He's still not feeling fully recovered, but it's enough to push on once again. "Hey kid, you ain't leading me on some kind of wild goose chase are you?" says Peleton. His color remains an ashen white, about the color of hawk bait.

"No, hell no. I know exactly where we are," says Vaughn. With no obvious landmarks, and the confidence of a seasoned guide, he pushes a quarter mile further down a sandy trail. His eyes soon scout the area to the left of the path as though he's looking for an indicator of some kind. Satisfied he's still on the right course, he signals to Peleton to follow him down a rather obscure track leading into what appears to be cedar scrub. By this time, the sheriff is trailing by a good fifty feet. Trying his best to give the impression he's still in charge, Peleton calls out, "Hang loose a minute kid. I want to check a few things out before you get too far ahead of me."

Peleton is still not feeling as though he's fully recuperated from the climb but confident he'll make a quick enough recovery. So far, Vaughn has led him deeper into a valley that's lined with walls of heavy hardwood growth. Looking at the possibility of yet another climb, Peleton is hoping to buy a little more recovery time.

No sooner are these words out of his mouth than Vaughn points to a spot in the scrub just ahead. Straining his eyes to see what Vaughn is silently pointing out, Peleton's senses finally begin to make out what may loosely be described as a man-made object. It's nestled into the cedar grove well enough that anyone not acquainted with its location would walk by, never seeing it. The only giveaway this place has served as a habitation for humans is the number of empty cans littering a twenty-foot perimeter.

Otherwise, this dwelling could almost be described as an aberration of nature.

Not sure what he may be encountering, and in spite of how bad he feels, Peleton kicks into sheriff mode. Putting his finger to his lips, he signals Vaughn to remain quiet and to stay put. With pistol drawn, he begins to slowly make his way toward the shack. He hears what he believes to be movement inside. Getting within twenty feet of the hovel, safely behind a tree, he shouts out, "Sheriff's Department! Show yourself with hands up!"

Prepared to shoot if need be, he catches a glimpse of movement behind the window. It's not a threatening movement, but it's one of non-compliance with his order to come out with hands in the air. Taking precautions, he raises his handgun. Suddenly, without warning the unlatched window pops open and a huge raccoon slithers out, leaps to the ground, and hightails it to the nearest tree. It sends a shiver of adrenalin through his body, adding to an already overloaded system.

A mixture of disappointment and relief overcomes Peleton. Surmising a raccoon wouldn't be occupying the same dwelling with a human, he determines the site to be free of human occupation. Lowering his sidearm, he cautiously moves forward with his eyes searching around every tree and bush. Satisfied there is no impending danger, Peleton holsters his pistol and begins his investigation of the premises.

With hands and eyes free to focus on the debris, one item catches his attention immediately. First, he uses his foot to uncover what appears to be a wadded clump of greenish cloth, half-buried under a covering of fallen leaves. As he reaches down and pulls it free, his excitement rises. He realizes this is exactly the kind of evidence he had been hoping to uncover. Taking a bag from his pocket and a ballpoint pen, he inscribes on the label *one army issue sock.*

In another sweep of the area including the interior of the shack, another piece of potential evidence catches his eye. This happens to be the vegetable tops. Since there isn't any indication of a vegetable plot close by, he can safely assume they had been connected to a vegetable grown somewhere else. A noteworthy observation is that these are similar to the varieties he had observed in Mrs. Jensen's garden. He doesn't bother to bag these in favor of a simple notation.

Vaughn has since moved in closer only to be told not to disturb anything, but if he sees something he feels is worthy of

Peleton's attention to be sure and bring it to his attention.

As far as Vaughn is concerned, he is still under the impression Sheriff Peleton is only focusing on Dace's crime. He has no idea the scope of Peleton's investigation into the possibility of a meeting between Dace and Sid.

Peleton, despite how ill he continues to feel, is determined to finish this part of his investigation today, even if it kills him. There is no way he wants to make the trek here again. "You say your brother and cousin have used this shack to hide out in the past and that day you met them on the trail to the boat landing. What makes you believe they were here?" asks the sheriff.

Using the toe of his shoe, Vaughn flips up a filter from a spent cigarette. "This right here, sir," says Vaughn. "This here is off a Winston. The only person who smokes 'em is Whitey 'cuz he steals 'em off his ma. I knowed they'd head fer this ole shack first. It's where they always go when they get in trouble," says Vaughn, with the assured tone of one who has been down this road several times himself.

Continuing to press Vaughn, Peleton asks a question that so far, he has avoided. "You described how you wanted to spook your brother and cousin along the trail. Did you happen to see anyone else while you were up here?"

Vaughn hesitates for a moment. "Like who?"

Sensing a reservation in Vaughn's answer, the sheriff presses forward. "Oh, I don't know, anybody at all," answers Peleton, avoiding any sign of this being anything other than a routine question.

"I was hopin' ya wouldn't ask, but I did see Sid Powell. I heard he was back here AWOL. I stayed back in the brush. He didn't see me an' that's just as well. He's always been crazier 'an a shit house rat," says Vaughn.

This is going better than Peleton had expected. Still not wanting to sound overly concerned with this information, intending to downplay it, he continues, "Yeah, I received a notice the military police were looking for him, but I got other things to be concerned with rather than doing their work."

Peleton desperately wants to take this lead to the next level, but he doesn't want to display the least sign of anxiousness in getting there. "You don't suppose your brother and cousin got tied up with him, do you?"

"They hadn't when I saw 'em. All's they said they was gonna do was hang around til things blew over."

"That's been nearly a day and a half now and I don't see any signs they're still hanging around this place especially after I seen that raccoon living in here," says Peleton. "Where do you suppose, they could have disappeared?"

Feeling the sheriff is trusting his opinion because of his sleuthing abilities, Vaughn can't contain himself. "I think they proly hopped a boxcar gettin' loaded fer Wisconsin."

"What makes you believe that?" asks Peleton.

Affirming this declaration with a touch of finality and recalling a few years earlier when he had done the same thing, he declares, "Cuz that's what I'd ah done."

CHAPTER 16

Vaughn's assertion involving a boxcar catches Peleton on his blind side. This is a possibility that hadn't occurred to him. Without letting on, whether Vaughn's reasoning is plausible—and why wouldn't it be—Peleton considers this to be a sure-enough game changer. After all, when he weighs the other options, it's the one he would have chosen himself.

Having spent the better part of the afternoon investigating and evaluating his assumptions, Peleton is ready to get off the hill. Instead of waiting for Vaughn to take the lead, he feels familiar enough with the terrain to lead off on his own. He's sweating profusely and his arm and shoulder are aching. Within minutes his breath is becoming labored. He needs to sit down fast or risk falling over. Barely able to get to a stump leading out to the trail, he begins to pass out.

Watching him grab his chest and helplessly slump to the ground, Vaughn has no clue what may be going on with Peleton, but he's sure whatever the problem is it's greater than he's capable of managing.

"Sir, are you okay?" asks Vaughn. He's almost sure he isn't going to get a positive response, but is inclined to go through the ritual of asking.

"I don't think I can get out of here on my own kid. I may need a little extra help?" says Peleton, in a voice that's nearly a gasp.

Feeling himself slipping deeper into a bad situation, Vaughn labors to phrase the right question. "Should I get a doctor, sir?"

By this time Peleton is lying nearly flat out on the forest floor, still clutching his chest. Looking up at the face of what should be nearly a man, he hears the inept question of a child. With a nearly inaudible whisper, he manages to say, "Yes, I think that is what you should do."

Vaughn's thoughts are banging around in his head. His feelings of incompetence are overshadowing his decision-making capacity. He's having difficulty realizing that he's in charge and is going to have to act like an adult.

Still not sure what his next move should be, he begins a rapid paced half-run, half-walk back toward town. His mind begins running through her options. *What are you going to do? Who are you going to get help from?* In a moment of clarity, the name Doc LaRue shoots through his thoughts. *Yes! Doc LaRue! That's who I'll get!*

Doc lives in Elbertport not far from the trailhead. He's mended nearly everyone in town at one time or another. He also owns a four-wheeled drive army surplus jeep he uses on difficult house calls during the winter. The trail leading up to where Sheriff Peleton is lying is a former logging trail, wide enough to permit a vehicle, but too steep for just any vehicle. "Doc's jeep can get back up the hill fer sure," calculates Vaughn out loud.

The next thing he is aware of is standing on a porch facing a shingle reading *Frank J. Larue Physician and Surgeon*. He barely recalls how he made his way there. The lobby door is always left unlocked allowing those wishing to see the doctor a small waiting room out of the elements. The sign below the doorbell reads *ring for assistance*. Still out of breath when the door opens, Vaughn stands mute. The medicinal smell of the doctor's office along with the presence of Mrs. LaRue, both wife and nurse, meet the wild-eyed young man standing speechless in the lobby. Like most of the young people in Elbertport, she recognizes Vaughn. After all, between herself and her husband, they have delivered most of them, taken out their tonsils, removed their appendixes, set their broken bones, cleared up their whooping cough and a myriad of other ailments. Finally, she asks, "How can I be of assistance to you, Mr. Kidman?"

"Somethin's wrong with Sheriff Peleton ma'am. He collapsed on me up in the hills," says Vaughn between short breaths.

Not waiting to get any more details, she recognizes this whole state of affairs as dire. Immediately she calls back through the open door, "Frank, can you come out for a moment?"

Coatless, but still wearing a tie and vest, the doctor appears at the door. By this time, Vaughn has recovered enough to give the doctor a more comprehensive overview of what Peleton was experiencing. The doctor listens without saying a word. Still not acknowledging Vaughn, he turns to his wife saying, "Ellen get a room ready. If he's still alive we may be able to help him."

Grabbing his bag, the doctor removes a few medicine bottles from a cupboard and places them in his pocket. Throwing on a coat and his fedora, he motions for Vaughn to follow. As Vaughn expected, the doctor's next move is to open his garage and fire up the jeep. With another impatient hand signal, Dr. LaRue motions for Vaughn to get in.

"We have no time to waste. We must get to him right now! Tell me exactly where we have to go," is his next imperative.

Once again, in just a matter of hours, Vaughn finds himself in a role of responsibility with another of Elbertport's leading citizens. Being seen speeding through the streets first in the sheriff's car and now in the doctor's jeep vaults him to a position of importance that he can only imagined.

He is already rehearsing in his own mind how he will respond to the attention he expects to reap from his role with the sheriff and now with the doctor.

But focusing on guiding the aging doctor up the unaccustomed trail is all Vaughn can handle for the moment. The track has its share of precarious ruts and overhanging branches, all attempting to dissuade the jeep's upward motion—not to mention the doctor's slower unrehearsed reactions in meeting these conditions. Vaughn's youthful impatience with the doctor's cautious progress is evident by his frequent shouts such as "Gun it! Turn left!" By all accounts, the doctor is out of his area of expertise and lacks the skills to maneuver the critical twists and turns in this terrain. With only one other alternative to meet this dilemma, Dr. LaRue stops the jeep on a small plateau. He sits for a moment looking up the hill at the long ride yet to go and then at the young man who has spent much of his recreational time challenging his driving skills through these old logging trails.

"Young man, you sound better equipped to maneuver this trek than me. Take over and get us up there," says the doctor with the same pragmatism he approaches all areas of life.

Quickly making the switch from passenger to driver, Vaughn is in his element. This is truly the best day of his life. He's been engaged with adults today in ways he's never experienced before. He can barely imagine how he's going to exploit this revolutionary status with his peers.

Scarcely grinding the gears, he slips this ancient veteran into first gear. The old vehicle lurches forward digging its tires into the side of the sandy hill. Charting his course as he has countless other times up this same hill, and after negotiating it with vehicles hardly designed for this kind of punishment, he manages to bring Doc's four-wheeled wonder to the very crest with ease.

Doc LaRue can't help but marvel at the youthful dexterity of this young man handling his old war horse. "Good job Vaughn, now just get me to my patient." Doc says in the same matter of fact tone he responds with in all his dealings.

In less than five minutes, Vaughn parks alongside the trail where less than an hour ago, he left Sheriff Peleton prostrate, and on the face of it, near death. Much to Vaughn's chagrin, the sheriff is sitting on a stump smoking a cigarette as though nothing had happened. After all of Vaughn's chasing around to get help and especially after he had painted the worst of scenarios, now to find Peleton patiently sitting there as though nothing unusual was happening is hardly tolerable. He finds himself wishing Peleton was dead, so he would have a more alarming scenario to boast about.

On the other hand, Doc LaRue is far from convinced everything is fine with the sheriff. Giving Peleton a hard look, in seconds he has a stethoscope on him going from one point of his chest to another. In a few more seconds and after some pertinent questions, the doctor has slaked his suspicions. "Miles you're undergoing cardiac arrest and I don't believe you're out of the woods yet, so we need to get you out of these woods and to my office." This message is presented with the same delivery as if he were telling the sheriff it's time for lunch.

There is no panic, solely a concise use of time and energy in assisting Peleton to the jeep. To insure an intact and viable trip back down the hill, the doctor places the disabled sheriff in the back seat along with himself. Positioning him in such a way that if Peleton should go back into cardiac arrest, he'll have the doctor's full attention.

Doc LaRue is very aware at this juncture the best he'll be able to do is to prevent Peleton from toppling out of the jeep. Vaughn is cognizant of his role as driver and is fully prepared to let anyone on the street become aware of his new role as an emergency ambulance driver. The jeep lacks the siren Vaughn would have preferred, but does possess a high-pitched, tinny-sounding horn precisely centered in the middle of the steering wheel. A little disappointed he can't have a more masculine sounding warning signal, he nonetheless is dead set on making the most of his opportunity. Hardly able to attract the attention he is hoping to promote, Vaughn presses hard on the horn's cover as he makes his way through town running every stop sign and ignoring the posted speed limits.

There are the usual hangers on dotting the streets. These are not the people Vaughn was hoping to see. At this point he craves the attention of presidents and kings. So far, he has barely caught the attention of old Charlie Morgan a six-foot-tall recluse plodding along in a cast-off army overcoat. Old Charlie could be in the middle of the biggest happening of the century and not have a clue what was coming off. He possesses the personality of a man who would be impressed with nothing less than Vaughn being on fire.

Doc would have preferred a less ostentatious entrance, but with Vaughn behind the wheel and a seriously ill man in the back, he opts to set aside Vaughn's theatrics and concentrate his efforts on getting his patient to his office. With a final flair, Vaughn whips the jeep around to the back door.

Ellen meets them with a look of concern that is only reserved for such emergencies. As with any well-oiled team, the two act in concert. They have the seriously ill sheriff out of the jeep and escorted to a room with a bed and a system of meticulously organized medical devices.

LaRue has always prided himself on being a country doctor but also one who has kept pace with any new medical developments. This emergency is bringing with it an opportunity to showcase his state of the art defibrillator. This innovation is heralded as a breakthrough for heart attack victims.

Speaking quite frankly with Sheriff Peleton, Doc LaRue pulls no punches. "From my observations and what you and Vaughn related, I believe that you have survived a widow-maker."

Peleton gives him a doe in the headlight look. "What does that mean?"

"It typically means that right now we should be delivering you to the funeral home instead of my office." Doc continues to talk as he gets the new equipment in order. "So far you're my miracle for the day and hopefully we can keep it that way. Your chance of having another heart attack in the next twenty-four hours is nearly a hundred percent."

Peleton continues to stare wide-eyed. He can't form words that will awaken him from what is becoming his reality.

"I want you to stay here so we can monitor you. If need be, I now have a machine that is capable of literally bringing you back from the dead," carries on Doc. "Hopefully I won't need to do that, but it's a nice precautionary piece of equipment to have if it comes to that."

Ellen is preparing the room around both her husband and the sheriff when she spots something very irregular. Peleton has suddenly begun to gasp, grabbing at his chest. She immediately drops what she is doing and alerts her husband. Doctor LaRue quickly readies two electrodes, forcing the tape to Peleton's chest, while Ellen struggles to physically make him lie flat.

He quickly sends a current of AC electricity into Peleton's heart. There is no response so he repeats the process again. Still no response. This causes LaRue to adjust the current to a higher level before repeating. The result is Peleton heaving himself nearly off the bed, but his heart has started and he is beginning to breathe again. Neither, Doc nor Ellen are ready to celebrate any success just yet. Monitoring Peleton is going to be a full-time activity for at least several days.

They spend the next half hour getting their patient settled into a bed.

During all this, Vaughn has not said a word and is trying to stay out of the way and in the background. As a final point, after Doc has finished with Peleton, he turns to Vaughn acknowledging him for the first time since leaving the hill. "You done a good job lad. I couldn't have done this without your help."

Notwithstanding his contribution, Vaughn is suffering the uneasiness that afflicts him whenever he is confronted with an adult—even more so with an adult as important as Doc LaRue.

As usual he's at a loss for words, between blinking steadily and swallowing, he finally manages to form the words, "Thanks, Doc. I'm glad I could help."

With all this ending, he's glad to get outside and away from the challenging company of these frightening adults. Smoking a cigarette gives him an opportunity to go over recent events and to plan his next play.

CHAPTER 17

Finishing the last drag on his cigarette, Vaughn flicks it aside. His thoughts have led him to the bottom of the hill he had only a few hours ago, descended—and with a cargo he never could have imagined he'd be carrying.

It's proving to be rather surreal looking. The sheriff's car is still parked exactly where the two of them had left it to begin their ill-fated trek up the hill. Things have happened so fast, he finds himself stopping to sort through them once again. For a reason that he can't quite put his finger on, he is compelled to return to where these events took place. It's as though the sheriff may have left some clue undiscovered; some bit of information interrupted by his inopportune courtship with death; something he may discover with an extra attentive scrutiny.

Feeling a rather personal connection with this trail after ascending and descending this same hill a couple of times in the past few hours, Vaughn finds his thoughts rolling over and over about what Sheriff Peleton may have been searching for. *I can't quite believe Peleton was as consumed with Dace and Whitey as he seemed. There must be something else.*

With his mind wheeling at near full capacity, almost unaware of anything other than his thoughts, he notices he has arrived at the very spot Sheriff Peleton collapsed. The disturbed forest floor reflects the struggle that culminated only a short time ago.

With the words of Sheriff Peleton warning him not to disturb the area and chance obliterating evidence still resonating across his mind. Vaughn finds himself not taking the risk of proceeding any further until he has adequately scrutinized the area. At first, all he sees are the ordinary things found on the forest floor such as fallen leaves, twigs, and small plants struggling for their share of sunlight. But with this calculated pause, he also notices something else that doesn't quite fit this wilderness. It's a coloration that is out of place. It is yellow—not the earth-toned yellow found with the surrounding debris. It's a much brighter yellow. Vaughn finds himself staring curiously at this bit of alien material. Conscious of the sheriff's warning, he takes extra careful precautions not to disturb any potential evidence as he makes his way to this mysterious scrap. Not wanting to damage the unidentified substance by uncovering it with the toe of his shoe, he intentionally bends down and carefully brushes away the forest clutter still concealing its identity.

What Vaughn discovers is that his fingers are not holding a random piece of discarded yellow paper, rather it's the cardboard covering of the very notebook in which Sheriff Peleton had been entering his findings. It evidently had dropped from his pocket unnoticed.

Vaughn fumbles through the notebook while nervously looking about. It's almost as though he expects the sheriff to catch him in the act. He undeniably knows he has come across a very private piece of property that Peleton would not be pleased if he knew fell into the wrong hands.

Since the sheriff is out of commission, Vaughn slowly convinces himself it's safe to do whatever he wishes with this artifact. Immediately, he begins a more methodical examination of its contents. Over the next hour, he pours over each page. The deeper he probes, the more enlightening its content becomes.

It's not surprising, every name in this log is a name he is very familiar with. What is strikingly evident is Sheriff Peleton suspects

Sid Powell is connected to at least two murders.

Vaughn is disturbed by Peleton's concern with a possible connection between Dace, Whitey and Sid. He was at least entertaining the possibility they may have made their escape the same way and at the same time—possibly together, whether wittingly or unwittingly.

Acknowledging Peleton's professional experience, Vaughn does not doubt the likelihood of Peleton's assessment. After all, didn't he spot Sid on the same trail leading to the rail yards? Vaughn hasn't always treated his brother and cousin in kindly ways, but this is a whole different kettle of fish. With the possibility—even more likely the probability—that Peleton's assessment is correct and knowing Sid, the way he does, Vaughn is suddenly faced with the sobering thought his brother and cousin may be in peril.

Once again, Vaughn makes his way down the hill. He has embraced what he believes fate has provided him to discover; the lost notebook. His thoughts are swirling relentlessly. He briefly considers returning the sheriff's property, but discards the idea in light of the sheriff's condition. Now he is thinking of how to make best use of the information himself.

Returning home, Vaughn is especially quiet through the rest of the evening. Rather than go out to meet his friends and glow in the coveted feedback on his less than humble behavior during the day's happenings, he stays in his room.

I know I can't sit by and do nothing. I have to do something even though I don't have a clue what that something involves. I can't just leave those guys to Sid's mercy. They may not even know he is with them, he muses.

Lying across his bed, he stares out the window at the sun beginning to drop below the very dune he had coupled himself to in so many ways over the past twenty-four hours. A former experience suddenly leaps into his mind. He recalls how he and Dick VanBrocklin hopped a freight a few years earlier and made the trip across Lake Michigan buried in the belly of a car ferry. It occurs to him that it's worth the chance he may be able to overtake his brother and cousin by doing the same. *Hell, it's been less 'an forty-eight hours. Those two peckerheads are proly still hangin around Kewaunee.*

Vaughn springs to his feet, grabs his old gym bag and begins to toss some clothing into it. Meanwhile his mother is in the kitchen putting supper together. Hearing the commotion coming from his room, she makes her way down the hallway. Standing in the doorway of his bedroom, she suspects something is going on when she sees him with a bag. Not sure what it means yet, she nonetheless has her suspicions. He in turn stares back without saying a word, dropping his bag only to announce, "Don't say a word, Ma. I'm goin' ta find Dace an' Whitey an' bring 'em home."

Brina stands nearly dumbfounded. She has lost her husband due to the war, her youngest son has left averting the law, and now her eldest son is preparing to desert her as well. With that, he gives her a peck on the cheek, picks up his bag and heads out the door.

"Vaughn wait," she pleads, "you have no idea where they went."

Hearing the anxiety in her voice, he says, "Don't worry Ma, I'll find 'em."

With the resolve of a cat watching a mouse hole, he throws his bag into the seat next to him, and turns the key firing up his custom '49 Merc. The original motor has been replaced with a Cadillac version adding greater horsepower. As the engine turns over, a blast of energy roars out through the special side pipes. This gives the whole monster an ominous, intimidating resonance.

At least for the moment, Vaughn has a single-minded purpose—get to the boat landing and find Gene McClellan. Gene is part of the yard crew in charge of loading the car ferry and Vaughn knows he will do favors for gas. Locating him on the loading apron, Vaughn approaches him and quickly negotiates five gallons of stolen gas for a free spot for himself and his car to be transported to Kewaunee.

"What the hell you gonna do in that craphole Kewaunee?" questions Gene as he transports the gas can from Vaughn's car trunk to his own.

"Hell, I dunno, maybe check out the chicks," says Vaughn attempting to maintain a cavalier attitude.

As is mostly true in railroading, everything comes and goes by a schedule. This evening is no exception. Gene has skillfully loaded the boat with railcars leaving just enough room to place Vaughn's car on the tail end of the ship. The great sea gate is lowered to prevent any unwanted spillage. Without it, cargo has been known to break loose and dump out from the rear of the ship.

Within forty minutes of his arrival, Vaughn is neatly packed in the cargo hold and shipping out on the first leg of the greatest venture of his young life—to rescue his brother and cousin.

CHAPTER 18

With the travel pass provided by Gene, Vaughn takes the three-hour travel time to climb up to the top deck. Finding a folding deck recliner, he stretches out for the duration of the trip. The weather is perfect allowing him a rare opportunity to gaze up at the constellations.

He recalls a happier time in which he and his father had a similar experience on a clear summer evening. To say that Vaughn misses his father would certainly be an understatement. Not only does he miss him, he often gets angry at him for getting killed and deserting him. This kind of anger is often expressed by Vaughn doing something irresponsible such as stealing or drinking or both together. Tonight, there is nothing left to do but try and sleep.

After a while, the smell of fresh baked bread wafts from the ship's galley. He's hungry and knows the cook is hired by the crew and doesn't supply food for passengers. He ambles by the galley's open door and notices the kitchen crew in the dining area smoking and drinking coffee. With the quickness of a mongoose, he snags a loaf of the cooling bread. Stuffing the whole thing under his jacket he makes his way back to his deck chair. Under the cover of darkness and out of any working area that would draw a crew member, he begins to consume his booty. He eats part of the loaf and puts the rest away for later. He wishes he had taken a moment longer to figure how he could have gotten a cup of coffee to wash it down.

Vaughn is awakened by a blast from the ship's horn as they prepare to enter the Kewaunee harbor. The trip across Lake Michigan has proven to be uneventful. The huge Great Lake's carrier is preparing to dock. Soon the captain has dropped the front anchor and uses its stable point to swing the ship's aft around to fit into an unloading slip. Everything must be perfectly aligned. As expected, he succeeds with the precision of a surgeon.

Individually, the crew wordlessly performs each of their well-rehearsed tasks. Lines are dispatched to waiting hands as each secures his to a piling designed only for that particular line. Within a quarter hour the captain has followed protocol, perfectly lining the ship's rail tracks with the tracks on the boarding apron, all fitted to disgorge his load of cargo laden railcars.

The first line of business is to remove any passengers and their vehicles from the ship's hold. That means Vaughn's vehicle is the first to be attended. By the time, he makes his way to the rear of the ship, his car is waiting for him in the parking lot.

Looking at his watch, it's nearly 1:00 A.M. He remembers this railyard from his trip made here several years ago, as a much younger boy. The lights in Maynard's are on, but the closed sign is in the window. It appears they use this time of the morning for cleaning.

He recalls a few years earlier how frightened he and Dick had been as young boys when they found themselves in this same spot. Rather than risk entering the hobo jungle, they had remained hidden in the brush only to watch. This time is different. Notwithstanding he will put those already there on edge, and with a healthy apprehension about entering such a sanctuary in the middle of the night, he nonetheless regards this mission as more important than his reservations. Setting aside his misgivings, he pulls out all the stops and goes for it.

Deciding to leave his car in the parking lot, he grabs his bag and an old furniture blanket stored in the car's trunk and makes his way down toward the glow of a fire flickering off to the side of the railyard.

By the time he's halfway there, he faces a number of faded, black-stenciled letters painted on white boards nailed to wooden posts warning trespassers they are trespassing on railroad property and subject to prosecution. He's soon joined by another warrior of the road just getting off a newly arrived freight. For no other reason than not making his entrance alone, he is taking comfort in the company. Silently, they make their way to the clearing. As usual there are many men already bedded down in various enclaves of brush or shacks. There are also the usual bums from town drinking anything and everything that contains a smattering of alcohol.

Aware these men are probably not inclined in any way to provide any meaningful information, he opts to bed down and wait for morning.

Abruptly startled by the clamor of iron pots, Vaughn shoots up like a scalded cat. It takes him a moment to realize where he is. It's morning and the sun is just beginning to make its way through the trees. Looking at his watch, it's 7:00 A.M.

There are several men gathering around the fire with various containers ranging from tin cans to tin cups. Each is sipping something that is loosely called coffee. Vaughn gathers himself together enough to pull himself out of his bedroll. Making his way to the gathering, he looks around not quite sure where he stands.

One of the men attending to the big iron pot looks up at him. He's a toothless, grizzled man somewhere between the ages of forty-five and seventy-five. All he says is, "Iffin ya gots somethin ta add ta the pot, yer welcome ta eat. But iffin ya ain't gots nothin' jes keep on truckin'!"

Vaughn is struck by the man's abruptness, but quickly gets the message. Laying on the ground is a soiled cloth that may at one time have fancied up someone's bathroom as a prized bath towel.

Now it's bedecked with various articles of food stuffs from canned goods to various vegetables. These are all being prepared to go into this pot of boiling water to simmer down into a soup.

Giving it a moment's thought, Vaughn pulls out the half loaf of fresh baked bread he heisted from the ship's galley the night before. The old geezer looks surprised to see something as domesticated as a fresh loaf of bread make its way into this hobo jungle breakfast.

"Yer in kid. I ain't seen nothin' like this since my kid days livin' in my grandma's house." With that, he tears off a small piece, slipping it between his toothless gums, he closes his eyes, shaking his head in disbelief, he smacks his lips as he savors it for a moment.

Continuing to look around, Vaughn has that look of not finding something he's looking for. The grizzled old hobo catches Vaughn's glances.

"Iffin yer lookin' fer a coffee cup, you'll find a cache ah cans over yonder in the brush. Most of 'em are decent enough ta drink outta," says the hobo, pointing behind Vaughn.

Making his way to the cache of cans, Vaughn tries to figure out how he is going to ask questions about Dace and Whitey without sounding as though he's nosy. Most of the cans he encounters have been used and reused many times over. Finally settling on the cleanest looking of all the dirty cans, he helps himself to a cup of camp coffee. At the same time, he measures his words to begin his inquiry.

"I'm tryin' to catch up to my brother and cousin. I know they hopped a ferry from the Michigan side in the last day or so and they had to come through here.

I'm wonderin' if any of you folks might've seen 'em?"

A code of silence ensues. As usual all is quiet as each listener unravels through his own thought process what has just been asked. In this community, very little is taken at face value. Most have found the best policy is to regard all questions with a suspicious ear until proven otherwise. Answering too quickly can bring on mistrust. Even in this underclass there are underhanded people along its fringe. Once one is held suspect as a snitch, word spreads and that person is forever shunned. The code is *I got a full-time job keepin' my own nose clean without stickin' it inta yer business!* As is true in most cultures, there are very few true confidants and many more potential adversaries.

Seeing the uncomfortable reaction people are exhibiting to his question, Vaughn backs off. He realizes bringing extra anxiety into this community of distressed nonconformists is not benefiting his mission. Instead, he finds a remote spot to drink his coffee; remote in the sense he's still well within the confines of the jungle, but outside of the main gathering around the fire.

Still savoring a piece of the homemade bread, the ole geezer flops down on an overturned pail next to Vaughn. "Damn good hunk ah bread ya brung."

"Thanks, sir," says a wary Vaughn.

"Ain't no call ta cuss me like that," says the ole geezer.

"Cuss ya, sir. How'd I cuss ya?" questions Vaughn sensing he's irritated a potential ally.

"Thar, ya went an' done it again!!"

Seeing Vaughn's frustration, the seeming antagonist says, "I ain't no *SIR*!! They call me Handsome Harry—you can do the same."

Vaughn extends his hand along with his most winning smile that is nonetheless causing his lips to quiver. "Pleased ta meet ya, S- - I mean Handsome Harry."

"So ya say. Yer lookin' fer a couple ah young guys 'at made their way through here? Wad they look like? You young fellers all look alike ta me," states Handsome Harry popping the last of the bread between his still grinding gums.

"They're a little younger than me. One is dark haired, the other is a blond with almost white hair," says Vaughn hoping he's framed each of them adequately.

"An ya say they jes passed through here the las' day er so?"

Not to sound too excited but grateful nonetheless, Vaughn ponders how to frame the next question. "Yeah, they got a head start on me. I was sposed to meet 'em here, but I had somethin' come up an' got me a late start on 'em." It's a conjecture on Vaughn's part, but he's hoping it's enough to convince Handsome Harry to supply the information he's seeking.

"Yer outta luck kid. They was here. But they done hopped a south bound ta Chicago yestaday."

"That's what I need ta know fer now, Si- I mean Harry-I mean Handsome Harry," says Vaughn, while quickly packing up his blanket. He heads back to the parking lot and his waiting vehicle.

Still in possession of Sheriff Peleton's notes, and following the entries, he begins to introduce his own inserts as an extension of the sheriff's information. It's like this is a brand-new movie. Not only is he writing the script and directing the action, but he's also starring in the lead.

CHAPTER 19

Though it's barely been a few days since Dace and Whitey left Elbertport, it seems eons ago. They certainly have nothing like a destination in mind, but it's a comfort to each of them to have the companionship of the other—after all, they've been backyard companions since they were babies.

The morning slowly gives way to the warmer afternoon. The train gives no indication of slowing, much less stopping. They are finding it nearly impossible to find a long term comfortable position. The platform affording them a seat is no more than three feet wide with open spaces on each side giving them a clear view of the awaiting steel wheels ever ready to grease the rails with their flesh.

The only alternative to sitting is to try and stand. Because of the cave-like configuration of grain cars, standing forces one into a hunched position. To fall asleep would be to risk toppling off the platform. This can only be imagined as a quick, gruesome end. Earlier in the day the goal was to successfully get onto the car—now the aspiration is to find a way off.

It's late afternoon before the train begins to slow. Unbeknownst to these weary passengers, they have crossed over the Oklahoma border into Arkansas. Neither Dace nor Whitey are confident enough to determine where a good place to jump off may avail itself. Keeping a wary eye on the railcar they suspect Cowboy occupies, they wait, gripping their bedrolls and positioned to leap at the first signal emanating from that direction.

It's not long before that moment arrives. Cowboy rightly suspects a crew change and that it's probably not a good idea to try and disembark with so many railroad personnel around. Instead he decides to get off before they enter the yards. Hopefully this tactic will elude the scrupulous eye of an overzealous bull. Signaling the two boys as to his intention, Cowboy hits the ground first and performs a tuck and roll maneuver he more than likely learned in the military. Quickly following his example, Dace and Whitey exhibit much more amateur results. Regardless, none of them are too much worse for the wear.

While in the process of brushing themselves off, they spot a conglomeration of trucks and brightly colored equipment in a field a short distance away. From all indications, it appears to be on the outskirts of a town.

"If this is what I think it is, we may be in luck," says an upbeat Cowboy, deciding to check it out.

As they get closer to this melee, Cowboy's suspicions are confirmed. The trucks with pieces of a Ferris wheel, a merry-go-round, and other amusements are still arriving. Cowboy is not looking at this through the lens of one hoping for entertainment, but rather as an opportunity.

"We're in luck! It's a goddam carnival!" says a delighted Cowboy. "I know damn well we can make some easy cash here!"

With the assurance of a good shot toward picking up some money, they wangle their way through a barbed wire fence in good order, and cut across an open field to the site.

There are a dozen or so shirtless men milling about with cigarettes hanging from their lips, all with various blurring amateurish blue tattoos adorning their arms and chests.

The individual who seems to be in charge of arranging the midway setup is a stout man dressed in a tweed sports jacket with leather patches across the elbows and a fedora on a very round, bald head. He is pinching an unlit cigar in his teeth. Between his shouted orders, Cowboy approaches him.

"'Scuse me, Sir. What're the chances of signin' up fer a job?" His inquiry is humble and to the point.

The stout man momentarily removes the cigar from his teeth and holds it between his fingers long enough to give them a once over.

"You ever set up a carnival before?" he asks. The abruptness in his question along with his no-nonsense gaze is enough to cause Dace to pull back. Fortunately, Whitey and Cowboy hold their ground.

"I worked for a circus once?" declares Whitey, with the conviction that the one time he helped set up a tent qualifies him as a bona fide carnival worker.

Cowboy speaks up in time to turn the tide. "We all are used ta manual labor. We can jump quick on anythin' you got fer us ta do."

The stout man gives them one more quick look and then adds, "Y'all go on over ta that silver trailer settin' over yonder. You tell 'em O.D. sent ya. They'll sign ya all up fer sompin'. Jes be ready ta go ta work. We gotta have this show set up an rollin' by tammarra mornin'!"

Jamming the cigar back between his teeth, he turns on his heel back to his prior business of yelling at a woman setting her sausage stand in the wrong location.

The trio head for the silver trailer. It's set conveniently at what appears to be the entrance to the still emerging carnival midway. The word *office* is plainly seen on a sign screwed to the trailer door. With a presumptive knock, the three step back allowing the door to be swung open.

What emerges is a hollow-cheeked, skinny man somewhere around forty. He's got a clipboard in his hand.

"Already know what yer here fer. I seed O.D. give ya the high sign and send ya over this way. We payin' fifty-cents an hour straight time. If y'all agree ta that jes sign who ya are on this here work sheet an I'll make sure-enough ya get yer wages what's comin' to ya."

All three agree and quickly sign—happy to get the work.

Their new employer continues, "My name is Billy Lee Wells. Y'all can jes call me Billy Lee—'ats what most folks do. If you boys ain't got no more questions, we gonna get movin' along." With both hands still gripping his clipboard, Billy Lee tosses his head as if it were a pointer. "Now y'all see that big nigger over there? His name is Albert." Not waiting for them to answer, he continues, "He know more about how all this shit go together than the man who invented it. Y'all gonna be workin' fer him. So jes throw yer bags under this here trailer an y'all mosey on over there an' get ta work."

With this settled, the three make their way over to where Albert is laying out long pieces of fabricated steel. Promptly introducing themselves, Albert stands for a moment looking at these three with the critical eye of an exacting employer. For a black man in these times, he has risen to the almost unheard of level of equipment foreman.

Albert is a big man. He carries himself well and has a commanding presence. Not about to lose this status through the ineptness of a trio of young inexperienced white crackers, Albert asks his first question. "Any ob you ebber do any kind ah wrenchin'?"

Cowboy speaks up saying, "I done some in the army."

"Thas good 'cause you gonna do some mo'," says Albert

with a knowing little chuckle. For a man dealing with transient laborers he maintains a kindly, patient demeanor. Turning to Whitey and Dace, still maintaining a wry sense of humor, he directs his next imperative, "You men gonna be ma heaby equipment operators. Dat der means y'all gonna unload dis here truck. Now listen up—ah wants it unloaded in da same order it's layin' in, y'all hear me."

Whitey and Dace take a quick questioning look at one another. It's just long enough to assure the other they're still on the same page. Whitey promptly takes the lead. In a flash, he climbs onto the truck bed and begins to hand Dace the contents. With a hard gaze and few more impatient directives, Albert satisfies himself the truck will be unloaded his way before he makes his way to another waiting project.

Electricians are busy everywhere. Their pressing assignment is to jury-rig a temporary power grid assuring high powered lights all designed to illuminate a whole lot of other tasks. Plumbers are also here to assure a steady supply of fresh water wherever and whenever it may be needed.

Like a welcome intruder, the morning brings with it a city of brilliantly colored structures which have nosed their way up and across the landscape in just a few hours. It's a gala event planned for the weekend, all designed to lift the spirits of children of all ages.

With the morning, our trio has been transformed. They're more like carny sages rather than hobo pillocks. Covered in honest sweat and dirt, they welcome the break. Gathering their belongings, they make their way to a line of showers put together by their ingenious boss, Albert.

There are four shower heads all separated by a series of makeshift curtains allowing a minimal amount of privacy. They're being serviced by Albert's wife, Elloise. For ten cents, she'll supply a bather with a piece of soap and a clean towel.

Whitey and Dace gladly pay the ten cents and bask in the lukewarm water as long as Elloise permits.

Cowboy is content to drink a beer with another mechanic, putting off a shower until Elloise gives him the option of showering now or getting into his bedroll, dirt and all.

Dace has found a spot beneath the trailer to bed down for a few hours. He's physically and mentally wiped out. It doesn't take long before he's dead to the world. Meanwhile, Whitey is sorting through his clothing looking for his cleanest dirty shirt. In a short time, he also grows weary from a night of replacing sleep with work and joins Dace under the trailer.

In keeping with Cowboy's clandestine habits, he is the last to bathe—after which, he disappears. This custom is disconcerting to the boys, but they have more or less come to accept it as Cowboy's way.

By noon Billy Lee is rounding up all the help that hasn't quit already and assigning them to the full-timers, hoping to teach them to operate a ride. He rousts both Whitey and Dace from their makeshift berth. "You boys is eighteen, right?"

Before either of them can answer, he hands them his ever-present clipboard. "Jes sign here after yer name," continues Billy Lee.

With that completed, he instructs them to meet with the operators of the Ferris wheel and the Tilt-a-Whirl. Within twenty minutes they've downed a sausage from the European sausage stand, a strong black coffee and are standing before their appointed carny trainer.

Dace has been assigned to the Tilt-a-Whirl. His instructor is a skinny, rawboned man named Til. His arms are a leathery brown and covered with an array of near featureless tattoos, almost obliterated by years of sun exposure. His face is of the same leather-like texture with deep creases and the kind of wet eyes that seem to accompany alcohol addiction.

Til would like nothing better than to be sleeping off the hangover he's induced with his daily ten rounds in the ring with John Barleycorn. This isn't new for Til. He's been in the grip of his demons most of his life. The familiar aroma of Prince Albert smoking tobacco and Til's nicotine-stained fingers give Dace a sense of belonging even if it's only on this lower slope of human potential. In some other ways, Dace feels superior to men like Til in that he believes himself to be above the adversaries these men have given in to.

It quickly becomes obvious to Dace that Til is much more dangerous to himself than he is to others. He's rather soft spoken and reticent in his mannerisms. His effort to explain in words the importance of safety in running this ride runs counter to the alcohol-induced shakes preventing him from doing so himself. Dace soon realizes he's going to have to learn much of the complexities of this task from trial and error.

Giving Dace a simple maintenance chore, Til excuses himself to take another long drink from a coffee mug he's tucked away in his toolbox. On his return, along with the sharp odor of fresh alcohol on his breath, his shakes are noticeably diminished.

Within the hour, Til has given Dace a crash course in operating the Tilt-a-Whirl, and leaves once again to get another bit of the hair of the dog.

Whitey is on the other side of the park. He is being indoctrinated by a man introduced as Archibald Axelbroken. He claims to be of Arapaho Indian descent and maintains he was an iron worker on many of the skyscrapers in Chicago. A series of brushes with the law and outstanding warrants have left him hiding among the ever-wandering tribes of carnival vagabonds.

Archibald brags without hesitation about being brought up on the reservation under very traditional Indian ways. This lifestyle has been nearly obliterated by the twentieth century's lust for technology. He readily admits, "The main problem with the traditional Indian upbringing is there ain't no damn place in this country ta be a Indian anymore." His frustration is clearly heard and has led him to act out in violent ways against the laws of the country. He sees these as enemies to his heritage designed to obliterate his people in the suffocating pit of modernity.

When it comes to erecting the carnival's hundred-fifty foot Ferris wheel, it makes sense to have someone accustomed to the heights of skyscrapers in charge. All the parts for these several hundred pieces of equipment are lifted in place by hand. Even with his resentment against the white man, Archibald's sense of pride insists that he create this work of wonder and beauty to perfection. His crew is putting the finishing touches on the big wheel when Whitey arrives on the scene. He's dutifully tagging along with Billy Lee who is in the throes of unveiling the work schedule for the day.

In this community, one would have to go a long way to find a carnival technician without a tattoo or who has a full row of teeth. There is nary a man here who has gone beyond eighth or ninth grade. Education for most has been in the school of hard knocks. However, one can't help but be amazed how creative these men are about maintaining these giant rides regardless of the negligence surrounding their personal maintenance and their lack of formal education.

Archibald makes his way down the high rigging in time to have Whitey introduced as a new hand hired to assist him with his other concession. Still in the dark as to what this job he's expected to do consists of, Whitey is willing to have a go at whatever he's asked to do.

Used to having transient laborers, Archibald isn't overly friendly or impressed with a kid the likes of Whitey. With no fanfare and a wordless hand motion, Archibald takes the lead toward a different part of the park.

Soon enough, Whitey catches the unmistakable pungent aroma of some kind of animal excrement. Being a town kid, he hasn't had a lot of experience separating the different varieties of manure by smell, but there is no doubt in his mind this job is going to have something to do with this smell. The next corner brings the odor into reality. What meets him is a stable of at least a dozen miniature horses.

Archibald's whole demeanor changes as he greets these pigmy equine species as if he had fathered each of them. They in turn respond with what appears to be a loving whinny. This relationship fulfills Archibald's need to practice some of the Indian skills he had learned as a young man on the reservation dealing with horses.

Whitey finds it unsettling to be in an environment of livestock for the first time in his young life, especially under the tutelage of the likes of Archibald who is obviously right at home with these foul-smelling, four-legged creatures.

Archibald soon turns his attention to this greenhorn. "Watta ya know about horses, kid?"

Even more unsettling is a question like this. There is no room for flimflam here. Whitey is going to have to be honest. If he could fake anything about this job, he'd do it in a heartbeat.

"Nothing sir, other than with which end they eat," admits Whitey in the hopes his attempt at humor won't put him in a bad light.

Archibald takes Whitey's playfulness as the kind of humble admission he's hoping for.

"That's all you need ta know for now. I'd rather work with a guy with a clean slate than have a guy who has to unlearn everything he thinks he knows about horses," says Archibald with a tone that spells relief. "What I'm gonna teach you about these horses is all you gonna need ta know ta get along with me," he adds with a knowing nod of his head.

Concerned that each horse be recognized as special, for the next hour and a half Archibald traces over the proper use of tackle on each of his ponies. "Babe here, she don't like that wide-strapped harness an' Dominick, don't like being cinched too tight." Never sure he's furnished enough information, the time finally arrives to begin placing mostly smiling children on the backs of these long-suffering steeds. Just as Archibald has accommodated himself to a world he wasn't prepared to meet, so it seems these beasts have for the most part accommodated themselves to meet the mixture of smiles and screeches these small broods are prone to.

The hordes of merrymaking, sticky-faced children are never ending. The afternoon soon wears into evening with new lines of merrymakers and weary parents.

Across the midway, Dace is becoming an old hand at running the Tilt-a-Whirl. The mobs of carnival revelers are just as intense here as they are with Whitey—maybe even more so. Unlike Whitey, Dace is not used to working hard. Operating this carnival ride is the most physical thing he's done since his high school gym class.

To make matters worse, the sun is beginning to heat the afternoon to an uncomfortable eighty-five degrees. When this becomes nearly intolerable, Dace feels a spray of liquid he suspects is coming from some unseen carny wetting down his concession stand. It's almost welcome as he involuntarily runs his hand across the fresh moisture. It takes only a moment for the texture to deny itself as fresh water.

"What the hell!! Somebody's puckin'!!" screams Dace at the same time trying to duck, not knowing where it's originating.

When this happens at a carnival, it's usually after an elephant ear, a hamburger, a hotdog, and a bag of cotton candy have been consumed earlier under happier, calmer conditions. A ride such as the Tilt-a-Whirl will almost always cause many a stomach to surrender its mulled-up contents. In this case, the culprit shared his meal with enough g-force to take out all those finding themselves within ten feet of the Tilt-a-Whirl's perimeter.

When Dace is finally able to stop the ride, the participants are barnacled with substances that provoke non-words like, "AARRGGHH and EETTHH!!" Not waiting to discover its disgusting source, they squinch in revulsion, trying to escape the *ill-*effects stuck to their skin, hair, and clothing. Several are gagging on this dripping wet barf they're left to themselves to try and deal with.

It quickly becomes apparent who the offender is. It's a greenish-colored man, the last to stagger away still retching and unaware he has single-handedly become the deep south's chief puke distributor.

Having to tell the next group waiting in line, "I have to close for maintenance," while covered in puke, carries as little confidence in him as a doctor telling his next patient, "I'll be with you as soon as I clean this guy's guts off me".

Dace's quick search produces a hose nearby. He's soon sharing it with several other would be revelers. It's been made available for the sole purpose of washing down equipment splattered with vomit. After turning it on himself and several other fellow sufferers, he sprays and scrubs every seat on the Tilt-a-Whirl.

Learning from some of the other carnies this is common happening, he has a better understanding of why Til stays drunk most of the time. The thought of having to do this work for the rest of his life is intolerable.

Whitey's experience is proving to be just as bad. Some parents are arguing with him about putting all three of their children on the same horse in order to save the cost of three horses. Others want him to choreograph the horse and their child to fit a photograph they have in mind or want to place a child under four years of age on a horse because the child is throwing a fit over the age restriction.

Whitey and Dace finally get a break. Neither have set eyes on Cowboy since the showers. Although the two of them have known him for only a short time, they have become familiar with his strange ways. That's not to say they aren't curious about his sudden disappearances and a seeming clandestine acquaintance with Sid Powell. It's puzzling and disconcerting to say the least, especially in view of Sid's legacy of pathological behavior.

Now, Cowboy suddenly reappears stating he has been on the far side of the park assembling the large roller coaster. "Hello boys," he announces, while munching on the remains of a Polish dog. "Ain't nothin' in the world ta give a man a better appetite than hard work."

Dace is by nature a bit more suspicious of Cowboy's behavior than Whitey. Whitey feels Cowboy has the answers for yet unseen situations. While it's Dace's opinion that he and Whitey can make it on their own, rather than deal with Cowboy's erratic behavior. In Dace's view, the headlight Whitey sees is rarely scrutinized as a speeding train rushing toward him until it's too late to get off the track.

"Ya ain't been out borrowin' cars again have ya, Cowboy?" asks Dace. His voice carries more than a little cynicism.

Taking Dace's wisecrack about stealing cars in stride, Cowboy comes back with, "Ain't seen you gettin' out any an walkin' none."

Whitey recognizes his cousin's penchant for what he views as *poppin' up ghosts where there ain't any*. He in turn is more inclined to go along with a program until the train is about to hit him.

"I seen ya workin' over on the roller coaster. How's that goin'?" questions Whitey.

"It wouldn't be so bad, if we could keep it runnin'. Seems like there's always one bolt ready to pop an' leave the whole damn thing in ah big scrap pile, but hell ole Albert can fix anything with a little bailin' wire," says Cowboy.

While Cowboy is speaking, Billy Lee is darting across the lot toward them at a full gallop. There's fire in his gait as well as his eyes. Still some twenty feet from Cowboy, he begins what quickly develops into a rant.

"What the hell ya doin' off the job? You was supposed ta be watchin' an makin' sure 'at track was stayin' put! Now the goddam thing is stuck with a pile ah people hung up sixty feet off the goddam ground. Get yer ass off my lot, yer fired!"

Cowboy continues to finish his lunch, wipes his sleeve across his mouth and quietly says, "Give me my pay and I'll be outta here."

With that, Billy Lee lets loose with a haymaker that catches Cowboy's jaw. He hits the ground like a pole-axed steer.

"PAY! PAY! You think you gonna get paid? Hell man, yer lucky we ain't gonna collect what we're loosin' outta yer sorry ass!!"

Still face down, Cowboy slowly and methodically puts his sun glasses on. He gets to his feet, brushes himself off, and makes his way off the property.

Whitey and Dace watch all this happen so fast they have no time to even let their jaws drop. It's still not mentally processed, it's still an abstract brainwave that's just beginning to materialize when Billy Lee turns to the two of them and says, "We gonna be tearin' down tonight an headin' fer Wichita Falls, Texas. You boys is good workers an' yer welcome ta stay on." Still not fully in possession of their faculties and not knowing what else to do, they shake their heads in agreement.

Befuddled, both boys return to their concessions to finish out the day. To say the least, they're both stupefied by this startling turn of events. It's been in both their minds to find a way to divorce themselves from a dependence on Cowboy. Now that it seems to be happening, it's as though their lives are spiraling out of their control.

The carnival closing time is 10:00 P.M. Neither Whitey nor Dace have had time to connect long enough to devise a plan for going forward. That opportunity doesn't appear to be anywhere on the immediate horizon as Billy Lee is rushing around, along with Albert, to get this operation broken down and on the road by daybreak. These men and women are often expected to work around the clock before they are given time to get a few hours of sleep.

Many of these are people who have chosen this life to avoid the responsibilities of paying rent or child support. After all it's difficult to track a person down who has no permanent address. It's not a coincidence that many have a criminal background and find it nearly impossible to find work in family-oriented communities of so-called normal people. In any event, this community is built around an underclass that affords many a bond with one another and a meaning to life within these ever-changing carnival surroundings.

It's not unusual for carnies to work for wages below the minimum standards. Nor is it unusual for the carnival owners to supply sleeping trailers at a cost to the worker. This often leaves only enough money for food, cigarettes, and booze.

Nonetheless, this doesn't prevent Billy Lee from trying his best to keep a crew. Between people quitting and the law catching up with a worker because he or she decided to test the local drinking ordinances, it often requires a personal visit with each worker to insure they are able to stay on.

The brightly colored lights that flashed and invited so many patrons are one by one being shut down. Overly tired carnies work earnestly through the semi-darkness expeditiously tearing down and packing this village into waiting trucks. As laborious as this project is, this is what carnies do—only to move to the next location and repeat the same process all over again.

Whitey and Dace are caught up in this ritual. Not sure they know what to do next, they dutifully try to be helpful and stay out of the way at the same time.

Whitey is alone, loading saddles and other assorted tack when he catches a glimpse of a familiar form leaving Billy Lee's trailer. The sight of this slightly hunched, lurking figure sends a jolt through his entire body. Before he can completely process this action, his mind shoots the message to his mouth. "SID?!" he shouts out loud.

Sid stops dead in his tracks and stares directly at Whitey, at the same time, he tosses a lit lighter back toward the trailer. Staring back more intently out of a mixture of dread and curiosity, Whitey is more than convinced the fleeing figure is that of Sid. The anxiety begins to build. He wishes Dace was here to support him.

In the next instant, a shout goes out that is never welcome, "FIRE! FIRE!" Swinging his stare away from the unmistakable slump-shouldered lurch of Sid Powell fleeing the scene and back toward a massive blaze roaring up in his wake. Whitey realizes the flames are engulfing Billy Lee's trailer.

A half dozen men, led by Albert, appear on the scene and start fighting the fire.

There is a strong lingering odor of an accelerant—maybe gasoline, kerosene, or fuel oil permeating the air. The empty gas can beside the trailer appears to be the culprit. In a moment, it too suddenly bursts into flames destroying any chance of recovering this apparently out of place piece of evidence.

Dace suddenly appears out of nowhere standing alongside Whitey. "What the hell is going on here?" asks Dace, with a tone of distress.

Whitey can't express how glad he is to see Dace. "You ain't gonna believe what I just saw."

"This ain't no time to be challengin' me with a dumb riddle. Whad you just see?"

Whitey can hardly contain himself. "Sid! I just saw Sid start that fire, then run away!"

It only takes Dace a moment to digest the impact of Whitey's

Sid sighting. "Are you thinkin' what I'm thinkin'?"

Whitey returns Dace's question with the temperament of one who has already decided his next move. "I'm thinkin' it's time we move on before we start bein' asked a lot ah questions we don't need ta be dealin' with."

Within minutes nearly every carnival worker on the lot is flocking to the blaze. What is conspicuous—even through the flames—is a shovel with its handle jammed against the door. Several workers attempt to remove it and get the door open, but are driven back by the intense heat. The sound of Billy Lee's fists hammering from the inside along with the desperate wail of his screams are left unanswered. It's obvious Billy Lee has been purposely imprisoned and is the target of a killer.

Whitey and Dace slowly, deliberately back away from the crowd. They quickly return to the trailer housing their belongings, pick up their bedrolls, and make their way back across the same field they had traversed in the other direction only a couple days before.

It's dark enough not to be seen and also dark enough to have to watch each step. With all the commotion still wreaking havoc behind them, they soon reach the rail bed. Never in their young lives did they expect to experience this overwhelming sense of relief and the mounting affection they're feeling toward this ribbon of steel. It may be difficult, it may be dangerous, but there is a growing sense of well-being, of being at home within this now familiar mode of escape.

With the ten dollars between them Billy Lee had paid out on the day before and the resolve of a couple of fledgling hobos, they make their way south down the track in hopes of beginning a new adventure.

CHAPTER 20

They begin their trek without needing words to link them together in purpose. It's as though they have but one mind between them—to put as much distance as possible between themselves and the carnival mayhem in the shortest amount of time. The frantic shouts of the carnival workers are the only sounds they are conscious of and these are becoming fainter as the distance between them becomes greater. Soon, they can hear nothing over the scuffling sounds of their own shoes meeting the rail bed and the tree frogs that chirp incessantly this time of year.

Even with the company of each other, they experience an overwhelming sense of loneliness that accompanies anyone left to stir around in the dead of night. They both feel what they imagine it may be like to be the only living beings left on the face of the earth.

Dace is the first to finally speak. "Sure as hell is spooky out here."

Whitey is pondering a more specific fear than Dace's generic apprehensions. "You ain't kiddin'. I hope that damn Sid ain't lurkin' around here somewheres."

Dace is silent for a moment. It's not that he's ignoring the possibility as much as he's looking for an alternative. Breaking his silence, he finally brings himself to question, "You sure it was Sid you saw?"

"Oh, hell yes. I can't tell you what his face might look like 'cause I never have got a good look at it, but I sure as hell know what that sneaky lope he's got looks like."

The boys trudge on with only desultory conversation. Walking on railroad ties is a near impossible task. They're not spaced to accommodate a normal stride. With determination, they continue to stagger along. Eventually, Whitey and Dace have managed to develop a smoother gait between the ties.

After walking for what seemed like hours, they notice a glow ahead on the horizon. Relying on the little experience they've had on the road so far; this glistening has always indicated a town. They trudge toward the light with the hopes of a better tomorrow. Adding to their rosy outlook, in the east another small glow is growing—it's called sunrise.

They find they're not the only members of the early morning outdoor population. A family of crows protest their intrusion step by step. Not to be outdone, the blue jays hold them in even higher contempt, scolding their every move as a personal affront to each of them.

With an unwavering gaze straight ahead, in the distance they spot what appears to be an outlying railroad building. Drawing closer, it proves to be a remote yard office of sorts. As far as they can detect, there is but one occupant. He's a middle-aged man wearing a blue uniform of the type usually worn by mechanics. He's sitting out front on a waiting bench, listening to a radio perched an open window sill. Above his head is a black and white stenciled sign saying *WHITES ONLY*, limiting who may use the bench.

Since he is not a mechanic, he has intentionally outfitted his shirt with a contrasting and well-worn greenish-colored bow tie, indicating he has a job of some importance. The ends of the bows have turned a darker green because of constant adjustments from grimy fingers. The name tag on the shirt says *Dewayne*. Strapped around his head of short-cropped, graying hair is a sun visor bearing the railroad's logo.

Not taking the time to fill their canteens before making their getaway and with the morning beginning to heat up, the boys have worked up quite a thirst. They have also caught the eye of this wary railroad veteran. "'Spose you boys are lookin' fer sumpin' ta drink?" This query is posed more as an observation rather than a question.

"Yes sir, we certainly are," speaks Dace for both himself and Whitey.

Placing a large tin cup under the spigot of a huge metal tank, Dewayne begins to draw a cupful. Handing it to Dace, he poses another question, "You fellers is Yankees ain'tcha?"

Looking at one another, they wonder what new unforeseen problem they are now facing.

Not waiting for an answer, Dewayne continues, "Yer accent tells me you boys is Yankees. I'm right ain't I?" Pointing up the tracks, Dewayne is still not ready to wait for an answer. "Them bulls up there in the yards like you Yankee boys. They make sure you get caught and sentenced to work a chain gang on ole man Woodcock's farm fer six months. Ole man Woodcock always give 'em a few bucks a head makin' it worth they trouble."

After managing to make their way this far with no law problems, this is not the kind of news they want to hear.

Taking a long drink, Whitey gives himself a moment to try and process where they may be standing with this railroad employee. For all intents and purposes, he is seemingly ready to give a couple of Yankee boys a heads up on the hazards ahead. This puzzles him as he hands Dewayne back his cup. "Why you tellin' us all this? You plannin' on turnin' us in fer a reward as soon as we leave here?" asks Whitey.

"Naw, I ain't got nothin' agin' you fellers. It's them damn company bulls I don't like. They make misery outta everything they touch. Hell, they as much agin' me as they is y'all. Them damnable rednecks is always lookin' ta make trouble," says Dewayne. "I jes like seein' you 'bos screw 'em over."

A little more conversation with Dewayne erases their doubts about his possible allegiance to his employer and the goon squad. Offering an alternative route, he points them to a dirt road leading away from the station.

"Y'all take this here road inta town. It's only a little over three miles. Whatever y'all do don't hitchhike. The law jes waitin' fer somebody 'at don' know no better ta stick 'em on a gawddam work gang."

"When y'all get inta town, go straight to the Rescue Mission. Ask fer Brother Tom. He'll give y'all a meal, a shower, and a bed."

After filling their canteens and drinking as much water as they can, Whitey and Dace thank Dewayne and begin the trek toward town. The road is dusty and worse when a car goes by. Even though tempted, the pair pay heed to Dewayne's warning about hitchhiking. Nonetheless, the hope remains that some kind soul will have mercy and stop to give them a ride. It doesn't happen.

By mid-morning they drag themselves into town. The heat is already hovering in the mid-eighties. From an aesthetic standpoint, it's not the kind of town anyone would choose to live in unless one was born here. It has a main street that starts with solid brick buildings, all connected. They're three stories high and ambitious looking. After a couple blocks, the buildings become much less impressive. Most of these become freestanding and made of wood. These have all been single family homes during better times—now they house a barber and beauty shop, a doctor's office, and a real estate office. At the very end is an old Victorian bearing a sign hanging from the porch announcing *Full Gospel Rescue Mission*.

Below that in smaller letters is their mission statement verifying, *We are a Christ-centered shelter for the physically, mentally, and spiritually poor*. The next sentence stipulates that there is to be no alcohol or tobacco use on the premises.

There are a few men hanging around the front of the building smoking. The melodious sounds of a piano waft out from inside. The music is distinctly an upbeat form of Christian hymnology popular among those who tend to be more demonstratively enthusiastic about their religion.

The pair are met at the door with a spirited handshake from a man in his thirties wearing a disheveled and out of date suit that is clearly too large, a shirt that had once been white, but has now taken on a grayish cast, slicked back hair that has been pomaded rather than washed, and bearing just as ruffled a demeanor. Without the suit, he would be nearly indistinguishable from the poor he has obviously placed himself here to serve.

"Welcome brothers. My name is Brother Tom. You're just in time for our Sunday worship. Please come in and find a seat."

Accompanying the handshake is a slight tug, pulling them inside the door. The music is certainly much louder and is combined with the distinct odor of un-bathed men. Behind the piano is a young lady in her late teens. She is manually amplifying the sound by the hard thrust she gives each note. She's dressed in quite a long dress reaching her ankles. Her sleeves are also designed to eliminate any chance of a man becoming sexually aroused by her bare elbows. What sets her slightly apart from this rather dour wardrobe is her blond hair pulled back in a rather stylish ponytail revealing a rather statuesque neck.

The vocalist is a rather hefty thirty-something woman also dressed in an ankle covering gown. Her hair has a pulled appearance as it is tightly packed into a prayer bonnet. The strained force of her voice is more enthusiastic than trained as she attacks the hymn "Bringing in The Sheaves". This is an obvious attempt to segue into beginning the service.

Dace is leading the way. He's very conscious of the direction he's taking. Unquestionably, he is drawn to the side of the room with a good view of the young pianist. Despite the attempt to make her look austere, her clear-skinned, natural beauty is undiminished.

As soon as the young pianist finishes, the thirty-something lady bends over to say something to her. The girl immediately, but ever so subtly removes the band around her ponytail and pulls her hair back and up into a traditional Mennonite prayer bonnet.

When the hymn comes to an end, Brother Tom, Bible in hand, marches toward the front of the assembly. He moves with the determination of one who has a message that must be shared immediately. It's a stark contrast to the slow, reverent processional Whitey's Lutheran heritage presents.

Brother Tom wastes no time welcoming the dozen or so congregants. He begins immediately praying for the Holy Spirit to play a role in any conversions that need to be made. He thanks God for the many blessings He has bestowed on His children. Another hymn is sung. When all eight verses are completed, he faithfully arises from his chair with the determination of one who has been swept to his feet by a Providential decree. Carrying his floppy, well-worn Bible, he methodically begins thumbing through the pages. Suddenly he stops, straightens his shoulders, and with the clear voice of one who has been, on the face of it, moved by an outside force declares, "Luke 10, the story of 'The Good Samaritan,' that's what I'm ah gonna preach on taday."

Brother Tom begins the lesson telling how this man had

fallen among thieves and was left in a ditch for dead. He details how several important people in society had passed him by without giving aid. Finally, an outcast of society took pity on the fallen man and bound up his wounds and made provision for his recovery.

With a handkerchief, he begins to blot the perspiration beading on his brow. The pitch of his voice begins to reach levels designed to capture and excite a listener. "Do you know why I wanna help bind up your wounded souls?" He looks about the room insuring he has ample attention to his question before continuing. "It's 'cuz I been that man in the ditch myself."

He then goes on to tell how alcohol had him in its grip and how he found himself in a rescue mission much like the one they are in at this very moment. There he heard a preacher explain how he could get saved and he surrendered his heart and soul to Jesus.

The tears are beginning to mingle with the perspiration on Brother Tom's face as he retells his salvation story. It's not difficult for anyone in the congregation to recognize Brother Tom's sincerity, but most are there to get a free meal and a bed. Attending services is part of the requirement to make the other two happen.

Dace has been exchanging glances with the pretty young pianist during the entirety of Brother Tom's sermon-testimony. Brother Tom is her father and the heavy-set lady vocalist is none other than her mother. This specific theme is the keynote topic of many of Brother Tom's messages. Considering how many times she has heard it, she is more than willing to entertain the attention of this young man and has found flirting with Dace much more exhilarating.

Brother Tom spends the next few minutes acquainting everybody with his wife, Norma Jean, and daughter, Grace, and thanking them for their unselfish love for the Lord in sharing their unique musical talents. In his next announcement, he makes it known any volunteer help in the kitchen to assist his wife and daughter will be greatly appreciated.

With the service at last concluding, Dace rushes to Grace to make sure she is aware of his willingness to help in the kitchen. A subtle change in her expression gives Dace the answer he is hoping for. It is just a quick, subtle glance, yet it still conveys a delicate sparkle at his offer.

Whitey is well acquainted with the dynamics of the budding attraction these two are exhibiting. It's only been a week since he last held his beloved Melody. A lonesomeness sets in as he watches Dace and Grace fumble with their insecurities in the presence of each other. It brings with it a longing to be with Melody; to have her body next to his, to taste her lips, to smell her hair, to feel the excited anticipation of their private moments alone. If he could magically transport himself, he'd be with her in a heartbeat.

Sitting alone at a table near a window, transfixed in his thoughts, Whitey's gaze suddenly catches a glimpse of a form that brings his daydreaming to a screeching halt. It's none other than Cowboy. His confident saunter is embellished with his usual flair as he makes his way up the mission steps. As he enters the door, it's as though he's been here before and is expected. Looking about the room, he spots Whitey. Sporting his big grin, he says, "Well I see you girls made it! When I din't see you in the railyard, I figured you either kept on travelin' or ya came ta town. Since this here is the only logical place, I figured I'd give it a try."

"By the way where's Dacey boy?" continues Cowboy, looking around the dining area. "You din't get separated did ya?"

"Naw, he's out in the kitchen flirtin' with the preacher's daughter," says Whitey.

Cowboy seems very relieved by Whitey's assurance. He has

exhibited an unusual concern since meeting them that they all stay together. He explains how he spent most of the morning hidden in the brush eluding the pervasive bulls, who were diligently checking rail cars for hobos. He had thought maybe Whitey and Dace got caught. Whitey, in turn, fills Cowboy in on what he's learned about the deal between the rail bulls and the local ranchers.

"'At's just like these rednecks. They all figure they're the only ones God created ta rule the world."

As they have been talking, the dining room has been filling with men of all sorts. Most are hoping to find work in the oil fields to the south in Texas. A few like Whitey, Dace, and Cowboy are willing to work, but have no actual destination in mind.

Then there are those who have no intention of working. Their only goal is another bottle of wine. They are happy where they are since the only cost for a free bed is to listen to Brother Tom and occasionally hit the *sawdust trail*. All in all, a wasted life is the high cost of low living. Anyone willing to undergo a change is Brother Tom's primary target.

After the meal, the chatter among these men with nothing to do continues through the afternoon and into the evening. Dace has managed to find enough things to volunteer for to keep him in the company of Grace. Together, they are spending the afternoon putting together sack lunches for the next morning as people will begin to move on.

Grace is more than a little curious asking, "What brings someone as young as you to a rescue mission? I mean everyone I see is old and down and out. You don't fit here."

Trying his best to make his life appear to be on the cutting edge of excitement, Dace pulls together some half-truths with which he hopes to dazzle Grace. "We're on the trail of a killer. He's supposed ta be in this area somewhere and me and my cousin, Whitey, are huntin' him down."

Despite Grace's exposure to the dregs of society, Brother Tom and Norma Jean have managed to shelter their nearly eighteen-year-old daughter from the influences of the world by maintaining a Mennonite household. She has been home-schooled and was taught the piano by her mother who has dedicated her whole life to this only child's welfare. But as things go with the young, there is usually a sense of entitlement rather than gratitude. To say that Grace has been protected from the ravages of society is not to say she isn't spoiled and more than a little naive.

Grace is all ears. This is the nearest she's been to teenage excitement in her life. "I've heard about killers, but I've never suspected there'd ever be one here in town," replies Grace with more than a little inquisitiveness.

"I ain't sayin' fer sure 'at this guy is here in town, but me and my cousin figure he pro'ly has sompin' ta do with that guy gettin' burned up out at the carnival," reports Dace with an air of authority.

Realizing he has captured the full attention of this sheltered girl, Dace pours on the bravado a little heavier. "We've been onto this guy for a week. We've tracked him this far from way up in northern Michigan. He knows we're on ta him, but he ain't showin' any signs of quittin' his murderin' ways."

Grace has been falling into a teenage funk over the last year. She is much closer to eighteen than seventeen and feels that everyone else her age has a much better life. She knows there is more to life than playing the piano at the mission, but her parents aren't willing to cut the cord holding her to her sheltered home life.

She can't contain her excitement over the possibility of being in even a very small way a part of something as electrifying as sleuthing out a murder. "What y'all plan on doin' with him if ya do catch him?" she asks. There is a clear tone of innocent curiosity in her question.

Dace had never considered she would go so far as to ask him a pertinent question such as this. He was hoping to enthrall her long enough to lead her to look on him as a swashbuckler—an action hero who always has the situation in hand no matter how dangerous the circumstances.

This question has clearly blindsided him. Immediately looking for an out, he glances through the small window in the door between the kitchen and the dining area. He spots Whitey and Cowboy sitting alone at a table. Pretending he hadn't heard her question, he loudly exclaims, "There they are, my partners! Come on out an' meet 'em." Not waiting for a reply and thankful for the momentary diversion, Dace swings the door open as he waves to catch their attention. They in turn, see him and motion him to their table. For the moment, Grace is free from the direct eye of her parents and is more than willing to see where this portal of freedom might lead her.

Dace considers her as a ray of sunshine in this otherwise rigid environment. She is enamored by his attention and he can't wait to introduce her to his waiting compatriots.

After the introductions, Grace nervously looks around for the ever-present eye of a parent. To justify her presence if she is caught in the presence of these near pagan young men, she has brought a dish rag and begins to wipe their table as if it's part of her chores.

Shortly, Dace joins Whitey and Cowboy in their discussion. Meanwhile, Grace is doing the best she can to overhear the conversation as she cleans adjacent tables. The talk quickly turns to the *Sid sighting* at the carnival.

Cowboy asks, "Why are y'all so scared of Sid?"

"You'd be scared too if you'd been through what me and Whitey been through with your shithead cousin Sid!" says Dace. It's not difficult to hear the disgust in his answer.

Cowboy is suddenly all ears. "What you sayin'? Sid do sompthin' bad?"

"Bad! If yah call burnin' a guy up alive bad, yeah he done sompthin' bad," says Dace with even more disgust in his voice.

Cowboy becomes very quiet. It's obvious he's contemplating something.

"I seen him comin' away from Billy Lee's trailer just as it started burnin'," adds Whitey in Dace's defense.

Cowboy continues his silence for a minute and finally says, "Sid never tol' me he done anythin' like that. Billy Lee never give me my pay an' Sid said he'd get it for me. That's *all* he done as far as I know."

Whitey is quite adamant. "Cowboy, you gotta get rid of Sid. He's a sicko. I don't give a damn how much you think you need him. Yer puttin' us all in danger keepin' him around."

Dace is next to speak his piece, "He's like a damn pit bull. Whatta we gonna do if we gotta confront him?"

Cowboy does what he does best; he creates another diversion that trumps the original question. "I think we need ta get outta here tomorrow morning before daybreak," says Cowboy. The concern around the *we gotta get outta here* is amplified by his tone. It's enough to make Whitey and Dace wish they were already *outta here*. They all agree to be ready to hop the first available freight regardless of where it may be going as long as it puts more distance between them and the carnival.

As Brother Tom makes his rounds, spotting his daughter so close to this trio of reprobates causes him to subtly motion her back to the safety of the kitchen. He also uses the opportunity to verify from these three how many beds he will need to supply for the night—and to let it be known these will be available immediately after the church's evening service. The only ones that appear to be anxiously looking forward to this obligation are Dace and Grace as it will hopefully provide another opportunity to have contact with each other.

CHAPTER 21

Brother Tom's zeal to save the lost is nearly equally met by those with a zeal to remain lost. To say his carefully crafted messages have no effect is a mistake. Like it has been succinctly put by a great saint in bygone times "Lord I desire to be righteous, but not today, maybe tomorrow." For many of his listeners, Brother Tom's preaching at the very least keeps this righteous end as a "right nice" goal.

The Sunday evening service is finally over. Fulfilling their customary habit, Brother Tom and his family stand at the door to shake hands with all those who participated.

Dace has purposely dawdled. As the last in line, he hopes to linger for at least a moment for an exchange with Grace—be it ever so brief. He has already met her gaze several times both during the service and now.

She smiles momentarily at each participant as they leave, but then quickly looks back toward him with an expectant glance.

Brother Tom is the first in line to grasp Dace's hand. With his most reverent expression, he bestows the same benediction he has given to each person. "God bless your evening.

We are happy to be able to worship with you once again."

Norma is next. She clasps Dace's hand between both of hers. Her grasp is uncomfortably lingering. With her most gracious smile, she wishes Dace the best, adding, "We've loved having you with us. Please come back again." Already looking to Grace, Dace forces himself to not pull his hand from Norma's clutch too quickly.

His anxiety level peaks as he looks into the face of Grace. Is it too early to call her his girlfriend? She in turn gazes back with a near painful sadness. After spending the afternoon together, the chemistry between them is working overtime. Grasping each other's hands, it takes all they have to prevent themselves from joining in an embrace.

Immediately, Dace's attention zeroes in on two major differences in her handshake—one, her hand is wet with nervous perspiration and secondly, she is pressing an object into his palm. Without attracting any more attention to their nervous exchange, Dace places the mystery article in his pocket.

With Dace being the last to leave, Brother Tom closes and locks the chapel door behind him. He then leads his family to enter their living quarters by a private entrance.

Finding himself alone in the hallway, Dace quickly retrieves the article from his pocket. It's a folded piece of paper. His hands are shaking a bit as he nervously looks around. Satisfied with his privacy, he begins to unfold the mystery paper. He's about to explode with anticipation as the hand-printed words meet his anxious eyes. It's a simple message reading, *I want to go with you tomorrow.*

Not sure what Grace may mean by this message, Dace takes a moment to analyze what she might have in mind. Wishing he could speak to her, he refolds the paper and places it securely back in his pocket. In a couple minutes, he has caught up with Whitey and Cowboy in the dormitory. Their discussion centers around the best way to make an inconspicuous exit the next morning. Brother Tom's rules stipulate anyone leaving after the service must be back before ten o'clock pm or find themselves locked out.

This means they need to plan carefully in order to not burn a bridge behind them. As usual, when he's present, Cowboy assumes the lead. "I think I should scout the railyards tonight. The last thing we need is to get caught by one of these rail bulls. You boys be ready to roll out by daybreak. I'll be waiting out back," assures Cowboy chewing on a toothpick, tilting his hat slightly back on his head.

Whitey and Dace barely remember how geared up they were to strike out on their own only earlier this morning. Once again, Cowboy has created another circumstance where he has convinced them of the necessity that they all stay together. Consequently, in the end, they once more readily agree to Cowboy's plan.

Satisfied to have a shower and a bed for the night, Whitey lies on his back with his arm outstretched holding a photograph of Melody. Staring at her senior school photo, she is flawless, her airbrushed countenance is angelic. The thoughts her image gives rise to refuse to set him free. His heart aches. He longs to be with her. His sudden departure didn't allow for any kind of explanation, filling him with a latent sense of guilt and remorse.

Dace, too, is quietly resting on his cot. His thoughts are filled with his own burgeoning romantic liaison with Grace. Still not quite sure of the full significance of her note, he unfolds it one more time. The words *I want to go with you,* have a disturbing effect. They pierce him to his very core. Although, he has been attracted to many other girls, he has never had a person of the opposite sex attracted to him with this intensity. On the other hand, he's sure by morning he'll be long gone. At least tonight he can fantasize.

Dace's next awareness is a hand on his shoulder shaking him awake. He hears Whitey's coarse whisper, "Wake up Dace, we've gotta get rollin'!"

With no fanfare, the two of them pick up their bed rolls and make their way to door leading to the backside of the building. The resonating click of the door locking behind them gives the promised assurance they won't be coming back inside anytime soon.

Immediately, they begin to check the shadows for Cowboy. These bodiless phantoms remain only empty forebodings. Despite their diligent adherence to Cowboy's plan to meet up with him this morning, so far, he is a no show. Within a few minutes, Cowboy is becoming more and more conspicuous by his absence. About the time they're ready to give up, the darkness produces a form. It's unquestionably a human, but it quickly becomes apparent it's not Cowboy, rather it is a kid.

Whitey and Dace both stand dumbfounded as the interloper comes toward them with suitcase in hand, looking like a refugee of sorts. It isn't until this form is directly in front of them that they realize this derelict is Grace! As best she could, she's dressed herself to look like a boy. Her long hair has been cropped short and covered by a ball cap. She's dressed in jeans and a sweatshirt.

Dace is the first to speak. "Grace?" Not waiting for her to answer the obvious, he poses another more straightforward question,

"What the hell are you doing here?"

As boyish as she is attempting to appear, her demeanor is still that of a young woman. Her eyes begin to well up with tears. "I have to get out of here. From the first moment I met you, I've hoped you'd help me."

Blindsided, Dace remains befuddled. All he can do is stand speechless and stare back.

Whitey is not so distracted. Noticing a light come on inside the Mission, he strongly suggests they forget about Cowboy and the present dilemma and get moving.

There is a path through a wooded area leading away from the mission down toward the railyards. It isn't much more than a ten-minute walk. As they get closer, they begin to hear voices. The speakers are still out of sight, but not out of ear shot.

One of the voices is definitely louder and more commanding. "Sit yer ass right there and don't move."

The three are sufficiently hidden by the darkness and the brush to remain unseen. In a whispered voice, along with a hand motion, Whitey tells Dace and Grace to stay put. Slowly and quietly, he methodically makes his way to the source of the commotion. It's on the far edge of the wooded area and barely inside the railroad yard. What comes into view is a large man hovering over a handcuffed individual seated on the ground. By the time Whitey is close enough to comprehend what he is seeing, a white pickup truck with the railroad's logo painted on the doors comes to a stop.

Another large man exits the pickup. "What ya got agoin' there, Del?" he asks.

"Got me another farmhand fer ole man Woodcock."

"Hell man, 'at there's the third this morning already," says the other man with a chuckle. "With the money that ole fart is willin' ta pay, we gonna retire early."

"Early Woodcock owns, as a good old boy from Arkansas has put it, damn near every acre somebody ain't buried in. Even then, he'd likely dig ya up if he could sell yer hide fer a profit."

The large man from the pickup truck has made his way to the captive still seated on the ground. As he gets him to his feet, there is enough daylight to get a fairly decent look at the unfortunate vagrant. What Whitey is looking at takes him aback. He almost reveals himself with a gasp as he thinks, *Oh my God, they got Sid.*

This new development is as unsettling as it is a relief. The unsettling part is these bulls have said they've taken in three others already this morning. To Whitey's thinking, since Cowboy is a no-show, he is probably one of the three. The relief is that Sid won't continue to be the menacing threat he's been since they started this trip.

Hardly able to contain himself with this news, Whitey makes his way back to the other two. After revealing what he has seen and heard, the decision comes down to whether it's better to chance getting picked up for trespassing on railroad property or getting picked up for vagrancy by attempting to hitchhike. "I think we should make our way back the way we came and get some advice from that ole fart, Dewayne. He knows this area better than we do and seemed willing to help."

Grace is the first to comment. "You talkin' about Dewayne out on Trowbridge Road? The old man at the railroad office?"

Whitey and Dace look at each other wondering how Grace knows about the old coot. Dace answers, "Yeah, that's the guy that told us about your dad's mission. Do ya know 'im?"

"Yeah, I know him. He's my uncle, my mom's older brother," says Grace with halting reservation apparent in her answer.

There is just enough hesitancy for Whitey to put his mouth in gear before he thinks. "I s'pose this is gonna be the beginning of you bein' a pain in the ass in joinin' up with us?"

With this remark, Grace has a choice to make—she can burst into tears like a school girl and run back home or fight for what she wants. "If you think you can get rid of me that easy, you got another damn think comin'. I've put up with a lot tougher guys than you comin' inta my dad's mission, so don't worry about it."

Whitey turns to Dace. What he's hoping for isn't coming. Instead Dace says, "Let's give 'er a chance. I think she can work out."

It's obvious to Whitey things between himself and Dace are beginning to change, and not necessarily for the better. Not yet ready to carry this attitude to another level, Whitey backs off. Instead, he places his prejudice in a drawer in his mind along with all his other unresolved conflicts of the past week.

With the circumstances surrounding their situation worsening by the day, there has never been time to resolve a problem—it's always shoved aside unresolved to meet the next crisis. Without a unanimous solution to their present situation, they agree the next crisis is already upon them. Along with the law, they now ought to prepare themselves for an irate father. They feel a sense of urgency in getting out of the area while the getting is good.

Ready to move on, Whitey recognizes Grace is not going to go away readily and her protestations are reaching a level that could easily draw attention.

"We're still going to have to make the trip out to the yard

office to hash this out with Dewayne," Whitey says. "He's our only hope to avoid the bulls."

Grace takes a moment to evaluate their options. "I know a way through the fields where we won't be noticed. It ends near Uncle Dewayne's office at a small grove of trees where I used to play when I was little. I'll hide out there 'til you and Uncle Dewayne get things figured out. My parents will probably lock me in my room forever if he sees me."

Grace takes the lead with just enough of the shadowed darkness left to conceal them. She adeptly guides them through a profusion of brushy fields toward Dewayne's outpost.

Arriving just as the sun breaks over the eastern horizon peeking through the trees with the promise of a fresh new day.

"I don't see Uncle Dewayne's car." As Grace makes this observation, a cloud of country road dust billows behind a maroon colored 1940 Ford making its way to the outpost. "There he comes now!" she cries with the hope this helpful observation validates her usefulness in the eyes of her new consorts.

The three watch as Dewayne parks his car in the same spot he has for twenty years, fumbles with a wad of keys, unlocks the door to the station, opens the windows, turns on his radio, and prepares his coffee. Satisfied his routine has accomplished its goals, he is ready to begin his work day. He takes his usual seat on the outdoor bench marked *WHITES ONLY*.

He is somewhat surprised to be confronted at the same time as the previous day, by the same two young Yankee boys making their way up the tracks with the same woeful looks.

"You boys still lookin' like y'all been rode hard an' put up wet. Din' ya get yer sleep las' night?" asks Dewayne with a curious note.

Not wishing to let on about the mishmash behind their strained demeanor, Whitey takes the lead. "Yeah, we got some sleep, but them bums snore so damn much a body can't stay asleep."

Seemingly satisfied with this explanation, Dewayne continues his curiosity. "So what y'all got goin' this mornin'?"

Still determined to keep his cool, Whitey continues, "Word got around the mission the bulls been real active this morning. We're hopin' you could help us get a freight outta here without any trouble."

Any time Dewayne can do something to put one over on the bulls, a smirk comes across his lips. Scratching his chin for a moment, he excuses himself.

A minute later he reappears with a work sheet for the day.

With a pair of spectacles perched on the end of his nose, he proclaims, "Says here they's gonna be a freight droppin' off a tractor here." With a moment of further study, he adds, "I spose 'at's 'cause they ain't got room fer it in the main yard."

Looking back to the sheet of stapled papers, he reads on. "They sayin' that there freight gonna be here in an hour an' then it highballs on down ta Wichita Falls, Texas."

"So, you think we can get on that freight before the bulls know we're here?" asks Whitey.

"I ain't sayin' 'at fer sure, but them peckerwoods don't get out of the main yards too much. Seems they got enough action without comin' clear out here."

Dace and Whitey take time for a brief goodbye. "It's been

nice meetin' you Dewayne. You've been more of a help than you know," says Dace, looking over toward the grove of trees and feeling a bit guilty knowing they're hiding his niece.

This part of the country is generally hot and dry much of the year. The grove of trees they are returning to is, by northern standards, a rather stunted stand. For them it serves as an umbrella against the intensity of the sun's increasing heat.

They briefly share with Grace the information they received from her uncle Dewayne. She is wide-eyed, quiet and pensive as she attempts to process what she is hearing.

It's the beginning of a new reality for her. This is not something she even imagined while sitting alone daydreaming up in her room at home. Her parents, out of sincere motives, but nonetheless with an over-developed sense of responsibility, have kept her almost totally dependent on them. As a consequence of their behavior, their nearly eighteen-year old daughter lacks the street smarts required to survive in this worldly environment. As it stands now, Grace is in the middle of the biggest change in her eighteen years and because of her naivete, 99% will rip by without her notice.

For no apparent reason, Grace looks straight into Dace's eyes. A little trusting smile comes over her that communicates she is blissfully ignorant and at ease with whatever plot they develop. Feeling they have fulfilled their obligation to keep her informed, Whitey and Dace turn to each other to plan their next move. With nothing to offer but an amenable demeanor, Grace sits quietly listening as they continue to strategize. She feels somewhat excited and grown up in just hearing their proposals.

In truth Whitey and Dace are not much more experienced than Grace in the ways of this underworld. After witnessing the fate of Sid just hours ago, and knowing the cousinly connection between

Sid and Cowboy, they can only imagine what may have become of their champion. Now, finding themselves without their mentor, Dace and Whitey, nonetheless, can portray a degree of reassurance in their merging of thought—at least to one another and for certain to Grace.

In an attempt to dispel the gloom, Whitey forces his enthusiasm to the forefront. "All we gotta do is make damn sure we keep an eye open for the bulls, find an empty car, and hop on."

Grace's contentment with her own naivete is challenged for the first time. "Hop on? You mean hop on a boxcar? What if it's moving?" The panic is clear in her voice

"I expect you'll run alongside and hop on," says Whitey. However, as much as he may be struggling to adjust his attitude, the clear overtones of a scolding sarcasm remain as he continues. "If you didn't think you could do this, why in the hell would you venture away from your nice, safe home in the first place?"

Dace quickly attempts to gloss over Whitey's abruptness with consoling encouragement. With a much gentler voice, he prompts Grace, "Just stick close to me and I'll make sure you get on. It's amazing what you can do when you have to."

Grace is finding very little relief in Dace's attempt to encourage her *inner boy*. Like many things, once they're explained, they become even more impossible to imagine performing. *I'm a southern girl—and southern girls don't hop boxcars*, is her prevailing thought. Looking once again into Dace's eyes, she adopts a soft-toned, southern lilt and with a childlike naivete says, "I'm useless with these things, but I know you'll be there to help me, won't ya Dace?"

There can be no mistake that Dace is smitten. Rolling his eyes, Whitey is well aware of the hopelessness of attempting to cure this affliction.

After all, if the truth be known, he misses his Melody something fierce.

Other than keeping an eye open, there is little to do for the next hour. As if on cue, Grace opens her suitcase to display a half-dozen sack lunches she lifted from the kitchen—the same ones she and Dace had put together the day before. While she and Dace giggle over some private discussion about putting these together, they joyfully begin to devour the contents.

Clearly feeling like the guy back at the carnival side show with a third leg, Whitey quietly sits off to the side. He keeps a wary eye and ear to any changes on the track.

As the time approaches, he makes his way the twenty or so feet to the steel rails. It's clear there is no one to see him except Dewayne. Using a trick he learned this past week, he squats and puts an ear to the rail. He quickly hurries back to their wooded lair.

"Get yer stuff together. We got us a train comin'," he says excitedly.

With hearts pounding like wide-eyed race horses, they grab their gear and begin the process of *catching out*. This involves keeping an eye out for an accessible car and praying it's not too much of a stretch to have a go at leaping on board with all their gear, each other, and their arms and legs intact—all this without being detected by an overzealous railroad bull.

"Dewayne said they were going to stop this train long enough to unload a tractor. That means when we see it startin' ta slow down, we gotta be ready ta pick a car an' get aboard," says Whitey. With Cowboy's absence, there's a newfound authoritative tone evident in his words.

Realizing the gravity of a wrong decision, the three silently begin to study their options. There are numerous flatcars loaded with everything from automobiles to large pieces of farm machinery. Flatcars are easy to hop because they provide a short ladder at each end. The downside is a person is left vulnerable to the weather as well as being easily spotted by the bulls.

One car after another rolls by with huge painted lettering declaring, SANTA FE, UNION PACIFIC, etc. The skies are beginning to cloud up, threatening rain so they are watching for an enclosed boxcar with an open door.

Whitey, in particular, is beginning to develop a sense of connection with these behemoths. He respects their power, but like all parasites who look to their host for sustenance, he has found their open doors to be their vulnerability. This is exactly what he sees coming down the track—a car with an unmistakable open door. The train as promised has slowed to a gentle momentum.

Springing to his feet with the precision of a combat officer leading a charge, Whitey shouts, "Let's roll!"

The gamble takes on a life of its own. The three leap out from the safety of their womb-like hideout and charge toward the optimistic safety of their waiting host. The point of no return has been crossed.

The three are now trotting alongside the railcar inviting them in through its open door.

With the dexterity of a young cat, Whitey is aboard. Looking down at the desperation of Grace, it's obvious she's at a loss to know how to board. His natural inclination to nurture the disadvantaged kicks in. Whether or not Whitey has a sincere inclination to practice this, his behavior is nevertheless, buttressed by earlier experiences in his life. His mother has always looked out for those in the community who may be underprivileged in any way. He inherited this concern, always feeling sorry for unfortunate kids like Julia Frotanelli, who stunk so bad none of the other kids would sit next to her in third grade. He could barely stand her smell of kerosene mixed with the foul stench only the unwashed can emanate, but he would take a seat next to her so she wouldn't feel the rejection. This was done in the face of the horrible harassment he knew he would suffer at the hands of his peers.

"Throw your suitcase on board!" he directs. After which, he extends his hand and grasping hers, jerks her aboard with Dace heaving himself up right behind her.

His safe landing is met with the familiar cry of victory of one who has once again defied the disregard this mindless contraption has for anyone's welfare. Happy to see Grace safely aboard, he congratulates her with a big hug. Having won this gamble, all three break out in a laugh of relief.

The railcar has the familiar odor of creosote associated with the treated wooden planking. Whitey and Dace have come to know how this type of travel is indifferent to the creature comforts shared by those riding in the luxury of a Pullman car. They are prepared to adapt and overcome.

Of course, the same can't be said of Grace. Her eyes dart from one end to the other. It only takes a moment for her to go from elation to depression. She heaves a deep sigh. The car is totally empty. The bleakness of the steel walls marred with dents and scrapes left by previous cargoes is a stark contrast to the comforts she has chosen to abandon in her parents' home.

Dace is busy attempting to arrange his bed roll in such a way that he and Grace can share it as a cushion against the car's incessant buffeting. Remembering Pappy's instructions, Whitey is busy laying his rail spike in the door's sliding track, to prevent it from slamming shut and locking them into an irreversible fate. All in all, the two boys are beginning to feel like old hands as they go about their chosen duties under the wide eyes of this newbie.

Still struggling with the surrealism of her situation, Grace innocently stands in full view in the middle of the open door, mesmerized by the speed at which the countryside is rolling by.

"Grace!" shouts Whitey, "Get yer butt out of that door 'fore them damn bulls see us!"

This imperative jolts her. She blinks a couple times waiting for her brain and body to function together before stepping off to the side. Dace catches her mixed look of intimidation and embarrassment. Smiling at her, in an effort to diffuse the bluntness of Whitey's commanding voice, he invites her to sit down on his makeshift couch. Obsequiously, she accepts the invitation. It's apparent she is totally out of her element. It is not that Whitey is taking a great deal of satisfaction in making Grace pay for her intrusion into his and Dace's life, but he's letting it be known he's not happy with this latest change.

In an attempt to soften his own abruptness, Whitey sits down next to them, reaches into his shirt pocket, and pulls out a rumpled package of Lucky Strikes. He puts one between his lips and lights it. Taking a deep drag, he passes it first to Grace. She flinches with her eyes unknowingly beginning to blink incessantly once again. She has never smoked a cigarette in her life. Once more her brain and body struggle to know what to do next. It's now in her fingers. What she notices is how nearly pure white the paper wrapping is. It looks inviting. Her heart pounds. For the first time in her young life, she places the end between her lips and draws in. Immediately, she leaps to her feet and spends the next few minutes hacking to rid her lungs of this invader.

With the tractor finally off the train, finding its new home parked to the side of the tracks and Grace eventually recovering, things are following the predictable pattern of car hopping. At first there was the intensity of waiting and watching for a desirable car, next fulfilling that desire by chasing the chosen victim as one would its prey, followed by the exhilaration of success. Now all that's left is simply the ennui of railcar travel. There are no nice diversions like a dining car, or a cozy sleeper, just a lot of the same blandness. They're solely left to bear under the hard jostling of the rail car much as one would an unbroken bronc in its seeming effort to punish those who dare attempt to ride it.

Still weighing the uniqueness of this experience, and maybe even the funkiness of it all, Grace finds herself drawn yet once more to the open door. Not wanting to risk Whitey's wrath again, she is careful to stand out of sight off to the side. Watching the panoramic countryside slide by as if it were on a movie reel gives her pause. Her yesterdays are forever a canceled check, tomorrow is only a promissory note that isn't here yet. All she has is the present. With this reality, she's content, totally engrossed in her *now*.

CHAPTER 22

Back in town things are churning. The authorities are in town investigating a possible connection of the murder at the carnival with a murder in a town up the rail tracks a few days back.

Now, Brother Tom's daughter has disappeared. Like many small communities, this southern village shares along with most other similar communities a common thread—gossip. Like it or not, with a self-justification construct of "just looking for the truth", it usually doesn't take long before the short cut of jumping to conclusions trumps a more thorough professional investigation. The amateurs are usually quick and will always guarantee a culprit—more often the wrong one—but at least someone. The suspects usually placed at the top of the list typically begin with those with the weakest defense.

In the case of the murder at the carnival, as soon as it came to light there was a negro man on the grounds and in a place of authority, all eyes automatically went in his direction. The emancipation proclamation was issued almost a hundred years ago, but has been very slow to change the thinking of the 1950's white southern communities. In this case, the accusations may have initially begun with Albert, but fortunately he was quickly ruled out. The entire carnival crew including the owner are all northerners and will have no part of this southern-style justice.

Albert is a negro and Archibald is an Indian. The word of neither of these men can, by the tradition of southern white men, be relied upon. Even though Til is a drunk, he's white and remains the only man the sheriff has talked to that commands his attention. "Them two Yankee boys disappeared soon's the trouble commenced. They was high-tailin' it across the back field toward the tracks.

I reckon they hopped a freight an' are long gone by now. No sireee-Bob they din't want no part ah stickin' around waitin' fer the fireworks," says Til with an air of importance.

Asking around in the next town along the tracks seems a logical next step in the sheriff's investigation.

Norma Jean is a rather thin-lipped woman and by nature a worrier. The extra strain of a missing daughter is adding still more to turmoil of her day to day life. "I know my daughter, Sheriff. She was smitten by that Dace kid. She was hangin' on him like he was some kind of Memphis singin' star. He had to have talked her into n'. She never would'a done anythin' like this on her own," laments Norma Jean, dabbing her eyes with a handkerchief.

"God only knows what kind of sin they may be leadin' my baby inta. Just get her back to us," she sobs.

Brother Tom has had an arm around his practically inconsolable wife since Grace didn't come to breakfast this morning. The note Grace left in her room merely said she was leaving. It didn't indicate where she's going, or why, or how, or with whom, and failed to give any details other than she would be in touch later. But Brother Tom, being an exasperated father, is also inclined to point the finger in the direction of these two recent visitors.

"It's hard tellin' with these kinds. I feed 'em with the Word of God, give 'em a couple meals, a bed and hope the Holy Spirit's gonna work somethin' good in 'em, but the devil has his way more often than not."

"Ain't that the truth. I see that goin' on everyday myself," agrees the sheriff.

By noon he has broadened his investigation and is linking Grace's disappearance to the murder. The evidence he's gathered is turning the eye of justice more and more toward a trio of young Yankee boys for both cases.

By asking around town, it doesn't take long for the sheriff to discover Whitey and Dace had been seen the day before walking from the yard office a couple miles out of town. This leads the sheriff to pay a visit to Dewayne.

Sheriff James Robert Thompson, known to the locals as Sheriff Jim Bob, is more than ready to get to the bottom of this fiasco—especially if it deals with outsiders coming into his county—and even more so if they're Yankee northerners. These will be a more rewarding catch than a Colored man or an Indian and without a doubt Jim Bob likes headline arrests. Now that he's fairly convinced he's got the perpetrators in his sights, his next step is to pick 'em off like fish in a barrel.

There isn't a whole lot of evidence to know what to charge them with, but in the sheriff's mind, along with the rest of the community, they seem to stand in the middle of every suspicious event and need to be questioned.

Dewayne is incensed that after all he had done for these two, they had been up to no good all along. "Them peckerwoods sure as hell had me goin'. I figured they was jes a couple young boys needin' a hand. Goes ta show ya a feller cain't trust nobody these days."

"That's fer damn sure. I'm dealin' with these kinds day in and day out," says Sheriff Jim Bob. He rarely misses an opportunity to let his constituents know how perilous his job is and how he risks his life nearly every moment to keep them safe. The community in turn gives him a free hand to wield justice as he sees fit. Often, he considers the ancient adage, *the end will justify the means* to be a perfectly legitimate investigative tool.

Not quite finished questioning Dewayne, the sheriff presses a bit deeper. "Ya didn't happen ta see yer niece, Grace, with them fellers did ya?"

Dewayne ponders the question for a moment, pulling his hat on and off his head several times in a seeming effort to overcome the frustration of not having a good solid answer and a way to cover the part he played in getting them on a freight. "Ya know only the two ah them boys come by. They was askin' about where I figured was a good place ta hop a car. I told 'em it was illegal an' I couldn't give 'em any information about it. They never give me any lip an' struck out toward 'at there clump ah trees over yonder," says

Dewayne pointing to the last place he saw them.

Sheriff Jim Bob hears in Dewayne's explanation more of an attempt to cover his own ass rather than an answer to his question. He tries once more, "Ya still ain't told me if ya saw a young girl with 'em."

"I seen three of 'em hop a railcar, but it looked like three boys," says Dewayne satisfied he's cleared himself. "The third one I ain't never seen before—leastwise I don't recollect ever seein' 'im."

"Could that third one have been yer niece dressed like a boy?"

Dewayne continues adjusting his hat as he gives this notion a second thought. "Ya know, come ta think of it that kid had a hell of a time gettin' on that freight. The blond-haired kid took all he had ta keep that one from slippin' under the gawdam wheels."

"So, you thinkin' it was a girl with them other two?" presses Sheriff Jim Bob.

"I never got a good look, but ya know—the way I'ma recollectin' it, the way that kid was runnin' toward that freight was more like a girl than a boy," muses Dewayne. Slamming his hat firmly on his head, he adds just as firmly, "Hell ya, yer dang tootin' 'at there were a girl—no doubt about it!"

Satisfied he's making headway, Sheriff Jim Bob continues his interview with Dewayne. He learns the freight is heading for Texas.

"What's the chances of getting' this train stopped?" questions the sheriff.

"Not much 'lessen you can convince the railroad they gotta do it by law," states Dewayne.

His matter of fact tone strikes the sheriff bluntly. This

exponent adds a new dimension. He's more used to calling the shots, now he's finding himself faced with a force he's not accustomed to dealing with.

CHAPTER 23

This part of Arkansas is a beautiful mix of mountains, flat lands, rivers, and lakes. The rail tracks follow precarious ridges around mountainous passes. With the railcar's door open, even the wash hanging on lines outside ramshackle homes situated in deep ravines referred to as *hollers* is easily viewed. This can be readily described as altogether very Arkansas.

Many of the people living in these areas have family ties that date back to a time before Arkansas was a state. This area is viewed as wild, certainly not ambitious nor bustling.

In her young life, the furthest Grace has been away from her parents' mission is when she visited her grandmother's home, which is also situated in one of these hollers in the southern part of the state.

Grace realizes she will soon be further away from home than she has ever been and finds herself sharing with the boys some of the experiences she's undergone at the mission.

"I remember a man who stayed with us, whose wife had tried to stab him for having an affair with her cousin who had gotten pregnant by him. She spent a month in the county jail. When she got out she hunted him down. Finding him at our mission, she finished the job. The last I heard, she is still serving a life sentence." It's obvious from her stories that despite her sheltered life, the world has made its path to her in its own way.

"You got a boyfriend?" asks Dace. The question makes him sound and look unsure. It freezes Grace for a moment a silence. The social climate between her and the boys is beginning to take on a life of its own.

The question brings back a distant memory. "When I was ten, my father took in a family that had found themselves homeless. They had a boy my age, named O.D. something. He just went by his initials," she recollects.

"He was messy in both his clothes as well as how he acted. I remember he had a tangled mop of brown curly hair that hadn't been cut in months. My dog had recently died by some kind of worms in his heart," recalls Grace. "I was lost in sadness over my dog."

She related how she had withdrawn herself to a backyard swing her father had built, and how she had little else on her mind other than her heartache.

"It took me by surprise to look up and find O.D. standing directly in front of me. I was scared by his rough appearance. I had previously ignored him. But for the first time, I noticed his eyes. They possessed a kindness I hadn't observed before. It made me wondered why I hadn't seen that until right then."

"I heard about yer dog. I'm sorry. My dog died last year," he said.

"I remember how I found his voice not so much sad, but oddly understanding. His next move was to jam his hand deep into his overall pocket, moving things around until he produced a half-filled box of Smith Brothers cherry-flavored cough drops. The box was dirty and folded. He spent a good minute carefully opening it. The candies had stuck together and I pulled two out. I unstuck them and handed him the other. We spent the next few minutes with him pushing me in the swing, savoring the shared cough drops. His family left the next day. If that's what a boyfriend is, I remember him well. But that was a long time ago."

Taking a pause, as if she were replaying a part of her story she hadn't shared, she harks back to Dace's question about having a boyfriend. Her face turns red as she takes on an awkward, self-conscious, inhibited behavior. Breaking her gawky silence, she answers, "Nooo!"

Dace, satisfied he has uncovered all he needs to be concerned with involving her personal life, moves on. He's had designs on this beauty from the first time he laid eyes on her. With her seated right next to him, he adjusts his position, enabling him to put his arm around her. Much to Dace's pleasure, he feels the warmth of Grace's body as she snuggles closer.

In the semi-darkness of the boxcar, their passions suddenly dominate them as they fall into the kind of kiss that rejects any suggestion of restraint. The result is two pairs of lips crashing together in a kind of grinding fashion. It's the kind of heavy breathing kissing the participants hope will never end and will unknowingly result in bruised, swollen lips later. For now, her hot, sweet-smelling breath is enough for Dace.

For Grace, this is a freedom she has yearned for. Up until this moment, her life has consisted of church, music and daily devotions. Now she finds herself shuddering in the arms of this unlikely paramour, leaving her with unexpected physical sensations she has never imagined. At this point, the fact this liaison is being fulfilled in a boxcar is not relevant to either of them. For now, they are more than content to just have a suitable partner with which to release their youthful passions.

He'd known since he was in kindergarten that girl cooties

were not only the most feared thing about getting to close to a girl, but also a very mysterious entity. Butch Langdon had told him how a girl had kissed him on the lips one time and how her cooties crawled up his nose and forced their way through the thin membrane separating his nose from his brain turning it into mush. Dace is wondering if this is what he's experiencing.

In this world's insistence on reality, this present experience is relatively new to Dace and brand new to Grace. Dace had a brief make-out fling in seventh grade when Vivian Albright trapped him in her garage. She was two inches taller, but by placing him on an upturned milk crate, she turned him into the Casanova she was hoping for. He was suddenly inches taller and when he kissed her, he fell to his knees breathless and faint, fully convinced the cootie theory had become a reality. *That was seventh grade. I was just a kid. Now, I'm nearly an adult. It's odd how similar the feeling is,* he thinks.

Both Dace and Grace are overcome with a complete body flush caused by increased blood flow and sweat. This only increases their arousal. They continue this course until they're sated and their lips are numb and unable able to feel the other's.

Whitey is once again feeling left out. A sense of desperate loneliness is creeping in on him. He longs for Melody and is wondering why he ever agreed to accompany Dace on this crazy trip to madness. Being in the presence of all this romantic frenzy with no way to escape leaves him feeling even more on life's sidelines—like the square peg abandoned to a world of round holes. *If I had a bottle of anything with alcohol, I'd drink the whole damn thing,* muses Whitey.

The cacophonous click of the steel wheels eventually interrupts his pity party and puts him into a strange land of semiconsciousness. It's a dream like-region giving neither peaceful sleep nor undisturbed wakefulness. It's the realm of demons creating nightmarish scenarios meant to frighten. In the lonely recesses of this crude conveyance, Whitey feels himself being shaken.

"Wake up, Whitey. Wake up!"

Jerking awake, he finds Dace and Grace peering over him with slight smirks. He's having a nightmare in the middle of the afternoon and they're finding it amusing. Even so, he's thankful they wakened him. The nightmare was a tortuous incident where he found himself running to catch a railcar and subsequently was thrown beneath the train. He is laying between the tracks, frozen in place, as axle after axle of a seemingly unending line of railcars rolls closer and closer to his face.

Thanking them, Whitey sits up in an effort to pull himself into the present. Grace marks the incident by producing yet another sack lunch. She feels good being able to contribute to this new alliance.

Whitey remains quiet, munching on a cheese sandwich and letting the present reality work its magic in crowding out the nightmarish incident. What *he* finds amusing is looking at the ridiculousness of his two car-mates with their red, swollen mouths. It's enough to humor him a little more into the present.

"You were hollerin' pretty damn loud," says Dace. "Wad ya have, a bull chasin' ya?"

Not wanting to relive any part of his dream, he's satisfied with Dace's assessment.

"Yeah, somthin' like that," says Whitey, quietly taking another bite of his sandwich. With another bite, he burps a loud gut release of trapped air bringing on Dace and Grace's laughter, the kind of simple laughter he needs a lot more of to pull himself out of his funk.

Sitting here eating a sandwich, Whitey's mind begins to drift in another direction. The tensions have been high since they left Elbertport. It's not been much over a week ago. There's a disturbing lump beginning to clog Whitey's throat. This may possibly be the lowest point in his young life. It started with Dace, when he believed he may have killed Orin back in Elbertport, but now it's grown to include Sid murdering people, Cowboy stealing cars, and now most recently harboring a young girl whose parents will surely blame him and Dace if and when they get caught.

As much as Cowboy has been a loose cannon in their lives, he always came through. Even though Cowboy frequently disappeared for long periods of time, he always reappeared just as they were entering head long into a looming crisis. Whitey realizes that as much as he had wanted to rid themselves of Cowboy, right at this moment, he misses his mastermind. *No matter what you got us into, you always got us out. Where the hell are you when we need you?!* screams an unrelenting frustration inside Whitey's head.

As has been the case since this whole debacle began, things are taking yet another unexpected turn. The train is slowing down. It stops and go into reverse for a short distance before stopping again. The next thing they become aware of is that the engine is moving forward—without them.

Knowingly, Whitey and Dace look at one another. They have been on the rails just long enough to figure out what's going on. Their car has been placed on a siding. This isn't supposed to be happening. Dewayne assured them this train was highballing straight to Texas. This is the downside to car hopping—the unpredictable behavior of the railroad.

The sun's position in the sky reminds Whitey and Dace evening is approaching. Certain things should be attended to. Since they have spent most of the day holed up inside a clamoring boxcar, finding a secluded place outside where a fire could be started is becoming a priority; as much for warmth as for mental consolation.

It has become nearly second nature for the boys to take notice of any hobo activity in the surrounding brushy areas. Within minutes they have come across the quintessential worn path. Among other things they have learned in their brief time on the road is that much can be discerned about a jungle by the amount of trash decorating the area. The more trash, the more likely the area is going to be occupied by local bums rather than by hobos. This former group is more concerned with being liquored up and will most likely find themselves under the wheels of a freight car in any attempt to catch out. These locals are more disposed to staying put. They're also more inclined to be hostile and ready to start trouble. No self-respecting hobo will engage himself for long with the likes of these dregs of humanity.

Since experiencing some negatives, Whitey and Dace have become a bit more apprehensive about barging into situations they haven't previewed. Considering they now also have responsibility for Grace's wellbeing, caution is even more essential.

In an effort to conceal her femininity, Grace has dressed in abandoned men's clothes pilfered from the mission's abandoned clothing wardrobe. Being a rather thin girl, the clothing she's picked is a size too big, emphasizing her slight appearance. Despite this attempt, including pulling her cropped hair up under a stocking hat, her girlish features only manage to make her appear as a sissy boy. This can be just as troubling as being a female in these usually all male subcultures. Many of these men have been in prison. The lack of women in those gated communities has developed a type of sexual predator whose sexual preferences can vary indiscriminately between young and old, male and female.

With this thought in mind, Whitey decides to take precautionary measures. "Lemme go in and check this place out before we all barge in," he says with an air of responsibility. Even though he regards Grace as a liability, he has unconsciously begun to regard her as he would a sibling. His upbringing makes him answerable for her welfare.

The path's moist black dirt has a particular shininess to it as it refracts the late afternoon sun light. It's not the kind of shininess that is pleasurable, rather it's the kind of sliminess one would avoid when barefoot. This observation along with the excess amount of trash, strongly suggests this is probably not going to be the kind of jungle they want to stay in.

Moving forward with quiet and apprehensive steps, Whitey soon hears the chatter of human voices. Still too far away to discern much, he cautiously moves forward along the path. Shortly, he can detect the low-pitched utterance of a man's voice and the higher pitch of a woman's voice. Now, within a few feet of the mystery mutterings and still undetected, he discovers their origin.

It's a disheveled man sitting on an armless wooden chair of no particular design or purpose relating to this outdoor setting. He has a half empty wine bottle gripped in his dangling left hand with his pants gathered around his ankles. His other hand is up under the blouse, cupping the bare breast of an equally disheveled woman with her skirt pulled up, straddling his bare midriff.

His unrestrained grunts are met with her squeals as they continue their uninhibited undulating. What is equally interesting is the dollar bill the woman is clinching during the entire tryst. She seems as riveted on the cash as she is the service she apparently is providing. Between the two of them their most glaring characteristic other than being disheveled, is that neither have any.

Whitey has never been exposed to the rawness of this kind of sex. He's struck with a mixture of curiosity and disgust. The whole affair is soon over with the woman dismounting, letting her skirt fall back around her bruised, blotchy bare legs. She smacks her snaggle-toothed lips to his forehead and lifts his bottle to her open mouth to take one last pull before she is ready to leave.

Not wanting to be caught and thought of as some kind of perverted voyeur, Whitey makes a hasty retreat.

Meeting Dace and Grace back near the tracks, and without explanation, he frankly says, "I think we need to find a better spot."

With that blunt tone, Dace figures Whitey will explain later and doesn't press him further. Quickly following him, they put a comfortable distance between themselves and this apparently unsettling site.

After walking a few yards beyond the tree line, they are unexpectedly met with an outcropping of another kind. On the horizon, appears a water tower. They all see it at the same time. It's a positive indicator they are on the outskirts of a town. If one is not cautious, this can be a blessing or a curse. Not sure where to begin to look for an agreeable place to spend the night, they decide it will be safest to find a spot adjacent to the tracks, but still near town.

With a bit of scouting, they agree on a small clearing in the middle of a stand of magnolia trees. It's ideal. It's only a short distance to their railcar. The remnants of a fire pit give evidence it's been used before. It's also thick enough to provide a barrier against the outside world, but still provide an avenue of escape if needed. What's more, discovering a carving on a log portraying a square without a top is assuring. Pappy had taught the two boys to be on

191

the look-out for the attitude of the locals and to watch for hobo symbols indicating safe or unsafe camping areas left by previous Knights of the Road. In this case, it is the hobo symbol for a safe campsite. Reassured by this positive mark, a fire is quickly started and they soon feel more secure.

Dace and Whitey find they are slowly becoming immersed in the hobo underworld deeper than either had ever imagined possible. In the beginning, their feelings toward their circumstances had been determined out of necessity, but now these feelings and circumstances have morphed into a real sense of community.

A phenomenon catching their eye is the red and green light atop the town's water tower meant to warn low flying aircraft. Within the heart of each of these young people, it's flashing serves as a beacon trying to lure them back to civilization. In these kinds of circumstances there are always lonely periods where the mind settles on home. To maintain this free-wheeling life style, one must fight against these periods as one would a relentless enemy meant to be defeated and brought to its knees. Sleep is often the answer with the expectation these feelings will pass away with the night.

With the sight of a new day, the hope is these sensitivities will be stuffed away. If this exercise is performed on a regular basis, these feelings gradually blur into other parts of the psyche—much like a virus that morphs into some other kind of disturbing disorder.

In the morning, the three awake refreshed and share a can of beans. With that finished, they put the campsite in order. It's the hobo tradition to leave things better than found. With all their chores completed, they soon strike out down the trail. Still remaining lighthearted, they share small talk until Whitey suddenly gasps, "What the hell?" The whole line of rail cars including the car that carried them here is missing.

The three of them stand speechless. There is nothing that can be said or done to change their situation. They're stuck and they know it. Dace is getting more nervous like he always does when things begin to fall apart. Aware they're standing out in the open with no place to go, Whitey breaks the silence, "Let's get back to camp and figure a plan."

Grace realizes things have changed again and once more finds herself with no clue what's happening. While waiting for the boys to come up with an answer, she simply remains confused. Stumbling along trying to half-drag and half-carry her overloaded suitcase, she feels dumb. She is fully aware of how totally reliant she is on these two Yankees.

In more than a little bit of a hurry and with Whitey in the lead, they anxiously, nearly mindlessly plunge back through the brush searching for the camp they had abandoned only minutes before. To add to an already hopeless situation, Grace's hat snags in the tangled thicket leaving her hair at the mercy of every lurching branch hell-bent on ripping every strand from her head.

Stopping for a moment, Whitey silently asks himself, *"What madness are we in? What would Cowboy do?"*

A moment later, almost as though he has somehow gained an insight he hadn't initially considered, holding his hands up, he all but shouts, "Stop! Let's just stop!!"

Like witless lemmings attempting to come to a standstill, the other two stumble into each other as his directive echoes off the walls of their minds. Standing breathless, without a clue as to what to do next, they all look to the other for a course of action. It's in this single moment after allowing some breathing space, they realize the clearing they are crazily searching for is right there beside them.

Whitey promptly follows up on his own directive, "Let's sit

a minute and think about this."

Wordlessly, Dace and Grace follow Whitey to the seemingly safe sanctuary they utilized the night before. At the very least, the place has a comfortable ambiance about it. With no thought, they take the same seats they had left only minutes before. In an attempt to conceal her anxiousness, Grace busies her hands pulling the tangles from her frizzled hair. Dace uneasily pokes a stick at the ground as though waiting for Providence to miraculously begin to guide the stick in writing some fresh new marching orders.

Whitey's eyes are fixed to an overhead spot in the distance. He's staring at the same water tower they spotted the day before. It seems to have an appealing allure. Mulling over its implications and not hearing any input from Dace or Grace, he makes a proposal. "Chances are we can sit out here 'til Jesus comes and never get on another freight. I suggest we take a stroll into town, maybe pick up a few cans of beans and fill our canteens."

Grace jumps to her feet as though someone had just pinched her. "If we do that, I'm not going looking like I do. I want to at least put on a dress," she declares in a tone as clear and concise as a female that has made up her mind.

Whitey and Dace both look at her blankly, giving a little shrug to their shoulders indicating their indifference. Grace doesn't wait for their approval before she grabs her suitcase and makes her way to the privacy of a nearby clump of trees. Not really knowing what to expect to come of this move, they continue their dialogue.

What catches their eye next is a total surprise. Grace suddenly reappears wearing a much more fashionable looking dress than either had ever seen her wear. It looks nothing like the clothing they had seen her in at the mission. Instead it's a pleated Scottish plaid skirt ending at the knee, rather than the ankle length flower prints she was obliged to wear in her father's house. The top two buttons of her blouse are undone with a knotted aqua-colored silk scarf encircling her neck. Even her heavy footwear has been replaced by a pair of black and white saddle shoes.

She had covertly acquired these "dishonorable" articles of clothing, hiding them in an outbuilding behind the mission. After getting her hands on a J.C. Penny catalog last winter, she secretly ordered this outfit and had it sent to her grandmother's house. Her grandmother being a more socially liberal Methodist wasn't big on her son's choice to become, in her words a "tight-assed Mennonite." Always sympathizing with her granddaughter, she helped her secretly buy the clothes. She has dreamed of the day she'd be seen walking through a city wearing such a stylish wardrobe. This is her first opportunity and she is beaming from ear to ear. With the reappearance of their newly acquired charge, Whitey and Dace are speechless. To say she looks stunningly out of place would be a gross understatement.

As they stash their gear under some loose brush, they are surprised to unearth a few hidden pots and other cookware. Now ready to head to town, make their way toward the water tower.

The town is an average size community of maybe ten or twelve thousand. It is big enough to supply an interesting downtown with several bars, a few drugstores, and among its eateries is a restaurant with the interesting name of *Snappy Joe's*.

Grace couldn't be more excited, if she had found herself walking the streets of New York City. This is the first time in her young life she has felt like she is a participant in the culture of her generation. Most parents are surprised when their children refuse to be an extension of themselves. This is most noticeable when offspring rebel against their parents' values or their world view.

Although Grace loves her parents, she already knows this outside exposure is developing a new mindset within her. She knows she will never return to the mission.

Their first stop is at Snappy Joe's for a bite to eat. It's a welcomed diversion. "Dace will you order for me?" Grace nervously asks and finally admits, "I've never ordered in a restaurant."

Dace couldn't be more pleased. He takes on this responsibility as though he were a seasoned cosigner. Making a bigger deal than necessary, he searches the menu ordering a burger with everything, a Coke and fries. Grace could not be more impressed had he ordered in French.

With their hunger satiated, they move back out on the streets. Grace's enthusiasm is like a kid in a candy store. She stops at every store window as though each display was prepared especially for her. Spotting a movie theater marquee, her excitement can hardly be contained. The marquee serves as a welcoming canopy with its endless stream of lights announcing *Rio Bravo*.

Dace couldn't feel more like a real man of the world in sharing these modern recreations with Grace for the first time. While looking at her naivete, a strange sense of enchantment overtakes him. It's a comfortable feeling as well as a tenuous one in the sense this may be too good to be true.

"I've never been in a movie house. My parents say these Hollywood people are all on their way to hell and we don't need to help pay their way," she relates.

"I don't know nothin' about that," admits Dace. "But I'd love to take you, if you'd like to see a movie. I been to at least a hunert of 'em."

Grace is beyond anxious at this invitation. She is trembling at the prospect of violating this Mennonite ruling, but nonetheless more than eager to throw off the harsh religious harness she views as repressive. In her boldest voice under these seeming avant-garde circumstances, wearing an uneasy smile that fails to stay in place, she grabs Dace's hand before her guilt can take hold, saying, "Let's do it!"

Everything that's happened to Dace, starting over a week ago in Elbertport, had to happen to bring him to this absolute high point in his life. If he had to kill Orin five more times to have this moment, he'd do it. This is undeniably the best day of his life.

Not willing to be the odd man out, Whitey says, "You two go ahead. I'm gonna scout around and see what the best way out of here is gonna be."

CHAPTER 24

With very little forethought, Whitey heads back toward the jungle that he had earlier forsaken to the copulating couple. He figures these underclass citizens are probably the most reliable people to talk to about the attitude of the local police toward outsiders. The sun has dried up the slimy dew left on the path from the night before, but the discarded trash remains the same.

Making his way to the well-worn setting inside, his eyes meet a couple of men. One he remembers as the man on the chair. The other is someone he has never seen before. The second man is a little shorter than the first, but just as grimy. It only takes a moment before it becomes obvious neither man is sober. Passing a bottle of rotgut whisky between the two of them, they pay little regard to

Whitey.

Thinking maybe he needs to start the conversation, he sits down on a large piece of broken concrete that gives no hint as to how it got here or what its function had been. Clearing his throat, Whitey says, "Hi—I'm on the road and need some information— I'm wonderin' if you fellas could help me out?"

Taking a long drag on a roll-your-own cigarette, chair-man bends his head a little, looking out of one squinting eye, he says, "'At there all depends on what yer willin' ta pay. Ya got any money, boy?"

Before he can answer, the other man chimes in, "Yeah kid, ya got any money? 'Cause we got all kinda information, only it don't come cheap—no sireee it don't come cheap!"

Had this hostile reaction been a week ago, he probably would have run off in fear. But things have changed quickly, hardening him to this kind of an opposition.

While making his way down the path, Whitey had already reached inside his shirt and unsnapped the small strap holding his knife in its sheath. A slight shift of his shoulder gives him a knowing certainty this weapon is available at a moment's notice. "Well I guess it all depends on what kind of money yer talkin'," says Whitey.

Setting the remains of the bottle of rotgut on the ground, chair-man puts on his squinty eye business face again. "Then 'at there depends on what kinda info yer expectin'."

"I need ta know what kind of law ya got around here for us 'bos that wanna catch out," says Whitey.

Both men give each other a quick look. To Whitey, it suggests they have this information. "Yeah, we can pro'ly hep ya out fer a buck," says chair-man.

Whitey begins to feel a tightness developing in his chest. "I ain't got a buck," lies Whitey, hoping to negotiate for a lesser amount. "Alls I got is a half pack ah Luckys." The tightness is causing his breathing to become shallow. He feels fortunate to have gotten the words out without choking.

The men look at one another once more. The short man says, "What if we decide ta check yer pockets ta make sure ya ain't lyin'.".

Knowing he needs to regroup quickly, he takes a deep breath. Whitey then slowly and in a very open way, reaches his right hand inside his shirt and draws out the silvery blade. He begins to methodically clean his fingernails. Looking them both square in the eye, he says, "I guess yer jes gonna have ta believe me on that one."

Things suddenly get real quiet. Neither man is looking anywhere except at the flickering of the late afternoon sun off the blade as it moves from one fingernail to another.

"I think we can do some business fer the cigarettes," says chair-man. "What ya needin' ta know?"

Throwing the half pack of cigarettes at the chair-man's feet, Whitey begins. "Me an' two ah my friends got dumped here last night after missin' a catch out. What I need ta know is where's the best place ta wait for the next freight outta here without havin' ta deal with the bulls."

The two reprobates glance at one another as if they are politely waiting for the other to divvy up a shared knowledge. Politeness is not their strength and they quickly set etiquette aside as both anxiously begin to speak over the other's words. Realizing this, they both opt to begin again only to do the same again. Finally, the chair-man desists, allowing the shorter man to speak. "I can show you the perfect spot. It's jes down the way here a piece," he says, pointing an unwashed finger on down the tracks. "Ain't seen a bull around these parts in some time. They's mostly payin' attention ta the downtown yards," says the short man with a convincing air of authority.

Whitey can't believe how cooperative these derelicts have suddenly become. Nonetheless, he's pleased to have created such an enthusiastic desire within them to want to be of help—at the cost of only a half pack of cigarettes.

Cecil, the chair-man, and Willis make the quarter mile trek with Whitey to investigate this ideal location. These two helpers are very precise and insistent in positioning Whitey and his yet unmet entourage into an exact spot. After at least an hour of planning, and sure that Whitey understands their instructions, they part ways, leaving Whitey on his own.

On his way back to the movie theater, Whitey mulls over his success. He's sure Cowboy couldn't have hashed things out much better. Proud of his negotiating ability, he can hardly wait to share with Dace and Grace the news of their good fortune.

His timing couldn't have been better. The movie has just ended and Dace and Grace are exiting the theater door. Grace is frantically attempting to arrange her disheveled hair and Dace is tucking in a disarrayed shirttail.

Whitey has a momentary distraction seeing the two of them once again with their swollen red lips, but opts to dismiss a berating other than a minor dig. "You two see much of the movie?" From the looks of them, if what they have done to one another was not consensual, they could have easily been charged with assault.

Ignoring Whitey's comment and ready to brush off any further discussion of their movie theater behavior, Dace says, "You shoulda come, it don't get no better than John Wayne."

Grace, still not sure of herself, attempts to smooth any apparent flaws in her clothes. This may only be a small Arkansas town, but after all, it is her debut. Attempting to sound sophisticated, Grace expresses, "It was a wonderful production, I thought the acting was superb."

Listening to Grace's attempt to sound classy, Whitey once more realizes how difficult it's going to be to get this naive girl street smart enough to be an asset. Nonetheless, it's time to move on. He begins to unfurl the happenings of the past couple hours with Cecil and Willis. He can sense in Dace and Grace's demeanor they aren't listening to him. It's obvious in the way they continue to cling to one another that they're still experiencing the afterglow of their two-hour movie make out session.

"Come on, guys. Snap out of it. We only got a little time ta get outta here, so get it together," pleads Whitey, giving them both a little push.

Reacting to Whitey's obvious concern, Dace begins to face their reality head-on. Grace, on the other hand is still basking in the newness of her city experience. She is hearing what is being said, but it's clear by her unruffled reactions she does not understand the seriousness of their circumstances.

Frustrated by Grace's nonchalance, Whitey takes a breath deep enough to empty the area of its oxygen. "Grace, if you plan on being part of this team, you gotta start acting as a team player. We can't afford ta screw up!"

Seeing Whitey's attitude toward Grace becoming hostile, Dace jumps to her defense. "Come on, Whitey, lighten up a little. We'll get it all done."

Realizing all that can be accomplished at this moment is done, Whitey opts to move on. "We don't have a lotta time ta wrangle. We gotta get our stuff an' get movin'!'"

Both Grace and Dace step up their pace. They're beginning to adjust to this new development. Within a few minutes, they've made their way back to the place they had earlier stashed their belongings.

Knowing what dirty conditions are awaiting her, there isn't anything in the world that can dissuade her from protecting her new wardrobe. "I need a few minutes to change my clothes," says Grace.

The brushy conditions concealing this area and the cooking pots hidden with care suggest it has probably been utilized as a stashing station for many a traveling Knight of the Road. With a little time to waste waiting on Grace, and a bit of curiosity, Whitey does a more intense search of the area. There are a number of discarded booze bottles ranging from beer and wine to whiskey. Something peeking out from under a pile of dead vegetation suddenly catches his eye. It has a familiar shape and density. He's soon on his knees parting the undergrowth. Next comes a smile. "Lookee here what I jes found!" he exclaims, pumping his arm in the air with the new-found treasure. It's a full, unopened bottle of Muscatel. Its history can only be conjectured. Obviously, it's been here for a while from the faded label.

Dace's facial expression changes from inattention to near ecstasy. "What the hell kind of luck you got, Whitey? You sure as hell gonna share ain't ya?"

They greet this find with the same simple-minded tradition they've had from the first time alcohol introduced itself into their lives.

Without a word, Whitey unscrews the top and sniffs its contents. Still wordless, he puts the bottle to his lips sipping a small amount and smacking his lips, as if this were a scientific test.

Passing the bottle to Dace, he in turn performs the same test mimicking the same procedure. Anticipating what Whitey is expecting from his examination, he says, "Tastes fine to me." With the testing finalized, he takes a big hearty drink, passing the bottle back to Whitey who does the same.

Grace, once again back to wearing her boy clothes, emerges from her brushy changing room only to be confronted head on with yet another brand-new life altering experience. Holding the bottle above his head and with a noticeable amount of condescension in his voice, Whitey questions, "Hey Grace, ya want a little bump?"

Having spent her entire life around her father's mission, she was never seduced by any of those visitors to join them in their drinking hi-jinx. Besides, her parent's paid careful attention to what she was exposed to. The men who frequented the mission were always the down and outers, the kind of people she had never had a reason to equate her life to. This is the first time her own peer group has invited her to participate.

Her mind immediately shoots out a warning she has heard from her father about the evils of alcohol. She has heard his story so many times she can literally mouth his words as he speaks them.

Looking once more at the hand passing her the bottle, there is a sudden mixture of dread and enticement. Not wanting to be viewed as a goody two-shoes and realizing she is no longer under her parents' tutelage, her hesitation lasts for only a moment. Taking the bottle, she holds it directly in front of them and looks both boys directly in the eye with the question, "Will this make me drunk?"

Already feeling the effects, Whitey displays his usual alcohol-induced cavalier attitude. "Hell yeah! Nothin' wrong with that!" Having taken advantage of the mission's facilities for bathing and washing his clothing, Whitey may be cleaner, but he has a young man's scraggly growth of beard he hadn't bothered to shave. Now along with an unkempt disheveled head of blond hair, and with a snoot full of alcohol, he has an eerie, almost sinister appearance.

Dace, on the other hand, is more reticent. Despite his lead toward getting this bottle empty, he manages to demonstrate a legitimate concern for Grace's welfare. "Grace, you don't have to, if you don't want to," says Dace.

Too late, the bottle has already been passed to her by Whitey. She stands looking one last time at her hand bearing this forbidden fruit. Her thoughts race through Mennonite judgments on worldly sentiments to what Eve must have felt like with the prohibited apple in her hand. Nonetheless, like Eve, she's ready to continue throwing off the yoke of her religious smugness.

With that settled, she closes her eyes—ready to test the waters as she tips the bottle back. Letting its contents run down her throat, she prepares herself for any bad effects. Instead, the taste surprises her. "This stuff is good, it tastes like grapes," she says wiping her lips with her sleeve. Suddenly emboldened by the reality she didn't explode or find herself in the pits of hell, she tips the bottle back for another brave pull. Its sugary bite creates a warmth she has never experienced from any previous beverage.

Fully aware what this can lead to, Dace stands ready to avert any chance Grace may have a bad experience. "Here, let me have another drink," he says, at the same time relieving Grace of the bottle. He's surprised how tight a grip she has on its neck.

Within fifteen minutes, they have drained its contents. For the first time in her life, Grace begins to feel a giddiness overtaking her she can't control. The euphoria is beyond any previous experience. She has never felt anything like this, not even while playing the piano—not even while making out with Dace. This is a brand-new sensation. Recalling all the sermons she has heard her father preach on the evils of alcohol, she is now confused. *How can anything that feels this good be that bad,* is her single thought.

Despite the alcohol-induced fog, Whitey is determined to get to the catch out location Cecil and Willis had sold him earlier.

It's becoming evident Grace is going to be a problem. Not only is she unable to carry her suitcase, she is apparently a *loud* drunk. Adding to this, she begins to dance a ballet. Straightaway, Whitey and Dace know they are in serious trouble. Catching out requires quick, coordinated movement.

Even in Dace's condition, he feels a sense of responsibility toward Grace and is desperately trying to calm her down. She's having no part of it. Still stumbling and demonstrating an unruliness in the place where inhibitions once gripped her, she desperately tries to pull him to herself. "Kiss me Dace. Kiss me like you did in the movie!" she insists, determined to pull him down on top of her.

It's all Dace can do to break loose. "Grace get a hold of yourself. We can't afford to get caught. Come on, we've gotta get outta here," he is equally insistent. "I promise, I'll kiss you when we get to our catch out place."

"Promise?" she slurs.

"I promise," assures Dace.

All three begin the quarter mile trek. Now because of their mental and physical shape, their walk is more of a stumble. Grace is still acting like a ballet dancer, leaping and twirling the whole distance, frequently falling, all the while singing a tune only she hears.

Evaluating himself, Dace feels like an old-time drinker compared to this novice. After all, this is Grace's first time dealing with the baffling, cunning power of alcohol. Consequently, since he bears much of the responsibility for her condition, he feels a strong sense of obligation to take care of her.

Even though she is having a wonderful time and enjoying a sense of freedom never before experienced, she continues to wonder how this good feeling can be altogether so sinful. It's an enigma to her, but for the time being, she is willing to halt any more thought on it.

Despite all the ruckus in getting to their destination, they finally arrive. Whitey is certainly feeling the full effects of his share of the wine, but is still able to navigate them to their exit point. As it goes in catching out, one never knows how long it will take, resulting in a fair amount of waiting. Today is proving to be no exception. The long wait is combining with the effects of the alcohol to bring them to a point of uncontrolled drowsiness. One by one they drop off into a deep slumber. It's the kind of unconsciousness one can only be brought out of by time or some extreme outside force.

In this case, it turns out to be an outside force. They're all feeling the compelling effects of something battering their rib cages, backsides, heads, arms, legs. With the residual effects of the alcohol prohibiting any kind of rational thought process, Whitey is flailing his arms at these seeming phantoms in a futile attempt to defend himself.

Dace is undergoing a similar reaction. The beating is accompanied by the coarse curses of very mean sounding male voices. It gradually becomes clear they are being kicked awake.

Grace is undergoing the same treatment, finding herself being beaten in a way she's never in her life experienced. She can't think. Every time she attempts to put a thought together, her head feels like it's about to explode. It's the kind of headache that is accompanied by nausea.

Not fully conscious, her mind is doing its best to warn her of the danger she's in. *My God, am I falling into a gorge? What's happening to me?* There's been so much packed into the past couple days since she left home. Now she feels like everything that made her feel good was just a set up to make her feel worse.

Ultimately, the beating stops and they find themselves being jerked to their feet by someone pulling on the backs of their collars. It's two good-sized, middle-aged men, red-faced from the exercise but wearing a satisfied smirk.

"You three peckerwoods jes stepped inta a whole new life fer yersefs. Yeseree Bob, I'm gonna put the whole lot of y'all inta mah retirement fund. Old man Woodcock pays damn good fer young healthy ones the likes of y'all."

Hardly sober enough to really catch the full impact of the moment, the three railcar ramblers are scarcely aware they are being decommissioned. The men handcuff each of them. As it turns out, one of the men is a railroad bull and the other is the local sheriff. Suddenly, Whitey realizes what happened. Standing off to the side, Cecil and Willis are grinning from ear to ear. "See here sheriff, we was tellin' y'all the truth all along about this here pack ah Yankees trespassin' on railroad property."

Without a word, the sheriff hands each of them a dollar. Cecil and Willis know when it's time not to push their luck. So, with an obsequious head nod, and a "Thank ya sir," they turn on their heels hightailing it for the liquor store before anybody changes their mind.

While the sheriff is busy handling the reward payout to Cecil and Willis, the railroad bull is getting identification information from the three perpetrators. Stopping dead in his tracks in front of Grace, the bull exclaims in a disturbing and antagonistic voice,

"Well I'll be go ta hell. Sheriff we got us a girl here!"

This turn of events gets the sheriff's immediate attention. He received a bulletin just this morning of a runaway girl in the company of a couple of Yankee boys. His attention turns immediately to Grace. He scrutinizes her as though she's a piece of livestock he's considering buying.

"What's yer name girlie?" asks the sheriff.

Grace's head is hanging on her chest out of a combination of fear, guilt, and shame. Without looking up, she mumbles in a weak, hardly audible voice, "Grace."

"Is yer daddy a preacher?" the sheriff continues with his face creating the same questioning look as his words.

Still not looking up, she replies in barely an audible whisper, "Yes."

Using a tone of voice that could intimidate the devil himself, he shouts, "Speak up girlie, I cain't hear ya!"

Grace begins to shake uncontrollably. She's hoping and praying this is all just part of the effects of the alcohol and it's just a bad dream that will go away. With her head beginning to clear, the acrid smell of male sweat emanating from her captors convinces her this is real. A strong sense of defeat overwhelms her. Grace knows she is on her way to hell and this is just the beginning of her eternal punishment for her egregious sins.

In a struggle to answer her captor's last question pertaining to her father, she begins to sob merely nodding her head in agreement with the sheriff's question about him being her daddy.

All her bravado about wanting to leave her parents and find her own way has all but evaporated. This is hardly the romantic ending she was expecting for her long-planned adventure. Now it seems it was all a lie designed by the devil to destroy her.

Being in handcuffs produces a feeling of having disgraced not only herself, but also her parents. The questions haunting her thoughts are unrelenting. *Why did you ever imagine this was a good idea? Why did you ever leave the security of home? You're no better than the drunken hussies you've seen at the mission all your life.*

Dace is beside himself with this tragic turn of events. He knows there's something wrong with this whole affair and there is something wrong with his part in it. His usual practice is to look for a scapegoat. Not this time. Acknowledging blame for failure and owning it is not easy. In this instance, he's torn between watching Grace have a meltdown resulting from her involvement with him and his selfish desire to have her regardless of the cost to anyone, including her.

Whitey feels ashamed for being so stupid as to be hornswoggled by those two losers. He is more embarrassed than fearful. *"I can't believe I let those two lowlifes work me the way they did. They must be laughin' all the way ta the liquor store."*

Raising his eyes to meet the other two, he can see the frustration they're both feeling. He feels a strong sense of responsibility for leading them into a trap he should have been smart enough to see coming. "Damn you, Cowboy. Where in hell are you?" he mutters under his breath.

Hearing him mutter, but not clearly enough to understand what he said, the bull takes offense whacking him yet again, "Cussin' me ain't gonna do ya no damned good so's ya might's well get used ta havin' somebody crack ya fer bein' a dickhead."

"I didn't cuss you, sir," says Whitey.

The bull cracked him alongside his head once again. "I din't hear nobody say they wanted ta hear yer whinin'. Keep yer damn mouth shut!"

The sheriff takes note of his cohort getting a little too rough with their subjects. Pulling him out of earshot, he says, "Axel, if these boys come in with broken bones 'at need six weeks ah healin' we ain't gonna get shit fer they worthless hides. If we 'specktin' ta make a profit on these Yankee boys, we gotta get them ta old man Woodcock heathy an' able ta sit up an' take nourishment, so go easy."

Taken somewhat back by the warning, Axel says, "Yer right, as usual, Gabe, but it's them sassy-mouthed Yankees I cain't stand."

The shared legacy of Sheriff Gable Beauregard and railroad Detective Axel Anderson dates back many years. They've been in cahoots along with nearly every other county lawman in taking "incentives" to keep Early Woodcock's enterprises supplied with labor. Of course, this is all done under the table, but when that many people occupy that many small chairs under the table, they create quite a vast network. What was once considered to be outside the pale of the law has become a normal way of life in these counties. Occasionally, a panel of concerned citizens will rail against these disgusting practices. Their voice is getting louder, but without teeth, it is still too weak to make a difference.

Satisfied they've tied up any remaining loose ends in bringing this detained trio to the county sheriff's office, Sheriff Beauregard gives Axel one last instruction, "Fill out the trespassin' charges and we'll get this show on the road."

Using her palms, Grace desperately wipes the tears from her cheeks. Her sobs have a gasping sound as though she's struggling for air. "I'm sorry, I'm sorry," she repeats over and over to no one in particular. Having been raised to believe every bad thing that happens to her is a consequence of her sins, she continues her penitence over and over. "I'm sorry, I'm sorry", she seeks absolution from anybody in hearing distance, but there's no one here to tell her she's forgiven. Somehow, at least for the present just letting her tears flow gives her some solace.

Dace's heart goes out to Grace. For all his previous strutting to impress her as a man of the world, his bravado has fallen into a failed, helpless ineptness producing unbearable guilt. "I can't even help myself. How can I help Grace?"

Initially shocked to the point of gloom, Whitey is beginning to pull himself together. For all that he's heard of southern justice, he's tried to rehearse for this moment in his dreams as well as in his waking thoughts, but dealing with reality is another thing. The overwhelming desire to just give up and see himself as a victim pulls at him like gravity sucking him down a hole. *"Don't give up Whitey, jes hang in there. Everything will work itself out sooner or later"*, he silently shouts over the dread of the unknown. He's struggling to see beyond the immediate future which by all accounts isn't going to be pleasant.

Remembering a prayer he learned from his grandmother as a small child, he struggles with recalling the words. By the time they reach the sheriff's office, he's pieced it together enough to make a stumbling attempt at communicating with God. *Hello, God. This is Whitey, your little screw up again. I'm askin' You to grant me the serenity to accept the things I cannot change, the courage to change the things I can, and the wisdom to know the difference.* He remembers there's more to this prayer, but he's hoping, at least for the moment, it's enough to get God's attention.

The trio remain cuffed and as common practice allows, they are methodically piled into the back seat of Sheriff Beauregard's 1956 DeSoto squad car. It's a large caged area with ample room for the three of them and maybe two more, if they're small.

Whitey and Dace have had their share of run-ins with the law, with everything from being a minor in possession of alcoholic beverages, to the trouble with Dace beating several people senseless—with this trouble still waiting for them back in Elbertport.

Grace on the other hand has never in her life had a brush with the law for anything. She has slumped into a quiet funk. Dace wishes he could just put his arm around her and draw her close. With their wrists handcuffed tightly behind their backs makes this movement impossible.

Within fifteen minutes, they are pulling around the rear of the sheriff's office. It is an imposing two-story, red, Romanesque-styled bastion of brick and mortar with concrete-arched windows built fifty years before. One portion houses the sheriff and his family.

Immediately to the east is a wing bearing the same architecture with the added distinction of featuring iron bars as window treatments. This area serves as the county jail. It's in this latter part where these three find themselves being driven into a garage with a huge door slamming closed behind them.

Here they are removed from the backseat and escorted into a waiting room. The furnishings are the austere type made from steel and concrete—easy to hose down. The walls may have held some variety of color at one time, but have long ago morphed into a dirty gray-black. There are rows of benches where greasy smudges from dirt-laden heads resting against the partitions have left their mark.

From here they are quickly processed and then separated with Whitey and Dace going one way and Grace another. Dace and Grace allow their sad eyes to meet one last time. Grace has a look of defeat and great sadness.

They both realize whatever may have been developing between them has come to a screeching halt and been replaced with the cold impact of defeat.

Whitey and Dace are led into a small room with a couple of chairs. They are still manacled and told to sit and not talk. At the end of the room is a high bench behind which a portly, sixty-something man is seated wearing a robe indicating he is a magistrate. They are brought forward individually. Within five minutes both boys are tried, found guilty of trespassing on railroad property, and sentenced to six months at hard labor, which translates to being sentenced to manual labor on one of Early Woodcock's farms.

They are next taken to another part of the building and told to strip. Their clothing is replaced with a set of black and white prison-striped uniforms. They're placed in a cell with several other inmates. It's located on an upper floor that's been transformed into a holding cage. The floors are wood planking with huge iron bolts holding the steel cage in place. The compartment is crowded with others who have found themselves with similar sentences. It's the kind of enclosure that can quickly foster claustrophobia.

What they didn't expect is the next person they see entering their cell, an hour later and wearing the same outfit, is none other than their brother and cousin, Vaughn. Even with him having a black eye and several other bruises, they are hardly able to contain themselves. Not wishing to draw any unnecessary attention to themselves, they try holding down their exhilaration.

Dace is nearly beside himself to be in the company of his older brother, even if it means meeting in this environment. Vaughn reacts in nearly the same way. The stark reality strikes home for all of them—they are completely out of their element. Individually, in their own way, each comes to understand they cannot trust anyone

213

else around them. Without any discussion, they quickly acquiesce to the common need to display a lower level of emotion.

Forcing himself to lower his voice, Dace is the first to speak, "How in the hell did you end up here?"

Vaughn manages a little grin. "I left Elbertport last week to come looking for you two assholes, before yer mothers die of worry," says Vaughn. "I got down this far like I always do, by siphonin' gas, 'til I got caught by some redneck takin' exception to havin' his tank drained. He beat the shit outta me, then called the sheriff. The rest is history. So wadda you guys have ta do ta have the luck ah me findin' ya so easy?"

They spend the next hour until lights out going over all the happenings they have each endured.

Morning comes early at 6:00 A.M. This is not a time for conversation as every person in the cell is waiting in line to use the only commode. Dace, Whitey, and Vaughn have little time to exchange anything other than pleasantries as they are quickly fed what is loosely referred to as breakfast and can better be described as *slumgullion*.

Next, they are manacled along with at least a dozen other men and led out to a waiting bus with the lettering on each side saying *WOODCOCK FARMS*. As soon as the prisoners are loaded, they are manacled to their seats. A large, burly man somewhere in his fifties, begins to address the busload. "My name is Mr. Flanerty. Y'all belong ta me from the time I pick y'all up at dawn 'til I bring y'all back at dark. If I tell ya ta stand on yer head an' whistle "Dixie" out yer ass, I'm 'spectin' ya ta do it with no questions asked. Iffen y'all cain't comply, we got the means ta convince ya otherwise. Any questions?" Without waiting for any response, he adds, "Good! Now we all understand each other."

It's a twenty-minute drive to their destination. A large sign announcing their arrival at *WOODCOCK FARMS* stands at the entrance. They are met by a formidable man, well-built and well-dressed with a neatly-trimmed, graying mustache, wearing a pair of special aviator sunglasses with golden rims and bows and a western-styled hat, and riding a large Thoroughbred. If this isn't enough to set this individual apart, he's holding a pump-action twelve-gauge shotgun across his saddle.

The prisoners are lined up single file and their manacles are released by men on the ground also wearing prison uniforms that say *TRUSTY* across the back. Once this is accomplished, the man on the horse begins to address them. "Welcome to Woodcock Farms. My name is Cap'n Willard Seagrave. I hope y'all understand this opportunity for y'all to work out your sentence here with us is a privilege. Y'all have freedoms ya ain't gonna experience sittin' in a little ole jail cell. If y'all wanna be treated like a human being out here, y'all better act like one. If any of you think otherwise, speak up now so we can fit y'all into one of our alternative programs, such as the one we'll demonstrate here in jest a minute." All of the prisoners maintain an uneasy silence.

With that said, the captain gives a nod of his head. Immediately a man is marched out by two trusties. He's taken across the lot to a barrel shaped wooden apparatus. He's subsequently bent over the barrel and his hands and feet are lashed to fixtures on opposite sides of this contrivance. Next his pants are pulled down around his ankles, exposing the bare cheeks of his behind. A large man, also wearing a trusty uniform, holding a huge belt some six inches wide and eighteen inches long is there waiting. At a signal from the captain, he commences to lash the tethered man—once, twice.... until he reaches twenty lashes.

When the sentence is concluded, the man's bindings are

released. The two trusties that had marched him out, straightaway commence to drag him back from whence they had come.

Whitey is the first to notice the peculiarities of this individual as he is marched by. There was something strikingly familiar about him as he was marched out earlier, but he couldn't put his finger on it until now. Even with this man's head hanging down, it's obvious to Whitey that this is none other than Sid!

Frantic inside and trying to remain poised on the outside so not to draw attention, Whitey catches a glimpse of Dace and Vaughn as they too are brought nearly face to face with Sid. What is even more alarming, is in spite of his injuries, Sid still manages to give all three of them a twisted sneer.

The group of prisoners stand stunned as they try and digest this archaic practice of public flogging. Our three Yankees, to say the least, are a bit more stupefied than the rest since the victim is undeniably one of their own. The black prisoners are also unprepared to have any Jim Crow tactics demonstrated on themselves as they prepare obediently for the next phase of their incarceration.

Taking full advantage of the shocking effect his demonstration has had on this new batch of fledglings, Captain Seagrave takes it to another level. "If yer wonderin' what kind of conflagration this here feller started ta get ah ass whoopin' like this, I'll tell ya. He stole another man's canteen of water. He got hiself twenty lashes fer that little bit a nonsense. Now I'm here ta tell ya if y'all thinks ya can steal, an' especially now after y'all seed what can happen, I'm more minded ta think maybe twenty lashes ain't enough. So's maybe thirty'll make ya think twice." Without another word, Seagrave turns his Thoroughbred around and rides off.

Nobody needs to warn them their troubles are only

beginning. They know they've been dealt a bad hand. It's a hand they can't win and can't quit. So far, there is no other choice than to play it out as best they can. To think about an escape now is foolhardy—it would get them at minimum twenty lashes. They don't have the slightest idea where they would go, even if they could escape.

But that doesn't mean some aren't keeping a wary eye open for any opportunity, providing it's a better than fifty-fifty chance of making a clean getaway.

As is the custom, everyone is given a quick aptitude test to determine where they can best be utilized. With that finished, it's time to give out their work detail for the day. Dace and Vaughn are left to clean out a calf barn. Manure has built up on the floor to the point the calves' heads are scraping on the already low rafters. Whitey, along with a few other prisoners, is transported to the cotton fields to hoe weeds.

The bittersweet thing about this experience for Whitey is how proficient he is at his hoeing assessment. The field boss has taken notice and lets him know he will be permanently assigned to his crew. His father has always had a big garden and hates weeds with a vengeance. It had always been Whitey's duty to eliminate every weed within sight or suffer his father's wrath. As much as he despised that work detail at home, at this point he would give nearly anything to be duty-bound to his family's garden plot, rather than to be a leased prisoner in the state of Arkansas.

With all the action of recent days, he hasn't had much time to think of home, but now he has nothing but time. Looking about at the group of strangers riding on the wagon along with him, he sees people he has very little to nothing in common with. It strikes him as strange how his mind, despite being a thousand miles away, can transport him back to Elbertport to share a kinship with all the people that mean the most to him.

He sees his mother more clearly than ever bustling about her duties, wearing an apron over her housedress. It's the kind of scene he had taken for granted, never giving it anything other than a casual notice. Now it has become a powerful image, capable of creating the most intense longing he has ever experienced. He hasn't told his mother he loved her since he was pubescent. Now he has no choice other than to merely say the words out loud with the hopes the wind will carry them to her.

Bringing Melody to mind in this environment is painful. It's only been a short time, though he feels he has been away from her for half his life. As part of the arrest protocol all his belongings were taken from him. Without her picture, he feels a disconnect as he strains to create a mental snapshot of her. Closing his eyes, he allows his thoughts to bring back images of everything he loves about her— the way her eyes met his when she tilted her head a certain way, the little sway in her walk as her hips moved beneath her dress, the fresh smell of her hot breath as she kissed him—and to place all this into a context of the tenderness she held for him. The enchantments these memories create are pleasures no one can remove, but they are also a reminder of where he is now. The latter is a source of great pain.

All too soon they arrive on the job site. Looking over the vast, treeless fields of cotton, Whitey only sees dryness. In the distance, there are any number of faceless human forms dressed in black and white striped uniforms carrying out robotic movements as they perform a single, repetitive task. He's distressed to the very bottom of his soul. This is the very lowest he has ever been. His thoughts are struggling against viewing himself as a victim in a corrupt legal system as he tries to take to heart his grandmother's prayer to *accept the things I cannot change*. "I'll get through this," he speaks out loud under his breath to reinforce a positive mind set.

To add to his feelings of disillusionment and abandonment, at the end of his wagon ride is a stark two story concrete building in the middle of this vast, treeless wasteland. It stands as a citadel to human misery.

This is Captain Seagrave's command center. His favorite Thoroughbred is being curried on the shady side of the building by another faceless man dressed in prison stripes.

After witnessing Sid's flogging, this display points up Seagrave's passionate regard for his steed and a seeming dispassionate disregard for his own kind.

This faceless currier suddenly turns, giving Whitey a better look. There can be no mistake. It's none other than Sid. As his tormenter, Seagrave has found yet one more way to humiliate this wayward young man, letting him know in no uncertain terms who his superior is.

At the same time, another inmate is cleaning and polishing an expensive pair of western-style boots. An overlooking window is filled with the form of an individual sipping a cup of something. Captain Seagrave is overseeing their efforts. He demands nothing less than unconditional surrender to his authority.

The last thing Whitey wants is to be noticed—to stand out for any reason. Seagrave, while taking another measured sip turns his attention to Whitey's momentary, but noticeable pause. *I just want to do my time and get out of here* is Whitey's only thought. With this, he takes an extra step to get in line with the others before he brings any more unnecessary attention his way.

A straw boss is giving strident orders while handing out hoes to each inmate. "My name is Gunther Meyer, y'all can call me

Gunner—that is as long as ya don't do nothin' ta piss me off—then yer gonna hafta call me Mr. Gunner. I ain't askin' y'all ta do anythin' I ain't done myself, so I don't expect no ass-draggin'. And it ain't no time ta be tryin' ta play a hand ya ain't been dealt," warns this no-nonsense man with a measure of simplicity.

Whitey takes his hoe with the assurance his prior training in his father's garden will stand him in good stead.

The work is hard and hot. Throughout the field, roving marshals armed with twelve-gauge pump-action shotguns loaded with buckshot keep a wary eye open for infractions. Toilet and water breaks are carefully monitored. So far no one in his group has been presumptive enough to stretch their luck. Each inmate is trying his best to do the job assigned and get all this hullaballoo behind him. Anyone who refuses the privilege to work may find themselves in solitary confinement or given a longer sentence.

Raised in a middle-class Yankee family with an immigrant father who still has one foot on the boat, Whitey soon exhibits a work ethic that is open and forthright.

At the end of the day, Whitey is exhausted, but has caught the attention of Gunner. "Ya done yersef proud taday boy. You keep that up an' you an' I ain't gonna have no problems. Ya gotta know I ain't no lawman. I work fer Mr. Woodcock an' we're always lookin' fer good, hard-workin' farmhands. When ya finish up yer time an' lookin' fer a job keep us in mind."

"Thank you, sir. I don't mind hard work, I been doin' it all my life," says Whitey, all the while knowing as soon as this sentence is finished, he will put as much distance between himself and his tormentors as possible.

Not wanting to appear presumptive, but with his curiosity getting the best of him, Whitey decides to take a chance. "Gunner would you mind tellin' me what the fella that got the floggin' this mornin' is in for?"

"You talkin' 'bout ole Silvon?" Gunner obligingly responds.

"Silvon? That's his name—Silvon?" returns Whitey, at the same time realizing he may not want to go any further with his prying. This is obviously a name Sid has managed to slip on himself.

"Who the hell knows what any ah you drifter's real names are. At least that's the name on his roster," replies Gunner with a knowing chuckle. "But fer yer other question, he's here fer the same damn charge you are—trespassin' on railroad propety."

With the day ending, they're soon all transported back to the county jail. The county provides them with meals taking the cost out of the small amount of compensation they're allowed for their labor. Usually at the end of their sentence and after all charges are paid, just enough money is left to assure the individual can buy a bus ticket out of the region.

The south has their own way of keeping cultural order—by segregating. This includes jails—Yankees with Yankees, Blacks with Blacks, Mexicans with Mexicans, etc. It's been said in these parts, "We ain't in the business ah changin' 'r way ah life ta fit the idea ah some pointy headed Yankee collage swot."

The two brothers and cousin are reunited in a cell together. In the privacy of their cell, Whitey is able pass on the small amount of information he has learned concerning Sid. Vaughn, in turn catches the other two up on the events with Sheriff Peleton back in Elbertport along with his suspicions surrounding the murders and connecting Sid. He also informs Dace that he hasn't killed anyone and Orin and his gang survived without much more than bad headaches for a few days.

Before the evening is over there is a sudden clanging on the cell door. It's the turnkey bringing another prisoner. "I done brought y'all another Yankee," with that pronouncement, he unshackles the prisoner, who if not the devil, is the devil's brother. It turns out to be none other than Sid. With his head deceptively bowed, he manages to carry on his peculiarity by bringing into play his quirky way of gazing up through his eyebrows at each of them. His head bobs and weaves like he's in some kind of prize fight, with his wild eyes turning one way and then another. Trying to get a good look at Sid is like trying to get a look at a contortionist going through his conjurations. It doesn't help that he has a head full of ragged, unkempt hair flopping around his face and he lopes like a skinny Quasimodo.

There is a definite moment of awkwardness as each tries to digest this crazy turn of events.

Vaughn is the first to speak. His mind is racing back to Sheriff Peleton's notes linking Sid to at least two murders. With a smirk, he confronts Sid, "Well if this don't beat all, the teacher and his student landin' in the same pokey a thousand miles from home. That gas siphonin' trick ya taught me got me inta this mess." When he doesn't get a reaction from Sid, he adds, "Wadda you here for?"

Sid is noticeably disturbed. Vaughn's question apparently has discomposed him more than usual. "A buncha bullshit!" is all he says, heading for the only vacant bunk left in the cell.

Puzzled, Dace and Whitey sit on the sidelines wondering where all this is going to take them.

CHAPTER 25

By 6:00 A.M. the next morning, the county jail is ablaze in lights. After a breakfast of coffee, grits, ham, and eggs, each inmate is given a sack lunch as they line up in front of their cells to receive their daily work orders.

The shift deputy carrying a well-used clipboard approaches the four Yankees. Looking first at his roster then at Dace, Whitey, and Vaughn, he states in a clear authoritative voice, "You yard birds are goin' out ta hoe cotton." Then looking to Sid, he says, "You goin' in the same direction as these three, but Cap'n got sompin' special in mind fer you, Yankee boy. You sposed ta report directly to him, hear?"

Sid doesn't look up, so the deputy places his nightstick under his chin and lifts before shouting directly into Sid's ear, "Didja hear me, boy?"

Obviously in discomfort, Sid twists his head away, cupping his ear with his hand, but still remaining defiantly silent. Even though these prisoners are the lowest security risk, they're still inmates and are reminded from time to time who's in charge—or in Sid's case—who isn't.

The four Yankees are loaded up in the same bus as yesterday and transported by Mr. Flanerty to the farm where they're met by the same wagon and retrace Whitey's path from yesterday. At the command center, Dace, Whitey, and Vaughn and are given hoes and assignments.

Sid is escorted by a shotgun toting guard into Captain Seagrave's cement bunker headquarters. Once inside, he's ordered to stand at attention and wait for Captain Seagrave to make an entrance.

In the meantime, outside, the two brothers and cousin along with other workers have been placed in a wagon prepared to transport them to their work location. With no notice, the door of Captain Seagrave's headquarters suddenly flies open. Sid Powell stands there, wearing Seagrave's aviator sunglasses and western hat, and holding a bloody screwdriver in his hand. Without a word, he throws all his booty into the tractor tool box. Then, with no warning, he lunges at the shocked tractor driver, sinks the bloody screwdriver into his throat, and dumps his still quivering body to the ground. With a flurry of movement, he slams the tractor in gear, throttles it wide open and with the wagon load of prisoners hanging on for dear life makes his way down a lane leading toward an open road.

It seems while waiting for the captain, Sid had spotted a forgotten Philips head screwdriver laying on a table. In a flash, he grabbed it and had its pointed shaft sunk deep into the chest of the unsuspecting guard. With no guard and no warning, the unwary Captain Seagrave entered the room only to meet the same fate.

The wagonload of prisoners is totally at the mercy of this maniac. Concluding it's much too dangerous to bail out without risk of serious injury, nevertheless, the fear of a wreck fills the thoughts of each of these terrified men left gripping anything offering them an anchor. All that's seen behind the wheel is the hunched back of Sid Powell. What each of these unfortunates is being forced to undergo is the madness of this maniacal killer.

With seemingly no thought for his own mortality, much less his human cargo, Sid powers the tractor down the gravel road with dust billowing up around a weaving wagon full of helpless captives.

Whitey, Dace, and Vaughn have much more insight into Sid's potential risk to all of them than do the rest of the stupefied passengers. He's a psychopathic killer, capable of the most unpredictable, untimely, and ultimately heinous crimes. His reckless disregard for the welfare, much less the lives, of this wagonload of passengers is indicative of his mindless sensibilities.

The eventual end game of this kind of erratic driving is soon met. The wagon flips over spilling a dozen flailing bodies along a hundred foot stretch of dirt road like so many bags of potatoes. Neither looking back nor slowing down, Sid continues to drag the remains of the crashed wagon down the road with an utter lack of concern for the fate of its spilled contents. Except for the cloud of dust completely obliterating the whole conveyance, it's soon out of sight, trailing splintered pieces of bedraggled wagon in its track.

The casualties slowly get to their feet—at least those who can. The rest remain in various stages of trauma. Two men are attending an unresponsive man with blood pouring out of his mouth. Others are holding their injured arms and legs.

Vaughn is one of the first on his feet. Other than a few minor scrapes, he is uninjured. Hurriedly finishing with his personal examination, he turns his attention to finding his brother and cousin.

Dace is moaning with what he hopes is only a bruised left arm. He barely remembers attempting to use it to break his forceful nose-dive to the road. Whitey is gasping on the ground with the wind knocked out of him.

Vaughn's mind is reeling at nearly Mach speed. Within a few minutes the reality of their situation has captured their complete attention. Vaughn has quickly surveyed their situation and what it can afford them. Looking to the other two for any opposition, he blurts out in no uncertain terms, "I think this here is our big chance ta make a run for it."

Dace looks at his brother as though he has lost his mind, "Are you nuts? They got dogs! They'll hunt us down and hang us by our balls."

Whitey is not surprised by Vaughn's proposition. He's more pragmatic about outcomes than Dace. It leads him to question how they can successfully pull this off wearing striped jail uniforms.

Vaughn has been hastily scanning the geography surrounding them. Pointing to an area off to the side, he answers, "You see that creek down there? There ain't a dog alive can follow a trail through flowing water. It's gotta lead to a river. We just gotta wade through that 'til we get outta this whole damn area."

Dace is still apprehensive. "I don't know, Vaughn. Sometimes you gotta way ah makin' bad situations worse."

Whitey is also looking the whole area over. "God knows how long it'll take for them ta figure out what become of their tractor an' their wagon load ah slaves. I agree, I say we make a break for it an' let the chips fall where they may. It ain't like we're felons an' their gonna spend a lot ah money an' time tryin' ta hunt us down. We can always say we was confused on what way led back to the farm. Besides, the only one they're gonna concentrate on gettin' back is Sid."

Vaughn begins to make his way around the scattered debris of farm tools and broken and confused inmates. He picks up bags of lunches and three hoes. "We may need all this. If we get caught with hoes, it'll reinforce our argument that we were just lookin' for our way back."

Whitey is also scouting around for any scattered canteens. Picking up several, he hands one to Dace. "You gonna just stand there, cuz, or you gonna join the getaway?"

By now Dace is left with no allies. Many of the other

prisoners that are physically able are already making their way off in every direction. Realizing he's pretty much in the minority, he reluctantly snatches a canteen saying, "Okay, okay, but if we get caught, don't say I didn't warn ya!"

With Vaughn in the lead, they begin their trek toward the creek. They soon discover it's neither wide nor deep. The best thing about this region is that it is farm country and sparsely inhabited. The banks along the creek have been allowed to grow wild, further increasing their chances of not being noticed. The further they travel, the odds of being detected are growing slim. Using their hoe handles as support enables them to more easily traverse the rocky bed of the knee-deep creek, permitting them a reasonable pace.

The hot afternoon drags on, it's well over eighty-five degrees. Having broken out in a sweat despite the cool water, they begin to relax and slow their pace. So far, it seems they have made a successful escape.

Stopping in an area affording sufficient shade and enough fallen trees to provide a ready seating arrangement, they break out a lunch. While Vaughn spends his time castigating his brother for being such a skeptic about everything, Whitey scouts the area for possibilities. In a couple minutes, he returns with the excitement of a carnival sideshow hawker. "Guess what I'm looking at boys?" Not waiting for an answer, he quickly continues, "Not more than three hundred feet from here is a clothesline with a ton of men's shirts and pants hangin' out ta dry."

In a moment, all the bickering between Vaughn and Dace has ceased as they both jump to their feet and follow Whitey's lead to the opposite edge of the creek bank. "Well, I'll be go ta hell, if that don't beat all. Just looket all them clothes," says a jubilant Vaughn. Of course, staring at them and coming up with a plan to wear them are two distinct logical stages.

Noticing the large size of the clothing, Dace makes a comment in a low negative tone. "None of them look like they're gonna fit any of us. That guy's gotta be a big fat ass."

Looking with a degree of scorn at his pessimistic brother, Vaughn answers with the same disdain, "Well, little brother, unless you can come up with a loom, we ain't gotta lotta choices now do we?"

Not willing to respond, Dace returns to his more recent custom of looking to Whitey on important matters. Not wanting to be in the middle of bickering brothers, Whitey tries to be a peacemaker. He suggests, "Dace you can have all the small stuff." Then considering the practicalities of their circumstances, he adds, "Maybe we should wait 'til dark before we take a chance of bein' seen."

It only takes Vaughn a moment to nix that plan. "We can't wait that long. If this here were our moms' wash, they'd have those clothes off an' in the house before any damp evening air spoiled the fresh smell. I think we gotta move while it's still too damned hot fer any ah these folks ta come outdoors."

Whitey and Dace know Vaughn has a valid point. They both concur they need to make a move soon. What they don't have a plan for is the habit of every southern farmer in this region to have a coonhound. This one is tied between them and the sought-after cache of clothing. All three continue to stare as the clothing continues waving in the breeze as if motioning them forward.

Wetting his finger and sticking it up to get a feel of the wind direction, Vaughn follows with, "That damn hound ain't smelt or spotted us yet. If he hadda, he'd be singin' his damn lungs out. We gotta figure a way ah gettin' past him."

Figuring it's time to get his two cents worth in, Whitey says, "I think we can get close enough to that bugger to sidetrack his attention with one of these lunches."

The brushy area they are hiding in extends almost to the dog's location. While the creek makes a loop with the result of enveloping the yard between the two locations like a peninsula. They begin to rehearse a plan with Whitey volunteering to crawl through the brush to where he can quickly get the dog's attention with a sandwich, while Vaughn positions himself across the yard behind the canine and makes a break for the clothesline.

Dace is assigned to lookout duty. He is more than happy not to be responsible for anything riskier than sounding an alarm, if needed.

The plan is quickly, but cautiously implemented. Whitey slowly belly-crawls through the brush like an army point man. He carries a sack with a promising delicacy this hound won't want to pass up—a Spam sandwich.

As expected, the hound is initially startled. Finding an interloper invading his turf, his first reaction is to stare and stick his nose in the air until he gets a good take. He next lets out a little suspicious snort followed by a full-fledged bay.

A gruff male voice from an open window on the other side of the lines of drying laundry shouts out, "Bubba! Shut da hell up!"

Whitey starts tearing the Spam sandwich in pieces and tossing them to his new friend. There is no question, Whitey is no longer an intruder and the hound's attention has been successfully diverted and refocused on the next awaited scrap.

There are four lines stretched between two support poles. Assessing the situation, Vaughn elects to untie each end of the closest line. In less time than it takes for Whitey to parcel out the last of the sandwich, Vaughn is bundling up a whole line of clothing. Carrying a whole line of semi-dry clothing is more challenging than he expected. Whitey realizes the problem and hurries to help.

Within a minute, both arrive unseen back at their creek bank hideaway. The overwhelming desire to celebrate their success transforms into a second thought not to push their luck. Opting to get out of here in a hurry, they all agree it's time to move out immediately.

Within another half hour, they have put some distance between themselves and their clothes theft. Whether or not they are safe enough to consider changing out of their jailhouse stripes, they decide to chance it.

Winnowing through the array of jeans and flannel shirts, each looks for any article of clothing that may halfway fit them. Holding a pair of overalls, Dace remarks, "I'm sure glad we didn't have to meet the guy who fits into these things."

"You ain't tellin' me nothin'," says Whitey holding out the waist of a pair jeans he has on, "You can dang near fit the two of you in here with me."

With that, Whitey measures out a length of clothesline and cuts it with the sharp edge of his hoe. He feeds the line through the belt loops, cinches it tight, and ties it to form a belt. "I knew this thing would come in handy for sompthin'," he declares tossing the hoe aside.

Throwing a shirt on, he leaves it untucked hoping to camouflage the bunched material around his waist. He follows this by rolling the pant legs up a couple turns. Looking at each of his companions, he muses, "This sure as hell ain't turnin' any of us inta a Sears and Roebuck fashion model, but hopefully it'll turn the cagey eye of any lawmen away from us."

Dace and Vaughn aren't faring much better. Looking himself over along with the other two, Dace concludes, "I wouldn't care if I hafta wear girl's clothes. I'm jes glad ta get outta them godawful stripes."

Vaughn is having the same experience, but opts to be more positive about it. He turns his collar up, slouches, and with a sneer he's seen on Elvis Presley, attempts to imitate the legendary singer by mimicking lines from a memorable song,

> *Well, since my baby left me,*
> *I found a new place to dwell*
> *It's down at the end of lonely street,*
> *It's called Heartbreak Hotel.*

It's enough comic relief to give a well needed breather from all the stress and tension—but not enough to divert their attention too far away from the urgency of their predicament.

Vaughn initiates a conversation about their future. "We gotta take a minute an' come up with an idea on how ta get outta this hellhole. I came down here lookin' for both yer sorry asses with the idea I ain't gonna face my ma and my aunt without you two with me. I can't go back an' get my car, so we gotta come up with another program."

"We got here by hoppin' freights, an' we can probably get outta here doin' the same," says Whitey.

"Yeah, well that idea is what got us in this predicament in the first place," shoots back Dace.

It's obvious he's still smarting from getting caught and not ready to revisit the whole experience again.

"We definitely gotta be smarter about how we go about it," says Whitey, remembering how those two old drunks had hustled him, resulting in all three of them landing in the hoosegow. "We gotta find some rail tracks first and then figure out what direction they're headin'. After that, we hafta find a way to catch out without runnin' into another pack ah bulls."

Vaughn has another idea. "I think we need ta get out of this godforsaken state. If we can make it into Louisiana, we stand a better chance of makin' it home."

To Dace, this sounds like it could be risky. As is his habit, he mulls over what perils these two strategists are planning. "Just how do you propose we do that?" he asks, his voice brimming with his usual negativity.

With a more strategic attitude, Vaughn continues, "A good ole boy back in the jail told me all these creeks and rivers make their way down into the Louisiana bayou, and they all dump into the Gulf of Mexico. If we can get to the end of this damn creek, I believe it will empty into a bigger waterway where we can maybe steal a canoe and make our way outta here."

This idea catches the attention of both Whitey and Dace, but as usual in differing ways.

Dace knows his brother well and has never trusted him to keep them out of trouble. "We get caught stealin', we ain't never gonna get outta this miserable pit. Besides, we don't have a clue where in the devil we are right now," laments Dace. A coloring of hopelessness is the only clear tone in his challenge.

Whitey, being a bit more pragmatic is willing to consider this option; but because of past experiences with Vaughn, he is unwilling to cede to an unquestioning surrender to his older cousin's leadership. "That's fine and dandy," he says, "but there ain't no sense in kissin' the devil good morning 'til we meet 'im. Let's keep our options open for anything else that cuts the risk an' still gets us the hell outta here."

Vaughn is only half listening. He assumes he's going to automatically drift back into his usual dominance over the younger boys and consequently he hears little of what his younger cousin is expressing.

His mind drifts off to his fixation with Sid. He hopes for little more than to prove Sheriff Peleton's theory of Sid's involvement in the murder of George Powell back in Elbertport. Bringing Sid to an accounting is becoming as much of an obsession with Vaughn as it had been with Sheriff Peleton.

They resolutely continue following the creek in the hopes of reaching a larger body of water. In their singlemindedness, they failed to pay attention to conditions around them, including the changing weather. The hot, still weather pattern from the morning hours has become considerably windier this afternoon. The dark ominous clouds just to the south are unquestionably brewing up a storm of some sort.

In less than a mile, their hope of finding the end of the creek reaches fruition. The creek empties into a river. It's a good-sized river—maybe a quarter mile wide. The wind has picked up from a breeze to a near gale creating white caps across the river's surface. The trees are whipping around like tortured souls. The clouds abruptly unleash a sudden torrent of water that nearly knocks them off their feet. The weather has no regard to the danger it is imposing on these three. They have no apparent protection against its increasing fury.

The heavy blasts of rain cut visibility drastically. Fifty feet in front of them they can barely discern the faint outline of something that resembles a building.

Without a word, they make their way toward it in the hopes it offers some shelter.

It turns out to be an antiquated, rained-soaked, unpainted boathouse. It's barely able to resist the hurly-burly of the storm. An opening that probably at one time had held a door is now just a gaping hole. Once inside, they quickly discover another danger. The old building is shivering as though this may be the last storm it will suffer.

The sight of something else grabs their attention. This structure houses the very escape apparatus these beat-up veterans of the road have been hoping to run across. It's not exactly the canoe they were hoping to commandeer, rather it's a small, flat-deck barge supported by two rows of four fifty-gallon barrels bobbing up and down with the swelling waves.

While Vaughn and Whitey are considering the strength of the storm compared to the strength of the raft, Dace is filling canteens from water pouring off the tin roof.

"If you're thinking what I think you're thinking, we need to talk about it," states Whitey, facing Vaughn head on. Especially with something as uncertain as this contraption, he's not willing to have a decision made without his input.

Without consultation, Vaughn boards the contraption and begins monkeying with the ropes securing it in place. He also takes notice of the latch holding the double doors keeping the craft inside.

"Yeah, maybe I am," says Vaughn. His mood is pensive. "I think we can take advantage of this storm, if we got the balls ta do it."

"Let's hear your plan," says Whitey, willing to contemplate

a reasonable strategy.

From his vantage point on the raft, and after his eyes have adjusted a little better to the darkness inside the building, he notices a group of tools hanging from hooks nailed to the side walls of the old shed. There is a variety of implements including a couple of long poles and a hatchet.

Vaughn hops off the bobbing raft with his eyes glued to these hanging implements. Pointing in their direction he says, "I think these poles are used to propel this slug through the water. If we get outta here while this storm is still blowin', we got a chance of not bein' seen."

Dace listens to his brother's proposal with his usual pessimistic ears. "How in all that's holy we gonna fight this wind? It'll blow us all ta kingdom come," he agonizes, imagining the difficulty.

Whitey is analyzing Vaughn's proposal and is measuring their potential for success. "The wind is shiftin' around in our favor, Dace. If we can get this thing outta here, we can let the storm blow us down river. Alls we gotta do is steer it," simplifies Whitey.

Vaughn has already laid the poles and hatchet on the deck and is opening the doors, a gust of wet wind slaps him in the face. A flash of lightening darts through the open doorway illuminating the entire inside, as an answering clap of thunder booms overhead.

"Come on, Dace. Grab a pole and help us get this rig outta here," shouts Whitey, over the howling wind.

As is normal with Dace, he quickly caves in and becomes part of the team. Within a few feet of leaving the safety of the shed, they find themselves facing the full brunt of the storm. They rapidly become slaves to the elements. Not only can they not see beyond a few feet, the river's currents and the wind are seemingly at war with one another, causing the raft to twist around in one direction then another.

The poles brought along to guide them are all but useless against these foes. All three have succumbed to the obvious—the storm is greater than themselves. They soon find themselves reduced to white knuckling it, hanging on to anything that holds the promise of keeping them on board.

Whitey is praying like he always does when he finds himself powerless, Vaughn is cussing, and Dace is fighting his fear with a panic attack. All three responses are a human reaction to impotence—one is positive, two are negative. An hour later Providence has its way, in spite of their reactions. They have been blown several miles downriver and meet clear, sunny skies.

CHAPTER 26

The temperatures are beginning to rise along with a stifling humidity that these folks in the Mississippi delta have endured nearly every day of their lives. The wind is still and the currents are willing to propel them with only an occasional correcting pole in the water keeping them on course.

"Do you guys think we've crossed the state line yet?" asks Dace.

"I don't have a clue, but I know we're headin' in the right direction ta have that happen sooner or later," answers Vaughn.

The day wears on with little evidence of the storm's fury except as a memory. Even their oversized clothing is beginning to dry with its tendency to sag around their lanky bodies making them look like living scarecrows.

As with all young, hunger is a driving factor. They have a few slugs of fresh water left in their canteens. But they are now without food, having lost to the storm the remainder of the lunches supplied by the county jail. Without even discussing it, they know they are all on the same page. Going a day or so without food isn't going to kill them, but none are anxious to test that assumption.

The afternoon is beginning to wane and Whitey is the first to point out a factor all three have been silently concerned with for hours. "We need to find a place ta get settled in for the night and we need food and water."

Vaughn is silent for a moment, then surmises, "I remember we had a full moon last night. I believe it's still gonna be there tonight. I say we take turns sleepin' while two keep us on course— besides we ain't got them damnable bugs out here."

Hunger and fatigue gnawing at the three of them flavors their thinking process, it's also becoming apparent they'll have to continue suffering some, if they're going to succeed in this undertaking. Surprisingly, Dace doesn't have a negative comment and is still willing to be a team player. Whitey also agrees to these new terms by readily volunteering to let one of the other two take the first rest period.

"I'm good for a few more hours, too," says Dace willing to join Whitey on the first leg of their all-nighter.

Vaughn is okay with this, agreeing to let these two take the first watch. For these three would be musketeers, life has calmed enough to be approaching the brink of boredom. It occurs to him that in times like this, the absence of turmoil may be just good enough. If it wasn't for the incessant gnawing in his empty stomach, it would actually be enjoyable.

In an effort to convince his base nature to deal with his hunger, Whitey recalls a time during Lent when he gave up desserts. In deference to this more noble avenue, he is attempting to present to his brain's hunger center that he is doing this out of a commitment to God in the hope the discomfort of it all will ease. To assure the deity he *wants* to do this, he begins to recite the *Our Father*. He has learned it in both English as well as from his father in German. He does not feel any immediate relief, but assures himself God will be pleased with how he is addressing his situation. Certain he's on the right path, he decides, much to the dismay of Dace, to also vocalize the liturgy along with his prayers. All in all, the diversion seems to be working—at least in the sense that it's taking his mind off his hunger.

The night waxes as does Vaughn's prediction of a full moon. The river is no longer the tumultuous up-swelling that hours before had driven their barge carrying them helplessly along. It is amazing to see this same water now, glittering in the moonlight like so many independent photoluminescences, as if all wired to an underwater grid rippling light across the surface. It's as though the river is voicing a peaceful truce, declaring all is right with the world—that is until there is a different blaze of light. It's a beacon of light behind a Brobdingnagian, a big dark shadow breaking the surface—at least at this time, it appears as a shadow. They quickly become aware that the shadow is moving. Not only is it moving, it's moving toward them.

Both Whitey and Dace respond in kind to the apparent disaster. "What the hell!?" is the singular response from both boys as they realize they are directly in the path of this looming, mysterious, and very ominous, shadowed form bearing down on them from behind. It has become evident this is a mammoth barge being pushed by a tugboat.

As much as they put their backs to the long poles, frantically sticking them into the river bottom, attempting to pry this Lilliputian raft out of the track, they realize the near futility of their efforts.

Adding to their panic, the tug lets out a deafening blast from its horn. It serves as notice to get out of the way or risk being overtaken, rammed, and sunk. A barge and tug cannot be maneuvered with any dexterity.

The two life reactions to danger usually incite one to fight or flight. Often preceding these is the moment of indecision that if not overcome creates a third reaction of freezing.

The blast awakens Vaughn just in time to assess what is about to happen. His adrenalin surges. "WE GOTTA JUMP NOW.!!!" he shouts. He's the first off the side of the raft, quickly followed by Whitey and Dace. They're swimming as hard as the can in the hopes of avoiding being run over by this river monster.

Ten seconds is all they had before the hollow, drum like resonance of the scow striking the small raft echoes across the water. Anyone accustomed to the sounds a barge like this makes as it strikes floating trees and logs would pay little attention to these noises. In this case, the tug boat had sounded its warning blast, indicating those aboard were aware of the small craft but unable to avoid a collision.

Responding to the emergency, the tug's props are immediately thrown into neutral. Still moving forward by momentum, the tug silently slips by the three boys bobbing helplessly alongside. Immediately, the tug's crew drops its anchors in a frantic attempt to prevent any further drifting.

A blinding spotlight illuminates the whole area. It's obvious some type of recovery operation is being initiated as the frenetic sound of men's voices echo across the water. They've only been in the water a few minutes when a small motorized craft is launched and making its way toward them. Soon the rescue crew is plucking the boys out of what could have been their watery graves.

Once on board, they're each given a blanket and hustled into the warm engine room to recover with a bowl of hot beef soup, coffee, and cigarettes. Each catches the attention of the others with the same thought, *We couldn't have had better luck.* Safe, warm, and well fed, the sonorous sound of the tug's powerful diesel engine soon induces enough drowsiness to put them to sleep.

The best part is they're back underway, pressing on downstream at a rate they doubtlessly couldn't have achieved with their cumbersome raft even if they had been Olympians.

They awaken in the morning to the clangorous symphony of various metals scraping and banging as they clash against one another with the punishing sounds that accompany docking the barge.

With a few questions directed to the crew, they quickly learn they have indeed crossed the border and are now guests of the state of Louisiana.

Having concocted a story among themselves of losing their identification in the tragedy, they give false names while assisting the captain in making out his accident report. At this point, the captain offers to give each of them twenty dollars if they sign off relinquishing any further compensation. Barely able to believe the turn of good fortune graciously blessing them, each signs their a.k.a. in return for the money. They thank the captain and crew for their benevolence and make their way to shore.

They encounter a typical small southern town. It's just after daylight and the town is beginning to awaken. Milk trucks with their distinctive rattle and clanging are making their rounds throughout the neighborhood. Bakeries in the downtown area are loading their delivery vans to begin their business day. The grocery, drug, and dry good store owners are rolling out their store's awnings. All this in normal preparations to meet the daily needs and wants of their community.

The money they have in their pockets adds to their sense of contentment. They are beginning to once again feel some of the lightheartedness they took for granted as young men back in Elbertport. Finding a table in a local beanery, the boys are soon enjoying a southern breakfast of ham, eggs, and grits.

Not wanting to burst their bubble, Vaughn waits as long as he can before he brings up the subject of Sid. "I don't believe for a minute with what you've told me, and what Sheriff Peleton suspected, and what I've seen with my own eyes that Sid is anything less than a psychopathic killer. I believe that he knows that we know that he's guilty as hell." Pausing in thought for a moment, he continues, "I know him well enough, an' for that reason, I don't think he's done with the likes of any of us yet."

Dace is listening intently to his older brother. He recalls how Sid used to scare him by telling him that he had killed at least a dozen cats and dogs. "So, don't piss me off or I'll kill *yer* dog, too," he would add.

Whitey is also paying attention to Vaughn's concerns, but his mind is elsewhere. He's had just about all he wants of this vagabond life. Since they've been pretty much assured by Vaughn that Dace is off the hook for what happened to Orin and his buddies back in Elbertport, he feels it's time to return. Careful not to come across as wimpy and homesick, he carefully measures his words and tone, "I think we oughta be thinkin' about how were gonna get back home."

This thought hits a nerve with Dace. "Yeah, Vaughn. What say we figure a plan to make our way outta here before we get in any more trouble and make it even harder? We got us some money. We can get us bus tickets an' be home in a couple days."

Vaughn thinks about it for a moment. "Problem with that little brother is we ain't got but half the money we need ta get those tickets. Then those tickets are gonna take us right back inta Arkansas, where they'll be more than willin' ta give us a new home an' God only knows fer how long." Thinking about what he just said, he makes one more point, "Nah, I ain't willin' ta make that mistake again."

"Well just what the heck is your bullshit plan then?" shoots back Dace with a distinct sarcastic tone.

Vaughn uncharacteristically remains patient with his brother's obvious hostility. "I'm thinkin' we spend a little time lookin' around for some work an' put together enough dough ta get us some train tickets."

Since neither Whitey nor Dace have a better alternative, they agree they need to rid themselves of the stolen, oversized clothes and purchase some that look more presentable.

After finding what they need in a secondhand store, they decide to split up, scour the town for some sort of employment, and meet back at the beanery later in the afternoon.

Whitey has assigned himself to scrutinize the southern part of town, mainly a residential area, in hopes for lawn or garden work. Dace is taking the downtown business district, and Vaughn is looking into a couple of small industrial sites on the northern edge of town.

This small southern settlement is a typical close knit community. As usual, they're always aware of strangers and concerned with their purpose in being there. Walking through the neighborhoods, Whitey becomes aware of people peeking through their curtains, keeping a wary eye on this young stranger.

He has stopped at a couple different residences that appeared to need some repair work, but with suspicious eyes, they turned him away. Feeling a haunting despair beginning to work its way into his spirit, he turns down yet another street in hopes things will change.

While saying a silent prayer for a little divine intervention, he spots a crew paving a driveway. This fits his idea of a good paying job. Calculating his chances of getting on this crew, he picks up his step. There are three men, two younger and one middle-aged. They're all busy with the task at hand. One of the younger men in particular catches Whitey's attention—he's wearing a western-style hat and aviator sunglasses. With both hands on the end of a large broom, he's spreading the tar-like sealer across this asphalt driveway.

Suddenly the melancholy rushes out of Whitey, as if he'd just won a big cash prize. "Is that you Cowboy?" he cries out.

Looking up with a surprised expression, the young man stops his work as if he'd been struck with paralysis. "Well I'll be go ta hell, if it ain't ole Whitey."

Surprised beyond expression, both stand staring with a momentary loss for words.

"How the heck...." They both exclaim, talking over the top of the other.

Cowboy yields with a gesture toward Whitey to talk first.

With a look that can only be described as searching, Whitey begins his inquiry. "How the heck did you end up here?"

"My mother's cousins live down this way—they're Travellers."

"Yeah, who ain't nowadays?" says Whitey.

Cowboy's signature grin breaks across his face, "No, I mean they're Irish Travellers."

"Yah mean like Gypsies?" enquires Whitey with a curious grin of his own.

"Yeah, somethin' like that," returns Cowboy.

"My ma used to threaten to sell us kids to the Gypsies if we didn't behave—they still doin' that?" asks Whitey.

"Naw, we're more inta sellin' stuff than buyin', besides she wouldna got much for yer sorry ass," rejoins Cowboy with the same assuring smirk. "But I'm askin' you, the same question. How the heck did you end up here?"

"It's a long story and it ain't pretty," says Whitey.

"Lemme finish out this part of my job an' I'll take a lunch break. You can tell me all about it."

With that section of the driveway broomed smooth, Cowboy meets Whitey under a big sycamore tree in the front yard. "So, let's hear about how you guys managed ta screw yerselves up without my help," begins Cowboy.

He listens with interest about how they got arrested, and met up with Dace's brother. As Whitey continues, Cowboy's interest becomes a more serious concern for all the details, especially when it comes to Sid.

"So, did ya see him kill that cop?" asks Cowboy, referring to Captain Seagrave.

"No, but it was pretty obvious he'd done somethin'. Especially when he come out with a bloody screwdriver in his hand and then attacked our wagon driver. For all I know he's dead too."

Cowboy listens to every word with studied thought. It's as though he's vicariously living the experience through Whitey. Then, in a strange way, his demeanor abruptly changes from serious to frivolous. Once again Cowboy manages to lighten the conversation, shifting mental gears as though he has resolved some serious thought. "Sounds like you girls missed me," he says with a little laugh.

As strange as Cowboy's behavior seems, Whitey welcomes the more frivolous Cowboy. "Well we managed to get by...so where did you go that morning we left the mission?" asks Whitey with a serious tone of his own.

Cowboy returns to his previous thoughtful pose. This is one of the few times Whitey has seen him this apprehensive. It appears as though, Cowboy saw the circumstances that morning as a life or death situation for himself. "The bulls was thicker than flies that morning. I seen 'em grabbin' 'bos left an' right. I managed ta get inta a boxcar 'for they spotted me. 'For I knowed what was happenin' that damn train cleared outta there with just me in it...sorry 'bout leavin' you and Dace. I decided ta hop off in this place. I'll be hanged if I didn't run inta a whole slew ah my cousins workin' through this area."

Whitey's intently listening to Cowboy with one side of his mind. There is something about Cowboy's explanation that isn't sitting straight, but since he can't quite put his finger on what it may be, the other side of his brain is working on something simpler—a plan to ask him about getting some work.

"Like I was tellin' ya earlier, Dace an' me run into Dace's

brother at that godforsaken work farm. So, the three of us need some work ta get enough dough ta get us back ta Michigan. What's the chances of the three of us joinin' up with yer crew long enough ta make that happen?"

Cowboy's first response to this question is not to move, staring off in the distance as if weighing something else on his mind. Then just as always, in the end, he moves once again from pensive to a reassuring lightness. "Lemme talk to my cousin. He's the boss, but I'm willin' ta bet he's gonna welcome some cheap help."

With a mixture of hopefulness and powerlessness, Whitey watches Cowboy as he begins to entreat the older man. This forty-something man is undoubtedly Irish in appearance. He possesses a head of reddish-blond, graying hair and a ruddy complexion. He moves with the assurance of a man who knows his work.

It doesn't take long before Cowboy is back. His grin tells the whole story. "You got it! My cousin says he's got a roofin' job he needs stripped ah shingles. You and your girlfriends up fer that?" Not waiting for Whitey's reply, he continues, "Not only that, but as part of yer pay we'll put ya up, room and board."

With a deep sigh of relief, Whitey welcomes the news. "Tell me what we gotta do next."

"We gotta few hours left on this job. In the meantime, you round up the rest of yer crew an' meet us back here at quitin' time."

With no fanfare, Whitey makes his way back to the beanery in time to find the other two. Their long faces tell the whole story. They hadn't had any luck at all. Hardly able to contain his good fortune, Whitey begins to relate all that happened since they separated earlier.

Vaughn is listening intently, even to the point of interrupting

Whitey. "From what you told me earlier about this Cowboy guy, he and Sid are tight. Did he say anything about seeing Sid?"

Considering this as an irrelevant diversion to all his good news, Whitey hesitates before answering. He's not quite certain why Vaughn considers this more important than hearing about work. "No, he didn't." But then as if he had a new revelation, he adds, "Come to think of it, he did have a worried look though, when the subject of Sid came up."

Dace, on the other hand readily accepts the good news about the job and the offer for room and board. It's not that he considers news of Sid as unimportant, but as he says, "Sure as hell beats canned tuna and sleepin' under some bridge."

Vaughn decides to join his brother and cousin in their elation over the seeming answer to prayer. The outcome of Whitey's search for work is just as delightful to Vaughn as to Whitey and Dace, but for different reasons.

To his brother and cousin, Vaughn has always been different, but now he's different in a brand-new way. His fixation with Sid is using more time than Whitey or Dace want to spend. Unfortunately, Vaughn lost Peleton's notes when he was arrested in Arkansas. Nonetheless, he had already poured over them enough to know the details by heart. Now to get to the point at hand, he knows how important Sheriff Peleton had regarded this investigation. With strong circumstantial evidence of Sid's role in the murder of his own father, Vaughn is beginning to see an opportunity to play a significant role in solving it without Peleton. "I'm gonna prove to everybody I'm not just some gas siphonin' derelict."

To drive his interest in this case a bit further, Vaughn looks forward to his meeting with Cowboy. He senses there is more to Cowboy and Sid's relationship than anyone has been aware of. After all, these are two very dissimilar people. In spite of their totally differing outlooks on life, they have clearly attached themselves to one another in a weird sort of an alliance.

He's trying to remember who Sid hung around with. Sid couldn't make friends among his age group though he was able to impress a younger age group with his bluster. Sid is several years older than Vaughn and it's been nearly a half dozen years since he hung around him.

He pushes his cousin and brother to tell what they have observed, being careful not to leave details to chance. The result is less than satisfactory for this budding sleuth. He is very aware he is going to have to pursue much of his investigation without their aid.

CHAPTER 27

At five o'clock in the afternoon, the three refugees meet with their new employer. Cowboy makes the introductions on his side and Whitey on his.

For now, Vaughn continues to size up Cowboy, taking note of anything out of the ordinary. Something he notices immediately is that the unique sunglasses and western-style hat Cowboy is wearing have a familiar look—he's just not able to put his finger on it for the moment. He locks it into a recess of his mind in hopes of drawing on it later.

The older man among the Travellers is named Billy McQewen. He's smooth talking, likable and able to get a person's confidence without a lot of effort. He spends little time basking in the introduction, rather he gets right to the point of what he wants done.

"Any of you boys ever done roof work?"

The three of them spend the next few seconds looking at one another as though one of them will come up with an answer.

Billy doesn't wait for a reply, the perplexed looks on each of their faces tells the tale. Already knowing the answer, he piles them into the bed of his pickup and drives them across town to a jobsite. Watching for any negative reaction, he says, "This is where you'll start earnin' yer pay tamarra' mornin'. Got any questions?" Not waiting for a reply, he announces with an assured air of finality, "Good!"

Still seated in the truck bed, the three of them stare at this roof as though it had just landed there from some alien world. Leaving them to mull over their assignment, Billy gets back in the cab and drives them to yet another unknown location. Still not sure where all of this is going to land, they hang on for the ride.

Billy turns down a tree-lined, two track leading into an open field. There they confront a caravan of a dozen vehicles—they are more than trailers—they're fancy wagons with ornate colors and scrolling with cut glass windows. They're obviously meant to be lived in. This is a community of *Irish Travellers* a name they prefer to the that of *Gypsies*. It's made up of family names the likes of McQewen, Murphy, and Gallagher.

Cowboy has laid claim to the McQewen clan through a connection with his deceased mother. It seems she disappeared years ago. A few years back her family received word her body had been found. She had possibly been murdered. Cowboy claims he barely knew his father and that his mother had raised him until she disappeared when he was in the seventh grade. Since then he has been on his own, traveling all over the country.

Billy brings his pickup to a stop in front of one of these

caravan trailers. It is a horse-drawn wagon and is highly decorated in bright, bold reds, greens, and blues. There is an outdoor campfire where several men are beginning to gather, smoking cigarettes and holding large glasses of beer. They're coming in from various jobs they've found from barn painting and tarmacking, to roofing.

The children have segregated themselves in their activities: girls with girls and boys with boys. The boys, being much more animated, have begun to fight among themselves. Fists are flying as well as ill-spoken words meant to denigrate their opponent. One of the boys in the middle of this ruckus is Billy's twelve-year-old son, Donny. Making his way to the center of the commotion, Billy grabs the two boys and lets loose with a torrent of cuss words of his own.

"You boys wanna donnybrook...that's good...only you both know the rules...it's gonna be a fair fight...do ya understand?" says Billy still hanging on to the collars of each of them, preventing further unsanctioned fighting between them.

The conflict began when Donny McQewen's maleness was held in contempt, diminished by his cousin, Kevin Gallagher, calling him Kate instead of Donny in front of the others. When a boy comes of age in this clan, he is encouraged by family members to seek reprisal for any kind of disrespect from anyone. Since honor plays a large role in the Traveller community, fist fighting is an accepted way of solving disputes—it's both quick and concise.

The action has also drawn a crowd with divided allegiances. Members within each family loudly back their kinsman. All family members support this system of retribution. When the call comes to take part in violence it's hard to step aside as a non-participant.

Another adult male has made his way to the increasingly noisy gathering with a couple pairs of boxing gloves. As it goes with many of these disputes, it requires an outside, disinterested adult to set the ground rules for the scrap. The referee in this case is an uncle of both boys. Gauntleted and made aware of the rules, in minutes the two twelve-year-old contenders are facing off against each other.

Shouts from the father of each boy abound, along with everyone else in the crowd. "Keep yer hands up...don't lead with yer head...jab! jab! jab!"

Both these young fighters are coming of age and know they can only leave this arena either as a winner or totally beaten and physically unable to fight. Protecting the family pride is reason enough to never give up.

The concept behind this approach settles each dispute as a single situation, so it doesn't linger and raise resentments that explode into a larger aggressiveness later. Considering they hold to the concept of protecting family honor, this kind of exercise insures that when a family member needs assistance it will be available with everyone of one mind.

The youthfulness, the determination, and the skill of both of these young pugilists holds the promise this contest is going to go on for quite a while. Forty minutes pass with the fight first going one way and then another. Finally, with one fighter so arm-weary he can't protect himself any longer, the referee ends the fight. With a noble grin forming around swollen eyes, Donny McQewen allows the referee to raise his arm, declaring him the winner.

Both boys have reddened skin promising to hurt much worse tomorrow than at the moment.

They manage to shake hands confirming a satisfactory resolution has been met, and despite only one declared winner, they both leave knowing neither has dishonored their family.

Billy couldn't be prouder. "Ya done good, Donny, me boy. Ya held yer own like a McQewen."

Not to be left out of this celebration, Margret McQewen, wife and mother to this family, besides sponging the blood, sweat, and dirt off her "Donny boy," has laid a good-size cut of beef aside for his supper.

Vaughn, Whitey and Dace are invited to share a meal with the McQewen's. Afterwards, they enjoy a beer or two, smoke a few cigarettes along with everyone else and soon find themselves assigned for the rest of the night to a tent outside the McQewen wagon.

Within a couple hours, the couple beers consumed have worked from their stomach down to their bladder. All three find themselves waking at the same time with the urgent need to relieve themselves. Quietly making their way out of their tent and across the way to the designated outhouse, they hear voices.

Considering it unusual to hear conversation at this early morning hour, they soon discover it's coming from the small wagon that has been assigned as sleeping quarters for Cowboy. They stop to investigate. They quickly recognize one voice belonging to Cowboy the other is unrecognizable at first, suddenly they realize it's the voice of none other than Sid Powell!

In the unquestionably argumentative conversation, Sid's voice is dominant. "I was all set to take those two lunkheads out while we was back on that work farm till that moron, Vaughn, showed up."

Vaughn becomes more attentive when hears his name mentioned. Immediately the three eavesdroppers are all ears.

"Just take it easy Sid. There ain't no sense in gettin' all het up over this. These boys ain't no threat ta you no how. They ain't seen enough ta make a tinker's damn." This voice is clearly that of Cowboy.

It's clear to Whitey, Cowboy is referring to him witnessing Sid kill the railroad bull a couple weeks ago. To hear a conversation pertaining to one's own demise is, to say the very least, a very disturbing experience. Notwithstanding the apparent danger, and in an effort to hear every word, they take a bit more daring initiative by quietly moving in closer to the wagon.

"You can bet yer sweet ass I ain't gonna stand by an' take that chance. Gimme the right time when the circumstances favor a good killin', I'm gonna make damn sure there ain't even the chance they gonna tell anybody anythin'," says the voice belonging to Sid.

"Sid, you gotta quit all this killin'. It ain't right," pleads the voice belonging to Cowboy.

"If I didn't need you, I'da had yer sorry ass a long time ago. You ain't nothin' but a whiny punk," says Sid noticeably irritated.

"You'd kill me like you killed my ma wouldn't ya Sid—*just like ya did her*, wouldn't ya?" Even through the walls, the bitter tone of Cowboy's voice is apparent.

"She had it comin', ya can't say she didn't—runnin' off with 'at sales guy the way she did," Sid's voice is clearly retaliatory.

Their original mission to the outhouse is abruptly aborted. Making their way back to their tent as unobtrusively as possible, they try desperately to keep their voices from reflecting the new fear gripping them.

Whitey is the first to speak. "We can't hang around here any longer. This guy's a real psycho. I've seen with my own eyes what he's capable of doing.

I can't live my life watching every shadow and looking behind every bush for Sid."

Dace is right behind his cousin in full agreement, "I'm with ya, cuz. We need ta get in the wind while we still can."

Vaughn is quiet, but not inactive. He too recognizes the imminent danger lurking outside their tent—a mere fifty feet away. Along with the other two, he is quickly gathering up his stuff, his mind is spinning. "We've gotta have a plan, but for now, you're both right, we gotta get outta here."

As quietly as they can, they begin to make their way back out of the clearing, through the tree-lined entrance, and out onto the same road they had entered ten hours before. By the time, they reach the edge of town, the crack of dawn is announcing itself across the eastern skyline.

Sid has put them in the right frame of mind and the trek provides plenty of time to throw out ideas and come up with a plan.

"We need to get back to Elbertport," says Dace. "I'll take whatever punishment they have waitin' for me. I can't hardly handle this crap with Sid any longer."

"I'm with ya on this one, Dace, besides I'm the one he wants ta kill," bemoans Whitey.

Vaughn, by his silence, appears thoughtful and contemplative. It's been obvious all along he has a special interest in this whole affair. "You're both right. We need ta get back ta where we're on ah even playin' field. We got enough money ta get bus tickets to somewhere further north, then we'll have ta figure somethin' else."

Relieved they have a plan and are all in agreement, they make their way to the beanery for a bite to eat. Having quickly finished with this, the next step on their agenda is to get to the bus station. It's only a couple blocks away and takes less than five minutes to get there. It's a typical, small town station with a ticket window, a couple rows of chrome plated armchairs with maroon-colored seat cushions, and a sign pointing to colored and white drinking fountains.

The place is deserted except for one lone person sitting in a corner seat. The three of them stop dead in their tracks on discovering this lone person is Cowboy. Simultaneously, the same thought shoots through all three of their minds, *CRAP!*

"What the Sam Hill are you doin' here?" asks a nervous Dace. He, along with the other two, is staring at Cowboy as if he had employed some unholy agency in transporting himself here.

"I saw you boys leavin' early this mornin'. I figured ya probably heard Sid rantin' and it scared ya off," says Cowboy. His voice is colored with an apologetic tone. "I fear as much fer my life as you do. I believe he'd jes as soon take me out, same way he did my ma."

"We did hear you arguing. When my seein' him kill that bull came up in his talkin', I knew right then an' there, I had ta get in the wind. I don't know why ya keep hangin' with that crazy psycho," questions Whitey.

"I figure if I stay close enough, I'll know what he's up to. And I keep thinkin' and hopin' maybe he's gonna change. He is my cousin ya know," says Cowboy. It's as close to an apology as he's going to get.

Vaughn is having his own revelations about this relationship and Cowboy's involvement in it. "Where'd you get that hat and sunglasses yer wearin'?"

"Sid give 'em to me when he caught up with me and the caravan. His mother was also part of the Gallagher clan," replies Cowboy.

"Did he tell you where he came up with them?" further questions Vaughn.

"No, he just said they weren't his style and I needed them worse than he did."

Vaughn is staring directly at Cowboy when he makes his next assertion. "Since he didn't tell ya where he got 'em, I'll tell ya for him. He took them off a dead prison guard named Captain Seagrave, after he murdered him on a prison work farm back in Arkansas. We was there when it happened."

"That don't surprise me fer a minute. Whitey already told me some of this but he didn't mention the hat and glasses. Didja see him do it?" asks Cowboy, in a matter of fact tone.

"Nobody saw him do it or they would be dead along with the captain. But I gotta believe the guard driving our wagon probably didn't fare much better neither, especially after yer cousin stuck a screwdriver inta the poor bastard's neck. We all saw that one," further reports Vaughn. "He hit the ground like he'd been poleaxed."

Cowboy is attentive to all that's being said. Finally formulating an answer, he says, "Well that explains Sid's obsession with all you guys. He's sure you seen enough to put him away for a long, long time. He didn't come right out and say what he'd done, but I know how he thinks. If he's on the trail of you boys like I think he is, he's got his reasons, an' he ain't gonna be satisfied 'til we're all dead, an' that includes me."

Dace is pale as ghost. This is not the kind of talk he does well with. "What the hell we gonna do? This psycho shows up every place we go. He must have the devil controlling his every move. We sure as hell can't fight that."

Seeing Dace begin to fall apart, Cowboy is ready with his plan. "We all gotta stick together. We can't fight him alone, he's too damn hellish. I told you boys weeks ago, I can protect you from him, but lately he's become a lot worse. Right now, I'm the only one who can keep him at arm's length and I don't know how long even I can do that."

Vaughn is quietly contemplating all that's being said and the odd relationship between Sid and Cowboy. *I'm sure the key in this case lies somewhere between these two.*

With his mind far from forming any kind of definite conclusions, Vaughn struggles to remain open-minded. "Okay, Mr. Cowboy yer on. I hope you know what all of us are in for if ya fail. So, what master plan you got goin'?" is Vaughn's immediate comeback. It has the definite tone of a sarcastic challenge rather than a simple inquiry.

On the other hand, he also entertains hope. *Suppose I'm wrong about this guy. Suppose he really does have a way of getting us safely back to Elbertport.* This sentiment remains a persistent thought that is competing with his unsettled side.

"It's damn certain we can't go back through Arkansas—it's way too risky especially with what's waiting for you boys there. With what money, we have left, I suggest we take a bus inta Texas and figure how we can start hoppin' freights back ta Michigan," Cowboy offers.

Whitey signals a silent time out by lighting a cigarette. Taking a long drag and filling his lungs, he then passes it to Dace, who does the same and passes it to Vaughn.

Cowboy is the last to share. Inhaling deep, he finally exhales along with the words, "So what's it gonna be?"

Whitey is quiet as he appears to be waiting for some kind of divine intervention. Dace is also fidgeting, trying not to make it obvious, he continues to look to Vaughn for a sign.

Finally, without looking to anyone, Vaughn barks out, "I don't see any hooks in anyone's ass. Let's make it happen!"

Since Vaughn's encounter with Sheriff Peleton, he has assumed a completely different persona from his former days of dissipation. In this instance, he is going along with anything Cowboy comes up with, but keeping a wary eye out. Pooling what little monies each of them have left, they purchase bus tickets to Beaumont, Texas.

CHAPTER 28

The bus trip itself is uneventful. It serves as a respite from their usual mode of transportation which always requires a watchful eye for an overzealous bull. The comfort of the seats, and the warmth of the sun through the windows soon has them enjoying a restful nap; something that has eluded them for some time.

Several hours later they awaken to find themselves in Beaumont, Texas, and once more in the dubious circumstance of unwittingly wandering the streets in a strange municipality. Not sure of this community's attitude toward nomads, they try and move as though they have a predetermined destination. In a sense, they do have a destination—the railyards—it's just that they're not sure of the location. To give the impression they know what they are doing while doing something else has its challenges. Once they find the district, the next challenge is to discover the whereabouts of the bulls and how active they may be. This must be done inconspicuously and takes a person capable of lying convincingly. As the most experienced, this task falls upon Cowboy, but not before they find a way to satisfy their growing hunger.

Of course, he has a plan to fix this problem, too. They're in a neighborhood that has several different types of retail outlets. One of these is a corner store with the name *Byerly's*.

It's typical of a family owned dry-good facility with groceries on one side and a mixture of hardware, clothing, and appliances on the other.

On the corner of the next block, Cowboy leads them to a grouping of wooden benches clustered under a shade tree. Motioning them to sit down, he speaks with a self-assured tone to his voice, "You boys know we are facing a situation which is growing more dire by the hour. I believe, in order to meet these extraordinary emergencies, we're goin' ta have ta set aside typical ways of dealing with these conditions. Do you agree?"

"Depends on what ya mean by *typical*," says Dace.

"I mean we may have to cross a line in the law, an' do what we have ta do ta stay alive and healthy," says Cowboy.

"Ya mean like stealin'?" asks Whitey.

"Since ya put that way, I guess that's what I mean," replies Cowboy.

"Ya mean like holdin' somebody up and stealin' their dough?" asks Dace. It's obvious he's not comfortable with this scenario.

"No, I'm sure we don't have ta go that far. I mean I got another plan that's easier and guaranteed ta work without gettin' anybody hurt," declares Cowboy in a hushed tone as though he could be overheard.

Over the next fifteen minutes, Cowboy introduces his game plan. It's a trick he learned while with the Travellers. Normally Travellers aren't willing to share their gimmicks with outsiders, but Cowboy considers these three as kindred spirits and is willing to break with tradition.

It's a quickly laid plan. Coming to an agreement as to how and who will fulfill each role, they take a few minutes to rehearse.

With the simple plan clear their minds, they get down to business. They have chosen to target the Byerly store.

Cowboy and Vaughn enter the store first. After a few minutes for them to get in position, Dace and Whitey enter the store as normal shoppers. Taking notice of the area where Cowboy and Vaughn have placed themselves, they gradually make their way to the opposite side of the store. On cue, Dace falls to the floor as though he is undergoing an epileptic seizure.

He mimics a scene he recalls of a time when a classmate, who suffered with epilepsy, would go into a grand mal seizure.

Whitey responds by rushing from aisle to aisle, all the while yelling as loudly as he can, "Help! Help! Somebody please help, my friend's having a seizure."

Dace is playing his role to the hilt. His arms and legs are flailing, knocking any merchandise in his way completely off its moorings. His whole body is in complete turmoil as he continues his charade. Meanwhile, Whitey's calls for help and the mayhem surrounding the whole fiasco have summoned every able-bodied man, women, and child in hearing distance to answer the call for assistance. Most are concerned and trying to be of some help, others are more of the onlooker type and always manage to get in the way of those who have a sincere desire to assist. Those attempting to make their way through the aisles, find them cluttered with cans, broken bottles, boxes of macaroni and spilled pickle juice running from cracked jars.

The whole lampoon takes no more than ten minutes from beginning to end. The owner is more than happy to see Dace recovered and on his way, overjoyed there have been no more casualties than a few cans and bottles.

Making their way out of the store with the blessings of all involved, Whitey and Dace quickly make their way back to the park benches out of sight of the store. Arriving at this predetermined shaded retreat, they are met by Cowboy and Vaughn both loaded down with sleeping bags, food, cigarettes, and assorted bottles of booze. While Dace was drawing the attention of all the people who could have given them trouble, Cowboy and Vaughn helped themselves unmolested to a waiting cache of supplies.

The smiles and pats on the back celebrating their success are quickly put aside. They all know they still run the risk of discovery. It's imperative to immediately put as much distance between themselves and their victims as possible. All four have tasted southern justice firsthand and have no desire to revisit it anytime soon.

Cowboy takes the lead. A city bus stops across the street and with a simple hand gesture, he directs them to follow him. At this point it doesn't matter the bus's destination, as long as it's far away from this neighborhood. Fumbling with the fare, they board as orderly as they can with blasts of adrenalin still shooting through their every fiber. Making their way with their ill-gotten gains toward the very last seats posted as *whites only*, they plop down, ready for this phase of their adventure to be over.

Determined to ride until they meet with a better alternative, they begin to relax. The time speeds by. A half hour ride brings them in sight of a railroad yard, which stirs a yearning within them. The cars carry a familiar moniker, *Union Pacific*. This sight is certainly not the best life has to offer for most people, but for this foursome there is a sense of community in this vagabond existence. As miserable as it can be at times, it's at least a predictable misery.

All four knowingly look at one another. Without a word said between them, Cowboy pulls the overhead cord alerting the driver to stop. Still silent, but very aware of what lies ahead, they disembark. Without so much as a glance at the departing bus, all four have their eyes firmly fixed on the moving railcars. With all their past experience coming into play, they realize this is the obvious workings of a railroad crew beginning to build a train. Now all they need to do is determine what time it leaves and in what direction it's heading. In order to do this effectively, it's necessary to have inside information.

Searching through their inventory of loot, they discover a bottle of Jack Daniel's sipping whiskey. Cowboy snags the bottle up. It's obvious he's formulating a plan.

Turning the bottle in his hands, while softly caressing the label, he says, "I think to the right person, this here can buy us tickets outta here."

The next step is to search out a jungle, so as to get their bearings. The neighborhood in which they have arrived is in a rundown section of town. It is characterized by small neglected, ratty homes, crumbling sidewalks, beat up or otherwise abandoned cars, front yards littered with assorted children's clothing and toys, and broken down porches furnished with abandoned appliances and old worn out couches. They know they're on the right track for a hobo jungle, it's just a matter of sorting it all out.

Another half-hour of patrolling the vicinity results in the kind of success only those living in this underbelly of society appreciate. Whitey is the first to spot what they have been keeping an eye open for. "Lookee there!" he says pointing toward a well-worn and littered path leading out of the neighborhood into a secluded area of unkempt brush and scattered trees.

The other three are on it like they have discovered the path leading to the Holy Grail. The trail leads downward into a ravine where they find a holding camp for those awaiting a freight car out of here—or for the local bums to find a secluded drinking area. There are the usual makeshift benches made of repurposed railroad ties carefully surrounding a fire pit along with the typical shacks made of abandoned sheets of tin. Without intending to be intimidating, these jungles are far enough outside the mainstream of American culture to keep the curious-minded away.

There is a sense of satisfaction in finding this alcove even though it's empty of occupants. It's a welcoming environment for these four young vagrants. Even so, there remains the task of finding a freight heading north. Cowboy is prepared to meet this challenge. Still cradling the bottle of Jack Daniel's whiskey, he makes his next announcement. "I'm going to take a walk into the yards and see if I can't find a switchman with a thirst fer some good ole fashioned sippin' whiskey. They usually got the inside track on what's what with the direction these trains are goin' in. They don't care fer the bulls any more than we do and with a little encouragement," he holds the bottle aloft, "most are willin' ta help us out."

Dace is quietly studying Cowboy's exuberance. "You ain't gonna disappear on us like ya been doin' are ya? Or are ya gonna go meet up with that no-good Sid again?" he questions.

These questions cause Cowboy to stop for a moment. Nervously blinking like he'd just been caught with his pants down, he says, "It ain't my intention, but if I don't show up by tonight, you boys hightail it outta here without me. Ya understand?" Fidgeting with the bottle, he adds, "If things change so's I can't get back, I'll catch up with ya back in Michigan."

Whitey is also dubious of Cowboy's intentions. They have all learned with Cowboy's weird behavior one must hope for the best but be ready for the worst. "I'm gonna tell ya right now, if you ain't back here shortly, you can bet yer sweet ass I ain't waitin' till some bull decides he needs ta bust a skull. I'm outta here," declares Whitey in no uncertain terms.

Up until now, Vaughn has not witnessed Cowboy's peculiar behavior. This is all new enough to leave him curiously sitting back without much to say.

The next few minutes find Cowboy making his way into the railyards, leaving Vaughn, Whitey, and Dace sitting alone, left to their own devices.

Vaughn remains curious about all the spoken and unspoken tension Cowboy is able to provoke between his brother and cousin. This generates a strong desire to seek out some more information. "Tell me again everything you guys know about Cowboy. I want to know how you met him, why he keeps showin' up, and especially about this relationship he has with his cousin, Sid."

The boys spend the next hour passing around one of the purloined bottles of wine and bringing Vaughn up to speed on Cowboy's elusive behavior over the past several weeks. When they've exhausted their recollections along with the wine, Vaughn lights another of the many cigarettes he's consumed during this period. Taking in a deep drag with a ponderous balloon of thought over his head, he hesitates for a moment before exhaling, *There's gotta be a heck of a lot more ta this story than these guys know about.* With this thought firmly entrenched, he wanders off mulling over all he's heard in the past hour.

Dace and Whitey have nothing else to do but wait. They are not ready to give up on Cowboy quite yet. "You think he's gonna come back?" asks Dace.

"I'm thinkin' he ain't," returns Whitey.

There's another long pause in the conversation as they try and digest the consequences of Whitey being correct in his thinking.

Whitey decides to change the subject to another of his puzzling thoughts. "Dace, you notice anything different about Vaughn?"

Without thought, Dace says, "Like what?"

"Like he acts like he's some kind of adult."

Taking a moment, Dace says, "Yeah, come ta think of it yer right—I couldn't put my finger on it. He ain't been quite so smart-assed with us, is he?"

The day wears on with Vaughn having rejoined them. They've eaten, smoked, drank and napped the afternoon away with no sign of Cowboy. Now that it's becoming early evening, they're convinced his chances of returning are slim to none.

Looking straight at his brother and cousin, Vaughn says, "I think we all believe we're pretty much on our own. You boys know a helluva lot more about this freight hoppin' crap than I do, but sittin' here in this jungle ain't getting us closer ta home. I suggest we get ta figurin' how we're gonna get outta here."

Dace has always been nervous about making decisions and quickly turns to Whitey. Caught off guard, Whitey's eyes dance around for no longer than a second before realizing the predicament in which he's been placed, even so, he quickly begins to formulate an exit plan.

"We gotta start watchin' the direction of these trains better, an' most of all watchin' out fer them damn, sneaky bulls. Rumor has it this yard ain't too hot with 'em. Nevertheless, I suggest we break camp an' start walkin' along this drainage ditch along the track 'til we can find a catch out point an' a good car ta hop."

The decision is unanimous: They will stay under cover along the brushy ditch paralleling the railyard and keep an eye open for any opportunity to catch out. The bulls have their own ways of staying out of sight. They will often hide between tracks loaded up with railcars waiting for a group to break out of the brush, then chase them back until the train is moving too fast to hop.

"I think our best bet is ta get on down the tracks away from the railroad property and hop a freight on the run," says Whitey, fully playing up his car hopping expertise to his still inexperienced older cousin.

There is little reason to have much discussion over this and they begin the arduous task of remaining concealed at the physical expense of making good headway through a trail of tangled vines and thistles. They have barely traveled a quarter mile and Dace is straggling in the rear when he gasps, "Oh, my God! Oh, my God!

His bellowing startles Vaughn and Whitey enough to stop them dead in their tracks. Like a dog on point, Dace is frozen staring at something off in the brush. Within a second, Vaughn and Whitey are staring at the same image. There can be no mistake this is the body of a man. He's lying dead, bug-eyed, mouth agape, clad only in his underwear, with an empty Jack Daniel's whiskey bottle cast alongside. His body is covered with only a few broken branches.

Continuing his investigation of this dead body, and before either of the other two can make another response, Vaughn is fast-tracking into detective mode. Tearing at the tangled mass of brush, he makes his way nearer with the hope of getting a better grasp on the situation.

"This guy's been murdered—there ain't a doubt in my mind," is his abrupt conclusion, pointing to a cord tightened around the victim's neck. On further examination, he posits, "And it ain't been that long ago, I can still smell whiskey on 'im."

"I'll bet some local jungle buzzard rolled 'im," concludes Dace while looking at the surrounding area, all trampled down as if there had been a struggle of sorts.

Whitey is also paying attention to some of the details that could get overlooked. "If this were for robbery, why would the perpetrator strip 'im? Seems like takin' his money would be enough."

Vaughn isn't answering, he silently continues his examination of the corpse. "Look here," he says, pointing to a small puncture wound on the man's neck above the cord. "It looks like whoever did this stabbed the guy at some point, then finished him off with the cord."

"But why would that make sense?" hazards Dace.

Vaughn is trying to wrap a motive around all this when something on the ground off to the side catches his attention. It takes only a moment to identify the object as a screwdriver—a Phillips head screwdriver. Now Vaughn's wheels are beginning to turn. Without touching it, he examines it a bit closer. "This here looks like the tool Sid was carryin' after he kilt Captain Seagrave." In another moment, he makes another connection, "I'll bet the puncture on this guy's neck came from that same screwdriver," continues Vaughn.

"Yeah, maybe, but why would whoever did this not just finish the job with the screwdriver?" further questions Dace.

Whitey begins to speak excitedly, "Cuz he didn't wanna get a lot of blood on the clothes. Whoever did this wanted the clothes, notice how he tied that cord below the wound ta keep it from bleedin'."

Vaughn is mulling all this in his head. His face suddenly lights up as he adds, "Whitey, me boy, I think yer on ta somethin'."

Dace is getting more nervous by the minute. "If we don't get the hell outta here, we're gonna get tagged with this guy's murder."

Neither Vaughn nor Whitey responds to Dace, instead they continue to search for more clues. In low voices, they agree to turn the body over.

"Bingo!!" says Whitey as the unexposed area suddenly produces the kind of evidence that opens a window to solving this mystery.

"Wadda ya seein'?" asks Vaughn. The excitement reflected in his voice is unmistakable.

Whitey reaches down with nimble fingers and produces a half-buried brass key.

"This here is a switch key. My dad has one of these. All railroad workers carry one."

In his excitement, Vaughn grabs the key, fingering it over and over as though it were a piece of precious metal.

Whitey continues with his opinion, "You thinkin' what I'm

thinkin'? This guy works for the railroad and the guy that done this wanted those clothes ta get by the bulls."

"That there is a viable theory," says Vaughn, attempting to sound professional. "But it stays a theory 'til we get more evidence."

"Sid did this, din't he?" says Dace, wanting nothing more than to get out of there. It's all he can do to keep from having a nervous breakdown. Now he has something more to add to his closet of worry.

Not willing to wait around for trouble to find them, they wipe their fingerprints off the key. Leaving it where they found it, they give in to Dace's escalating concern to get away from this predicament.

They haven't gone far when they cross a clearing. It's a spot where they can easily see everything going on in the railyards, but it also allows them to be seen. A train is approaching, lumbering along at a slow speed. They spot a rail worker riding a ladder on the end of a boxcar. He looks directly at them. Dace is the first to notice and he lets out a gasp. Hearing Dace, Vaughn and Whitey look for what spooked him. The form is the familiar hunched over form of Sid Powell!

The nervous chill that ran first down Dace's back has also attacked Vaughn and Whitey in turn. For a moment, they stand dumbfounded.

Now, Sid has also spotted them and is staring directly toward them. There is no doubt in any of their minds, Sid is wearing the dead man's clothing. Still staring straight at them, he slowly and methodically makes a finger gesture of a knife crossing his throat. This sends yet another chill down their backs. In the minds of these three, the mystery is now solved, but it only adds more fearful apprehensions. Vaughn and Whitey have already concluded this murder is Sid's handiwork. They resume following the rails looking for a likely catch out spot.

"That damn Cowboy is never here when we need him," bemoans Whitey.

"He assured us he's had Sid under control. It don't look like anyone's got this psycho under anything resemblin' control," further laments Dace.

With all this added stress coming at them, they failed to notice they have left the railroad property. Whitey is the first to discern this detail. The train is still lumbering at a slow enough pace that if they hurry they can hop it. The concern with Sid takes a backseat to getting on this freight. Watching for a car with an open door becomes their main focus. The right amount of darkness with shadows makes the bulls' job more difficult and the people catching out more successful.

"There! There's one!" yells Vaughn triumphantly.

"Good eye, Vaughn," says Whitey as he takes the lead. They quickly scramble up and out of the ditch while carrying their loot-laden sleeping bags. The train is steadily beginning to pick up speed. Whitey throws his sleeping bag on board, managing to follow it by nearly catapulting himself inside. His railcar hopping skills have unquestionably improved in the past few weeks. Once he is safely aboard, he turns his immediate attention to Dace, who is struggling. Extending a hand, he manages to pull Dace on deck. Next is Vaughn. He's running for all he's worth with his heavy sleeping bag banging against the undercarriage of the moving car. It's apparent this burden is hampering his effort.

"Toss it up!" yells Dace, referring to Vaughn's gear. At this point, Dace is fearful his brother may not make it.

With every bit of strength, he can muster while still trying to maintain a pace faster than the train, Vaughn heaves his heavy baggage on board. As he releases this burden, he manages to plant his elbows on the boxcar floor. Despite this, his strength is quickly draining. This is far as he can heave himself and he begins to slide backwards. With Whitey on one side and Dace on the other, they come to his rescue, hauling him on board totally exhausted.

Trying to get to his feet on this moving train, Vaughn finds himself thrown to the floor again. It's obvious to him, as well as his brother and cousin, he's going to have to make some adjustments if he expects to stay on his feet. Vaughn proves to be a fast learner getting up again, only this time sporting an especially wide stance. With a mindful awareness of his recent relationship with the floor, he manages to stagger to a wall, using it to support himself.

With a clear memory of his struggle to get aboard, and with more humility than either Whitey or Dace have ever heard from him, a great departure from his usual braggadocio, Vaughn says, "I wanna thank you guys. I honestly didn't think I was gonna make it. All I could imagine was those wheels would either miss me or I hoped they'd do the job fast an' get it over with."

Whitey takes the whole experience to another level. "We're all in this together, Vaughn. It's best we remember we're only gonna make it if we stick together."

"Yeah, we're like the Three Musketeers, 'All fer one, an' one fer all,'" adds Dace breaking into a little dance along with the first smile he's had in days. "It sure feels good ta be back on the road again."

Whitey has already begun to scrounge around for any discarded trash on board that will promise some creature comforts. After a minute of searching the car's dark corners, he rises with a triumphant grin declaring, "Look what I found." He holds up a fistful of straw, leftover from the packing material of some previous cargo. "There's enough for all three of us ta make into a cushion an' keep our bony asses from bouncin' off these miserable rails."

With a bit of interior design, they finish making themselves as comfortable as possible. With nothing left to do but ride, they begin to search through the stash of foodstuff squirreled away in their bedrolls. In a short time, they enjoy the luxury of a full stomach once again.

There is no question the days are becoming shorter, bringing darkness earlier. Successfully back on the road once more and finding the safety of a railcar for a night along with the natural undulations only a train can produce, they settle into its rhythmic pattern as though they are riding a magic carpet. Whitey and Dace feel life is good again as they fall into a restful slumber.

On the other hand, this kind of travel is all new for Vaughn. Still wide awake, he finds himself sitting in the doorway feeling the sway of the car as the steel wheels meet the unevenness of the track. There is nothing fragile about this much iron charging at sixty miles per hour down a narrow steel ribbon only inches wide. Like many before himself, he begins to appreciate a kinship with this instrument. It creates a kind of mental and physical elation with a wonderful mix of relaxation. The unregulated squeaks and moans these cars make, by and by become a cacophonous orchestra bringing about a hypnotic sense of peace and contentment to a rider.

For many travelers, and now including Vaughn, traveling on a northbound "hot shot" reworks a moment like this into a world that's a much more manageable place—whether real or imagined. It's an exhilarating experience, bringing about a sense of well-being like he's never experienced before.

Doing exclusively what trains do, this huge behemoth continues its uninterrupted race through the night, sounding its woeful whistle at every crossing, only adds to the surrealism. Unable to delay the inevitable, Vaughn soon joins his compatriots in a long sought, restful slumber.

CHAPTER 29

RUUUMMMBLE, RAAATLE, CRASH, BANG!! These are the first sounds heard by the waking Musketeers, followed immediately by a hard jolt against their boxcar indicating some alteration is taking place in the makeup of their train. Whitey and Dace are immediately up and on their feet, peering through the open door into the semi-darkness. They soon determine their boxcar, which so far has dependably sheltered them, is being placed on a siding.

"So, what do we do now?" asks Vaughn. It's obvious the fanciful feelings he experienced just a few hours before are quickly evaporating, and being replaced with feelings of abandonment.

Looking around, Dace has an uncomfortable expression. "We could be here for five minutes or five days," he bemoans. A slight chill races across his skin causing his hair to stand on end as he senses something foreboding about this place. After hours in a noisy, clamoring boxcar, the quiet is eerie. Not even a bird is chirping, nor is there the slightest movement of a breeze. There is an ominous fog hanging in the air. It's a haunting kind that accompanies thoughts of evil. There are sinister places in this world that seem to render a sense of the unholy more so than others.

Even after the length of time they have been on the road, the only thing that remains certain is uncertainty. At least Whitey and Dace have come to expect these surprises. Vaughn on the other hand has yet to experience the full reality of riding the rails. With this turn of events, they all recognize a new strategy needs to be forthcoming.

Without a clue as to where they are, yet not to be daunted, Whitey notices a slight rise in the landscape off to the side of their boxcar. It's a wooded area and appears to provide the type of seclusion they will feel most comfortable in. It also provides a vantage point from which they can keep an eye on their railcar in the event things change. Getting the attention of his cousins, he makes a recommendation. Pointing off toward the spot, he says, "Let's get outta this car and make a fire and eat somethin'."

The fall weather this far north is cooling down. The fog along with the cold air is bone-chilling. Whitey knows a good fire will provide the therapy needed to give them all a lift.

With nothing more than an approving nod, Vaughn and Dace gather up their gear and join Whitey's lead. Once on the small knoll, they discover they are on the back side of a farm. This area is used as a scrapyard for cars and farm equipment that are no longer viable. Finding an old rusted license plate attached to an abandoned car, it suggests they are somewhere in Missouri.

Wasting little time, they busy themselves with gathering enough wood to get a fire going. The warmth and a little food in their bellies begins to work its magic. The day drags on as days do in the culture of train hopping hobos.

With a bit of scouting, they discover a pond on the property. The tracks around its periphery indicate it serves as a watering hole for livestock. Not willing to take a chance at drinking its water without boiling first, they fill a hubcap from an old hood-less

DeSoto with a tree growing through its engine compartment. Setting it over the fire long enough to bring it to a rolling boil produces the purification required. These tasks keep their minds and hands busy enough to ward off any boredom.

Vaughn begins a discussion about the object of his obsession--Sid. "I'm convinced Sid is crazy. The only thing predictable about Sid's kinda crazy is that it sure as hell ain't predictable."

Dace listens to his big brother in earnest. He also has his thoughts. "I agree with ya bro'. But what's sure-fire is he's gonna show up again like a bad penny when we ain't ready for it."

Whitey is also ready to share his concerns. "We can't be damn sure we ain't gonna see Sid 'for we see Cowboy first. Them two is like two peas in a pod."

"Yer sure as the devil right about that," says Vaughn. "Din't ya tell me Cowboy tol' ya he's gotta have Sid around ta do his dirty work?" further questions Vaughn.

"Thas' what he tol' me a few weeks ago," recalls Whitey. "He said they gotta lotta stuff on each other. If it weren't for them bein' cousins, they'd ah proly kilt each other by now."

"That's what bothers me," says Dace. "We got stuff on both of 'em. Cowboy says he's here ta protect us, but he ain't never been around when Sid gets all crazy killin' people."

Realizing many of Sid's atrocities have been committed in states other than Michigan, Vaughn is more interested in keeping Sid following a trail back to their home turf where he believes he can be dealt with more effectively. Sharing his ambitions with Dace and Whitey, he hopes to entice them into his eagerness to bring Sid in.

Whitey has remained silently intrigued with this change in

Vaughn, but is now finding himself curious enough to ask, "When'd you get all this here junior detective thing goin'?"

Vaughn has been so engrossed with his obsession to bring Sid to justice, he looks back on his prior life as a distant past. Along the way, he has picked up another notebook since he lost Peleton's to the work farm in Arkansas. He spends a good part of his time pouring over points he's entered, believing they're pertinent to bringing this case to a head. With dusk settling around them, Vaughn concludes he's surprisingly comfortable enough in this setting to consider Whitey's question. Over the rest of the evening, he relates his experience with Peleton, going into minute detail.

After listening intently, Dace asks a question out of brotherly concern, "Do ya think Peleton's still alive?"

"I ain't sure, but if there's anybody in this world who can make it happen it's ole Doc LaRue," answers Vaughn with the sureness of a loyal believer.

The day comes to an end with no indication the boxcars dropped on this remote siding are going anywhere soon. They are left with the choice of either waiting it out or beginning a long walk to God only knows where. Thanks to the efforts of Whitey and Cowboy, they have enough pillaged food along with canteens full of boiled pond water to last a few days. They decide to sit it out in the hope these cars will be moving again soon.

The night air is taking on a heaviness as a fog begins to settle around them. The crackling, popping of burning wood is the most prevalent sound in the still damp air. These three young men are silent, staring into the fire. Each is lost in their own thoughts and is taking comfort in this shared company of silence. It seems less lonely being in the presence of others.

This solitude casts Dace's thoughts back to the captivating time he enjoyed with Grace. He recalls how innocent her laugh had been, how they melted into each other's kisses. He aches to think he may never see her again.

Whitey is also alone with his own reflections. His thoughts are on his parents and his sister, then without warning, they jump to how he and Melody had professed their love to one another. He sees her in the arms of an unidentified male, filling the role he has abandoned. This vision carries with it the most inconsolable regret to have to go to sleep on.

Vaughn is also having his own struggles. He recalls the selfish things he's done over the years. After all, this is the first time in his young life he's been alone with himself like this and not had an escape route ready to sidestep any serious introspection. Many of these derelictions are things he would ordinarily not give a second thought to. But now a deep desire to change and a regret for the foolish things he's done compel him to heave a deep sigh.

Without words, they arrange their sleeping bags around the fire. Even though wordless, each is grateful for a warm fire and the company of one another, especially with a shared sense of something evil—real or imagined—inhabiting these grounds.

In the throes of sleep, without warning RRRUUUUM, CLUNK, RATTTTLE! A shot of adrenalin propels its way through their unconsciousness, immediately shifting them from a state of deep sleep to near total alertness. This sound is all too familiar. The rail cars are being hooked to a diesel engine. All three shoot up as though they had been asleep on a catapult, wide-eyed and immediately out of their sleeping bags.

They are up and on the move. A train is a respecter of no one, it comes and leaves at will. Swiftness and clear thinking are the only weapons they can muster against being marooned in this desolate place.

Each is aware of the very, very short window of time they have.

Gathering up as much of their provisions as they can immediately lay hands on, they bolt through the darkness toward the tracks. Stumbling and tripping under a combination of their load and the unfamiliar terrain, they hasten toward the barely visible opening of the boxcar. As the train begins to move, they force themselves and their baggage up onto this impatient titan.

Vaughn is the last to board. He's happy it's as dark as it is so the others can't see the panic on his face. Every fear he experienced the first time he attempted to hop a freight has roared back to the forefront of his mind. In this darkness, he's sure his life is in as much or more danger now as it was the day before under the same circumstances.

Humans don't do well standing upright in a mobile darkness. These boys are no exception and find themselves thrown to the floor and then tossed around by each jolt as the lead engine pulls the slack from between the cars. Not able to see anything in this windowless transport, they choose remaining on the floor as a sensible position to prevent unwelcome injuries.

Within an hour, they are well on their way, speeding through the night as parasites securely entrenched in the belly of this indifferent host. The hours pass into morning bringing with it a near light-less charcoal colored horizon.

Despite the ashy light this cloudy morning is willing to share, Vaughn carries on the best he can to update his notes based on their conversations the day before. Whitey has also awakened and takes an inventory of the supplies they managed to save.

"We've barely got enough grub ta get us ta Wisconsin," Whitey announces. "We left half of it layin' on the ground last night."

Dace is surprisingly positive, saying, "Hey man, if we hadn't got outta there when we did, we'd ah starved ta death anyway waitin' for another train. I'm damn glad we're movin' again."

Dark rain clouds continue to meet them as they speed north. The highballing train aptly chews through the cold rain, spitting and spewing it aside as one would a bad tasting drink. The further north they push, the lower the temperature drops, forcing the boys to spend much of the time wrapped in their sleeping bags. Generally, people in the northern states welcome cooler fall temperatures after hot summers, but then, they are not usually given to riding in drafty boxcars.

Even though this conveyance is generously offering itself as an escape vehicle, it doesn't extend itself to provide onboard entertainment. The repetitious composition this car produces as it's drawn along this ribbon of steel creates a mental stillness of boredom. Today Whitey has a different reaction. He begins to add words in a chant-like response and choreographing dance steps to the wheel's unusual symphony of monotonous clicks, squeaks, and moans. Vaughn and Dace soon find themselves joining in by clapping to the beat and adding vocal sounds of their own. Quite pleased with their creative innovations, they break out the last bottle of wine, which miraculously had managed to escape with them, and begin to pass it among themselves.

Generally, alcohol brings with it a peak of euphoria and then begins to drop its collaborators into an abyss of dysphoria. The three of them pass through the gamut from the lighthearted fun alcohol promises to the final phenomenon of passing out. The wet, drizzly conditions outside buttress a perfect pretext to give themselves over to their dream-like comas.

Impervious to their condition, the train continues its relentless northern quest passing through Missouri and into Illinois. Having slept off the effects of the wine, one by one the boys begin to stir anew.

Whitey is the first to begin to question where they may be. "I hate the thoughts of going through those damnable Chicago yards, but I don't see any way around it. We gotta stay hid."

"Yeah, I know. If those bulls pull us off there, we'll be stuck 'til Jesus comes," agrees Dace.

Vaughn doesn't fully understand the concerns his brother and cousin are expressing. Due to his limited rail hopping experience, he is perfectly willing to take a backseat in any decisions as to how to handle the next leg of their homeward journey.

"We gotta keep this door closed. We can't risk bein' seen an' gettin' tossed off," says Whitey, jamming a rail spike in the track to prevent it from locking them in. Being stuck in a nearly dark railcar for twenty-four to forty-eight hours isn't appealing, but the risk of being thrown off the train is an even grimmer thought.

"With a bit of patience and a little luck, we'll be back in Elbertport before the weekend," assesses Whitey.

This pronouncement is met with mixed emotions. None of them are sure this homecoming will be met with open arms. Nonetheless, it's time to go home.

CHAPTER 30

Vaughn is being as patient as he can bear under the circumstances. As many times as he's had moments of peaceful pleasure during this escapade, it has never been his idea to make an extended adventure out of freight-hopping. What has made it palatable up to this point has been the desperate necessity of getting out of some area as quickly as possible. Now that much of the immediate danger has subsided, reality is taking its place. It is sinking in just how much he is missing his '49 Mercury. "That fat ass Arkansas sheriff is proly happy I ain't able ta come back an' claim it," he laments.

With the railcar door nearly completely closed, despite the ever-present clamor of steel wheels converging with steel rails, there persists a strange kind of quiet with these three children of the road. Each, alone with his thoughts, is struggling to decipher something in the dark that will give them the key to making sense of their lives over the past few weeks.

They are coming to understand just how much the experiences they've endured have marked the end of their childhood. Each day, the world silently turns. The perceived groaning sound is not from the earth itself, rather it's the voices of those ill-prepared to meet its new challenges. In this period, they've repeatedly been called out by life's vicissitudes to make adult decisions—not by choice, but rather out of a need to survive. As the train races to its destination, so these three are racing from adolescence to young adulthood.

Their eyes have grown accustomed to the semi-darkness of their wheeled cabin. Vaughn strokes his weeks old beard. It's gone from a prickly stubble to a soft pelt.

He's as comfortable as one can be, considering all he has is a pile of leftover packing materials to cushion his body against the continuous pounding of wheels accosting rails.

As one can grow weary of talking, so one can just as readily tire of silence. It's time once again to acknowledge one another in conversation. It begins with Dace's concern with how much food they have left. It's a simple start for a conversation.

"All we got left is some jerky and two canteens of water," reports Whitey. "But I ain't worried about it. At the rate we're goin', we'll be in Kewaunee by tomorrow. We can hit a street mission and restock."

With each click of the rail, they share an unexpressed delight. They're performing the noble function of moving—heading north—homeward bound. As cool as the air may be, it's fresh northern air; it's *their* air. Because of all the trials and tribulations they've faced over these past weeks, in being thoroughly out of their element and overcoming anxieties and fears in a unique way, they share together a sense of victory. There has been a cleansing nature to being on the road. Being a little hungry or thirsty is a common occurrence nowadays—nothing to stress over, it's all part of their valiant escapade.

The simple act of chewing on some jerky and passing a canteen together renews their connectedness as family. They begin to recall with some delight the close calls they've encountered and how, by the grace of God, they managed to find a way out.

None of them knows for sure what lies in store when they reach Elbertport, but there's an overwhelming feeling that if they stick together everything's going to be okay. It's all ahead of them. The hope prevails they are leaving trouble and madness behind.

It's a bright, new dawn. They are arriving in Kewaunee as

Whitey had hoped. The chance of their freight highball running non-stop through Chicago, without some kind of divine intervention, was by all accounts next to zero. The hand of Providence has truly been their companion.

The railyards are just as they left them weeks ago. The paint-peeled sign announcing *Maynard's* is still in place with the same red shingles spelling out the word *EAT*. The same car ferries line the harbor like so many monster whales readying to make their sixty-mile journey across Lake Michigan. All are patiently waiting to fill their empty bellies with railcars.

Vaughn couldn't be more delighted to escape his wheeled dungeon. While it has been exhilarating, overall, it's not been his favorite experience to ride around in a dirty, noisy, drafty railcar.

Whitey and Dace, on the other hand, approach their circumstances differently. With a thought to their next move, Whitey says, "Most of this train is going to be loaded in each of these boats, we gotta find out which one is heading for Elbertport."

Making their way toward Maynard's, Whitey recognizes one of the jungle buzzards checking the grounds for long cigarette butts. He's one of the local vagrants referred to as "Switchman." Over time, the story behind some of these monikers has been lost with only the nickname remaining. All that can be remembered is Switchman at one time worked for the railroad but lost his job when John Barleycorn took over his life. After they fired him, he continued to hang around the railyards as a local vagrant.

With the boldness of a seasoned hobo, Whitey approaches Switchman, "Trade ya a cigarette for some info."

Without a pause, Switchman fires back, "Make it two and ya got a deal."

Fishing two cigarettes out of his shirt pocket, Whitey hands them over to the nicotine-stained fingers of his informant with the question, "Which of these boats is leavin' for Elbertport?"

With one of his newly acquired cigarettes firmly between his grizzled lips, Switchman lights its end. He sucks in its fumes in such a way his toothless gums appear as though he's about to swallow his entire head. Each word is accompanied by a waft of exhaled smoke. "Ya gotta get on the *Ann Arbor Number 3*. It's the only one sailin' ta Elbertport."

"Ya got any idea when it's gonna be leavin?" further asks Whitey.

Pointing in the direction of the siding they just got off, Switchman says, "Soon's hey get them cars on deck. The hostler is fuelin' the yard engine right now, so's he can load 'em. It ain't gonna be more 'an about a half hour."

"Good we'll make sure our behinds is on it. Got any news up an' down the tracks?"

Switchman's eyes suddenly take on a look of fright. "Foxy Mike got hiself kilt last night fer his goddam boots, right back here in the jungle. Ain't that some shit—a man gettin' kilt fer a goddam pair ah boots. They was brand new, he got 'em at the Salvation Army an' then some sombitch come by an' kilt 'im. Slit his goddam throat," deplores Switchman, still shaking his head in disbelief. "I was drinkin' with 'im an' musta passed out fer a while. When I come to, he was barefoot an' dead," he further adds in disbelief.

Realizing the anguish this poor soul is suffering in his loss, Whitey thanks Switchman and hands him another cigarette for his co-operation. Turning next to Dace and Vaughn, Whitey gives his assessment, "We ain't got enough time ta get ta town. We're just gonna have ta get a bite here at Maynard's an' call it good. We gotta get back on that railcar 'for we get stranded here."

This is not what any of them want to hear, nonetheless, they all agree. While Dace fills the canteens and Whitey gets a takeout order, Vaughn entertains himself by supplying Switchman with a few more cigarettes for some more of the lurid details of Foxy Mike's murder. His sleuthing juices have been well stirred by Switchman's account. There is no doubt in Vaughn's mind, he can make a connection with Sid.

With a bag of cheese sandwiches and to not waste any more time in Kewaunee, Whitey employs Switchman's expertise once more. "You got any idea where the bull is hangin' out this time ah day?"

"Ain't seen 'im since they come an' got poor ole Foxy Mike this morning. I suspects he gots stuff ta do 'bout all that," says Switchman.

Whitey quickly interprets this information to mean they have a short window to get back in their boxcar before they could be seen by the wrong people. The last thing any of them want is to be thrown off this close to home. Without any discussion, they begin their slog across several sets of tracks back to their waiting railcar in the backside of the yards. They are possessed with only one thought, *get home*. Once on board, Whitey slides the huge door nearly closed to rest against the rail spike.

Switchman's forecast proves to be on the money. Along with their line of cars, they soon find they are heading toward the slip holding the *Ann Arbor Number 3*. It waits empty, with its huge jaw-like sea gate open wide, like a huge water slug waiting to be force fed.

Once they are on board, they experience a rolling sensation. This all undergone in the darkness as the ship receives the rest of its cargo. The sounds of uncoupling rail cars inside the ship's belly take on a hollow echoing resonance as they vibrate off its steel walls. This is followed by the rattling, clanking noises of deckhands setting chained breaks designed to secure each car. This procedure is to prevent any boxcar from breaking loose in high seas, crashing through the sea gate, and plunging headlong into Davy Jones' locker

Suddenly a familiar sound makes its way to the listening ears of these would be stowaways. Someone is pulling the spike holding the door open from its track. Whitey jumps to his feet as though he has just been snake bit. In a split second, he is at the door, jamming his foot into its six-inch opening. There he is met with the shocked look of a deckhand falling back as though he'd just come face to face with the bogeyman. It's obvious as an explosive fulmination of rhetoric begins to pour from the startled man's mouth. "You dumb son-of-a-bitch. What the hell you doin' hidin' on my boat?"

Before Whitey can answer, Vaughn, recognizing the voice of Gene McClellan, has made his way to the door. With an impish laugh, he announces, "Gene it's me, Vaughn Kidman!"

Gene, still attempting to process all this, blinks a few times as though his brain will gain some clarity in the process. Finally recognizing all of them, he forms some words, "Yesterday it was that loon Sid Powell. Today it's you guys. I ain't even gonna ask what you dumb asses are doin' hidin' out in a boxcar on a boat in Kewaunee, Wisconsin."

"Good!" jokes Vaughn, hoping he can make light of a situation that could turn ugly very fast, "Cause we ain't gonna tell ya anyway."

The very mention of Sid Powell's name sends a shot of anxiety through the minds of these three. Vaughn takes the lead on this new development. Not wanting his anxiety to reflect in his attitude, he continues his lighthearted verbosity in a thoughtful, but concise manner. "You say you saw Sid? I sure gotta agree—he's a loon." Hoping to get the information he's looking for without appearing to be overly anxious, Vaughn continues his inquiry, "Where'd ya say ya ran inta Sid?"

"I saw him yesterday. He was crawlin' outta a boxcar that had just been unloaded in Elbertport. I gotta say, he's one creepy dude."

"Did you see if he went towards town?" asks Vaughn, still trying to measure his words.

"The last I saw of 'im, he was crawlin' up the dune," says Gene.

"Yeah, that's more his style. He can roam around up there—come down at night—steal a little food, go back up again and never be seen," says Vaughn.

"Word around town is that the sheriff is lookin' fer his sorry ass," continues Gene. "Come ta think of it, all yer names been comin' up." With this thought swirling, around in Gene's mind, he pauses just long enough to conclude, "I think I seen enough of you guys. The last damn thing I need is ta get sucked inta any more bullshit than I already got. Stay in this car an' don't come out 'til we get ta Elbertport—ya hear me?"

"Ya got a deal Gene—we stay hid an' you keep yer mouth shut—right?"

"Humph!" is all Gene says as he walks away shaking his head.

Eased their secret is not in jeopardy, at least for the present, they retreat back into the dark shadows of their sanctuary.

They've been gone for the better part of a month, although to them it seems like light-years. Like many transitions in life, this one is coming faster than they had envisioned. Now, they have only the next three hours before they arrive in Elbertport to contemplate their next move.

With the ship making its way to Elbertport, they opt to keep their concerns to themselves—for the present at least—and try to snooze the time away.

CHAPTER 31

It's a beautiful sun-filled day as the ship arrives in Elbertport. The thick forests covering the massive dunes are all ablaze in fall colors. They appear pleased to welcome the ship as it makes its way through the channel to its assigned berth. It's truly one of those warm October days Michiganders refer to as Indian Summer. It also marks one the high holy seasons—deer hunting with bow and arrow.

With the proficiency of men who have repeated this operation hundreds of times, their boxcar is soon deposited on a rail siding to await the next leg of its journey—which will be to their delight without them.

At last able to slip out of their sanctuary on familiar turf, Vaughn offers, "I think we're gonna have ta pull a 'Sid' an' lay low 'til we can get a better handle on where we stand."

The three prodigals agree and decide to spend a day or two in the dunes, to get a feel for what they may be facing in town.

"I suggest we head toward Dud's shack. At least there, we got some protection against the weather," proposes Vaughn.

Slipping between railcars in the hopes of not being spotted, they make their way to the trail leading up the dune. It's the same trail Sid reportedly used only the day before.

"We don't have a clue where that damn Sid might be lurkin'. We need ta stick close together an' be on our toes. Keep an eye out for anywhere he could pop outta," says Vaughn. At the same time his eyes scour the ground around them. It's loaded with fallen limbs of all shapes and sizes. "We need ta hunt around for a good sturdy club. We may need 'em."

Whitey and Dace don't need to question this suggestion. They know exactly what Vaughn is getting at. For the next few minutes, they kick around the forest floor. Testing the strength of several would be weapons by whacking them against trees, within minutes each has armed himself with a club-like cudgel, stout enough to break bones. Feeling less vulnerable and keeping a wary eye out for any movement that may be regarded as suspicious, they make their way along the two-mile trail toward Dud's shack.

Their thoughts are mixed. There is an excitement at being back home in a familiar environment, but also a concern for what may be awaiting them—not only from the law, but from a known killer lurking about and capable of ambushing them at any time.

There is very little conversation between them as they try to be as silent as possible—a task made more difficult by the rustling beneath their feet of the already fallen leaves. If this were not enough, the blue jays have assumed their innate responsibility to warn the entire forest of their intrusion. After a time, the noisy shuttlecocks become bored with them and fly off to look for more interesting trespassers. This allows the boys to listen for other sounds—sounds that may alert them to any imminent danger trying to surprise them.

Dace is the first to stop dead in his tracks. His eyes are fixed on a sight he could hardly have prepared himself to confront. Following suit, all three find themselves frozen, gazing forward. It's the body of a man hanging from a tree by a tether fastened around his waist. He appears to be lifeless.

Their first thought is that it's a bow hunter who fell from his tree stand. With eyes darting in every direction as a precaution, the three slowly and methodically make their way to get a closer look.

"This here is Fritz Bencke!" says a startled Whitey. "He musta fallen...Oh my God!"

This last exclamation brings both Dace and Vaughn close enough to capture the full impact of this grizzly setting. What they behold is a gaping, blood-stained wound in the center of his chest. Another anomaly is he seems to have a portion of a sandwich gripped between his teeth.

All three have the same thought at the same time. *This is absolutely the work of Sid Powell.* The reality of their vulnerability has them spinning around looking off in every direction. To imagine there could be more than one person in this small town capable of this kind of handiwork is ludicrous.

"We gotta get the hell outta here!" is Dace's singular response.

Whitey isn't too far away from agreeing with Dace. For all of Cowboy's supposed insights into Sid's psyche, enabling him with special powers to protect them from the seeming senseless rants of his cousin, they have once again been left on their own. All the same, he isn't quite ready to throw in the towel without a more pragmatic reason than fear.

Speaking directly to Whitey and Dace, Vaughn is ready with some horse sense. "One of you has gotta go into town. We need to get the sheriff up here as quick as possible."

The words are hardly out of his mouth before Dace's hand goes up. "I'll go!" he volunteers.

Vaughn instructs Dace to go directly to Doc LaRue since he's the county corner and inform him of what happened to poor ole Fritz.

Dace couldn't be more relieved than to have this benign assignment. Eased for the moment, within seconds, he's on his way, leaving Vaughn and Whitey to fend for themselves.

Alone, Vaughn and Whitey sit down on a nearby fallen log to share a smoke and further discuss their situation. "Wadda ya think Sid's motive is behind all these killin's?" questions Whitey.

Taking an extra-long drag on the cigarette, Vaughn considers the question. "I don't think there's any kind of outside motive. I think he carries this within himself. He's had a lifetime of hate buildin' up inside and it comes pourin' out in violence against anybody standin' in his road."

Amazed at Vaughn's unusual insight, Whitey says, "I think we gotta be real smart from here on."

"You ain't just ah kiddin'," acknowledges Vaughn. Each takes a last drag on the cigarette before Vaughn stomps on it and together, they make their way back to the trail.

Certain there's nothing else that can be done for Fritz, the duo cautiously continues their trek toward Dud's shack. With one final look at Fritz, still hanging helplessly alone and dead, Whitey says, "You keep watch on your side of the trail. I'll keep an eye on mine."

It's not until they are within shouting distance of the shack that a loud disturbance stops them in their tracks again. Both become aware of it at the same instant. It only takes a moment to realize the ruckus is coming from the direction of Dud's shack.

Now that they are almost within sight of their goal, they become even more guarded. Still unwilling to back off, they begin to steal their way down the last segment of the trail. Much of the summer foliage has fallen, making the shack visible at a greater distance. The closer they get, the stronger the voices grow. Not only are they louder, they're recognizable.

"I'll be go ta hell if that ain't Sid Powell bellerin'!" determines Vaughn.

"The other's Cowboy!" says Whitey aghast. "I'd know that voice anywhere."

Sid and Cowboy have evidently made the same journey twenty-four hours earlier.

Obviously, a dispute has broken out between them. It seems Sid is arguing with Cowboy and both are becoming quite hostile.

Vaughn surveys the area looking for a place he can creep up to the shack unseen. Speaking to Whitey, Vaughn whispers. "You stay here and cover me.

I'm gonna get a better look at what's happenin' with these two."

Bellowing at the top of his voice, Sid makes a statement that gets Vaughn and Whitey's attention, "I can't afford ta have these punks around any longer. They've seen too much and know too much. If it weren't fer you, I'da had them dead and outta my life a long time ago."

Cowboy is just as adamant, "Well, I'll tell you this Sid, if it weren't fer me hidin' you, the law woulda had your sorry-assed neck stretchin' rope a long time ago."

"Don't be preachin' ta me like yer some kinda Sunday school boy in all this. There ain't one ah them guys I took out 'at you didn't get somethin' out of it. Them damn boots yer wearin' din't drop outta the sky. They come off a bum over in Kewaunee. The only reason I kilt the worthless asshole was 'cuz you said you liked them boots. Well now ya got 'em!"

Cowboy can't help but admire his new boots, but is still not willing to agree with Sid's reasoning. "All the money you took from those people was used to hide you out and I'm the one that made sure that happened," Cowboy responds.

"Yeah, maybe so, but you an' yer punk friends woulda starved ta death a long time ago if I hadn't got you money. Jes like you hadn't ate in two days when I kilt Fritz, so's you could have his lunch."

Vaughn is crawling on his belly through the brush between himself and the commotion. Despite his attempt to be quiet, he inevitably snaps a branch just close enough to the shack to be heard.

The next scene is so crazy, so disturbing, so insane, so unnerving that regardless of the danger standing before them, Vaughn and Whitey become so unhinged at what they see that they freeze in astonished disbelief.

A lone wild-eyed figure has emerged from the shack. It, he, they are wearing a cowboy hat, a western boot on one foot and an army issue boot on the other, army issue fatigues and wielding a buck knife. The frame of this physical body appears to first be that of Sid, then in a split second it takes the form of Cowboy. The wild swipes this figure is making with the knife has Vaughn rolling around in a horrified attempt to avoid its edge.

Still carrying his club, Whitey rushes to Vaughn's defense. With his thick cudgel raised over his head, Whitey charges forward with a primordial roar, He brings the weapon down squarely on the head of this ominous figure and drops him in a shuddering heap at his feet.

By a miracle, Vaughn had managed to avoid the slashing blade. Getting to his feet and rushing to his cousin's side, both stand petrified at the grotesque figure lying unconscious on the ground in front of them. It's clearly Sid, but at the same time, in a weird way, it also appears to be Cowboy.

The undulating sound of Doc's Jeep forcing itself over the uneven turf comes from the main trail. In the heat of their battle, neither Vaughn nor Whitey had consciously paid attention to it. Within a minute, Dace is standing beside his brother and cousin. Doc and a recovering Sheriff Peleton are directly behind him. They all stare at the crumpled body lying on the ground.

Not wasting a moment, Vaughn kicks the knife aside. A small grin begins to make its way across his face as he continues to stare at this anomalous human. He is finally able to assure himself his hunch had been right all along. *Sid and Cowboy are the same person!!!* He had entered this suspicion in his notebook a week ago, but not wanting Dace and Whitey to think he had lost his mind, he kept the thought to himself.

The boys quickly bring the sheriff and Doc up to speed as to what had just taken place. Sheriff Peleton secures the awakening Sid with handcuffs while Doc LaRue tends to the concussion he's sure to have.

Once again fully conscious, Sid continues his argument with Cowboy.

"I told you a month ago, we needed to take these guys out—but no, you wouldn't listen to me. Now look at the mess you got us in."

"Shut up Sid, I'm done tryin' to protect you. I don't care if we are family, I'm done with ya," says his counterpart.

This wrangling between Sid and his alter ego continues as a manacled Sid is loaded into the back of Doc's Jeep along with his victim's body—poor ole Fritz Beneke. Relieving Doc of the tenuous task of driving them out of here, Vaughn takes the wheel.

Loaded with all these participants, he once again proudly drives into town among the buzz that begun a month ago.

By now the news has spread enough to line the streets with finger-pointing onlookers as Doc's Jeep cavalcades first to the funeral home to deposit Fritz, then on to the village holding cell to deposit a still wrangling Sid—or Cowboy—whichever was, for the moment, in charge of the body they share.

A week goes by with plenty of hubbub. Doc LaRue unofficially releases his diagnosis of Sid as a *dual personality syndrome*. This is enough to keep Sid's future in the hands of those who understand the ramifications of such a diagnosis. But this doesn't reduce the conjectures of the townspeople who speculate as to its cause and subsequent outcome.

"I knew damn good and well nothin' good was ever gonna come outta that family. Those parents oughta been horsewhipped," says Harlan Pierce, concerning Sid's family.

Within another week, Sid is ordered by the court to be placed in the Traverse City state hospital for an evaluation. The decision is to keep him there until he can be suitably tried in a court of law.

The boys are regarded as celebrities as they willingly share their many adventures with anyone willing to listen. Whitey has resumed his job at the bowling alley and has picked up where he left off dating Melody. Her parents along with the rest of the community have taken the position that these three boys are heroes and have forgiven them for any infractions that pale in the light of bringing a killer in their midst to justice.

Vaughn's adventure has given him a more mature outlook on life. His tenacity in solving this crime has caught the attention of Sheriff Peleton. With the encouragement of the sheriff, Vaughn is seriously considering a future in law enforcement.

He's getting information from a university in Michigan's upper peninsula that offers a course in police work.

Dace is without a doubt the most unsettled of the three. He stays to himself quite a bit, refusing to bask in the attention he could be receiving from his peers. There is something about this adventure that has left him bottled up with his own thoughts. He knows exactly what it is, but is unable or unwilling to express it to anyone.

Another month goes by. As he leaves school for Christmas break, he encounters an unexpected apparition. He spots a very familiar-looking girl in a pair of men's coveralls, carrying a bedroll. He stops dead in his tracks looking at this female hobo in all her glory.

"Grace!" he exclaims. There is no way he can hide the

excitement this sweet hobo girl brings to him.

A smile breaks across her face as he makes his way to her. In a moment, they are locked into an embrace they had left unfulfilled far too long ago.

"What in the world brings you here?" is the only question Dace can muster at the moment.

"I never went back home after we were picked up. Instead I went to live with my grandma. She got tired of me moping around. I knew all along what I had to do. What say we get back on the road and finish this adventure?"

A smile breaks out across Dace's face. "Ya don't have ta ask me twice!!"